Sally

Secrets and Lies

Lesley Elliot

Sally
Secrets and Lies

For Mom with love.

Table of Contents

1

Just as Ann raised her hand to the front door, Bill opened it. He gazed solemnly at her, for a minute with his nostrils flaring, then turned away and sauntered into the kitchen.

Ann followed him, noticing the milk and teapot on the kitchen table and feeling the warmth from the fire, which was competing with the winter sun streaming into the room. She stood with her head bowed. 'I'm sorry, Bill,' she said.

He remained silent and leaned against the door to the backyard, looking anywhere but at her. His knuckles stood out; white against his weathered skin as he grasped the teacup. Distant sounds of wood chopping punctuated the silence, but Bill didn't hear it. He was waiting for Ann to start blaming him for her absence as she usually did. He was ready to tell her to shut up and get out of his sight, but she didn't move or continue to speak. Her uncharacteristic behaviour disconcerted him.

'D'you want a cup of tea?' he asked, breaking the uncomfortable silence.

'Yes, please.' She kept her head down as she unbuttoned her coat and carried it through to the living room where she threw it over the back of the sofa, and then reluctantly returned to the kitchen.

Bill poured her a cup of tea then leaned back against the door while they both drank.

Ann deliberately kept her voice low key. 'You'll be late for work.' When Bill hadn't moved after a couple of minutes, she tried again. 'Look, can't we just leave it? I've said I'm sorry. Go to work; we'll talk about it tonight when you come home, eh?' She eased herself onto the corner of the table and continued to sip her tea.

'I'm not going to work.' The loose, brass doorknob rattled as he took a step towards her. His lips set in a stubborn line.

Ann gave a disbelieving snort, and her head flew up, lips parted. He always went to work on Saturday. He was just determined to have a row before he went.

Her lip curled. 'Oh, and why not? Made of money now are we?'

'Don't bother starting Ann; I've had enough. You want to live with your mum – you can do just that – I'm leaving.' Although Bill said the words steadily enough, he was seething. How dare she come waltzing back home again, and think that saying sorry made everything alright. She hadn't even asked how Sally was, or where she was. He placed the teacups into the sink and washed his hands.

Ann was stunned as his words sank in. He was leaving her, leaving *her* to bring up Sally on her own. She just couldn't. The shock made her go cold inside. Her tongue thrashed about finding words to hurt him and start a fire to warm her again.

'Oh no, you're not leaving,' she hissed. 'Running out on your wife and child, what sort of man are you? A weak, useless, spineless bastard, that's what! Doesn't take much for you to break your marriage vows, does it? You might as well have joined up and got killed. At least I'd be able to hold my head up in the street.'

Ann's outburst was so sudden and fierce that she visibly sprayed spittle as she moved across the kitchen with her arms flailing. She wanted to injure him. She wanted to scratch and bite and kick and hurt him as much as he'd hurt her. How could he expect her to have a baby and then cope on her own? Why should he return to a carefree life? She'd expected his anger, even his contempt, but not to be punished like this. Her panic escalated. As she reached Bill, she struck out at his face and upper arms with her fists. She was so intent on inflicting pain that she couldn't hear her screams and grunts neither could she see the hatred that coloured her face a violent shade of red. She took a step back and slammed into him again, landing a solid punch on his cheekbone – her hands then bent like claws and reached up to scratch his face.

Bill flinched and drew his head back. 'For God's sake, Ann, control yourself – you crazy cow,' he shouted.

Fearing for his eyes, he grabbed her wrists and held her to him. He could feel the heat from her head, pushing through his shirt and vest as though he embraced a furnace. Ann continued to struggle furiously while calling him all the coarse names that she knew. Long minutes passed then suddenly she became limp and slumped forward. The animal noises that she'd continued to make gradually subsided into tearful sobs.

Bill held her as gently as he could, feeling remorse that he'd provoked such an onslaught. He relaxed his muscles but kept her enfolded until she was quiet. He felt

3

lightheaded and tried to take deep breaths. A few more minutes passed then Ann jerked herself out of his embrace and stepped away from him – now entirely in control.

'I'm going back to my mother's,' she spat the words at him. 'You can do what you fucking well like.'

She began to walk rapidly out of the kitchen into the living room, but something about the tilt of her head and the swing of her backside as she flounced out, caused Bill to react. He crossed the room in two strides knocking aside the table with his hip. The jug of milk wobbled then smashed on the floor; spider patterns formed on the worn red tiles. Bill neither heard nor saw it happen.

He'd no idea what he meant to do until his hand made contact with the small of Ann's back. He gave her an almighty push. Even as he touched her, he tried to stop himself, but it was too late; her forward momentum increased. She flew into the air in slow motion, her feet tangled in her coat which had fallen from the sofa. She twisted around as she fell until she was facing him. He noted with anguish the rapidly changing expressions of surprise, shock and horror that chased across her face. Her head struck the edge of the sideboard with a sickening thud, and she landed gracelessly in an unmoving heap.

Bill began to shake uncontrollably as he saw the blood pool under Ann's head. 'Oh my God, I've killed her.' He said aloud. Then he collapsed onto the sofa, unable to look at what he'd done. He broke down and sobbed.

Much later, he slowly raised his head and wiped the wetness from his face with his fingers. Whatever made me push her, he berated himself? He'd never suspected that he possessed such an explosive, childish temper. He immediately understood that his vindictive behaviour would send him to prison – he'd probably hang.

The horror unfolding in his mind left him breathless and weak. What would happen to Sally then, he panicked, she'd be looked after by strangers. Ann's mum wouldn't take her, he felt sure of that, and neither would his sister. Even if Clarissa would raise her with her own three children, her husband, David, wouldn't stand for yet another mouth to feed. God almighty what had he done?

He rose stiffly to his feet, carefully avoiding looking at the result of his insane behaviour. He walked back into the kitchen and stood with his eyes closed for several minutes; ways in which he might avoid the appalling consequences of his actions whirled around and around in his head. There didn't seem to be a solution that would enable him to carry on with his intention to raise his daughter. He felt trapped and useless.

He rejected one unworkable plan after another until a scheme occurred to him that would allow him to look after Sally for as long as possible. If he left Ann's body where it was, and took Sally with him, it might be a few days before anyone missed them. Perhaps he would be able to disappear permanently in another city, or maybe go to America. He knew he was naive and grasping at straws, but he couldn't think of a better solution. He convinced himself that if he stayed in Lincoln, it wouldn't help Ann or Sally. He finally decided to travel to London hoping, with a little luck, to lose himself in the large, and somewhat transient population which he knew existed there. He was unsure of everything except his need to take care of his daughter

He dragged his mind back into the present and galvanised into action and avoiding brushing against Ann, he crossed the room and quickly climbed the stairs. Sally was still asleep, lying on her side with her thumb firmly placed in her mouth. She didn't stir as her father picked her up, laid her on the bed, changed her napkin, and began to dress her. It was never an easy task to put her into the knitted dress, coat and bonnet, which his mother had made in soft, white wool, but he persevered.

He could see his Mum sitting by the fireside, needles flying. He imagined he could smell the talcum powder, which she'd used to make her hands sweet and dry while she carried out this labour of love. How he missed her; he felt sure that if she'd been alive, she could have helped to prevent the disaster that he had caused.

He shook his head and tried to concentrate. He needed to plan carefully if he was to avoid prison or worse. He finished dressing Sally, checked he had everything vital, filled her bottle with milk, shoved it into his jacket pocket, and then left the house. As he shut the door, Sally startled awake, and immediately began to wail.

'It's alright, my darling just go back to sleep,' he whispered, 'Daddy will feed you when we're safely on the train.' He rocked her gently, and without a backward glance strode towards the busy High Street and the railway station with its imposing stone columns.

2

Birmingham

Abigail buttoned her old, black coat, stuck a pin through her hat and tucked in her hand-knitted scarf as she prepared to leave the comparative warmth and peace of the church where she'd been praying for the happiness of her daughter's soul.

She treasured her visits to St. Martin's where she gained comfort from the familiar smell of polish, incense and fresh flowers that pervaded its atmosphere. Since her daughter, Grace's death five years earlier, Abigail could be seen many times each month entering her sanctuary. The solemn ritual of lighting a candle and saying a short prayer had enabled her to go on with the life that she felt was empty. Many of the clergy and other parishioners had listened when Abigail was at her lowest ebb. They had become her friends when she hadn't been able to hide her grief, and time had done little to diminish her anguish. Jim wouldn't listen. He maintained that she'd had ample time to grieve, and her infrequent tears seemed to annoy him, often causing him to leave the house and seek brighter company elsewhere. He usually returned home the worse for wear and feeling amorous, but thankfully incapable of remaining awake long enough to insist on having sex. His apologies were always profuse the following day, but Abigail felt hurt and alone with their loss.

Jim was a prosaic man, and Abigail was well used to his ways after ten years of marriage. But familiarity didn't stop her resenting the fact that he'd so quickly put the past behind him even though he'd loved his daughter. He often told Abigail in no uncertain terms that she should be sensible and follow suit. They rarely mentioned their daughter's name now, and Abigail considered it hardly surprising that they'd grown apart in many ways. Although she blamed herself for the coolness between them, she wished Jim was more understanding. She'd never cease to mourn their daughter's passing and couldn't begin to see things from his point of view.

Taking a last look around the peaceful church with its beautiful stained-glass windows, Abigail inwardly thanked no one in particular and went out into the fresh air. She hurried through the stone-flagged vestibule idly wondering if Jim would prefer some herrings for his tea instead of smoked haddock. He worked as a slaughterman and brought fresh meat home every weekday. Each Saturday, they had fish from the market in the Bullring depending on what was available. Abigail loved all types of fish and shellfish. Sometimes she would buy crab claws, and Jim would keep her company using a hairgrip to poke and pull out the succulent flesh. However lonely Abigail felt while living with her husband, she was glad that both his age and occupation exempted him from being away in the armed forces.

She may well have continued to concern herself with mundane matters, but a small child, who started to cry, drew her attention. Abigail's brown eyes met the blue ones of the young man who was sitting on one of the pitted stone seats placed either side of the vestibule. She thought he looked exhausted as he gently rocked the child in his arms. She smiled and stayed her footsteps; he seemed somehow out of place sitting there. She noticed their rumpled clothes were clean and further rapid scrutiny gave her the courage to speak to him. He did not have the downtrodden appearance of a vagrant about him.

She looked with interest down at the squirming bundle. 'Is it a boy or a girl?'

The man returned her smile. 'She's my hungry daughter,' he said, 'her name is Sally.'

Abigail nodded in the direction of the metal-studded church door. 'Are you waiting for your wife?'

Bill hesitated, he wondered how much he could safely tell the kindly looking woman. Then he chose a lie. 'No, my wife died giving birth to Sally.'

'Oh! You poor thing – I'm so sorry – I shouldn't have asked.' She turned away from him, her cheeks flushed. She felt sad and embarrassed to think that she'd intruded on the man's sorrow. Abigail speculated that he'd probably been visiting the church for much the same reason as herself. She began to walk away, but he spoke again.

'It's alright,' Bill said quietly, 'nice of you to take an interest. I don't know Birmingham. I was just sitting here trying to decide what to do next. We only arrived by train a couple of hours ago.' He seemed to run out of things to say and started to pace about with Sally, making small shushing noises.

Abigail noticed the battered suitcase for the first time. She wasn't usually an impulsive or nosy person; she prided herself on her ability to mind her own business. Sympathy for the tall, gentleman who was having problems caring for his daughter, led her to act against her nature.

'Do you have somewhere to go?' Abigail asked Bill and shook her head as she put the question. She already knew what the answer would most likely be; it didn't take a fortune teller to guess their immediate plight.

'I'm afraid not, I don't know anyone in Birmingham,' he paused for a second, 'I didn't intend to come here, but here we are.' Bill was well-spoken, but Abigail couldn't place his accent.

She smiled once more, tilting her head a little to encourage him to continue.

Tentatively Bill did. 'I thought maybe the vicar might be able to …' he looked searchingly down at her, 'do you know of anywhere we could stay just while I sort myself out?'

Abigail replied immediately, having already made up her mind what she was going to suggest. 'Why don't you bring Sally and come home with me, it'll give you time to catch your breath, and we'll see what my husband has to say?'

Relief flooded through Bill, but he hesitated to show how eager he was for some help. 'You're very kind,' he said, tugging his cap down more securely onto his short hair with his free hand, 'are you sure that would be alright?'

Abigail nodded and held out her arms to take the still whimpering child. 'I suppose you'd better tell me your name, mine's Abigail Tildesley.' She looked expectantly at his smiling face.

'I'm called Bill, erm, William Brooks.' As the words left his mouth, he realised that he should have given her a false name.

Feeling disinclined to question his good fortune any further; Bill gratefully handed Sally, who ceased crying in surprise, to Abigail and picked up his belongings. He briefly surveyed the dark, brown hair and eyes of the woman who looked kind and reliable. He followed her from the churchyard

3

Lincoln

Ann groaned as she became conscious; she thought it was morning – she had to get up and feed Sally. She could hear her crying in the distance. The wailing ceased, and Ann became aware that her head was throbbing painfully. She touched the hairline at the back of her head where it hurt the most; it felt wet and sticky. Blood covered her hand. Where was she, and why did she feel so cold? She felt her eyelids close under their own volition. She couldn't answer her questions; she couldn't think properly.

Minutes passed, and Ann woke as she tried to turn over. She knew with certainty that she wasn't in her bed; she opened her eyes and gazed around the room. Instantly her memory returned. The bastard had pushed her, and she must have hit her head on the sideboard. She could still feel the imprint of his hand on her back. Ann guessed that Bill had gone to get help; she could sense that he wasn't in the house. Please hurry Bill she thought and hoped that Sally had gone back to sleep. Even if her daughter started to cry again, Ann couldn't get up to see to her. She felt too ill, and her legs seemed to have disappeared; she couldn't feel any trace of them. Bill was usually such a gentle person; he hadn't meant to hurt her like this.

Ann's head was painful, and her neck felt cramped from being pressed up against the leg of the sideboard. Tears of fear and self-pity oozed between her eyelids and ran down her cheek, tickling uncomfortably on her nose, as they trickled to the cold, hard floor. She kept her eyes shut and tried to think of nothing except Bill's return. Small moans escaped from her dry lips, but Ann was only aware of the pain in her head and neck. Hurry Bill, she thought as her eyes closed. I need you.

Ann opened her eyes, but she could see nothing except shadows of furniture. It was night, and Bill hadn't returned. She tried to sit herself up but cried out with the pain from her head and neck and let her head fall again to the floor. How had she allowed this to happen? Where were Bill and Sally?

She remembered that Bill had pushed her after they had rowed, but she couldn't believe he had taken Sally and left her there to die. She felt too weak and lay still running over in her mind the cause of the row. She remembered walking home from her mother's house and aiming a kick at a tabby cat that sat on a doorstep, meowing to be let in. It shrieked and ran off. She had wanted to kick Bill, not the cat, and being cruel had done nothing to lighten her mood.

Bill had never really loved her or even cared very much for her. They'd married because it was the thing to do after she became pregnant; they both regretted it. Ann believed that he loved her, and thought that she was in love with him, wanting only to please and make him happy. She understood now how naïve she'd been. At least she knew he was delighted with his daughter.

Thoughts of Sally triggered strong feelings in Ann. She told herself that all their problems stemmed from her prolonged and challenging labour. But at times she knew this wasn't so; a loveless marriage was too difficult for them to maintain.

A recollection of Sally's traumatic birth filled Ann with nearly as much horror as the event itself. She remembered screaming and cursing everyone, especially Bill and her mother. She didn't know how she had coped with the intense pain that went on for hours. After producing sweat by the bucket load, but no baby, forceps had been used. She had wanted to die. She'd intended to ensure that Sally would be an only child, but Bill had continued to insist on his rights, and she was in constant fear of becoming pregnant again

Ann had seen nothing beautiful about the red, wrinkled bundle that needed so much attention. She didn't even like the scent of her daughter. Alarm bells began to clamour as the days went by with a continued absence of maternal feeling, and she had eventually confided in her mother.

'Give it time love,' Rose had advised her, 'this often happens to young mothers, you'll soon grow to love her.'

It hadn't happened. Nearly two years tied to a frequently crying child, endless feeding and rocking, and the disgusting task of napkin washing had brought no feeling of love for her daughter. Her life seemed to consist of chores which made her wrinkle her nose, and she put off carrying them out as long as possible. Ann remembered some woman saying that a line full of white nappies blowing in the breeze was a beautiful sight, but when her elbows sank into stinking, shitty water, she believed they must have been insane

Ann knew that in the beginning, she had been as eager as Bill to find opportunities to be together. She readily lied to her mother to gratify their lust. Both of them had wrapped events up in a pretty ribbon, and frequently referred to their sexual encounters as making love, but Ann knew better. She no longer wanted Bill to touch her. She was miserable and knew that Bill was unhappy too.

During her reluctant journey home, Ann had decided that their marriage would have to end. She'd wondered how Bill would react. The idea brought a frisson of fear. She'd given no thought to the consequences for Sally.

Ann felt her forehead; she was hot. She tried again to sit up but only slid an inch along the lino. Surely if she lay still, someone would come.

She remembered speaking to her friend, Enid, as she passed her house that morning and telling her that Bill had practically raped her the previous night, she'd begged him not to come inside her, but he'd taken no notice. Enid had commiserated and said that she'd see her this evening. Perhaps she would arrive soon.

Ann's tears ran freely down her face as she pictured again, when almost home, a milkman's horse as it tossed its head, snorted and then moved, with little prompting, along the cobbled street to its next stopping place. It had stood still as milk got ladled into a jug held out by a child dressed in short, grey trousers and a non-descript jumper that hung from his thin shoulders almost to his bony knees. Then the milkman gave a gentle click of his tongue against his cheek, and the horse moved on. Another click from the rugged faced man and the horse waited patiently until the

15

next short walk. Ann thought about the mysterious understanding between the man and his willing beast and had idly wondered how long it'd taken to develop their close teamwork. If they could work so well together – surely Bill and she – but her thought trailed away. She remembered her loneliness.

4

Bill listened to the wheels of the train as it rolled through the countryside and held Sally close to him. To his relief, the rhythm had sent her to sleep as soon as she had finished her milk. He stared miserably through the window and pondered the sequence of events that had led him to become a fugitive.

Only yesterday Bill had left the Lincolnshire building site where he was employed as a bricklayer and was hurrying home. He wanted nothing more than to remove his tightly-laced boots, ease his feet into a steaming bowl of water liberally laced with mustard, and soak the bone wearying ache from them. He couldn't know that he would never see that site again.

As he neared home, his gloomy thoughts about his life ceased when he heard the sound of crying that he knew was his daughter, Sally. He opened the front door and kicked the worst of the mud from his boots before crossing the un-scrubbed step. The cry changed to a wail.

'Ann,' he called. He called again – louder this time. Damn the woman, why didn't she answer and do something to stop the crying.

He strode past an imposing, old sideboard that Ann's mother, Rose, had given them. The bevelled, ill-fitting mirror rattled as it fleetingly reflected his passing. It brought to mind his mother-in-law's abusive reaction when he had confessed that her daughter, who she considered could do no wrong, was three months pregnant. She had called him a sex-crazed madman who should be locked away

He tried to put negative thoughts aside as he hurried through the living room and stepped down into the kitchen. Sally ceased to cry. The silence gave an eerie feeling to the empty room. He livened up the meagre glow from the fire and swung the soot-blackened kettle over the coals. He shrugged his broad shoulders and frowned as he pictured Ann sitting in a comfortable armchair at her mother's house. She'd be giving out her orders, and Rose would do her bidding as she always had. Fetch me a cup of tea mother – I'm cold get me a blanket. His lip curled, and the image faded as Sally began to whimper.

He threw his old, brown work jacket and flat cap on a scrubbed wooden table – the only piece of furniture in the small kitchen. Returning to the pokey living room, he threaded his way past a faded, horsehair sofa, and yanked open the door that hid a steep flight of stairs.

'Alright Bab, hold on Daddy's coming.' His gravelly voice softened when he spoke to his two-year-old daughter. Bill hadn't expected to feel anything for the baby that he hoped would be a boy. Living with Ann and the lump, as he'd referred to the baby, represented the end of his freedom. But he fell in love with his bald, scrap of a child the minute he was allowed to see her.

He took the stairs three at a time cracking his head on the slope of the ceiling at the top of the narrow flight.

'Alright, alright little one,' he said. He bent his six foot two, lean frame down and scooped his daughter up from her bed.

It was cold in the dimly lit room, but Sally's face was hot and sticky, tiny tufts of golden hair stuck wetly to her forehead. She had been sick on her blanket. He inhaled the smell of sour milk as he hugged her close to him, and rocked her gently until she settled down to a quiet whimper.

'Come on my love, let's get you something to eat, you'll feel better.' He continued to rock her in his arms as he carried her downstairs.

'Where's your Mum, eh?' he asked, 'as if you care now that your Daddy's here.' Sally rewarded him with a toothy smile and lifted her hand to touch his scratchy face.

As he changed his daughter's napkin, he felt overwhelmed with love for her. She was so small and utterly dependant. In his opinion, Ann was once again neglecting Sally, and this thought drew his lips into a thin line. He thanked God that he hadn't yet been called up. He'd had to register and knew that it could happen anytime. What would happen to Sally then? He wouldn't be able to keep an eye on her. He tried to imagine carrying a rifle and shooting someone. He wasn't a coward, but he knew he couldn't do it.

He and Ann had had endless arguments about her neglect of Sally, and often these arguments morphed into ones about sex or more frequently about her slovenly housekeeping. Bill regularly came home and found that he had to dump clothing off the sofa before he could sit down, or wash the breakfast dishes up, because Ann had spent her day reading or round at her mother's house.

When Sally had been fed, with bread soaked in milk and sugar, and was babbling happily to him, he brewed a pot of tea then sat on the sofa with her on his lap. He poured some tea into his saucer, blew on it and allowed her to take sips while he listened for the sound of a key in the front door. Eventually, she drifted off to sleep with his index finger gripped tightly in her small, pink hand.

Bill withdrew his finger from her tenacious grasp and lay her down using a cushion for a guard at her side. She fluttered her lids a few times but slept peacefully on. He studied her relaxed face, she really was beautiful, and closely resembled her mother. How Ann could resist loving her, he couldn't fathom.

He fetched his coat from the kitchen, covered her, and then sat beside her to untie his boots. He eased them off with a sigh of relief. Thoughts of soaking his feet fled as his head sagged onto his chest. Voices, faces and images spun around and around. Strain as he might, he couldn't quite follow what they were saying. Ceasing to try to understand, sleep claimed him.

As his slumber deepened, lines of worry, that lately seemed to have become a part of his features, smoothed out. His attractive face, ready smile and friendly manner endeared him to many people. He often caught the eye of both single and married women, but he rarely noticed.

Bill snored and moved his long legs into a more comfortable position. Even in sleep, he seemed aware that Sally slept beside him. One of his ungainly looking hands rested lightly on her feet where they touched against his thigh.

The clock on the mantle shelf ticked on unheard, the shadows outside the small window, curtained with off white nets, lengthened. The moon disappeared behind a cloud, shrouding the living room in darkness.

Bill shivered as he woke. The house had become chilly, but Sally slept on with her thumb in her mouth. He rose carefully and stretched, bringing his muscles back to life. He removed his coat and fetched a blanket that his mother had knitted to cover Sally. His stomach growled.

Bill yawned as he took a box of matches from his coat pocket, pulled down the gas lamp from the ceiling above the sofa and lit it. He strode into the kitchen to make a pot of tea and find something to eat. He swore under his breath as his foray into the range oven in search of a dinner proved to be in vain.

He sorted out some bread that was stale but edible and cutting a thick slice spread it with a scrape of dripping. He ate slowly, silencing the lion in his stomach, but not the irritation that continued to gnaw away at him.

Perching on the edge of the kitchen table and sipping his tea he looked with distaste around the cheerless room and noticed a piece of paper on the worn, stone floor by the door. He recognised Ann's writing. The note was simple and to the point – I've gone for good this time – don't you try to find me – I've fed Sally – Ann.

He threw the paper aside. Ann had left three times before and gone to her mother's; returning when she'd ceased to feel sorry for herself. He sat down again and stared blankly at the whitewashed brick wall in front of him. If only she'd stay away this time, he could raise Sally on his own; he'd manage somehow.

Bill thought that Rose was to blame for many things. He believed that she'd spoiled Ann to compensate for her father's death while she was an infant.

According to Rose, Ann's father, Reginald, was estranged from his family, who came from Nottingham. He already owned property when he'd met Rose in Lincoln Cathedral. He was a prosperous grocer until he became ill, and had to sell the shop and one of the four houses that he owned.

When he eventually died from a brain tumour, Rose had inherited everything. Although she'd published details of his death in The Nottingham Post, no one attended his funeral that she didn't know.

Ann became her world, and she hated Bill for taking her away.

Bill shrugged his shoulders and ran his hands through his straight, blue-black hair. He decided that Ann had had her chance – he wouldn't have her back again.

His parents were both deceased and other than his twin brother Arthur and their sister Clarissa he cared little for anyone other than Sally

He and Clarissa often shared their worries about their good-humoured brother who had joined the navy when he was fifteen years of age. Since the outbreak of war, they'd heard nothing from him or about his ship, HMS Acasta and were both extremely concerned.

5

Birmingham

Abigail walked quickly, taking tiny steps and laughed as she said, 'I'm afraid the fish market's our first stop, do you eat fish or do you prefer meat?'

Bill answered, but Abigail failed to notice, she was too engrossed in the small face that peered up at her. She tucked the knitted shawl firmly around Sally's shoulders while making a mental note that someone had loved her enough to make her some beautiful clothes. It felt wonderful to be holding a child again, even though she wasn't her own, and wished she could keep her. No sooner had this thought entered her head than Abigail scolded herself, and put a block on her imagination. Thinking along those lines would lead to further unhappiness. She determined just to enjoy the child while she held her. As they climbed the stone flight of steps leading into the fish market, Abigail's thoughts turned to her husband. Whatever would he say, would he think that she'd taken leave of her senses bringing a stranger and a little girl home with her?

Although she felt apprehensive, she wasn't too perturbed. Jim had his faults, but he was usually an affable man who wasn't averse to doing a good turn for people in need. He may question her motives, but she knew his support, and sound advice would not be lacking. At least she hoped she still knew him that well.

Bill trailed closely behind Abigail as she rapidly completed her shopping. He offered to carry Sally a couple of times, but Abigail denied the need, preferring to make her purchases hampered by her welcome burden. Sally seemed to be happy with the stranger, who smelled of flowers and held firmly on to her. She searched Abigail's round face and looked around occasionally for her father, but she made no protest.

Abigail rushed about so quickly through the crush of people that it was all Bill could do to keep sight of her. His eyes, ears and nose were popping with all the sights, sounds and smells which assailed him from the fascinating, busy streets that they passed through. Since he'd stepped from the train at New Street Station and negotiated his way through the bustling passengers to the ticket barrier, his mind had been bombarded with unfamiliarity. He felt ashamed and frustrated by the circumstances that had brought him here. He would have enjoyed exploring this new-found city if only he were free from the worry of his actions.

Birmingham was much bigger than he'd envisaged. There were masses of people milling in and out of shops catering to the wealthy, and stalls selling clothing and goods that had seen many previous owners. They'd surrounded him on his way to the quiet haven of the church where he'd met Abigail. Considering that there was a war going on, he thought, there seemed to be plenty of goods to buy and people to buy them.

He looked at Abigail's retreating backside and thanked the Lord for her. He had no idea what he'd have done if not for her kindness; it was too cold to be out late with Sally. He found himself smiling his gratitude at her hastily receding, plump figure, and wondered, not for the first time, why she'd decided to do a stranger a good turn?

After leaving the fish market, Abigail bought vegetables from one of the barrows as they walked down the cobbled hill towards Jamaica Row. The wooden carts with their big, iron-rimmed wheels and cheeky, weather-beaten vendors, who called out raucously to potential customers, lined the street as far as Bill's eyes could see. Dusk had just started to fall, and many of the barrows had oil lamps standing in amongst the wares, spreading little puddles of light around the iron weights and scales. It was a scene that Bill repeatedly saw over time, but one that never ceased to give him an inexplicable feeling of comfort.

A strong stench of rotting vegetation wafted towards him as they neared Jamaica Row. He breathed through his mouth as he spied the source; a pile of trimmings from cabbages and other waste was decomposing against the wall of a building that Abigail informed him was the rag ally.

Bills eyes lighted on a hunched-up woman who appeared to be a hundred years old. Dressed in a dirty, tattered shawl, that was held together by a large brooch which was missing all but one blue stone, and a worn-out black skirt that dragged on the ground while she stooped to root about through the discarded rubbish. She shook as though with the ague and muttered to herself as she scrutinized each piece that she picked up. Leaves and other acceptable bits and pieces were shoved into a threadbare hessian bag that she pulled through the garbage. She could have been invisible; attention only being paid to her by a scruffy, black mongrel that vied with her in her search for food.

Abigail didn't seem to notice the woman; she was intent on heading home where she could comfort Sally who'd become restless. Though quite a well-rounded woman, Abigail could still make haste when she wished and proceeded to hurry Bill along towards the River Rea.

Shifting the suitcase and various shopping bags around to redistribute their weight, he dogged her footsteps. He was trying to work out a plausible story to explain to Abigail and her husband, why he'd brought his daughter to Birmingham. Bill wondered yet again if someone had found Ann's body, and if the police were looking for him. He didn't think they were magicians, but they would probably be able to trace his whereabouts – and so would the Army. His spirits sank; he could hardly tell them that he'd killed his wife, he thought wryly, even if it was accidental. He decided to keep his story as simple as possible to avoid having to remember the lies.

Bill could hear Abigail puffing along. 'Nearly home,' she said, and as they crossed the road, she waved a hand and continued, this bit is Cheapside, and this here's the corner of Birchall Street. They walked in single file through a covered entry to the back of a Post Office building. He felt all his confidence evaporate. He doubted his ability to lie convincingly, and he could imagine Abigail's husband throwing him out into the cold, damp night. Then where could he take Sally? Her immediate comfort was his primary concern. He just had to get by.

Praying that his luck would hold out, he followed Abigail across the blue, brick-paved yard. He became aware of just how tired and hungry he felt as they entered the homely kitchen where the white-painted brick walls gleamed with pots and pans. There were bunches of dried herbs, hanging from nails hammered between the bricks. They scented the air with thyme and sage mixed with other sweet odours that Bill couldn't identify.

Abigail called out to her husband that she was home, and that she'd brought visitors. She climbed a small step with Sally in her arms and disappeared, but Bill hung back and chewed his lip while he waited for an invitation to enter.

6

Quiet voices from the other room reached Bill's ears, but he couldn't make out the words. He stood twisting his wedding ring round and round until a man's voice called out, 'Don't stand out there lad come on in and tek the weight off y' feet.' The strong Birmingham accent startled Bill as Abigail had spoken with a faint Welsh lilt, but he obeyed and entered the comfortably warm living room.

Abigail's husband rose quickly from his chair by the fire and stepped forward hand outstretched. 'Nice to meet you, Bill, I'm Jim.' They shook hands. 'Sit y'self down lad.' He gestured towards the sofa that was placed by the range where a coal fire blazed. Bill sat gingerly on the edge of the seat. 'Kettle's nearly boiled; you'd like a cuppa?'

'Yes, please, I'm parched,' Bill said. He surveyed Jim as he sat back down and then smiled his thanks at him. He was just about to ask the whereabouts of Abigail and Sally when a door in the corner of the room opened, and Abigail stepped off the last stair. Her face was beaming.

'There,' she said, 'all changed and comfy.'

Jim disappeared behind his newspaper.

Abigail set Sally down on the floor by Bill's knees. Sally quickly held out her arms to be picked up. Bill obliged, and she settled onto her father's lap. Her thumb went into her mouth as her eyelids drooped wearily.

Abigail eyed Bill then her husband; smoothed her dress down on her hips and walked towards the kitchen.

'I'll see to her bottle and make a cup of tea then we can relax and have a good chinwag. Make yourself at home, Bill,' she said.

Bill eased himself back onto the sofa and began to rock his daughter on his knee. He was surprised that she wasn't clamouring for food. It was some time since she'd last had anything. Perhaps she senses that she has to be on her best behaviour, he thought gazing at her with pride.

Bustling about, Abigail efficiently produced both Sally's milk and a slice of bread and butter for her to eat. She passed a cup of strong tea to her husband and then one to Bill.

'Can Sally feed herself, or shall I?' Abigail asked Bill.

'What about your tea?' Bill said.

'Don't you worry about me lad, I'd as soon make sure that Sally's fed first, I'll have mine in a minute,' Abigail held out her capable arms, 'give her here then. Come on, little darling; you must be famished.' She soothed the child with her voice while testing the heat of the milk on her hand. Holding onto the bottle, Sally sucked greedily the instant the teat entered her mouth. When it was almost empty, she dropped it to the floor and started to eat her bread. For a while, a comfortable silence reigned in the homely room.

Bill drank his tea and felt his body begin to relax while the warmth from the fire seeped into his bones. His eyes wandered around the neat living room taking in the sewing machine, and a mound of clothing nearby.

'I'm a seamstress,' Abigail said, following his gaze, and Jim's a slaughterman at the meat market around the corner, we do alright for meat and clothes in this house, we're fortunate really.' She gave a smile and a nod in her husband's direction.

Despite her smile, Bill thought he detected wistfulness in her last remark. Jim didn't seem to notice anything amiss; he placed his empty cup on the hearth and turned to face Bill, a question in his eyes.

Bill's heartbeat quickened. 'I'm sorry we've turned up like this, but I was becoming worried about Sally, and your wife seemed to think that you wouldn't mind.' He took a breath and waited for Jim's response.

'Oh, I'm used ter Abigail's lame ducks, no offence meant,' he chuckled, 'what's brought you to Birmingham lad if y'know no bugger here?'

Mentally crossing his fingers, Bill told them a story of his wife's death during childbirth, and with no second thought, went on to blame his mother-in-law for his flight from Lincoln.

'But why did Rose blame you for her daughter's death,' Jim asked, 'seems unreasonable to me?'

'She blames me for getting Ann pregnant. Can't say I think she's wrong in a way. Ann was too young, and she wasn't ready for marriage.' Bill couldn't look at Abigail as he talked. Sex wasn't a topic that he'd generally mention in the presence of a female, and he thought she'd be embarrassed by his frankness.

Abigail raised her eyebrows but said nothing.

As he took responsibility for wrongdoing in his mother-in-law's eyes, Bill admitted to himself for the first time that it *had* been his fault. He should have kept Ann safe; she'd been too young to know what she was doing. The insight left a bitter taste in his mouth as he quietly continued with his storytelling.

'Rose wouldn't leave me alone. She was forever round at the house telling me how to look after Sally. She constantly interfered although she refused to help me out by sometimes looking after Sally while I went to work. I had no choice but to leave her with a neighbour. Everything came to a head yesterday. I couldn't take it anymore and decided on the spur of the moment to make a fresh start in London.' Bill poured the story out with scarcely a breath; he couldn't wait for the lies to be over.

Jim nodded and pulled on his pipe which he'd been filling with sweet-smelling tobacco while Bill had been talking. He blew smoke from the side of his mouth, and then spat a stream of brownish liquid into the fire, where it sizzled for an instant.

Jim gazed intently into the fire. 'In London?'

Before Bill could reply, Abigail stood up with Sally who'd gone to sleep; she handed her to her father, and he cuddled her into his chest.

'I'll see to our tea now,' Abigail said, 'I'm sure you must both be starving?'

While she busied herself in the kitchen, the two men continued their conversation. Bill, keeping it as simple as possible, talked about missing the London train connection, and on impulse boarding the Birmingham one. Jim's cautious curiosity seemed to be satisfied; he closed his eyes and nodded off with his pipe threatening to fall from his hand. Bill decided to ignore it; he didn't want to disturb Sally.

7

Lincoln

So cold – she had to move and get help, or she was going to die. Ann turned her head slowly to see where dust balls lay undisturbed under the sofa. Her eyes paused to watch a small spider busily weaving its web; running to and fro where hessian touched the metal caster on the couch. The spider's concentrated technique held her interest until, once again, cold intruded on her consciousness.

Gripping the barley twist leg of the oak sideboard Ann tried to bring herself to a sitting position. Her legs were useless – two dead weights. She eased her hands under her thighs, dug her fingernails hard into the flaccid muscles, and pulled in an attempt to bend her legs at the knees. The pain in her neck swiftly flared into unbearable agony. Her efforts only resulted in permanent scarring to the back of her legs. Her breathing came in short bursts; if I don't get some help, I might be paralysed forever, she thought. A rush of much-needed adrenalin helped her to reach the front door by pushing against furniture and pulling herself inch by inch along the shiny floor. Her frantic banging and cries for help quickly alerted passers-by.

Unable to open the door, they'd forced entry at the back of the house. A tear-stained, dehydrated, hysterical young woman had been carried rapidly to her mother's house. Her two-day ordeal, much of which she had been unaware of, was at an end. For three days Ann was too ill to answer questions, and then she'd concocted a version of events which had satisfied everyone except her mother.

Ann knew she was fortunate; the temporary paralysis of her legs was caused by swelling that had put pressure on her spinal cord. As the swelling reduced, the use and feeling in them gradually returned. Any thought of blaming Bill for her injuries to make him suffer too rapidly fled from her calculations. The realisation that he could go to prison, and she'd once again be responsible for her daughter's welfare, prompted her to hide the truth.

Rose instinctively knew that Ann's tale of an accident, where she'd slipped, tangled her feet in her coat and then hit her head on the sideboard after Bill had left, was not the complete truth. She'd had enough experience of her daughter's prevarications in the past not to recognise the signs. She couldn't imagine what the truthful version of events could be, but she wasn't at all surprised that Bill had left and taken Sally with him. They should never have married in her opinion. Ann was too young, and she'd led a sheltered life.

Rose was secretly overjoyed that her only child had returned home where she could look after her. Had she been challenged about her attitude, she would've been bewildered by the questions. She had no insight into her motives for wanting to keep her daughter a child as long as possible. She wasn't a reflective person and saw very few negative consequences in sheltering Ann from life's realities and responsibilities. Conversely Rose had little or no interest in her granddaughter, barely acknowledging her existence. If she thought about her at all, she excused both herself and her daughter by believing that Sally was Bill's responsibility.

Rose pretended to believe Ann's story. She was sure that her daughter would confide in her at a later date, and it didn't matter why Ann had been able to return home, as long as she had.

'Make us a cup of tea Mum.' Ann called from her bedroom. The door was open, and she could hear her mother moving about downstairs. Rose always got up early; otherwise, her arthritic joints stiffened up and became more painful.

Ann raised her head and listened; she could hear her mother as she raked embers from the fire. Bugger it. She must have forgotten to bank it up with potato peelings and slack before she went to bed – the fire had gone out.

Irritated by her mother's forgetfulness, Ann flung herself on to her side, pulled the blankets and eiderdown up around her face, and tried to go back to sleep. All the time that Rose spent nursing her daughter back to health, Ann had failed to appreciate the devotion that her mother showered on her. She was unaware of the pallor, or the lines of weariness and pain that were on Rose's gaunt features.

Ann turned onto her back and stretched; taking pleasure in the luxury of single occupancy. Sharing with Bill had been repulsive to her for more than one reason. Thinking of Bill made her wonder briefly, but without concern, how Sally fared. She knew he'd care for the child; so why was she feeling apprehension and guilt? She certainly didn't want her present situation to alter, and self- recrimination was a waste of time. Shaking off thoughts that troubled her, she allowed herself to think of Dr Marlow.

An image of his kind face and gentle hands brought a warm flush to her body. He'd promised her a change of scenery today she remembered with anticipation. Always a creature of swiftly changing moods, Ann was buoyed up: she was free of responsibility; she was alive and recovering from her ordeal, and she would soon see Dr Marlow.

Her index finger probed the irregular, ridge of tissue at the back of her head. The soreness had almost disappeared. Ann closed her eyes and allowed her mind to wander; her hands ran lightly over her winceyette nightgown. Her fingertips lingered, caressing the contrasting rough lace that decorated the smooth nap of the bodice. She hesitated for a moment then gently stroked inwards and upwards with both hands manipulating her nipples. Enlarged since the birth of Sally, the erectile tissue stiffened in response to her familiar touch. An unheard moan escaped her lips as spreading her fingers she allowed palms that had heightened in sensation to move lightly in circles, skimming the erectile tissue. She masturbated. But it wasn't Bill's face that appeared in her fantasy.

Ann's thoughts were turning with increasing frequency to her married doctor. She'd tried with little success to redirect her daydreams, but she continued to weave stories linking them together whenever she was alone. The unwitting thoughts, and memories that had caused her body to betray her, brought a shamed flush to her cheeks. She turned on her side and clasping her hands firmly together allowed her mind to dwell on desires which she'd naively thought had disappeared from her life forever. During these musings, however, the face of Doctor Marlow was displaced by that of her husband. She'd re-lived their last argument repeatedly in her mind, and her mouth drooped to find she was doing so yet again.

A faint tap on the panel of the door presaged Rose's entry into the bedroom. 'Are you awake dear?' Rose whispered, placing her hand gently on her daughter's shoulder. Ann kept her eyes shut; afraid they might betray the riotous thoughts that had been running through her mind.

Rose sat on the edge of the bed and waited. After a couple of seconds, Ann stretched her arms above her head, yawned, pretended to rub the sleep from sticky eyes, and opened them slowly. 'Morning Mum, what sort of day is it?'

'Need you ask? It's been raining cats and dogs all night, and I forgot to bank the fire up before I came to bed. It's taken me ages to get it going again; the kindling was so damp. I must remember to buy another basket and keep some in the house like we used to.' Rose answered her daughter in her usual clipped manner. She buzzed about the room, pouring water into the pink, crock basin from the matching ewer, and helped Ann to sit up and freshen herself.

'I can get up today, can't I Mum? Dr Marlow said I could,' Ann mumbled from under the voluminous folds of her nightgown as she pulled it impatiently over her head.

'Are you sure you feel up to it, it's only been three days since you regained the complete use of your –'

'Oh, don't fuss, Mum, I feel alright. I'm on top of the world, and I'm bored of staying in bed.' Her mother sighed and nodded.

8

Birmingham

Abigail set the table, all the while humming softly to herself. When they were seated, the two men found that their shared interest in the war gave them a topic of conversation. They talked enthusiastically throughout the meal. Abigail poured tea and buttered bread for them, allowing their voices to flow over her head, her thoughts and glances filled with the child who lay asleep on the couch.

Abigail had always refused to consider the likelihood of war. It scared her so much that she ignored any references to the subject and wouldn't contemplate the thought that Jim might eventually have to join in the fighting and could die. She was grateful that, for her sake, he had resisted his initial intention to volunteer even though he felt it was his duty.

Jim took a bite from a piece of bread and butter, swallowed a mouthful of herring that had been dipped in flour and fried in lard, then wiped his mouth with the back of his hand.

'Yer welcome to stay with us f' now,' he said, nodding his head in Bill's direction, 'it'll give yer a chance to find a job an' get yerself an' the babby a place to live. I know my missus won't say no t'lookin' after the babby for yer,' he turned to Abigail, 'will yer love?'

She beamed. 'It'll be a pleasure, and we have a spare room and a small bed which we can fetch up from the cellar for Sally.'

Hardly able to believe good fortune was holding out for him, Bill thanked them both profusely. Thanks which they brushed aside. He already had a fondness for Abigail who reminded him of his mother, and this feeling now spilt over to her husband. Their kindness almost overwhelmed him, but he was a fugitive, and he could imagine the horror his new friends would feel if they knew the truth. Had they found Ann's body yet? Was it only this morning that the row had taken place? It seemed years had passed. Hopefully, they'd never have to know he thought. He'd be out of their lives as soon as he could find a job and a furnished room to rent, and someone reliable to mind Sally. Luckily, he had enough money to tide them over until he could earn again.

Lost in his thoughts, he was surprised when Jim invited him to go for a pint. Although Bill was agreeable, he hesitated. He didn't want to offend Jim but believed that he shouldn't put upon Abigail to mind Sally, she'd done enough.

Abigail, however, had other ideas. 'Go on out,' she said, 'I'll enjoy putting Sally to bed.'

'Mind you fetch the bed up first though,' she reminded her husband, 'I'll need to air it in front of the fire. Come with me, Bill and bring your bits and pieces. I'll show you your room.' She led the way up the steep wooden stairs. Bill followed, banging awkwardly into the side of the door jamb with his suitcase.

'Mind the paint lad,' Jim said and chuckled.

Bill knew that he spoke more to put him at his ease than out of concern for his paintwork, and any lingering tension left him.

'Here's your room, and ours is there,' Abigail pointed to the opposite door. 'I hope you'll be comfortable, Bill. I'll get Jim to put Sally's bed next to yours. I've already made it up with fresh sheets, and I've put a towel on the chair for you.' She pointed to a cane chair in the corner of the surprisingly large room they'd just entered. 'If you need anything else, just ask – oh, I forgot to say that there's water in the ewer if you want to wash. We're the only ones in the yard who've got a sink and water tap, so I change the water every day.' Her voice dropped to a little more than a loud whisper. 'I know you've already found your way down the yard, but we share – the middle one's ours – well it's the one I keep clean anyway.'

Bill patted her arm. 'Thanks, Abigail, I don't think I'll ever be able to say it enough.'

Abigail smiled and patted him back.

Having imparted all of this vital information, she hurried back downstairs to comfort Sally who'd begun to cry. Jim was just about to call her. He always said that he didn't know one end of a baby from the other, and he wanted it to stay that way. Babies, in his opinion, were women's business. He much preferred his task of transferring their daughter's bed from the cellar to be aired.

Abigail would have been amazed and deeply touched if she'd witnessed Jim's display of emotion as he picked up the thin mattress. Feelings which he'd buried forever, so he thought, surfaced and briefly held sway. Jim missed his pretty little daughter. He couldn't share his hurt, especially with his wife, although he wouldn't have been able to explain why. He only knew that thoughts of Grace made him feel weak and vulnerable, and they were best kept hidden.

'C'mon Bill,' he called as he climbed up from the cellar, 'I need a beer.'

9

Abigail tried not to think too deeply; aware that she mustn't become attached to Sally; she couldn't count on her being with them for long. Today was the first time that she was truly alone with a toddler since the death of her daughter. As she hugged the little girl to her, cathartic tears coursed down her face.

Sally didn't stir as Abigail continued to cry out her feelings of grief and guilt until at last, she seemed able to accept their loss for what it was – a tragic accident.

Sharply defined images and words, despite the passage of time, once again thrust themselves onto the battered screen of her mind. She pictured her daughter running, gleefully calling out, 'Here you are Mommy,' just before she tripped over a rag rug and fell down the step into the kitchen. Her favourite china eggcup, in the shape of a chicken, held out in one hand, and her small egg spoon clutched in her other one. Abigail could still hear the sound of the egg cup breaking as Grace tumbled. Her precious child died from a brain haemorrhage while she held her; much as she rocked Sally now. The egg spoon had entered through one of Grace's large, grey eyes, piercing her brain and severing an artery. Life had rapidly left her daughter, and Abigail could do nothing. It was some hours before she could bring herself to accept that her daughter had gone. She'd continued to sit on the stone step, with Grace in her arms, until Jim returned home expecting his lunch to be on the table. Abigail screamed and cried and carried on pleading for the return of their daughter for hours after they'd taken her body away. Eventually, in desperation, Jim had paid the local doctor to give her something to make her sleep. Abigail's recall of the days that followed was sketchy.

For several weeks she'd barely eaten or left the house unless forced to do so. She blamed herself for leaving Grace on her own for even the few minutes it took for the tragedy to happen. It counted for very little when friends tried to help assuage her guilt. After the funeral, Abigail took to her bed for several days until Jim insisted that she venture downstairs. Her devastating grief was exacerbated by the knowledge that she couldn't have more children. Giving birth to Grace had been complicated, and Abigail knew that further pregnancies could mean an early passage into the next world for her.

Their marriage was under a lot of pressure, and sexual intercourse, which had become very infrequent to prevent further pregnancies, ceased altogether after Grace's death. Abigail was aware that her love for Jim had died at some point in the last five years, but it had been a gradual process. One that had made it possible for them to remain, friends, as their relationship changed. She knew that she would never cease to blame herself for Grace's death, but a feeling of peace began to steal over her as she sat with Sally. She kissed her charge on the cheek and vowed that she would stop grieving so bitterly and try to satisfy her maternal needs by helping some of the many unfortunate children where she lived.

Abigail laid Sally on the sofa, needing to make supper for Jim and their lodger. Several hours seemed to pass, but the clock on the mantelpiece told her that they had only been gone for an hour and a half. She felt as though she'd had a gift of extended time, as she prepared the bedding for Sally. She hoped that her tears while holding the little girl would bring about a change in her life, but knew that only time would tell.

10

Lincoln

'Come on lazy bones, get up it's a lovely day, and we're going shopping.' Ann said. The novelty of being allowed out hadn't yet worn off. She tugged playfully at the pink and green bedspread drawn up to her mother's chin. Her playfulness ended abruptly as she saw the disfigurement of her mother's deathly pale face, and realised with dawning horror that something was wrong.

'Mum, what's wrong Mum?' Ann's voice seemed loud and harsh in the stillness of the early morning.

Her mother lay unmoving, but she opened her eyes and looked beseechingly up at her daughter. The left half of her face seemed to have slipped somehow while her mouth grimaced as if she tasted something sour. She attempted to tell her daughter that she couldn't move, but the only sounds that emerged were garbled. Ann leaned closer to understand, but a stench that filled her nostrils as she drew near, caused her to recoil.

Her reaction to her mother's plight filled her with shame. She took her mother's cold hand that had twisted, claw-like towards the wrist, and tried to impart some warmth to it by gently rubbing it between her own.

'It's alright, Mum – I'll go and get help.' Ann gently placed her mother's hand onto the eiderdown. She turned to go to summon the doctor but stopped as her mother again made an effort to communicate. Rose's eyes rolled as she gasped for enough breath to speak. Saliva dribbled from the corner of her mouth as her lips moved uselessly, fishlike, still uttering gibberish. Ann ran crying from the room.

11

Birmingham

'Stop running about like a headless chicken,' Abigail admonished Bill, 'it's not going to get you there any quicker, you're already late.'

Helpful though her words were, he continued to rush around gathering his coat and cap together before thrusting his feet into his work boots. Abigail breathed a sigh of relief when he eventually plonked on Jim's chair and proceeded to tie his laces. Then he was up again and heading for the door. He retraced his steps, to where she stood with Sally on her hip, and bending over, tenderly kissed his daughter goodbye. With a hasty, 'Tara, see you later,' he was gone.

Sally's face crumpled. She held her chubby arms out towards the door and called, 'Daddy come back.' Abigail cuddled her to her cheek and planted another kiss there.

'Daddy's gone to work, but he'll be back later, my love. Shall we have our breakfast now?' Sally sniffled and stuffed her thumb into her mouth. As they walked to the kitchen, she used her other hand to grab the gold chain, which Abigail always wore around her neck. Abigail absently disengaged Sally's hand and repeatedly clucked to distract her. Rocking her hips, and continuing to make amusing noises, she succeeded in making tea and toast and a bottle of warm milk, which the little girl drank with relish. When she'd finished drinking, Abigail pulled apart pieces of buttered toast and passed them to her charge. Sally was a tidy eater and became dismayed when some bits ended up on the floor.

'It's alright my love,' Abigail said. She picked up the pieces and blew on them saying, 'God bless, no germs,' and then popped them back into Sally's eager hand.

Contentment exuded from both participants in this daily ritual which took place as soon as Jim and Bill left for work. Abigail thought it was the best part of her day. She was able to pretend, rightly or wrongly, that Sally was her daughter, and no one was there to dispute her flight of fancy.

During the couple of months that Bill and Sally had been staying with them, Abigail had tried hard not to become too involved. She loved Sally with all her being and refused to contemplate the day when Bill would move on and take his daughter with him.

After Bill had spent a few weeks doing odd jobs, cash in hand, Jim had spoken for him, and he'd begun work at the slaughterhouse. Abigail knew that he wasn't happy being involved with the killing of animals, but it enabled him to earn enough money to rent a place for him and Sally. She was relieved that there'd been no mention of their living arrangement coming to an end as yet, but when she couldn't help but think about it, she felt sure that the status quo wouldn't go on for much longer. Jim, true to form, had said nothing, but she knew he wouldn't want Bill to live with them forever. Whenever Bill started a conversation with her lately, her tension increased. She'd begun to avoid him whenever possible, and she thought that he'd become aware of distance developing between them. It saddened her. Her common sense told her that she should discuss her feelings with either Bill or her husband, but she hadn't. She wouldn't risk precipitating the inevitable parting of the ways.

After breakfast, surfaces clean and tidy, and elbow grease having achieved a deep shine on the furniture and hearth; Abigail gave Sally her favourite toys and set about finishing off the current sewing orders. She worked hard to ensure her reputation, and her name was well known. She knew that there were other good seamstresses out there just biding their time.

12

A light knock on the kitchen door announced the arrival of Mrs Evans, who was both their landlady and a good friend. She opened the door as usual and stood just inside. 'Ow do Abi am you in?'

Abigail smiled to herself, hearing her friend's daft question. She always announced the start of their well-established morning routine with this greeting. The mid-morning cup of tea and gossip that they shared had begun after the death of Grace. Initially, Abigail knew she'd been less than welcoming, and had at times turned the key in the kitchen door and pretended she was out. But Ellen had persisted, and a deep and trusting friendship had developed between the two women. They now resembled close siblings who shared joys and sorrows alike. Not that Abigail had felt sorrowful since Sally's advent.

Following the death of her husband, in a train accident, Ellen had continued to run the post office with the help of an assistant. Usually content with her lot, she now took every opportunity to pop – round the back – and give a hand with Sally. One of the primary bonds between the two women was the fact that Ellen too knew the heartache of a childless marriage.

'Come on in and shut the door, the kettles on.'

Ellen entered the room quickly, as usual. She was a tall, plain-looking woman. She had a beaky nose and way of pursing her lips that made Sally think of a bird waiting to peck at seeds. Ellen was born and bred in Wednesbury and proud of her Black Country heritage. Sometimes when she was teased about her broad accent, she hit back jokingly about being a Brummie only by marriage not by preference.,

Ellen sat down and cuddled Sally until Abigail put aside her needlework, poured boiling water over the tea leaves in her favourite blue teapot, and then set it down on the hob.

The two women relaxed into their familiar routine; glad to be in each others' company. As usual, Abigail brought Ellen up to date with Sally's progress since the day before. These simple tales gave the two of them considerable pleasure, and Sally loved the attention. This morning was different, however, as Abigail wanted to share a worry.

'Bill got a letter yesterday,' she sipped her tea, 'I think it must have been some good news; he slept soundly last night for the first time since he's been here. I don't know who it was from, but it made him late getting up for work this morning.'

'Oh, yes.' Ellen coughed, tickled Sally's hair, and gazed intently at her friend as she waited for her to continue.

'The postmark was from Lincoln; you know he comes from there.' Abigail gave a deep sigh and made a helpless gesture with her hands. 'I can't help thinking that he may be going to go back and take Sally with him.' Her face tensed as she tried to stop the tears that had begun to rain down her red cheeks. 'I can't bear to lose her Ellen.'

Ellen sprang from her chair and placed a comforting arm around her friend's shoulders. 'Now, now, yow'r jumpin' the gun ain't yow? It's probably somat and nowt, don't be gettin' upset till yow've talked to Bill. It's about time there was a little plain speaking atween yow two anyway, yow've bin livin' with this 'angin over yow'r 'ed fer wiks now.'

Abigail fished under the bib of her pinny, and mopped her eyes with the handkerchief she kept tucked away. 'I know you're right, Jim's already told me that if I don't talk to Bill soon, and find out what his plans are, then he will.'

'I'll mek us another pot, this 'uns stone-cold,' Ellen strode off towards the kitchen, 'yow'll feel much betta when yow know summat definit.'

Abigail's wet eyes followed her friend's back. 'I know, I know, I'll try and talk with him tonight. You're a good friend, Ellen – I don't know what I would've done without you these last few years.'

When Ellen returned, she kissed her friend on top of her head and then handed Abigail a cup with plenty of bubbles on the surface.

'Ere, drink yow'r tea, an' stop yow'r mitherin, I cor do without yow either. And we're upsettin' the babby.'

13

Bill strode down Bradford Street counting his blessings. He whistled in time with the click, clack of his metal-studded boots as they hit the uneven cobbles that sustained a daily beating from cattle driven from Curzon Street Station to slaughter. Traffic and people also took their toll, but Bill wasn't thinking about anything so mundane.

The sun was shining, and he could hear a robin singing, his brain sang too as he passed a derelict factory where a few straggly buddleias struggled to live. He hadn't killed his wife. He could feel the sun on his face – he hadn't killed his wife – Sally had a comfortable home with caring people – he hadn't killed his wife – it felt like Christmas – he wasn't wanted by the police, and he hadn't killed his wife.

Bill felt young and bursting with happiness. He had a job, not an enjoyable one, but it was one that paid. Good fortune smiled. He knew he'd never be able to adequately repay Jim for speaking up for him or Abigail for looking after Sally, but he vowed to try one day.

He leaned against the stone gateway at the entrance to the abattoir adjoining the meat market and took his sister's letter from his jacket pocket.   He re-read her welcome scribble.

Our House

April 1916
   Dear Bill Well you might have let me know where you were sooner. Shes alright, no thanks to you!!!!! You can breathe a sigh of relief you bloody fool you could have easily killed her. Shes at her mums but shes been through a hell of a lot I tell you. She was out of it for two days before she managed to attract the attention of someone. Why she hasnt told the police it was you that shoved her and caused her injuris I carnt understand. Anns stickin to her story after youd taken Sally she tripped over her coat and banged her head on that old sideboard, but her mum dont believe thats what really happened and shes been round here wantin to know where youd got to. I told her you hadnt been in touch with me, and I dont know where you are or what happened. Mind you if you ask me I think shes so glad to have her daughter back where she can mollycoddle her that she wont be makin much fuss if you stay away. She never even asked after Sally. Unatural thats what the pair of them are. How can you not love your own baby and granchild eh? Anyway Anns getting better and that nice Dr Marlow has been goin in to see her and says she will soon be on her feet again. If I was you Id stay well clear and start a new life. Theres nothing left for you here is there. Id have you both here but you know how Dave is he woudnt stand for it.

Write again when your more settled. The lady whos taken you in must be a really kind person. Cant you stay with her at least while the wars on?
Your loving sister
Claris
Ps I was glad to hear from you. Take care of yourself and give Sally a kiss from me. X

He smiled broadly and replaced the paper in his jacket as though it were a precious jewel. Content, for now, he entered the small gate that set into the imposing wrought iron double gates. He continued to whistle, feeling glad that he didn't have to deal with the animals until after they were dead.

He ceased to whistle abruptly as he crossed the threshold into the noisy atmosphere, and found himself surrounded by the smell of death. He stood just inside the vast hall and watched as a new herd of cattle entered the holding pens. The animals were channelled into the wooden enclosures where they would spend a short time before being led one by one, to where the slaughter took place. They seemed to sense the fate that awaited them, and some tried desperately to break away from the herd, bumping and banging into each other as the stockmen prodded them back into line. Their panic-stricken bellowing made Bill feel sick; he knew they must be able to smell blood, just as he could.

He strode around the hall to where boots, overalls, and leather aprons hung. He could sense his happy mood drifting away as he considered the changes in his life. Would he ever be able to feel the touch of a gentle breeze on his face or smell freshness while working outdoors again? He reached for some protective clothing. He knew that his life would continue to change; just another day to get through, he reassured himself.

14

Birmingham

'I dunno 'ow true it is,' Jim leant forward, selected a spill from the jar on the hearth, lit his pipe and sat back. 'Some of the blokes was sayin' as we've lost a lot of our soldiers at a place called Ypres,' he found the word difficult to pronounce, but continued, 'sounds as though the Boche aren't getting off any better either.' He pointed with his pipe at Abigail's back. 'I'd 'ave volunteered loike a shot, but I promised 'er I wouldn't. I think I've missed out on a lot of fun and games.' He spat his usual stream of brown saliva into the fire and watched as it sizzled and evaporated.

Bill frowned; his hand hovered over his tobacco tin. 'I heard as much Jim while I was hosing down at work, it doesn't sound like the picnic they keep telling us it is though, does it?' He opened the tin and began to tease out strands of rich brown tobacco and lay them along the folds of a Rizla paper. He tamped them down with a yellow-stained index finger and then rolled a thin cigarette.

'Time enough to fight when it's compulsory in my opinion,' he shook his head, 'I can't bear the thought of killing.' He paused for a few moments. 'I don't know if I'll go anyway. My service is just deferred you know–'

Jim's head jerked up towards Bill. 'What d'yer mean?'

'Come and have your dinner and shut up about the war please.' Abigail spoke sharply as she plonked their plates onto the white, embroidered tablecloth and sat down.

Jim nodded and giving Bill a conspiratorial wink took his place at the table. Bill stuck his nubbed roll up behind his ear and joined them. Abigail was an excellent cook, and he was ready for his dish of lamb stew. It'd been making his mouth water for the last hour or so. The three adults ate in silence, busy with their thoughts while Sally, who had eaten earlier, continued to play quietly on the floor with some shiny, green sycamore leaves that Bill had picked for her on his way home from work.

Abigail smiled as the men murmured their appreciation of her cooking. 'Well I hope you aren't thinking of going out again tonight, I need to talk with you both about something, but I want to clear up and put Sally to bed first.'

'Alright love, I'll just have a read of the paper.' Jim left the table, settled into his comfy chair, gave a loud belch, placed his unlit pipe between his teeth, and started to read the Birmingham Gazette – noisily turning the pages and smacking them into place.

Bill volunteered to wash the dishes while Abigail took care of Sally. Some evenings he put his daughter to bed, but he knew that Abigail felt sad when she didn't tuck the child, who now called her mommy, into her bed.

'What do you want to talk about?' Bill cheekily ruffled Abigail's hair as he went to the kitchen.

'Hey you,' she protested with a chuckle and shoved him out of her way, 'wait a bit, I'll tell you when we've all sat down.'

A little later, Jim stood warming his backside in front of the fire; he frowned at his wife then raised his bushy eyebrows. 'Well, what's all the mystery about then?'

Abigail gave Bill a worried look. 'I don't quite know how to put this, but I have to know where all this is going? I've come to love Sally as if she was me own and I'm very fond of you an' all. I need to know what your plans are Bill, you don't say a lot, not that I'm saying you're secretive like, but I need to know.' She started to cry. 'I can't bear to think of losing Sally now, and I know you won't want to stay with us forever.' She came to an abrupt halt and dabbed at her eyes with the bottom of the faded, flowery pinafore.

Bill got up, put his arm around her, and dropped a kiss on her wet cheek. 'Don't cry Abigail, I'm sorry, I've been thoughtless, but I've just been so happy to be here. I felt that we'd come home. I haven't stopped to consider how you might be feeling.'

He looked over at Jim. 'What about you, Jim? I suppose you'd like a bit of peace and quiet back round here, wouldn't you?'

Abigail held her breath and stared blankly at the mantelpiece over the range. She thought Jim would say that it was about time that Bill and Sally moved on, but he didn't.

Jim thought for a minute and scratched at his thinning brown hair. 'I won't deny that at first, I thought you'd be gone by now, but I've bin pleasantly surprised at 'ow we've all gor on t'gether. Its bin loike 'avin a younger brother an' a niece stayin' with us. Despite the war, I've bin lookin' forward ter next Christmas, even though it's a long way off. I dunno what your plans are, but I'd be 'appy to see nothin' change.'

'Christmas,' Abigail chuckled, 'it hadn't better hurry itself.' She took a step towards Jim. Did she know her husband she wondered, amazed by his words? She put her hand on his arm and stroked it.

Jim smiled affectionately at his wife. 'I must say, Bill, I aint sure allowin' the missus to become so attached to Sally was a wise move on my part though.'

Jim had confided in Bill when they were at the pub one evening, and Bill understood that he feared a repeat of Abigail's distress at losing another child. Now I pay my debts he thought as he looked from one to the other. He took a deep breath, then spoke in a quiet formal manner.

'Jim, Abigail, I want you to know how grateful I am, and always will be that I found two of the best friends anyone could have when I came to Birmingham. I'd like it if we could continue as we are if that's alright with you.' He reached for Abigail's hand. 'I know what you went through when you lost Grace, and I know that Sally can't replace her, but I wondered if you'd consider being Sally's foster parents and bringing her up for me?' Red in the face now, he paused and listened as Jim noisily cleared his throat, and Abigail peered at him through her tears. 'If you say yes, I want to make you a promise Abigail,' he continued quickly wishing this evening could be over. 'I promise I'll never change my mind, you could bring her up as though you were her mom, and I'll always pay for her keep, and after I leave, I'll come and visit as often as I can. But I want her to know me as her father – I'll always be that.' He was breathless as he finished his speech and slumped back against the scratchy material of the sofa.

'Sounds alright to me,' Jim said, looking at his wife with a grin, 'what d'you say love?'

'I think it's Christmas already.' Abigail laughed as she dried her eyes, and then gave first Jim, and then Bill a hug. 'Would anyone like a cuppa?'

15

Lincoln

'C'mon hurry up, Betty will wonder where we've got to.' Ann's friend, Enid, called up the stairs.

'I dunno if I can be bothered to go out, I'm not feeling so good. It's all this sorting out and moving furniture. I feel too tired; you go and play cards with Betty. I think I'll have an early night.' Ann appeared at the head of the stairs. Her face was pale.

'Y'do look a bit peaky, would you like me to stay here with you?' Enid asked.

'No thanks, good of you to lend me a hand, but I'd sooner be on my own now if you don't mind. Say hello to Betty for me, and I'll see you tomorrow if you'll come and help again. I've still got a lot to do here.' Ann managed a smile and waved languidly.

'Alright, if you're sure, see you tomorrow then.'

Ann sat on the edge of her bed and listened as Enid shut the front door to with a bang. Noisy bugger, she thought and went to the window where she peered through the crocheted, cotton curtain, and watched her friend as she ran through the gently falling rain. The sky loomed menacingly over the neat houses opposite, promising more rain to come. Merely looking at the gloomy weather caused Ann to shiver and draw her cardigan close about her lean frame. She picked up an old black shawl that had belonged to her mother; wound it around her shoulders, and lay down on the bed where she inhaled the familiar smell of lavender water. Oh, Mum, she thought, why did you have to die and leave me? You'd have known what I should do.

It had been late in the afternoon when she'd started to feel faint and slightly nauseous. The realisation that she was again late with her curse hit her. She'd sat down on the top stair and calculated that she'd missed three months in a row. She'd put the first two months down to all the upset. Bill's desertion, her injuries, her mother's funeral, but with dawning horror, she knew she was pregnant again. Ann recalled trying to relax when Bill was having sex with her the night before he decided to leave. She'd grown to hate his hands on her body and dreaded the possible consequences.

She'd wanted to scream in disbelief as she thought that the bastard had dropped her in it for a second time. Although she couldn't have gone out to her friends as planned, lying on the bed trying to keep her panic under control, she wished she had. She couldn't think why she hadn't confided in Enid who she knew would stand by her. Ann wondered if her friend would help her when she understood her determination not to have another child, and what she now intended to do about it. She knew that Enid wanted children and found Ann's dislike of them strange.

Contrary to her expectations, Ann slept soundly until Enid knocked insistently at nine o'clock. Enid went into the kitchen to see to the range and make a pot of tea. Ann prepared herself to face yet another dreary day disposing of her mother's possessions and trying to believe that her memory and addition were faulty.

Her pregnancy was confirmed for her, however, when she took a mouthful of tea and promptly vomited yellow bile into the sink. 'Oh, God no,' she said, 'not again oh, please God not again.' She'd been sick all through her last pregnancy.

'What's up with you?' Enid asked, 'you in the family way again?'

Ann burst into passionate sobs. 'I bloody well think so,' she said, 'I've missed three times now.'

'Eh don't take on so, it might just be all the upset,' Enid said, 'Bill's been gone nearly three months hasn't he, and you weren't getting on too well before that were you?' She tilted her head and surveyed Ann intently; her eyebrows pulled up almost to her hairline as questions balanced on her lips.

'No! I bloody well haven't been doing anything I shouldn't with anyone else,' Ann said. 'It's Bill's alright,' she spat his name out, 'and I'll tell you something else, I'm not going to have another bloody baby.' She clutched her friend's arm. 'You've got to help me, Enid.'

'Alright, I believe you, but I don't know what I can do to help. Do you know where Bill's gone?'

'No, and I don't care, I'm not going to tell him, I just want to get rid of it.'

Enid sighed. 'You don't know what you're saying, and you're too upset, you'll change your mind when you've had time to think about it.'

'Please Enid,' Ann said, 'I've heard there're ways. Didn't your Elsie do something last time she caught?'

Ann looked so distraught and desperate that Enid reluctantly agreed to find out what she could and left her to carry on clearing the bits and bobs accumulated over her mother's lifetime. Ann resented having to sort everything out before she could sell the three houses that now belonged to her. Trust Mum to have collected rubbish that no one else would like she thought. Pieces of china, jugs, elephants and a variety of inexpensive figurines had all been hoarded despite their lack of value. Ann flung them carelessly into a pile.

Later that afternoon Enid returned and without taking her coat off said, 'I've got these for you.' She handed Ann a cone-shaped paper packet filled with two smaller twists of paper that contained black, bean shapes, and a bottle filled with some clear liquid. 'You've to give me half a crown, I've promised to take it straight round to where I got these from, and I can't tell anyone where that is either.'

Ann's mouth dropped open. 'I'll get my purse.'

'You've to swallow the beans with some of the liquid leaving two hours between each one.' Enid looked embarrassed. 'Then after two more hours, you've to pour steaming water, not boiling mind, into your bucket and sit astride without your drawers on so the steam can get into your private parts. You have to finish all the liquid too.'

'I'm ever so grateful Enid. I'll never forget what a good friend you are. Ann kissed her on her cheek, fetched her purse, and pressed half a crown into her hand. 'Is it gin?' Ann asked. She uncorked the bottle and sniffed the contents. 'D'you think I'll get drunk? What d'you think will happen?' Her voice dwindled to a whisper.

Enid shrugged and opened the front door after pulling her old coat around herself. She then replied without any disapproval in her tone.

'I dunno we'll have to wait and see. I'll come back in the morning to see how you're doing. The person said the sooner you do it, the better it'll be.' She hurried out after a brief farewell. She was concerned for her friend and didn't approve of the course she was taking, but her sister had been fine. She hoped Ann would be too.

16

Coventry

23rd June 1916

Dear Mabel,

How are you and Ronald? It was lovely to see you again at Mom's funeral even though it was a sad time for all of us. I miss her more than you can imagine. No one will ever love me the way that she did. I wish she was still here; I feel so lost without her.

But enough of that she's gone and I have to get on with my life I know. That's the reason I'm writing now. I need some help, Mabel, I'm in trouble.

I still don't know where Bill has gone and taken Sally. It's not that I want to see him, but I found out last week that I'm expecting again. I'm three months gone, and just in case you're wondering; I haven't had anything to do with another man. Bill's the father but I don't want him to know after the way he has treated me.

Anyway, I'm selling up all three of Mom's houses, and I wondered if I could come and stay with you while I sort myself out?

I'll not be short of money so I won't be a nuisance and I'll pay my keep. It's just that at the moment I feel too scared to be on my own. We spent a lot of time together before you married your nice Ronald so I know you won't mind me asking for your help.

Please let me know soon Mabel, I am starting to show and as you know Bill's sister lives just around the corner, she's a nosy cow and I don't want her to notice and tell Bill.

I'll be looking out for the postman. Please, please say yes, you won't regret it.

Love Ann XX

She put her pen down and sealed the envelope. She ran her hand over the small mound of her abdomen. Ann already hated the life that was growing inside her. She'd tried everything she knew to get rid of it: jumping down a few stairs many times, taking the vile tasting stuff that Enid had obtained for her, and drinking bottles of castor oil – but nothing dislodged her problem.

She'd drawn the line at Enid's suggestion that she go and have it removed. She'd heard stories about people going to old women, who knew a thing or two. She couldn't do that; sometimes, something went wrong, and it was more than the baby that died. She was too scared to put her life in danger. After many hours of crying and cursing, she'd decided to have the baby and give it away, although she dreaded the thought of another painful birth. It was after this decision that she'd come up with a scheme to leave her baby with Mabel and her husband.

Ann remembered a conversation she'd had with her mother regarding Ronald's possible failure to have children; as a result, she'd decided to coerce Mabel and her husband into bringing up the baby as their own. She planned to ingratiate herself with them by making it appear that she was helpless and vulnerable. She hadn't thought it would be as easy to take advantage of their trusting nature, as it turned out to be.

Mabel's letter arrived after a few days telling Ann that she would be more than welcome. Ronald had enlisted in the army and could soon be called up. She wrote that she'd be glad of the company and there was plenty of room.

A couple of weeks passed, and Ann arrived in Coventry. She was impressed by the large, detached, red brick house that was surrounded by well-kept gardens. Ronald had told her on one occasion that it had been in his family for generations. It gave the appearance of being an ancient part of the landscape. She soon settled in and was relieved to be told that they wouldn't hear of her leaving to give birth on her own.

When Ann had initially asked for her cousin's help, she'd thought no further than the birth, and the certainty that Mabel and Ronald wouldn't be able to resist keeping the baby after they'd looked after it for a while. Ann's devious plan worked better than she'd hoped. During her first month, Mabel became the answer to her prayers. She asked Ann if they might keep her unwanted baby. Ann pretended to be surprised and said she thought they didn't choose to have children. Mabel had dismissed this assumption and explained that their lack of children wasn't a choice. Ann listened impatiently while Mabel gave her a potted history of their lives; most of which she already knew.

Mabel was a kind, nervy woman who'd had an accident to her face as a child; it had destroyed her confidence. When Ronald told her that she had gorgeous hair and a lovely smile and that she'd always be beautiful to him – she agreed to marry him. Ronald had confessed that it was unlikely, that he could become a father. Mabel who loved children and hoped to become a mother one day told him that she'd leave it in God's hands.

Ronald was a cheerful, easy-going man, always laughing and playing tricks on her; he was a perfect foil for her periods of self-doubt and anxiety. During the three years that they'd been married they'd tried to start a family, but gradually gave up any hope of becoming parents. Neither of them understood or had any empathy with Ann's lack of maternal feelings, but Mabel saw it as a possible solution for all of them. It never entered her head that Ronald might die in the wartime fighting.

Ann readily agreed to give them her baby but stipulated that they could never tell the child who its birth parents were. They had to say the mother had died in childbirth, and the father lost his life in France. Ann had discovered that she could not have the baby legally adopted without Bill's consent. Still, Mabel would have agreed to almost any condition and made no demur about fostering the child.

She was delighted when on the 10th of November Ann gave birth to a healthy boy, and immediately handed him over to her cousin's care. She agreed that he could be called Frank Barnes, but later that month Ann registered him correctly as Frank Brooks, after deciding that she didn't want there to be any possible trouble with the authorities at a later date. Ann hadn't, once again, seen or felt anything appealing in the child – even though his birth had been relatively easy. She had no qualms about rejecting her son.

After searching for a couple of months, Ann bought a large house in Wolverhampton. Although she could afford to, she couldn't stand the thought of living alone, and so she planned to take in lodgers. This way, her income would increase, and she would always have company. Ann had no intention of doing chores and employed a married couple who were willing to do all that would be necessary for the smooth running of the house.

Ann sometimes paid a visit to Mabel, but she never looked at or offered to hold her child. He didn't exist for her. She was pleased, however, that he wouldn't exist for Bill either.

17

Birmingham

Bill grinned at Abigail as Sally turned unsteadily in a circle while holding out the hem of her new dress with both hands. She promptly fell against the table leg, got up and ran into Abigail's outstretched arms.

'Coat Mommy,' she said. Abigail laughed at the demand, but fetched her daughter's coat and dressed her ready for the journey.

Bill picked his bag up from by the door. 'Thanks, Abigail, she looks lovely, I'll be proud as Punch showing her off to Clarissa.' He smiled as he took Sally's tiny hand in his. 'I know you'll miss her, but we'll only be gone two days so it'll soon pass. It'll give you a chance to catch up on a few things; you've not had a minute to yourself lately.'

'Don't you be worrying about me – I'll find plenty to do. Just mind how you go and come back safe.' She answered brusquely to hide her feelings. 'Go on, give Claris my love and tell her it's her turn to write.' She gave them both a resounding kiss and watched as they walked towards the entry. They turned around before they entered the gloomy tunnel and Sally waved.

'Hurry,' Abigail called, 'don't miss your train, and mind the horse road.' She thought what a lovely picture they made as the sun chose that moment to light up the fact that they were both nicely dressed, thanks to her tailoring skills. She was proud of the coat and matching bonnet that she'd run up using excess material from a customer's order. She should have handed it on to the customer, but it was just enough for Sally's clothes. A mid-green, lightweight linen; the shade suited Sally's curls which were becoming darker by the day. The thought that her daughter would have dark brown hair, like her own, gave Abigail intense pleasure. With an image of a crowded train foremost in her mind, Abigail began her chores. She was already missing her darling and prayed that she wouldn't be too frightened of the soldiers, or the noise.

18

Lincoln

'Now then, come on in, you look fit to drop.' Clarissa hugged her brother and niece in one big armful then lifted a reluctant Sally from Bill's arms, and began rocking her up and down and making daft noises. Sally began to cry and attempted to get back to her father who'd carried her from the station, but Clarissa walked her into the back room, leaving Bill to follow. 'Come on duck, don't be a mardy bum, look who's waiting to play with you.' Three small boys who were naked from the waist up surrounded her. 'These are your cousins, this is Harry, John and Billy, and I'm your Aunt Claris.'

'Come here love, let's take your coat and hat off, you must be too hot.' Bill took her hand, picked up their bag and went upstairs to the boy's room where they were to sleep. Sally was a well-behaved child and was soon comfortable and playing happily with her cousins under the draw leaf table by the window. They seemed fascinated by this little girl and treated her gently looking frequently at their mother and big uncle for approval.

'You're a sight for delight Bill.' Clarissa chuckled as she used a childhood saying that her twin brothers had often teased her with.

'It's lovely to see you too,' his wide smile turned to a frown, 'have you heard any news from Arthur?'

'No, I was hoping you'd heard from him. I've got a feeling that his ship's patrolling in the North Sea.' She dumped the boys clothing off a chair onto the floor and flopped down into the space with a sigh. 'If he'd been hurt when those German warships were chased off after shelling the coast around Hartlepool we would have known. I heard there were about a hundred killed and many more injured that day.' She shrugged and shook her head, 'I couldn't sleep for a week after I heard that.'

'I know what you mean, how's David feel; he's not going too is he?'

'No, thank God, he's exempt, but he's working longer hours than ever now. So many of the labourers have joined up, they need him there, and I need him here too. I never know what time he'll be home though.'

'I suppose you've heard about the losses in Ypres – and what the bastards did to the Lusitania?'

'Of course, I know we're quite isolated here, but we still hear things eventually. Bad news travels fast.' She gave her habitual dismissive shrug and glanced at the playing children. Sally was sucking her thumb and carefully observing them. 'Well, I think no news is good news, so let's try not to worry. He'll turn up sooner or later, full of himself I don't doubt. Right, I'm going to feed this lot. When they're in bed, we can talk.'

Clarissa refused Bill's help, and he was grateful to sit back and close his eyes while she fed her brood and Sally with jam sandwiches which they ate, without making a mess, while remaining under the table.

When they'd finished Clarissa said, 'All right you grufty lot, line up.' The boys scrambled obediently to stand, in age order, within reach of their mother. Sally climbed sleepily onto Bill's lap.

Dipping a piece of an old towel into a basin of tepid water, Clarissa gently wiped her boy's faces and hands – Bill did the same for Sally.

In no time, the children were all sleeping soundly in the large feather bed that had belonged to their grandmother. Clarissa and her brother settled themselves, tea in hand, on the wooden bench in the yard, where they could enjoy the mellow evening sunshine.

'Haven't, they all grown Bill?' she said. 'Sometimes they're naughty, but they're good most of the time. Dave would tan their backsides if they weren't, and they know it.' She lowered her voice and pointed at the wall, which separated their yard from next door. 'That old cow next door plays merry hell if the boys make a noise, she always complains to Dave when he's home, she makes our lives unbearable at times.' Clarissa grinned at Bill. 'I'm sure she'll have summat to complain about when she knows you've been staying here. Not that it's any of her business, and I'll tell her so an' all.' She made a rude gesture at the wall behind which faint rustling noises could be heard. Her childish behaviour made them both giggle, but their mirth was short-lived as Clarissa said, 'I'm sad that Mum isn't here to see how lovely they are, she'd have loved them to bits, wouldn't she?'

'I'm sure she can see them wherever she is, I'm sometimes glad that she isn't here to be scared by this war.

75

It's going to get worse before it ends, you know. Asquith kept telling us that conscription wasn't going to happen, but I don't know who believed it, I certainly didn't.' He held his hands out as though to question the sky. 'What was all that registration business for I'd like to know? They thought we were stupid enough to believe that it was just for census purposes. They wanted to keep track of us all for call up even then, is what I think. I don't trust any of 'em.'

Clarissa placed her hand firmly on his arm. 'Shut up will you!'

'Sorry sis, I don't mean to scare you, but I think we're losing too many men, it's only a matter of time before we're all in it. They're getting more, and more women to take on men's jobs now y' know.'

'You don't mean you though, do you Bill?'

Hearing the anxiety in Clarissa's voice, Bill lied about his thoughts. 'Don't worry your head about it, my love. But I'll never forget how I felt when I thought I'd killed Ann. I'll be buggered if I'll willingly kill some other poor sod: no matter what the reason. To tell you the truth, that's the reason I wanted to come. Remember, when I wrote about joining St. John's Ambulance?'

'Yes, did you?'

'I've been going to their meetings and helping wherever I could ever since. I've learned a lot, and I've become one of the first blokes called on at the meat market. I've had to deal with some awful injuries. I'm good at it too.' A note of pride had crept into his voice. Clarissa noticed and smiled with sisterly affection; he'd always had a bob on himself.

'Good for you,' she gave his shoulder a weak punch. 'But what's that got to do with this visit?'

Bill took a deep breath. 'I've asked to join the Royal Army Medical Corps. If they'll have me, I believe I can be of use without actually having to fight. It doesn't mean I'll be a coward; I'll just not be expected to kill anyone.' He turned to look his sister in the face. She was staring at him, her eyes wide. 'You know I'll have to go when they send for me anyway, but if I'm in the RAMC at least, I won't have to carry arms. What do you think?'

Clarissa got up slowly and went into the house. She was running water into the kettle as Bill came up behind her and rested his head on her shoulder. She shrugged him off and said, 'I can't think right now duck, I've worried so much about Arthur, and I can't bear the thought that you'll be putting your life at risk too. You've come to say goodbye, haven't you?' Bill didn't answer. 'What about Sally, what'll happen to her if you get killed, eh? Have you thought about that? How d'yer know Abigail will be able to keep her? Ann might decide to take her away if she finds out where she is.'

'Nothing's going to happen to me, but I know that Abigail and Jim would look after Sally as if she were their child.' He followed his sister into the living room and sat down at the other side of the table. 'As for Ann, there's no chance she'll find her and even less chance that she'd want to look after her. That's why I took her away in the first place if you remember. Ann hates children.'

Clarissa pursed her lips. 'Well she might hate them, but I reckon she was having another one before she left here. I can't be sure, but she'd certainly put on some weight in the right place after her mother's funeral. I wouldn't be at all surprised.'

'Well, I would.' Bill shook his head. 'I wonder where she's gone; I don't know anyone who she might keep in touch with.' He shook his head again and looked questioningly at Clarissa.

'There's her friend Enid, and she may be writing to Betty, you know – the fat girl – who lives in James Street with her loose mother. I could ask when I see them out shopping. I don't suppose they'll tell me anything, though.' She handed Bill a cup of tea.

'Ta, no, don't bother Claris, I don't suppose they would, and there's almost no chance she was expecting, and what's more, I never want to see her miserable face again.' He rubbed his hand, wearily across his hair. 'D'you mind if I go up, and leave you to say hello to David for me?'

'No, you go on up,' she kissed his cheek, 'I'll just clear up here, and then I'm sure Dave'll be home. He's looking forward to seeing you. We've some news for you, but he wants to be here when I tell you.'

'You're not having another one, are you?'

She laughed as her cheeks turned pink. 'You'll just have to wait. It's good news though, so don't be worrying. Night, night love, sleep well.'

19

Birmingham

'Now, now Abi Luv, there's no use you mekin a fuss. 'His minds med up – mark my words there'll be no blokes left in this country shortly.'

Abigail stilled her feet on the treadle and swung round to face her husband. 'Are you saying you're going too?' She threw the dress she'd been making onto the top of the sewing machine; it slid to the floor in a heap of crushed red velvet. 'You promised me you wouldn't go.'

'Keep yer 'air on, I'm doin' nowt of the sort yer silly bugger, but since we all 'ad ter register, it's always bin possible I'd 'av' ter goo in the end, yer know that. I just think Bill's wise ter try and choose where 'e thinks 'e'll be able to help, now, before 'e's pushed God knows where.'

Abigail's hand closed over her mouth. 'No, he's got Sally they couldn't make him –'

'Hush love it's for the best. With the first aid trainin' an' experience that 'e's got there's a good chance 'e'll be allowed to join the medics, or oi'm fairly certain that 'e'll become a conchie an' God knows where that'll land 'im.

But I'll not be followin' suit so stop yer mitherin' and let's 'ave a cuppa eh?'

Abigail stomped out and filled the big iron kettle usually kept steaming on the hob. She swung it over the fire and sat down at her sewing machine. 'I'm sorry love, I know you wouldn't go and leave me unless you had to. But what about Sally, eh? She'll miss her daddy, and what if anything happens to him, eh? What then?'

'Nothin's gonna 'appen to 'im and anyway Sally'd be alright here with us, wouldn't she?'

Abigail had no time to answer as Bill's cheerful voice called from the kitchen. 'I'm back.' He looked around as he stepped into the living room. 'Sally having a nap, is she?'

Abigail nodded. 'Kettles on, tea won't be long,' she raised her eyebrows, 'well – have you been and done it?'

Bill glanced at Jim, who shrugged his shoulders and disappeared behind his newspaper. 'Yes, they've made an exception and allowed me to join the RAMC now. I should receive my papers in about a week then I'm off to Aldershot for training. At least I won't be expected to carry any weapons, thank God.'

'What will you be doing then?' Abigail sounded surprised.

Jim lifted his eyes to the ceiling. 'Don't be daft, Luv, 'e'll be given other jobs ter do, loik peelin' spuds, an' mekin' beds and probably carryin' other soldiers about when they've bin wounded. 'e's a big strong bloke – 'e'll be fine – wun't yer Bill?'

'Of course, I'll be alright, and I'll be sending most of my pay here so you won't have to worry about Sally.' He grinned, looking very boyish. 'Actually, I'm looking forward to doing my bit to help finish this bloody war off, sorry Abigail, but it's dragging on far too long now. You know I'll miss you all, and I know you will look after Sally. It's okay, I'll fetch her down,' he said, as his daughter began to call him from the bedroom.

'Hey there pretty girl,' Bill said, as Sally plonked down at the top of the stairs and proceeded to bump her way on her bottom down each step, 'wait for me.' Abigail always told him off for allowing Sally to come down ahead of him, so he scooped her up just before they entered the living room. He nuzzled her neck, inhaling the sweet smell. 'I'm going to miss you,' he said.

'Me come wiv you.' She planted a kiss on his soft cheek.

'Not this time, my love.' He kissed her springy brown curls and set her down on the floor with her favourite teddy bear. She immediately climbed onto Abigail's lap dragging her toy up by its chewed ear.

'Dink Mommy.' She tugged at the wide strap of Abigail's pinafore.

'What do you say then?'

'Dink please.'

'Good girl.' Abigail gave the two men a hard look to make sure they noticed how well Sally was learning manners.

'Good girl,' they chorused.

Abigail wasn't sure if they were playing her up or praising her charge. She muttered to herself as she went to fetch a drink of milk with Sally trailing behind her. Jim smiled and winked at Bill nodding his head in the direction of the kitchen where they could hear Abigail singing the nursery rhyme, "Twinkle, Twinkle Little Star", and Sally's attempts to copy her rendition.

'It's wonderful to hear her so happy,' Jim said. 'I never expected to hear her laugh so much as she has since you and Sally arrived.' He settled back in his chair and closed his eyes.

Bill wended his way to the window and stood to gaze out into the bright summer day. The yard was deserted except for two small boys, playing a game of marbles, outside the end house where he knew Mr and Mrs Jenks lived with their four children. They were an obnoxious couple; disliked by all the neighbours for the way they carried on. They seemed to care for little except drinking beer at the White Swan.

Two of the sons were in the army, and the eldest son worked with their father at a factory in Deritend where they manufactured nuts and bolts for the shipping industry. He would often roll home as drunk as his parents. Most Saturday nights rows broke out and Margaret, their only daughter, could be heard trying to placate them and get them off to bed. She was about the same age as Ann had been when Bill first met her, but unlike Ann, she was the skivvy in her family. She did the cleaning, shopping and washing while her mother sat smoking a clay pipe on a backless wooden chair outside their house.

Bill caught sight of Margaret as she crossed the yard to the brewhouse with her head down as usual. He felt sorry for her. She looked so downtrodden. She was an attractive girl, but he avoided the smile that invariably lit her face up when she saw him in the yard. They hadn't spoken, and Bill had no intention of ever doing so; nevertheless, he acknowledged the attraction between them with an occasional smile. He'd decided he wasn't having anything more to do with troublesome females.

He supposed her parents and her brother were sleeping off hangovers. Sunday was usually quiet after a stormy Saturday, and last night was no exception. The family fought and disturbed all who lived in the yard until the early hours of the morning.

20

Bill turned away from the window and peered into the fire while his thoughts about going off to war troubled him. He felt some disquiet when he thought of the area where he was leaving Sally, but supposed she could do no better than be with the foster parents who doted on her. Their house was clean and tidy and had more facilities than the other five that surrounded them due to being built behind and above the post office.

He knew that Ellen was an excellent friend to Abigail, and she loved Sally too, so he suppressed his qualms about leaving his daughter. But he knew he had to ease his conscience – before God knows what fate awaited him.

He faced the room just as Abigail returned and sat on the wooden chair in front of her sewing machine. He sat down on the sofa and noisily cleared his throat to gain their attention.

'There's something I have to tell you before I ...' He hesitated, feeling his heartbeat quicken, his face became flushed. He gazed again at the fire instead of their expectant faces, took a gulp of air and continued. 'I want you to know that I don't think I had any choice but to lie to you when Sally and I arrived here.' He lifted his head and looked directly into Jim's then Abigail's face. Both wore a puzzled frown.

'Goo on,' Jim calmly knocked the ash from his pipe into the fire, 'what about?'

'About Ann, Sally's mother.'

He was unable to go on, his mouth had become dry and time seemed to slow as he took in every detail of the vases on the mantle-shelf. The hunting scene on a jug that held candle stubs was brought sharply into focus, and he could feel the blood pounding in his neck.

'Spit it out, no use beating about the bush.'

Abigail spoke sharply and brushed her hair back from her face. She stood and lifted Sally into her arms, holding her protectively close to her body. Sally's thumb went into her mouth, and she sucked quietly, sensing the tension between her loved ones.

Bill told them the whole story; blaming himself where he could. It was some time before Jim asked why he was telling them the truth now. Bill explained that he thought they needed to know in case anything should happen to prevent him from returning from the war.

He managed to convince Abigail that Ann didn't know where Sally was and that she wouldn't claim her even if she found out. That being Abigail's primary concern, they agreed that they understood why he'd lied, but extracted a promise that he would trust them in the future. Relieved that his confession hadn't had disastrous consequences, Bill invited Jim to join him for a pint, and they left Abigail to her favourite bedtime ritual with Sally.

As soon as Sally settled, Abigail knocked out her secret code on their adjoining whitewashed wall, sending a signal to Ellen that she would appreciate her company. Her friend arrived shortly afterwards, gave her customary greeting and was soon oohing and aahing as Abigail told her Bill's story in confidence.

Ellen's hand flew to her chest. 'Well, it sounds as if he was lucky not to 'av killed 'er.'

They both shuddered, but they spent an enjoyable evening speculating about Ann's character, and her whereabouts. Speculation that kept them occupied on and off until well after Bill caught the train from Snow Hill Station to Aldershot two weeks later. He promised to write as soon as he could

21

Birmingham

'Hard day love?' Abigail knelt and unlaced Jim's well-worn boots tugged them off and placed them neatly on the hearth to dry. She eased his knitted woollen socks away from his wet feet, hung them over the wire that stretched under the mantle shelf, and then replaced them with dry ones that had been neatly darned at heel and toes.

It had rained heavily for the last couple of weeks, and everyone was struggling to keep their clothing dry as they were soaked to the skin each time they ventured outdoors. Abigail knew that their family was lucky, as many didn't possess any spare clothes. She'd always helped out where she could, but her charitable nature had taken a back seat since she'd known that Sally was to remain with them. Abigail had a secret reason to save every penny. She intended to buy a house of her own in a better district as soon as she had enough money. To this end, she worked long hours at her machine and sat up sewing by candlelight long after Sally slept.

'Thanks luv.' Jim relaxed back into his fireside chair, having removed his outer garments in the kitchen. He sighed contentedly as Abigail handed him a steaming cup of tea, and then gave the beef stew, that had been simmering for hours over the fire, a quick stir.

'Mm smells good love,' Jim said. He held out his arms to Sally. Come and give yer Uncle Jim a big 'ug.' He spoke gently to her. She'd been sitting quietly on the sofa watching him since he'd returned from work.

'Wet.' She pulled a face and hid behind the sofa.

'Oh, come on, oim dry now, come an' 'ave a drink of me tea.'

Sally looked to Abigail for reassurance then climbed onto Jim's lap and slurped from his proffered cup.

'Tell Uncle Jim what came today, Sally.' She bustled about laying the table.

'Daddy letta,' she chuckled, 'you see.'

Abigail handed Jim Bill's letter. 'Abaht toime too.' He grumbled, but he was pleased. They had been waiting over two months for news from him.

Jim passed the letter back to Abigail. 'Yow' read it luv.'

Dear Jim and Abigail, sorry it's taken so long for me to write but it's taken me ages to get my bearings and have some time to myself. I hope you are all well and Sally's not missing me too much. How I'd love to see you all and get a big hug from my lovely daughter.

The time here is rushing past and I'm starting to feel very fit. We are up with reveille at five-thirty am and out on a route march before we have breakfast at seven-thirty. Then it's lectures and practical teaching for first aid and sanitation. This can cover a really wide range of general information that we need. After more marching we have foot inspection as our feet need to become hardened. Then it's dinner at one p.m., then any jobs that have to be done. I've asked to be put on kitchen detail as I don't mind peeling vegetables, but I hate some of the other tasks we are ordered to carry out.

Would you do me a favour Abigail? I would love to have a photograph of Sally to keep with me. I know you won't mind so I'll enclose some money for you to have one taken at that place in New Street. Our letters aren't being censored at the moment so it should be alright to send it.

I want you to know how grateful I am for the letters, socks and balaclava that you've sent me. We certainly need them; it's sometimes very cold at night. I've got most of my uniform now, including, I'm glad to say, a greatcoat for blocking out the wind.

We've been told that we won't get much warning when we're in the next group to be posted, but I'll try to let you know as soon as I do.

Love to you all and a big hug for Sally.
Bill.

'E sounds alright dunt'e?' Jim laughed and gave Sally a squeeze. 'There's yer 'ug from yer Daddy now.'

Sally giggled and slid onto the floor then climbed onto her chair as Abigail ladled stew onto thick white plates. Jim tucked a cushion under her. She'd only recently been allowed to eat her meals with them, and she was always first to the table.

'I'll see about getting the photograph taken tomorrow and send it as soon as I can for him. He's sent far too much money, so I'll buy some material from the market to make Sally a nice warm coat and hat. I'm sure that's what he'd want me to do with it. You don't suppose he'll be somewhere else before I can get the photograph to him do you, Jim?' She looked anxiously at her husband as he noisily ate his meal.

'Stop yer frettin' 'e'll need more trainin' fust, believe me, 'e'll be around for a while.'

'I wish he were still here,' Abigail said.

'Well the fightin' can't last too much longer yow'll see,' Jim said and wiped his greasy fingers on the edge of the table cloth.

'I've asked you not to do that you dirty bugger.' Abigail snatched up the tea towel she'd used to bring the stew to the table and slung it at her husband. Jim caught it and grinned at her.

'Lovely stew darling,' he winked.

'Oh, you,' she said but noted with wonder the change of temperament that she'd seen in him since Sally's arrival. He was still full of surprises.

22

'Oh! Shit! Grab the bloody rope – grab it – swing 'im round – that's it.' The stockman shouted his orders to the three men that now surrounded the terrified bullock. It took all their combined strength to bring the beast under control – its black coat was glistening, slick with sweat – bulging eyes rolling madly as it bellowed out its anger and fear.

Jim lay still as death; his face relaxed – a grey mask.

The stockman continued to bark out orders. 'Get 'im onto that board before 'e comes round, his leg's broken, I heard it snap, he's gonna be in agony, fetch Fred, 'e'll be in the next shed.'

Fred had just finished immobilizing Jim's leg when he became conscious, and his face immediately contorted with pain. He reached out and grasped his gaffer's arm. 'Tell Abigail I'm alright.' His eyes closed.

'Alright Jim, I'll goo meself, I know she'll worry. I've arranged fer yer to be taken to Dudley Road; there's nothink more we can do 'ere,' Fred said.

Abigail knew as soon as she saw Fred standing on the threshold with a downcast face that something had happened to Jim. She paled, and her hand went to her throat as she took a step back into the kitchen.

'Jim's alright Abigail don't upset yerself,' Fred said, 'There' bin an accident but 'e's alright. If yer get yer 'at an' coat, I've gorra wagon and I'll tek yer to 'im. ' 'E's in the infirmary.'

'What's he done?' Abigail held on to the doorjamb for support.

' 'E's broke 'is leg. They're waitin' fer the gypsum bandages t'set now. It was a bad break though Luv, 'e slipped on the floor when a spooked bullock tried ter break loose. It trampled 'im underfoot,' Fred paused and placed a steadying hand on her arm, 'e's bin in a bad way. They gave 'im summat fer the pain a while ago an' 'e's bin askin' ter see yer.'

Ellen looked after Sally while Abigail went to see for herself that Jim was being cared for properly. She cried when she saw him in pain. Shortly after she arrived a nurse gave him an injection, and a little while later he was able to settle back into his pillows, and regale her with his sketchy memory of events.

He recalled slipping on a cowpat and the bullock's flank coming towards him then bringing its hind leg down full force onto his thigh as it panicked trying to get away from the noise and the smell. His next memory was being in agony as he was jolted off the wagon and carried into the hospital.

'Anyway, Luv',' he managed a smile, 'I want ter forget about it now an' get better so's ter get back ter work before they gimme the sack.'

'Don't you worry about that love, I've got a bit put by, and Bill's money comes in regular as clockwork so we'll be able to pay our way.' She squeezed his hand, 'Just you hurry up and get well, can't have you lazing around at home getting under my feet, can I?' She stayed holding his hand as his eyelids drooped, and he slid easily into oblivion.

'You should go home now,' a nurse told her, 'but you may visit again tomorrow for fifteen minutes.'

'When can he come back home nurse?'

'Well, it will depend on what the doctor says, but it's usually about three months. His leg will have to be in traction by tomorrow. It was a bad break, and the femur can take a long while to heal. I'm sure Doctor Morgan will have a word with you tomorrow if you ask.'

Abigail walked slowly home; she'd told Fred not to wait for her. She didn't understand what traction or a long time before Jim could walk again meant. Visiting the next afternoon, and seeing Jim's leg was being held in the air by pulleys, the reality of their situation sank in. Abigail realised that their future would probably be harder than she'd ever known, and knew she'd have to work even longer hours at her sewing. She was thankful for Sally, who was a well-behaved child and helped where she could. Most people didn't have the money to afford new clothing, but many required alterations or old garments patched. She'd turn her hand to anything and make the best of it. Jim shouldn't have to worry when the change in their situation wasn't his fault. She determined that Sally would still have everything that she needed.

It was just before Christmas that Fred visited and handed Abigail a packet of money from Jim's workmates. 'It isn't much,' he'd said, 'but they've given all they could spare. This time of the year and the war, everyone needs every penny for themselves. But they all send their best and hope it won't be too long before he's on the mend.'

Abigail had thanked him profusely and taken the money that she knew they had given with a good heart. He'd then wished her and Sally, who was clinging to her legs, a Merry Christmas, and plodded his way through the snow to their entry.

When she told Jim of their kindness and good wishes, all he said was, 'I'll goo cowin' crackers if oime off work much longer without anythin' t'do.' Abigail was annoyed with his ingratitude and didn't visit for a couple of days.

Jim hadn't understood how serious his injury had been, and he became increasingly cantankerous as the months wore on. Abigail visited him less and less frequently as his mood worsened, and her patience wore thin. She'd stopped attending church a few months before his accident after a pro-war sermon had incensed her; now she returned; feeling the need of comfort that it gave her. She also wanted Sally to know about Jesus.

Eventually, Jim was allowed to return home using crutches, and both he and Abigail were touched and delighted when Fred, and some of Jim's other workmates, called round and took him to the White Swan for a pint or two. Jim had been popular, and when he'd eventually ceased feeling sorry for himself; he'd been overwhelmed at the generosity of his pals who'd given practical support to Abigail and Sally.

After five months he was advised by an orthopaedic specialist that his pronounced limp was due to curvature and shortening of his femur and that it would be permanent. He was despondent until he landed a night watchman's job at the meat market. He jumped at the position. He knew that he wouldn't be classed as fit to join the army, but that didn't stop him being called up. He attended the appointment and subsequently failed the medical. Abigail was pleased that he wouldn't have to go and fight, but she tried not to show it too openly as Jim was still inclined to be taciturn about his loss of easy mobility.

Life settled down into a routine for the Tyldesleys; until Sally was four years old. Along with many others in their yard, she became ill with influenza. Abigail didn't sleep for days until she knew that Sally would recover. There were several deaths, including Margaret Jenks and two of her brothers. Much to Abigail's, and most of the other neighbour's disgust, Mrs Jenks could be heard bemoaning the loss of her daughter, referring to her as her helper. She's well out of it Abigail thought, but wisely kept her opinions to herself.

The council eventually sprayed chemicals in the streets and advised people to wear anti-germ masks, but these measures proved to be ineffective. As she stood for hours at a time in queues to buy their rationed food; Abigail frequently noticed with dismay the absence of people that she usually saw daily.

Infrequent letters from Bill were now sketchy. Clarissa wrote and said that Arthur had met and married a nurse called Amy Long while in a hospital in Kent. He'd been wounded in a battle at a place called Jutland and was slowly regaining the use of his left arm, but he'd no hope of recovering his hearing on the same side. But he considered he was one of the lucky ones.

Lesley Elliot

23

Birmingham

The war seemed never-ending, but eventually, on the eleventh of November 1918 the Germans signed the Armistice in a railway carriage in a serene forest in Compiègne, and at eleven a.m. precisely the country went mad. Abigail, hearing the church bells clanging, knew that the war had ended, and scooping Sally up in her arms, ran outside to join her neighbours who were whooping, and crying tears of joy as they danced with each other in the street. They kept time with sirens and whistles that were making a tremendous racket. Jim soon found his way to the White Swan and stayed there all night celebrating.

In time, men, both young and not so young, came home to their loved ones. Thousands never came back, others took years to recover from their experience, and there were more than a few who never recovered at all.

Bill returned home.

Abigail laughed as Sally bounced into the living room, took one look at the soldier who sat talking to Jim, and ran into the kitchen.

'You daft 'apporth, come and say hello to your Daddy.'

Jim frowned. 'What's up with 'er?'

'What do you think? She hasn't seen Bill since she was two and didn't recognise him, and she's shy of course.' Abigail went to reassure Sally and after a few minutes led her back into the room.

'This is your Daddy Sally, he loves you very much, and he's been longing to come home and see you again. I've told you lots of times about how he's been fighting the war in France, now haven't I? Don't you remember him?'

Sally lifted her head and surveyed Bill intently. 'No,' she shook her head vigorously.

He returned his daughter's gaze and stood, then realising how big that would make him appear to her, knelt by the sofa where Sally remained clinging to Abigail. He knew he was a stranger to his little girl, but felt desperate to hold her in his arms again. Her dog eared, faded photograph, helped with the horrors that Bill coped with while in Ypres, for the majority of his war. He had achieved his aim not to be directly responsible for the death of anyone, but he'd paid a price that had left him with unbearable images in his head. They rarely disappeared from his mind for more than a short time. Sometimes he wondered if they would ever fade enough for him to be able to live comfortably with them. Often he was scared that he might reach a point where he could no longer bear to live with them at all.

He gently placed his hand on Sally's arm, but she cringed. He was determined to try to establish some rapport with the child that he adored, he left his hand where it was and said, 'You know Sally, I don't recognize you either. When I had to go away, you were a tiny girl.' He sat back on his heels, and taking his treasured photograph from his wallet showed it to her.

'That's you, Sally,' Abigail said.

'That's what you looked like last time I saw you,' Bill smiled at her, 'you've been all through the war with me, and I've looked at and kissed this picture every day that I've been away. I missed you very, very much.' He held her earnest eyes. 'I'm not going to force you to give me a hug, but I'll be glad when you feel that you can.' He kissed his fingers and placed them gently on her cheek. She turned her head away, but she also smiled.

'I go to school now,' she told him as she walked away.

'Wow, you are a big girl. I guess you're clever too?'

Sally tilted her head, her long curls falling like a waterfall down her back. 'I am, aren't I Mommy?'

'Yes you are, but let's show your Daddy how you help me to put the cloth on the table, and you can tell him all about school while we're eating.'

When Sally was tucked up in bed by Abigail that night; she chanted the prayers she'd learnt. 'God bless Mommy, God bless Uncle Jim, and God bless Daddy ... should I still say, please take care of Daddy and all the other soldiers, sailors and airmen.'

Abigail hugged her and said she thought it wouldn't hurt to change the words to everyone in the world now.

'What do you think – are you going to like your Daddy?'

'Oh, yes, he's nice, but he looks sad.'

'We'll have to see what we can do to cheer him up then, won't we? Come on now settle down and fly off to the land of Nod.' She kissed Sally's cheek and went to draw the curtains. As she reached forward, she noticed with a start that a giant black spider was lurking just where she'd been going to place her hand. Abigail hated spiders and usually called Jim to dispose of them, but she didn't want to scare Sally.

'What's the matter, Mommy?' Sally asked.

'Oh, it's just a spider love go to sleep; it's okay.'

She went out onto the landing, unsure what to do. Sally got out of bed, walked over to the window, climbed onto a stool and caught the spider. Abigail stood stock still in surprise as Sally passed her, holding her closed hand out in front of her. Unable to utter a word Abigail followed her downstairs and watched as her daughter opened the kitchen door and put the spider down on the duckboard just outside.

'Now, don't you come back in this house,' she told the spider,' some people in here aren't as brave as me.'

Abigail gazed in awe at her daughter's determined face. 'Was it hard to catch Sally?' she asked as they mounted the stairs

'No, it was easy,' Sally giggled, 'it just ran up one arm and down the other straight into my hand.' Abigail wondered what would become of her wonderful daughter who she felt deserved better than she'd had.

24

Birmingham

Jim and Bill were home by eight o'clock from their celebratory pint, much to Abigail's surprise. She'd expected them to stay until the White Swan closed, or even later if the landlord had a lock-in. Jim explained that Bill was exhausted and couldn't wait to drop into bed.

Jim and Abigail decided to have an early night too, and all was silent in their home by nine-thirty.

'Gerroff me yer Barstad, leave me alone, I'll get the perlice on ter yer.'

'Shut yer gob an' gerrinside yer drunken bitch!'

'Yer gonna mek me ar' yer?'

Mr and Mrs Jenks put on a show for the neighbours as they fought and fell over in the yard.

Mrs Price, who lived just across the yard from Abigail and Jim, and wasn't afraid of anybody, went over and tried to manhandle the couple into their kitchen without success. She received a punch in the eye for her trouble and showed this off to all and sundry for days, calling it her battle wound.

Bill woke with panic flaring; he could hear the shouts and firing of guns as if he were again in the midst of the battleground. He became wide awake and heard Sally, who was crying with fear, as Abigail tried to comfort her. Guessing who was causing the ruckus, and clad only in his shirt and combs, Bill stormed out into the yard. He grabbed the troublemakers by the scruff of their necks and banged their heads together with enough force that they were stunned into silence, and then half carried; half frog-marched them to their house and slung them through their doorway. 'Shut up and get to bed,' he yelled. His presence sobered them enough for silence to reign, and everyone returned indoors.

No one ever found out what he said to them the next day, but everyone heard him knock on their door and demand entrance. He reappeared after ten minutes and peace came to the inhabitants of the yard from that day forward.

Two weeks later, the remainder of the Jenks family did a moonlight flit. None of the neighbours heard them go, but they all breathed a sigh of relief when they heard the welcome news.

Abigail suspected that there was a significant change in Bill's make-up. He'd never shown any inclination to intervene in the domestic life of anyone, let alone be the one to sort the Jenks family out. She remembered how upset he'd been when he replied to her letter telling him of the death of Margaret, and her mother's reaction to the loss of her daughter. Abigail idly wondered if anything might have come of their undeniable attraction if Margaret hadn't succumbed to the epidemic that was responsible for who knew how many deaths. When she ventured to ask Bill how he'd felt about Margaret, he'd told her not to let her imagination run away with her. He'd said, much to her relief, that in the unlikely event that he should find a woman to love and trust enough to settle down with, he'd still be keeping his promise to her regarding Sally's upbringing. Abigail had felt somewhat reassured, but she was sensible enough to know that people could change with time and circumstances. She determined to treasure every minute that she could spend with her daughter, and keep hoping, as she told Ellen, that Bill could be trusted to keep his word.

The relationship between Sally and her father blossomed as they got to know one another. They would often sit close together on the sofa while they took turns to read and describe the illustrations in Sally's favourite books: *The Tale of Peter Rabbit* and *The Tale of Jemima Puddle-Duck.* Sally was a bright little girl who'd been able to read reasonably well before she attended school; due to the time and effort that both Ellen and Abigail had spent teaching her. They were all proud of her, but they tried not to spoil her or allow her too much leeway when she was naughty.

As time went on, there were many nights when the household was startled awake in the early hours by Bill calling out when he had a nightmare. It became part of their lives as it did for other families whose lives had been disrupted by the war and its aftermath.

During the day while Jim slept, Bill would be out tramping the streets looking for work. He took Sally with him sometimes to enable Abigail to get on with her sewing. He was determined not to apply to be taken on at the slaughterhouse again unless desperate. Both Jim and

Abigail understood and were supportive; they knew how much he had hated it.

Feeling down, Bill took Sally to stay overnight with Clarissa. Sally and Billy were soon busy playing together, but Harry and John went out with their friends, they now found Sally too young to be of interest. Clarissa introduced them to her daughter, Abi, who was now three years old. She'd been named after Abigail as a thank you for her kindness to Bill and Sally. She was a lovely looking child with jet black hair and startling green eyes. She didn't speak very well and followed Sally everywhere holding her arms out to be picked up. Sally treated her like a doll and took great delight in helping to bathe her and put her to bed.

Sally tugged on her father's arm the following day. 'Daddy please can I have a baby sister or brother one day?'

Bill replied more sternly than she'd ever heard before. 'No, you can't and don't bother asking me why not.' He turned away and went into the yard.

She never asked him again. She told Abigail when they were alone that she didn't want to revisit Clarissa, but she wouldn't or couldn't say why. Bill seemed surprised when Abigail told him what Sally had said; he'd forgotten about the question and the answer that he gave.

A week after their return to Birmingham, his old gaffer, Fred called in at the White Swan and went over to Bill where he was leaning against the bar.

'I've bin lookin' for you. Can I buy you a pint? Mind you; you'll owe me one in a bit.'

Bill swallowed the dregs. 'Well, now you've found me what's it about, eh?'

'Two pints of bitter please love,' Fred said to the barmaid. He turned to Bill. 'I've some good news fer you if you want it.' He pointed to a table in the corner, took his pint and plonked down on a wooden stool.

Bill followed suit. 'What's it all about then mate?'

Fred took a gulp of beer, wiped the side of his hand across his mouth and then said, 'I've put in a word fer you at Meridiths, the builders. They're in Wolverhampton, but they carry out contract work all over the country. You interested?'

As a result of Fred's recommendation and Bill's ability to demonstrate his skills to the boss's satisfaction, he got the job as a bricklayer on a trial basis. Out of practice and somewhat slow initially, he proved to be an asset and remained in their employ for many years, moving wherever the work took him. Fortunately, many of the jobs were to carry out building repairs in the Midlands, so he was often able to stay with Sally.

25

Birmingham

Bill's nightmares continued to disrupt everyone's sleep whenever he stayed over, and Abigail became increasingly concerned as Sally was tired and looked pale in the mornings. Abigail didn't know how to resolve the situation as she was both sorry for Bill, and scared of the possible consequences of any change. Everything came to a head one morning when Sally returned home in tears from her school that was just around the corner. Abigail was annoyed when Sally told her between sobs, what had occurred and showed her the palm of her hand.

After soothing her and washing her face, Abigail asked for the whole story, and Sally admitted that she'd been naughty. It turned out that she was supposed to have been copying writing from the blackboard onto her slate when she'd fallen asleep. Her teacher had used the wooden stick that she employed as a pointer, to smack Sally several times, hard enough to raise angry-looking red and white marks across her hand that she'd held tightly. When her teacher had walked away, Sally had picked an enamel inkwell from her desk and thrown it across the room at her retreating back. The ink had spilt as it flew, but Sally hadn't waited to see the results of her handiwork, she'd run out and home.

Abigail's annoyance escalated and after removing her pinafore, marched round to see the headmistress and show her Sally's injury.

The teacher was called into the office and told by the headmistress why Sally was so tired. She said that Sally shouldn't be punished further for her actions and Sally was happy to be sent out into the hall to sit and wait after she'd apologized for throwing the inkwell.

After Sally had left the room, Abigail warned the teacher politely, but firmly that if she ever hit Sally again, she would deal with her by involving the police. She then left, taking Sally with her. Sally was reluctant to return to school the following day, but when she did, it was to find she'd gained considerable kudos with her peers. The teacher ignored her for the remainder of the year, but Sally didn't mind.

When Abigail recounted the day's happenings, Jim and Bill tried to keep their faces straight, but couldn't help showing some mirth at Sally's spunky retaliation. Sally knew she shouldn't have thrown the inkwell, and Bill agreed that she shouldn't, but he found himself secretly admiring the spirit that was showing itself in his daughter's character.

Discussion ensued with Jim and Abigail, and Bill found himself a room to rent near to where he was working in Wolverhampton. Sally was upset that he was going away again and begged him not to go, but Bill promised to visit each weekend unless he was going to see Clarissa or Arthur. It took Sally a while before she came to accept the arrangement and stopped asking for her daddy at bedtime – but she began to sleep well again.

Near to Christmas Jim brought home a puppy as a surprise for Sally. It was a stray that had taken to visiting Jim in his hut and accompanying him on his patrol around the buildings. Jim knew there'd be trouble if reported by the surly individual who worked the weekend shift. Sally was excited and spent hours trying to decide on a name for the puppy that she adored as soon as she saw it's long, narrow face and gold and white fur. Jim thought it was probably a Collie, and became convinced he was right as its coat became long and luxurious. Its liquid, autumn brown eyes followed Sally everywhere. She decided to call it Rover until Jim pointed out that it was a bitch. Sally knew this was a swear word, and Jim became very bogged down in his explanations, much to Abigail's amusement.

When Sally still couldn't decide on a name after three days, Jim told her to choose one, or he'd decide for her as he was tired of hearing about it. Sally quickly decided to call her Tess and spent every free moment teaching her to be obedient and grooming her. They became inseparable. She soon knew what time Sally came from school, and would wait patiently outside the gate for her. Tess was friendly with the other children, but if a stranger approached Sally, she would growl a low warning until Sally said, 'It's alright Tess.'

Neither Jim nor Abigail felt too happy about having an animal in the house. Jim thought that animals, especially dogs, should be kept outside in a kennel. Abigail had to be extra careful where she put unfinished garments to avoid hairs or muddy paw prints; nevertheless, she was glad that

Tess had joined their family. She didn't have to worry so much when Sally was out of sight.

On one occasion, when Sally's Dad and his brother visited, Arthur pretended to take Sally's teddy from her. Instead of laughing, Sally thought he was going to keep it, and became distressed. Her cries caused Tess to snarl menacingly at Arthur, who quickly let go of the bear. Bill warned that if Tess bit anyone, she'd probably have to go. Sally didn't need telling twice. Tess stayed at home to avoid crowds of people. She didn't think she could bear it if anything happened to make her lose her dog. She promised herself that she wouldn't be such a cry baby in future, and explained at length to Tess why she shouldn't growl.

26

Abigail had been feeling under the weather for a couple of days, and as she perked up suggested to Sally that she might like to go into town with her. They both enjoyed a mooch around the market stalls where Abigail regularly bought new and second-hand material to make into clothes to sell. Since the war she'd become well known locally as someone who often had garments already made up, that could be altered to fit and weren't too expensive. The market traders frequently put aside pieces of material, especially velvet, satin and pretty pieces of cotton that they thought Abigail would like. She was always grateful, and while she wanted a bargain, wouldn't haggle about the price if she believed it was fair.

Sally's twelfth birthday dawned cold as usual, and she spent most of the day cuddled up by the fire and helping Abigail with some tacking. While Jim was getting ready for work, she took Tess for a walk and then played at skipping for a little while even though it was icy in the yard. She counted aloud as she completed as many doublers as she could before her feet tangled in the rope.

'C'mon in now Sally, tea's on the table,' Jim shivered as he quickly shut the kitchen door. Sally and Tess followed him inside after Sally hid the precious length of washing line inside the tin bath that hung on the outside kitchen wall.

As she opened the door, the aroma of Lancashire hotpot made her mouth water. She sped into the living room, where she stopped in surprise.

'Oh Mom, it looks lovely,' she said and gave Abigail a bear hug.

Abigail shouted out as Sally placed her cold hands on her bare arms. 'Gerroff you monster,' and gave an exaggerated shudder, 'do you like it?' She indicated the cake that she'd made and iced to celebrate Sally's birthday.

'Mm yes, do I have to share?' Sally grinned at Jim over Abigail's shoulder.

Abigail gave her a gentle push. 'Come on both of you before it gets cold,' She ladled the hotpot into bowls and sat down.

They ate in silence until Sally gave a loud sniff. 'It's lovely, but it's making my nose run Mom,' she said.

'Well, yer'd betta bloody well run arter it and blow it 'adn't yer?' They all laughed as though it was the first time that Jim had made that response.

Abigail wished that every evening could be like this; so happy all together. She was sad that she and Jim had continued to grow apart despite their shared love for Sally but knew she wouldn't try to do anything about it. She had Sally to love and look after, so her world would be alright.

Sally broke into her reverie. 'I wish Dad could have been here.' She spoke with a mouthful of Victoria sponge and sprayed a few crumbs onto the white, embroidered tablecloth that was only used on special occasions.

'Ere, piggy, piggy oink, oink,' Jim said.

Sally swallowed and coughed. 'Sorry, but I miss him, and he didn't come last weekend.'

'Now you know he had to work extra hours on the new housing estate. He'll be here on Saturday with a present for you. I've no doubt. You've had the lovely card he left for you. You'll have to be content with that for now.' Abigail pushed a packet she'd kept hidden across the table to Sally. 'Happy Birthday love,' she smiled at her foster daughter, 'it's not much, but it's just what you need, and I hope you like them.'

Sally beamed and removed the tissue paper carefully after giving her present a squeeze. Inside was a hand-knitted scarf and matching hat in pale blue wool.

'Ooo, thanks Mom, they're beautiful, and I never saw you knitting them.' She kissed Abigail on her cheek and snuggled her face into her new scarf. Does it suit me?' She stuck a playful pose.

'Mmm, 'ansome is as 'ansome does,' quoted Jim sententiously, spoiling the effect as his expression told Sally that she looked lovely.

'Ah, I did it while I was round at Ellen's and when you were at school – do you really like it? Try the hat on.'

'Hold on, let 'er 'ave this fust.' Jim lifted a large brown paper parcel from under his side of the table and passed it to Sally, 'appy Birthday, Luv.'

'Ooo thank you, Uncle Jim, I wonder what it is?' she said. She felt around its perimeter and gave it a gentle shake.

'Well open it, and y'll find out wunt yer?' Jim chuckled. He seemed nearly as excited as Sally as she carefully removed the wrapping.

'Oh, thank you, thank you,' she jumped up and hugged Jim, 'where did you get it? It's so beautiful.'

'It ain't new, but I knew yer'd like it, a bloke at work was sellin' it.' He broke off and watched with pleasure as Sally caressed the ivory inlay on the musical box.

'Oh, I love it and my hat and scarf. I'm ever so lucky, none of my friends at school has parents as nice and kind as you.' She leaned her head to one side and thought for a moment. 'And I've got a Dad as well,' she grinned, 'may I leave the table now and show Tess my presents?'

Jim and Abigail laughed at Sally's enthusiasm. 'Goo on then, yer daft 'apporth,' Jim said.

Sally settled on the hearthrug and wound her music box up while explaining to her best friend, Tess, what she was doing. Tess pricked her ears and appeared to listen intently to every word. She gave a brief perplexed whine as Sally looked underneath the box hoping to identify the music, but there was nothing except an initial C etched into one corner.

'What's the music Uncle Jim?' she asked. But neither Jim nor Abigail knew. It was many years before Sally discovered that it was Beethoven's *Für Elise* that gave her an appreciation of popular classics that would remain with her throughout her lifetime.

Abigail listened to the music and gazed at her growing daughter. She prayed silently that Sally would always be happy, and nothing would happen to change her fun-loving, kind personality. She wanted Sally to grow up but dreaded the day that she would probably marry, and leave home to face all the cares and responsibilities that were the norm. She chided herself for her unnecessary worries and humming along with the tune, went into the kitchen to clear up.

27

Life changed for Sally that same evening. Abigail had made faggots and peas to take to Jim in his hut for his midnight meal. She sometimes took it to him about ten o'clock so that he saw a friendly face to help break up the long shift. This night Jim could see how tired his wife felt and insisted that he take the basin himself. Abigail was pleased that he'd been more thoughtful of late and thanked him, adding that she and Sally would have an early night.

About two hours after he left, Sally found the basin of faggots, tied up in its cloth, still on the kitchen table. Abigail said it didn't matter, and she would take it as usual.

'I'm a big girl now Mom; I'll take it to him, you need an early night.'

'Alright love, but go soon though, I'll worry if you're out too late when it's cold and dark.'

'You old fusspot, I've done it before haven't I?'

'But that won't stop me mithering 'til you're back home. Your Uncle looks forward to heating his dinner up on that old stove where he boils his kettle. If we don't go, he'll only have cold fruit that he keeps in his hut; otherwise, we could give it a miss.'

'I know. I don't mind going, try to sleep though – I promise I'll wake you and let you know when I'm home.'

'You could bring us a cuppa; you'll be cold when you come in. I'm going up now love.'

'Okay, love you, Mom.' She blew her a kiss as Abigail disappeared through the doorway, and started to climb wearily up to her bedroom.

Taking the shopping basket from its hook on the kitchen wall, Sally placed the covered basin in its middle and padded it with an old towel to prevent wasting a drop of the aromatic contents. She donned the navy blue coat that Abigail had made for her at Christmas, and with her new hat and scarf in place, snuggled her hands into her mittens, picked up the basket, and went out with Tess into the frosty night.

The moon resembled a slice of orange hanging low in the sky with myriad stars twinkling in the heavens. Sally loved looking at the night sky and recognised many of the constellations. She liked to imagine that God hid behind the moon and watched over her, and when there was a halo, she usually narrowed her eyes and peered at it for a couple of minutes to see if she could discern any sign that he was there. But she only shared her fanciful notions with Tess.

There was a ring around the moon, and Sally stood still and carefully surveyed the fuzzy edges before making her way across the yard to plunge into the dark entry, with Tess at her heels.

28

Bill looked up at the moon and thought about Sally. He knew she liked to look at the moon at night, so he kissed his fingers and blew her a kiss via the heavens, sorry that he'd missed her birthday tea. He would have enjoyed seeing her excitement when she opened the presents that he knew her foster parents had for her.

He planned to see her at the weekend and had bought her some pink glass beads, some double-ended colouring pencils and a sketch pad. She enjoyed drawing and colouring in, even though she said that she wasn't very talented. He wasn't sure about the necklace as he wasn't very good with female fripperies – but he'd bought it anyway hoping that she'd like it.

He was just glad that he earned enough money to buy Sally a present. The firm he worked for had no shortage of building work, and he didn't think he'd have to join the crowd of men that were being laid off, or having their wages reduced. The newspapers were full of depressing stories of hardship now that the affluent days after the war had come to an end. Money was tight for many families whose men had returned from the war incapacitated; ex-soldiers who had lost limbs were frequently begging on street corners.

Bill tried not to think of the war. He knew that he was one of the lucky ones, although he found unbidden gruesome images in his mind at all times of the day and night. He'd been sleeping better recently, but he still sometimes woke shouting from a nightmare. His landlady had grown used to him and turned out to be an understanding, tolerant person. She appreciated the fact that he always paid his rent on time and occasionally brought her a bottle of stout home from the pub. Most nights he could be found on his own or drinking with a few mates at his local. Bill thought that a couple of pints helped him to sleep.

He usually frequented one of two pubs that were near his lodging house, but the night of Sally's birthday, he went further afield to meet a couple of his mates at a large landmark pub. Its well-painted sign featured an elephant with a castle on its back, over the main entrance. Bill liked the glazed, green-tiled facade, which felt smooth to his touch. It was in a more affluent area than the district where he usually drank.

Dressed in a smart black suit and overcoat topped by a trilby that suited his still handsome face, Bill strode confidently into the lounge where his friends, Bob, and Sidney, were already supping pints of locally brewed ale. Bob went to the bar and ordered a pint for Bill, and then they sat at a small round table by a roaring log fire. Bill gazed at the unfamiliar surroundings, admiring the hundreds of china and pottery jugs that hung from old oak beams which supported the ceiling.

'Fancy a game of dominoes?' Sidney asked.

'Just what I need,' Bill said.

Bob went to the bar and came back with a set of bone tiles in a fancy box. They were soon absorbed in their game. Bill found something soothing about the smooth feel and the clack of the dominoes as they were placed thoughtfully onto the table. The play was frequently interrupted by swigs of ale and the ritual of roll-ups. The fug of tobacco and wood smoke coupled with the strong smell of beer went unheeded.

As most of the tables became occupied, and customers relaxed, and the beer began to affect him. Bill excused himself and walked steadily in the direction of the gents. He passed by a table where two well-dressed women and a man were talking animatedly. He was startled when one of the women put out her hand and touched his arm. Bill's heart leapt in his chest, and his mouth became dry as he recognized the woman that he'd last seen lying on the floor, where he'd left her for dead ten years ago.

'Bill?' She quickly withdrew her hand. Bill thought how attractive she looked in a smart blue suit with a fox fur draped over her shoulders and a flowery cloche hat that sat snugly over short brown hair. He glanced at the other occupants of the table, trying without success to decide if the man and the other woman were a couple, or if the man was Ann's companion. He couldn't make up his mind but guessed they were all around the same age.

He tried not to allow Ann to hear in his voice how the sight of her had affected him as he said, 'Hello Ann, well this is a turn up for the books, I imagined that you'd still be living in Lincoln.' He spoke without warmth or animosity; she felt like a stranger to him.

Ann smiled, but her eyes remained dispassionate as she said, 'I moved here several years ago.'

Bill glanced again at her companions, who were watching this exchange with open curiosity. Ann did not attempt to introduce him. A couple of seconds passed. 'You look well, Ann,' he said and continued on his way.

He nodded to her as he returned, and Ann smiled briefly then turned back to her companions in a gesture of dismissal. Outwardly unperturbed Bill joined his mates.

'Who's that?' Bob grinned, 'nice-looking woman, you dark horse.' He laughed, and Sidney joined in with the good-natured joshing.

Bill shrugged his broad shoulders. 'Just someone I used to know. Now mind your own business and let's get on with the game.' He spoke firmly as he sorted out the five four domino and placed it onto the table. His friends knew that he'd said all he was going to, and let the matter drop.

Bill played and talked calmly for the next couple of hours, but his eyes often strayed to his wife, and his mind was anything but calm. He had many things to say to her, but his pride wouldn't allow him to try to speak to her again. As if she'd read his thoughts, Ann stopped by his table as she and her companions were leaving the pub.

'I think it would be a good idea for us to talk Bill,' she said, 'would it be possible to meet me here tomorrow evening about seven?' Bill nodded his agreement, and Ann followed her friends into the night.

Bob and Sidney again made a couple of ribald remarks but ceased when Bill pointedly downed his pint and went to the bar to buy another round. He left them to speculate as they wished but wondered what they'd say if he told them the truth. They were unaware that he was married. He

119

didn't feel married and had no idea what Ann wanted to discuss with him.

He drank more than usual that night and left the pub more than a little merry. Next morning when his alarm clock began its strident ringing, he was surprised to find he was back in his lodgings. He had no recollection of his return home or winding the clock.

Bill shaved while looking into the mirror, his landlady's pride and joy, and Ann's face flashed in front of his eyes. He felt a stirring in his nether regions when he recalled that he'd agreed to meet her the following night. He wondered why she wished to meet him and hoped that it was to ask for a divorce. God knows she was entitled to one. He was the one who'd walked out and made no attempt to find out where she was, or how she fared after her mother's demise. Bill knew a divorce was on the cards, but his eyes held a steely glint wondering if she'd changed enough to want her daughter back. He would never consider Sally leaving Abigail after all this time, even if Ann begged. Pulling a derisory face and whistling the famous tune "nobody knows the trouble I've seen," Bill walked down the stairs. He continued to whistle the same song on and off all day until his workmates threatened him with more trouble if he didn't – put a sock in it.

29

Sally walked at a steady pace along the familiar roads until she reached the small, Iron Gate that people on foot used. Usually, either she or Abigail would ring the bell, and her uncle would come out, have a word with them, and take his meal inside to the wooden hut where he spent his time between security checks. This night when she arrived, she found the little gate was ajar and full of fun she decided to go in and surprise him.

Instructing Tess to stay outside, she tiptoed up to the misted window which was divided into small panes and set high up in the side of the hut. Just as she was about to make her uncle jump by tapping on the glass, she heard a woman's tinkling laugh coming from inside. She lowered her hand and stood stock still, feeling shy and confused. She knew that her uncle wasn't allowed to let visitors into the market. She felt silly just standing there, and undecided what to do for the best she stood on tiptoe, and peeped through the dirty, steamed-up window. An oil lamp shed a dim glow, and she could just make out her uncle leaning back in his chair with his eyes closed, a strange expression on his face. A dark-haired woman was sitting astride him with her bare legs splayed out. Her hands were on his shoulders, and she was moving slowly up and down.

Sally's mind refused to register what she was seeing, she couldn't think what was happening, but she knew they shouldn't be together like that. In a panic in case they should see her watching them, she dropped the basket by the dark, wooden door and fled.

She ran, her breath coming in gasps. Her lungs felt as though they were on fire with the cold air that she sucked harshly into them. When she reached home, she leaned against the red bricks in the entry until her breathing slowed. She tried desperately not to think about the awfulness that was making her feel queasy. Tess sensed Sally was upset and pawed at her coat. She breathed warm air onto her hand as Sally petted her automatically.

'Its' alright girl, come on, let's go in,' they crossed the yard and entered the haven of their home.

Sally hung her coat up as Abigail called from the bedroom, 'Is that you love?'

'Yes, Mom.'

'You've been nice and quick – be a love and bring us up a cuppa, will you?'

'Okay, I'll be up in a bit.' Sally placed the kettle that was still warm, over the fire where it soon boiled up enough water to make a pot of tea. As she banked the blaze with slack and a large lump of damp coal to keep it in until morning, her thoughts skittered about wondering what, if anything, she should tell Abigail.

Sally didn't know what she'd witnessed, but she'd realised during her flight home that it was probably something to do with the way people made babies. Being the only child living in a house where Jim and Abigail were un-demonstrative with each other, and having a Dad who never even mentioned being close to a woman, hadn't allowed her to see, or hear any of the typical sights and sounds living within a large family would have. Some of her school friends talked about such things, but Sally remained on the perimeter, although she listened intently, curious to know what they knew, but embarrassed by conversations that she didn't understand, and couldn't join in. Now some of the things that she'd overheard were starting to make sense.

She wanted more than anything to talk to Abigail, but she knew she would upset her by telling her about the awfulness. She was concerned about what her uncle would have thought when he found the basket sitting outside the door, but she tried to stop thinking about it and put a smile on her face as she took the welcome cup of tea to her mom.

'Thanks, love – are you alright – you look a bit peaky; I hope you're not coming down with what I'm just getting over, it's made me very tired?' she sighed as she sipped the hot drink.

'I don't think so, but I am tired, so I'll go and jump into bed,' Sally leaned over and kissed Abigail, 'night, night Mom, love you best in the world.' At that moment, her father didn't even enter her head.

Sally undressed quickly and pulled her cotton nightdress over the top of her vest. Gritting her teeth, she snuffed the candle stub out, and climbed into bed, easing inch by inch into the centre, allowing time to adjust to each bit of the cold sheet before moving further over. She shivered, drew the blankets and eiderdown up to her neck, grabbed her old, treasured teddy bear and pulling him under the covers, cuddled him close. She ran her thumb over his brown, boot button eyes as silent tears rained down her chilled face.

Her thoughts were in turmoil, seeing the ugly picture of her uncle's face when she had peeped through the dirty window. She couldn't recall the woman too well as she'd not seen her face clearly, but repeat images of her legs returned vividly to her mind. She tossed and turned, trying to sleep, but it eluded her, and for the first time in her life, she knew what it was to feel alone with her troubles. She remained struggling with feelings of guilt and embarrassment well into the early hours of the morning. The feelings turned to anger and resentment towards her uncle for his betrayal and her father for his absence. Not knowing how she would be able to face her mother or her uncle in the morning, she eventually drifted into an uneasy sleep.

30

'Sally,' Abigail tugged the blanket that was almost covering Sally's head. As her daughter surfaced, she put her finger to her lips and said, 'shhh, your uncle's already asleep. Come on down. I've just boiled the kettle, and you can wash and get dressed by the fire.'

Sally threw off the bedclothes and landed a resounding kiss on Abigail's cheek before grabbing her clothes. They crept downstairs into the warm living room.

'Look.' Abigail pointed to the window where sparkling white snowflakes drifted lazily from a leaden sky. They stood watching as the flakes became miniature clouds, and began to stick on the yard bricks, and every other available surface. In no time, it was about an inch deep and everywhere looked pristine. The reflected light shone into the room and lit up areas that were usually a little gloomy.

In between washing, getting dressed and eating her breakfast, Sally peered out into the yard. She couldn't wait until it was thick enough for her to don wellingtons, and with a pair of Jim's old woollen socks pulled onto her hands and up her arms, go outside and build a snowman with her friend, Faith, who lived two doors away. Today, although the swirling flakes still called to her, she didn't want to go out and leave Abigail.

'It's nearly thick enough to build a snowman,' Abigail said, an hour later. 'Are you going to call for Faith?' Sally continued to stare out of the window and shrugged her shoulders. 'You'd better make the most of it.' Abigail was working her sewing machine treadle as if her life depended on it.

When Sally didn't speak, she stilled her feet and looked up. 'What's the matter with you – you've got a face as long as Livery Street?' Sally still didn't reply. Abigail sighed. 'If you're not going to tell me, I can't help. Now cheer up and move out of my way, I've still got lots of sewing to do – we can't all have days when we don't have to work, you know.' She smiled.

Sally returned the smile and sat down by the fire. Glad she hadn't told Abigail what she'd seen but wishing that there was someone to confide in and ask advice from before she saw her uncle. He must know by now that Sally was the one who'd left the basket, and he would probably have guessed that something had upset her. She'd always loved his slow way of smiling and enjoyed his teasing; she'd thought he could always be relied on to love and care for herself and her mom. Now she knew she'd never trust him again, or feel comfortable telling him her thoughts.

She looked across the room at Abigail's bent back and wondered, not for the first time, about her birth mother. Her dad hadn't said much about her, just that she'd been pretty like herself, and he was sad that she'd died while young.

She'd asked her aunt on one of their visits if she'd known her mother, but Clarissa hadn't wanted to talk about her and had quickly changed the subject. Sally hadn't liked to question either of them again.

She sat for a while in silence mulling things over then decided that she'd try to avoid being alone with her uncle Jim until she'd had a talk with her dad at the weekend. She picked up the knitting needles and wool that Abigail had provided. Her mom thought all girls should be able to sew and knit, but Sally was turning out to be all fingers and thumbs where knitting was concerned.

She was saved from yet another frustrating attempt to master the craft by a knock at the door. It was Faith. Sally ceased her worrying thoughts, threw down her knitting, and became all child again. She quickly wrapped herself up and went out into the bright day.

'Don't forget you said you'd take this sewing round to Mrs Plumber in Great Bernie Street, love, I've nearly finished it,' Abigail said.

'Okay, Mom, I'll just be outside here.' Sally skipped out, leaving an unhappy Tess to keep dry and warm on the old coat that lived under the table in the kitchen. After a few minutes, Abigail opened the door and let Tess out to be with Sally.

'I can't put up with the whining,' Abigail said quietly, 'she'll wake Jim. Just make sure you dry her before she comes into the living room.'

Sally waited until lunchtime when she was alone with Abigail to ask the question that had been uppermost in her thoughts since her birthday two days ago. She looked down at her plate. 'Mom, where do babies come from?'

Abigail smiled, she'd expected Sally's question as she approached puberty, and had spent considerable time deciding what her response should be. She'd been given no information by her own mother, who she thought had done her a great disservice. Abigail believed an honest answer was the best course to take. She too averted her gaze as she explained the facts of life as simply as she could without too much detail.

'Thanks, Mom, I think I understand.' She took the last bite of her corned beef and onion sandwich, jumped up from the table and went to look out of the window at the fresh fall of snow.

Abigail started working on a wedding dress that she was making for a woman, she knew from church, whose daughter was planning her wedding at St. Martins in March.

31

Sally continued to gaze at the snow-covered yard and tried to sort the facts that Abigail had presented, into something that made sense to her. Although Abigail had told her that when two people got married and slept in the same bed together, they could snuggle up close and make a baby, she still couldn't understand what her uncle and the woman she'd seen in his hut had been doing. Sally hadn't liked to ask Abigail any more questions but was very curious now. She was unsure whether to be more scared that Abigail would find out, or whether she could be happy that she would be going to have a baby brother or sister. Faith didn't know how lucky she was to have several brothers and an older sister. Sally had often longed for siblings. Taking two homemade biscuits from the tin – she went to call for her.

They headed for the brewhouse, which was their favourite place when the weather was inclement. After some women had been using the big gas boilers to heat water for their washing, it was sometimes warm. Today with the snow thick on the ground, they were out of luck. They shivered as they ate while sitting on the stone steps of the boiler house.

'Faith,' Sally spoke her friend's name softly, immediately gaining her attention as she sounded so uneasy, 'do you know where babies come from?'

'Course silly, don't you?'

'Not really, will you tell me?' Sally surveyed her boots.

Faith held her friend's hand while she graphically described the sex act. She showed no embarrassment as she moved up and down to show Sally clearly how adults did it and went so far as to make noises that she'd heard, in such a way that they both ended up falling about holding their sides. Then serious again, Faith told her about menstruation, but she called it the curse. She warned Sally never to let a boy put his hand up her skirt as they were dirty buggers who couldn't be trusted. Sally couldn't bring herself to tell her friend about her uncle and asked about sitting in a chair. Fully enlightened and realizing that sex wasn't just for procreation; Sally worked out that she wouldn't necessarily be having a baby to love. Her worry continued, however, about Abigail finding out what her husband had been doing; as he would probably carry on doing it. She resolved to try to forget about it. Her uncle hadn't mentioned the basket being outside the door, and she hoped he never would.

Sally kissed her friend on her cheek. 'Thanks for telling me Faith, I feel much better now.' She didn't ask Faith how she knew all the details that she'd imparted, and Faith didn't volunteer that information either.

'C'mon yer dafty,' Faith said, 'let's goo an' play in the snow ter ger us warm. Is yer dad comin' ter see yer tomorrow?'

Sally nodded. 'I think he'll be bringing me a present. Mom said he would.'

'Ooo, I wonder what it'll be, I'd love a present, if its sweets will yer share?'

'Course I will,' Sally said. The two friends crunched out into the snow. It made even their yard look bright. They immediately scooped up handfuls of the powdery stuff which they flung at each other. Their shrieks of laughter soon brought other youngsters, who lived in the other houses that surrounded the yard, out to join the fun.

32

Wolverhampton

'Got a girlfriend 'ave yer?' Mrs Pearson, his landlady, asked with a twinkle in her eye as she surveyed Bill. He was wearing his best clothes to go out for the second night that week.

Bill flushed and laughed his denial. 'Now who'd be daft enough to have me?' he said and glanced in the oval mirror that hung on the hall wall. He leaned forward and ran his tongue over his teeth to check that there was no trace of the green cabbage that Mrs Pearson had served up with a sausage and mash dinner.

'You'll do,' she said, 'whoever she is.'

Bill laughed again and bid her goodnight as he ran down the three stone steps that led into the street.

'Mind 'ow yer goo, and don't do anything I wouldn't do,' she said. Mrs Pearson shut the thick wooden door behind him and retreated into her cluttered sitting room where a flickering fire cast shadows on the walls. She settled into her favourite chair and lifted her ginger and white cat onto her knees where he began to purr loudly. 'We like Bill don't we Timmy; it'd be nice ter see 'im settle with a nice lass wouldn't it?' Timmy purred even louder as she ran her hands through his fur, and gently picked small bits of fluff from his coat.

Bill jumped off the tram and walked jauntily along towards the Elephant and Castle. He watched and listened to the tram as it pulled smoothly away along its track, making a high-pitched whine in the overhead wires.

His head had been full of questions and possible scenarios all day. He had mixed feelings towards Ann, and he wanted the meeting to be over so he could stop second-guessing the outcome. He felt guilty for pushing her and leaving her without checking to see if she could still be alive. But he also remembered how self-centred and uncaring she'd been to both him and her daughter. He wondered if it were possible that she'd changed with time. She'd certainly looked composed and affluent when he saw her; outwardly unrecognisable as the unkempt, moaning woman she had turned into after they'd married. He speculated about what had happened to her in the last ten years, and became aware that he felt a frisson of fear or excitement, he didn't know which.

He was determined, however, not to reveal his or Sally's whereabouts. He didn't trust her. He'd decided to ask her if she wanted a divorce. He saw no reason for them to stay married; neither of them was religious, and he'd never want to see her again after tonight. He didn't think that divorce was easy, but he felt that there must be a way of achieving it.

While he'd been mulling over old history, he'd arrived at the pub. He went inside to see if Ann had been bold enough to venture in alone; he wouldn't put it past her, she'd seemed at home in the Lounge bar. She wasn't there.

He went back into the cold to wait for her, only to find that it was starting to snow again. Bloody weather – it stopped him working outside – and in the present climate, it threatened his livelihood. He paced up and down for a few minutes before Ann appeared at the corner of Stafford Street and clip-clopped along in fashionable, if not practical, boots.

33

'Hello Bill, glad you could make it,' she smiled politely.

'I've been looking forward to it,' Bill said, in an equally polite tone of voice, 'shall we go inside?' He held the door open by its brass handle and waited for her to decide where she'd like to sit. Ann chose a seat close to the fire and allowed her silver fur coat to slide from her shoulders onto the blue, plush bench.

'What would you like to drink?' Bill asked.

Ann took a cigarette from her bag and asked for a port and lemon. Her eyes never left Bill as he went to the bar. How fit and well he looked – her lip curled – every bit the handsome gentleman. She idly wondered if he was still employed as a bricklayer and if he was living with another woman. Ten years was a long time for him to be living singly and bringing Sally up on his own. She was curious to know how he'd managed. She'd seldom thought about her daughter in the intervening years, but seeing Bill had started her thinking. What did Sally look like now – what had Bill told her?

Bill returned, placed Ann's drink on the table in front of her, and then sat down opposite. He took a sip from his pint glass and said again, 'Well this is a turn up for the books, isn't it?'

'Cheers, thank you.' Ann crossed her shapely legs at the knees and raised her glass.

Bill returned the salutation, thinking how much Sally was starting to resemble her mother; both had unruly tendrils of hair that framed their heart-shaped faces and even features. Ann didn't look much older now than when he'd first met her, still pretty too. Well, outwardly pretty at least. He thanked God that Sally's temperament was a vast improvement on how he remembered her mother's to be. He came swiftly back to the present as he became aware of Ann's long, well-shaped nails drumming gently on the tabletop. She'd quickly finished her drink and was looking around the lounge. He asked her if she would like another, and as he went to the bar found all his old feelings of dislike and resentment returning full force. He wasn't tight by any means, but she didn't care if he could afford the drinks he provided. He didn't think she'd changed one iota.

'What's this all about Ann?' he asked after she started to sip the fresh drink, 'what do you want to talk to me about?' He didn't wait for her answer. 'Before you say anything, I know I owe you an apology,' he took a deep breath, 'I am sorry, I'm sorry for pushing you and sorry for not staying to check if you were alright.' Ann could hear the sincerity in his voice, but the apology only served to exacerbate the feelings of hurt and anger that she'd bottled up over the years.

'Why didn't you?' she asked, 'stay I mean.' She watched his eyes, looking for guilt written there.

'I thought I'd killed you and I panicked.' Bill considered every word before he uttered it. 'If I'd known you were still

136

alive I'd have gone for help, you know I would. I thought I'd hang, and Sally wouldn't be looked after properly ...'

'Yes Bill, I do know that you would have, I thought that was where you'd gone when I first came round.' Ann didn't seem to feel any real resentment towards Bill as she went on to describe in a matter of fact way how she'd succeeded in getting help, been temporarily paralysed, and how she'd made a slow recovery. She finished by relating the circumstances of her mother's death but told him nothing of her life as it was now.

Ann knew he'd disliked Rose as much as she'd detested him.

He managed to murmur, 'I'm so sorry,' and then asked, 'but why didn't you let on that I'd pushed you?'

'I didn't want you to go to prison and leave me to cope with Sally.' Ann stated with a shrug.

Bill took a drink while he inwardly digested her words. Clarissa was right, she's a selfish unnatural cow, and she always has been.

They sat in silence for a short while, their eyes trailed around the warm, welcoming room, and the various people that surrounded them. A pot man cleared their empty glasses, and then Ann uttered words that Bill wasn't expecting.

'I want to see Sally.' She placed her glass delicately down on the table, took a cigarette from a tortoiseshell case, lit it, and inhaled deeply. She returned both the case and matching lighter to her handbag and sat quietly, waiting for his reply.

Bill felt as though she'd slapped him. To cover his alarm, he lit one of his own and inhaled deeply. 'Why? You never loved her, why do you want to see her now?' He shook his head slowly from side to side. 'No! I can't let you do that – she thinks you died when she was born.'

'I don't know why I want to see her, but I do.' Ann grimaced and took a drag of her cigarette then blew a trail of smoke from her red, painted lips. She took a sip from her drink before she carried on speaking. 'You're right, I was a lousy mother, but I was young, too bloody young.' She looked accusingly at him. 'I still don't like little kids, but Sally's twelve now, hardly a little kid. I want to see what she's like.' She ended emphatically, her lips in a determined line.

Bills tone was firm. 'Well this time Ann you aren't going to get what you want,' he tapped ash from the tip of his cigarette, 'she doesn't know you exist. How do you think she'd feel knowing I've lied to her all these years? What makes you think she'd want to see you anyway after the way you treated her?'

Bill was having problems keeping his temper now as he thought of the hurt and disruption it could bring to both Sally and Abigail's lives and the devastation that Sally would feel knowing he'd kept the truth from her. There was no way on earth that he was going to allow that to happen just to satisfy a selfish whim.

Ann's lips curled as she considered her husband. 'Sally won't know how I felt about her when she was a baby unless you tell her, will she?' Her foot began to wag up and down.

'Well I'm not going to be telling her anything – you're dead – and you're staying that way.' Bill spat these words out as he stood and picked up his overcoat. The meeting had been a mistake on his part.

'Hold on Bill,' Ann said, louder than she meant. The other customers in the lounge went quiet, sensing a row brewing, a few glanced at the couple who were glaring at each other, and then they quickly looked away, 'I haven't finished what I wanted to say.'

'You've said enough, Ann I'm not going to change my mind. It could only hurt Sally, knowing who you are.'

'You'll be sorry if you don't hear me out, Bill. It isn't about Sally either.' Ann spoke the words with menace in her voice, causing Bill to throw his coat back onto the seating and sit down. She held his gaze as he surveyed her intently; his curiosity overcame his need to get as far away from her as possible.

Ann had not had any compulsive feelings about seeing her daughter when she'd seen Bill by chance, but now he'd refused her request she was determined to meet her. How dare he tell Sally that she was dead, he'd no right. She was now going to do what she'd intended when setting this meeting up, but she'd let him stew for a few minutes longer. To this end, she lit another cigarette and removed an imaginary piece of tobacco from her tongue with her pink, varnished nails. As she opened her mouth to speak, Bill could contain himself no longer.

'Well?' he said, hoping she was going to ask for a divorce.

Outwardly calm Ann said, 'You have a son Bill.'
Her words caused his mouth to gape. It was exactly the reaction she craved.

34

Bill struggled to contain his emotions. 'Okay, you've got my attention – what the hell are you on about?' He knew she was lying; he hadn't been with a woman since he'd slept with her. He knew he hadn't fathered another child.

Ann didn't answer, she sat impassive, a sardonic smile drawing her mouth down at the corners, as she enjoyed her moment and waited for it to dawn on him that she was telling the truth.

He drew his fingers distractedly through his hair as he remembered what Clarissa had said when he'd taken Sally to visit her for the first time. He'd refused to believe that Ann could be pregnant when Clarissa had a notion that she might be before she left Lincoln. Now it looked as though she might have been right.

'How do you know it's mine, what about your nice Dr Marlow?' Bill spoke sarcastically without thinking he was betraying Clarissa's confidences. He wanted to wipe the mocking smile off Ann's face as he waited for her to explain.

Ann's laugh held contempt. 'That sister of yours is a lying bitch if she said I had anything to do with him. Believe it or not, as you please.' Her smile became more scornful. 'Being with you put me off men for life, my dear husband. There's been no one else. Frank *is* your son.'

Bill studied her face, his emotions in turmoil. He had a son. Ann giving him a name made him real. He wanted to know more but was reluctant to hand Ann a bigger stick to beat him with, as he knew she would.

Trying to sound casual, he asked, 'Why didn't you let me know sooner?'

'You'd disappeared with Sally, have you forgotten?' She ground her cigarette out in an ashtray. 'Mum did go and ask Clarissa where you were, but the spiteful cow wouldn't let on – she never liked me. What would you have done anyway, come back so we could go on with our happy marriage as we did before?'

'You're enjoying this, aren't you?' Bill said. He pushed his coat further onto the seat then strode to the bar where he ordered drinks for them. A son, he had a son; he'd be nine years old now Bill reckoned. Ann knew how much he would have loved to have a son – he'd gone on about it all the time before Sally was born. He tried to stay outwardly calm. He knew he'd probably have to negotiate with Ann to see him. He wondered as he carried the drinks from the bar – did Ann love Frank – she'd never been able to find any love for Sally. If the birth of her second child hadn't triggered her maternal instincts, he would have had a tough time so far. As the knowledge that he had a son sank in, Bill knew he would have to see him, no matter what Ann wanted.

Bill passed Ann her drink and took a pull of beer before sitting back down.

'Thanks.' She wasn't feeling as confident as she had earlier; Bill had surprised her by remaining calm.

'Where is he?' Bill asked, looking unwaveringly into her eyes as though he could see into her brain and pluck out the answer.

Now, she thought, now he'll lose control. 'I've no intention of telling you Bill; you'd only want to take him away as you did Sally.'

Bill gave a fake smile. 'I might have guessed it. I could always follow you home, you know. No one would prevent me from seeing my son, and I intend to see him, Ann, make no mistake about it. No one will stop me. Do you want this to be easy or hard? You knew when you told me that this is what I'd want.'

'Well, this time, Bill, you aren't going to get what you want.' Ann echoed his earlier words and delivered the cruellest blow she could think of, 'I had him adopted.'

Bill's head jerked back as though from a physical assault. 'That's where you're wrong you evil bitch. Even if you have had him adopted, I'll drag you through the courts unless you tell me where he's living.' He meant what he said; he needed to ensure the care of his son. He needed to touch him and imprint his image into his mind. His dislike of Ann turned at this moment into a feeling he'd hitherto reserved for the German war machine. She was self-centred, domineering, and narcissistic; a force that he now knew would go to any lengths to hurt him, and the rest of his family.

Everyone in the pub heard Bill's outburst, and Ann clutched her chest as she saw the expression that lit his face as he glared across the table. She'd wanted to hurt him and make him lose control, but she'd thought no further than achieving her aim. Ann knew that she had gone too far. She stood up, gathered her coat and bag and started to walk away.

Bill's sinewy hand grabbed her arm and prevented her from moving further. 'Sit down.' His words spat forcefully at her.

Ann was flabbergasted; she'd never heard Bill speak, or seen him behave like this; he had always been polite and easy-going. She'd expected him to be upset, and beg her to let him see Frank. She didn't recognize this resilient person who was refusing to be manipulated by her. She instinctively responded to his order, threw off his hand and sat down. She was shaking inside but tried not to give any indication of it.

35

As they paused for breath, the landlord appeared and stood looking down at them with a frown. He took in their animated faces and slowly shook his head. 'If there's any more noise or upset from you two I'll have to ask you to leave, you're disturbing my other customers.' He stood waiting for their response, while Bill, now in control, raised a questioning eyebrow at Ann who nodded her agreement.

'Sorry landlord,' Bill said, 'I think we'll be able to keep our voices down. We'd like to stay, we've still a lot to talk about, but we'll do it quietly.'

'Alright but I'll not warn you again, you'll be barred. Now, do you want another drink?' Bill looked in Ann's direction, and she nodded.

'Yes please,' Bill said, and gave the landlord a florin.

As he walked away, the landlord said, 'I'll have them sent over for you.'

'Thanks, and keep the change,' Bill said.

They sat in silence busy with their thoughts until a barman brought their drinks. He glanced curiously at them but said nothing.

The buzz of conversation and the clink of glasses had resumed when Bill asked quietly, 'What did you mean by you had him adopted? I'm his father how could you have done that without my consent, it's not possible.' He leaned back in his seat and raised his glass. He wasn't sure that was so, but he thought it was and started to add, 'I'm –'

Ann interjected swiftly. 'I didn't say it was legal. It was a private arrangement, fostered – I suppose that's the correct term. The couple who have him took him from the moment he was born. He's their son, and he doesn't know who we are. I swore they would be able to raise him without any interference from me, and I'd no intention or thought of letting you know he existed.' She spoke defiantly then seemed to run out of steam. Her hand shook as she picked up her bag.

Ann felt justified in leaving her son with Mabel but knew that Bill would never be able to understand how she could have turned her back on a second child. She mentally kicked herself for being silly enough to think she could set this meeting up and control the outcome. Bill had changed, he'd usually been amenable and avoided conflict wherever possible in the past, but now it seemed that he wouldn't give in just to keep the peace. She didn't know how to get out of the hole she'd dug for herself.

Bill noticed the tremor in her hands as she took a handkerchief from her bag and dabbed nervously at the corners of her mouth, smudging her lipstick. He felt no remorse as he continued to speak coldly. 'So, you know where he is then?'

'Yes.' Ann peered into the mirror of her Mother of Pearl compact, dabbed some powder on her cheeks which were glowing, then removed the smudges from around her petulant mouth. While she repaired her make-up, she was trying to think of a way to gain the upper hand. 'If you let me see Sally,' she paused and looked questioningly at him to allow her words to sink in, 'I'll take you to see Frank, but you can't let him know who you are, he doesn't know he's adopted.'

'He's not adopted,' Bill said. He considered her proposal for a while and then said, 'Alright, tomorrow morning. I assume the couple live locally.'

Ann nodded; her face a sullen mask.' And you won't tell him who you are?'

'If he's looked after alright and he's happy, then I won't tell him, but if he's not then, I'll move heaven and earth to have him with me.' Bill imagined how difficult it would be to look after another child. He couldn't ask Abigail to foster him, and if he was happy with the people who he thought were his parents, it would be wicked to take him away from them. It would be like taking Sally away from Abigail. 'Will it be alright for us to just turn up without warning at the foster parents' house?' Bill asked. He assumed that Ann didn't keep in touch with them.

'Oh yes, I sometimes call in on a Saturday or Sunday. Do you remember my cousin, Mabel, and her husband, Ronald Birch?' Bill nodded. 'They were desperate for a baby. They looked after me while I was pregnant, and I didn't see how I could keep Frank,' she said, omitting the facts. She hoped Bill might feel partly responsible for her plight as she painted it. She continued varnishing the truth. 'Mabel and Ronald stipulated that Frank should never know that they weren't his real parents.' Ann's eyes widened as she went on to spin a brief tale that she hoped would show her in a good light, or at least a better one than the truth: that she'd never given a damn about Frank.

Bills face relaxed. 'Well, at least you kept him in the family.' Bill recalled Mabel and her husband. He'd liked Ronald's lack of pretension even though he'd come from a good background. He'd also impressed Bill with his care of Mabel when she was suffering from her nerves. Recollections that led him to believe that Frank had probably been better off living with them than he would have been with Ann. 'Where do they live, and come to that, where do you live?'

'I'm not going to tell you,' Ann said, causing Bill to go red in the face again.

'You are Ann,' he said between gritted teeth, 'I'm not stupid enough to let you disappear, and not know where I can find you if you choose to renege on our arrangement.'

'What's to stop *you* doing just that, eh? I wouldn't know where you were either.'

Bill drummed his fingers on the table – he wanted this meeting to be over. He'd no intention of going back on his word, but he didn't trust Ann to keep hers.

'Look, Ann, if you want a divorce it stands to reason we're both going to know where the other one lives aren't we and—'

'What do you mean? I've never asked for a divorce; it suits me to stay married. I just don't want to live with you. Do you want a divorce then?'

Bill shook his head. 'It's a fight I can do without, and I've no intention of getting married again – ever.' He paused and emptied his glass; deep in thought. 'Drink up Ann I'm taking you home; I need to see for myself where you live.' Ann opened her mouth to refuse, but Bill carried on speaking. 'I'll give you my address, and you could always find me or get a message to me through Clarissa.

147

You needn't tell me where Frank lives now, but I'll meet you in the morning, and you can take me there, then I'll take you to see Sally in the afternoon, I promise.' He glowered and pointed his index finger at her. 'You have to promise that you'll never go there without me, or give her any indication of who you are. I won't have her hurt, and I wouldn't contemplate hurting Frank or Mabel either.' He stopped talking and picked up his coat.

Ann knew she had no option but to trust him; she'd lost the fight for now. Reluctantly she acquiesced, but she was inwardly fuming as they left the pub together.

36

When he'd escorted Ann home the previous evening, Bill's eyes had widened to see that she owned a large Victorian house that was well maintained. She explained that she took in lodgers, but didn't invite him in. As she unlocked her front door, he glimpsed a long hallway paved in red, blue and cream tiles that were highly polished. She quickly said goodnight and closed the door, preventing him from seeing any further into her world. That suited Bill, he had no intention of continuing to see her after their necessary arrangements were over.

Next morning as they approached Mabel and Ronald's house, Bill admired the neatness of the garden that featured a tall weeping willow tree whose bare branches cascaded gracefully amid the snow-covered lawn and small shrubs. The air energised him as it entered his lungs with biting freshness. It heightened his senses enabling him to hear water as it bubbled over shale in a nearby stream. They crunched along the gravel path to the front door with its open porch. Bill thought it was a lovely setting for his son to grow up.

Mabel quickly answered the doorbell and showed no surprise to see Ann early in the morning, but she blanched as she recognised Bill. She took a sideways step and leaned against the doorpost. Bill felt annoyed with himself as he realised that Mabel possibly thought he'd come to claim his son.

'What's the matter with you,' Ann said, 'you remember Bill, don't you?'

Bill stepped forward and took Mabel's hand in his own. 'It's alright Mabel don't be worrying yourself – I've not come to cause trouble – I just have to see him.'

Mabel attempted a weak smile. 'Won't you come inside Bill?' She ignored Ann as she turned and led the way down a thickly carpeted, cream painted hallway. She indicated a room on the right, followed them in and closed the door.

'He doesn't know –'

'I know Mabel; Ann's told me everything. I won't tell him I promise, but I think you'll understand that I must see him. Where is he?'

Ann had removed her coat and settled herself in a comfortable, chintz-covered armchair. She lit a cigarette and leaned back. 'There's no need to make a fuss Mabel, Bill's already promised that he wouldn't take Frank away so long as he's happy and well cared for, haven't you Bill?'

'Yes, where is he?' he asked again.

Mabel gave Ann a dirty look, 'He's with his dad in the potting shed clearing out pots and making sure everything's ready for planting seeds when the weather's right. They're both keen gardeners,' she added. Her pride in them was evident. 'You should have let me know that Bill was coming, Ann.'

'Oh, stop fussing,' Ann said.

Mabel took Bill's coat and offered to make them tea while she gave her husband and son a call. When they came into the kitchen, she told Frank to clean himself up, and as he ran upstairs, she quickly warned her husband that Ann had brought Bill with her. She explained that Bill had no intention of claiming his son. Ronald understood and followed Frank to the bathroom.

After a short while, Mabel re-entered the room bearing: a wooden tray with pretty rose-patterned teacups, a matching teapot and milk jug, and a plate of biscuits that she placed on a small table next to Ann – who offered to act as mother. The irony wasn't lost on Bill.

'They're just washing their hands and getting rid of the dirt then they'll be in,' Mabel said to Bill, as she sat down on the chair opposite Ann.

Bill had been admiring the red carpet and crystal wall sconces. Every polished surface from the piano to the small side tables placed either end of the sofa, where he sat, glowed with the patina that comes with age and care. The room managed to be elegant yet cosy he thought and complimented Mabel on her beautiful home.

She smiled but waved her hand and said, 'I can't take all the credit, most of this has been in Ronald's family for generations, I've just carried on looking after it.' She looked him squarely in the face. 'It will all belong to Frank one day.'

Mabel handed round tea as Ronald came into the room, nodded to Ann then strode across the room and shook Bill's hand. 'It's good to see you after all this time; you're looking well.'

Bill returned his greeting. 'It's good to see you too.' But his eyes were directed expectantly at the door.

'Come on in son and say hello to our visitors,' Ronald said, in a baritone voice.

Frank entered hesitantly, glanced at Ann, nodded, and then walked over to his Dad, who was warming his backside in front of a crackling log fire.

'This is Mr Brooks, an old family friend.' He gave Frank's shoulder a gentle tap.

Frank took the hint and shook hands with Bill, saying, 'Pleased to meet you, sir.' He went to sit on the floor at his Mom's feet.

Bill said, 'Hello, young man.' He beamed as he surveyed Frank, taking in his well-cut, thick, brown hair, bright eyes and rudely healthy cheeks. He looked neat and tidy down to his shiny black lace-up shoes. He presented as a well brought up, happy boy who loved his parents as much as they loved him, Bill thought gratefully.

They all sat talking about very little for half an hour, then Bill thanked them for their hospitality and said they shouldn't outstay their welcome. Ronald and Frank returned to their gardening after saying farewell.

Bill was interested to hear that Frank's, 'Goodbye Mrs Brooks,' held no warmth or familiarity.

Mabel saw them to the door, and as they were leaving Bill asked her if she would mind if he visited occasionally. She hesitated for a second and then agreed it would be acceptable, but she would prefer the visits to be prearranged, and infrequent. Bill said that he understood, and kissed Mabel on her cheek before following Ann, who was impatient to leave, down the path.

37

Bill was very quiet as Ann, and he travelled to Birmingham. They had exchanged very few words all morning. He found that the longer he spent with her, the more their mutual dislike became apparent. It was evident that there was no connection between their son and Ann, and Bill thought he would make any future arrangements to see Frank, without Ann's help or knowledge.

Shortly after they'd left Mabel's house, Ann had asked Bill what he thought of Frank, but he didn't tell her how proud he'd been when he set eyes on his son. He'd shrugged and was non-committal. Bill wanted to ignore his promise and tell his son the truth but knew he would never do that to Mabel and Ronald. Frank was their adored son, and they could provide him with more, in a material way, and equally as much love as he felt. Thanking God that Frank would not be brought up by Ann, he remained silent on the subject.

By the time they'd walked from the station to Birchall Street, Ann was feeling cross with them both. She moaned: about the cold, the crowds, and the way the cobblestones made walking difficult. At one point she said she'd changed her mind about going to see Sally.

Bill had stood stock still in the clutter of market stalls. 'Clear off then if you want to, but it's the only chance you'll get to see her so either go or stop bloody moaning.'

He'd strode off, his back ramrod straight. Ann had quickly caught him up, calling his name to make him wait for her before he disappeared into the crowd of shoppers. She apologised and excused herself by saying that she was scared Sally wouldn't like her. Bill's patience was at an end, and he told her that it wouldn't matter if she didn't as he was going to introduce her as a distant cousin. This visit was to be a one-off he reminded her.

They walked in strained silence until they reached the entry to the yard where Sally lived. Ann let out a shout of disgust as she trod in some dog mess that had been partially hidden by the melting snow.

Bill cleaned her shoe. 'Watch where you tread,' he said without sympathy.

Ann wrinkled her nose in distaste at her surroundings and averted her eyes from a group of small children, dressed in a motley assortment of ragged clothes, who were playing tag in the narrow, cheerless yard.

Bill didn't usually have any snobbish thoughts, but he couldn't help comparing the place where his daughter was being fostered, to the surroundings that he'd found his son was enjoying. It confirmed that he was right in deciding not to tell Sally that she had a brother. Both Sally and Frank were loved and cared for in their respective homes, and Bill could see no good reason to change anything for either of them. He decided that, for now, ignorance of each other's existence should continue. He hoped there might come a time when he could enlighten them, but felt sure that it shouldn't be now.

Bill told Ann to wait outside while he asked his friends permission to bring a visitor in to meet them. She raised her eyes to the sky and pursed her lips but agreed.

Bill went into the kitchen and called, 'Hey you lovely people, anyone at home?'

Sally flew out of the living room and threw herself into his open arms, hugged him, kissed his cheek, then said with a beaming smile, 'I thought you'd never get here.' She led him into the living room where Jim sat in his chair, reading the previous day's paper, while Abigail sat on the sofa, knitting.

'I'm sorry to spring it on you,' he said, 'but I've brought someone with me, I hoped you wouldn't mind.'

Sally's eyes widened with surprise at the unwelcome news, and she immediately went to sit by Tess.

Jim said, 'Well don't leave 'im standing in the cold bring 'im in.'

Abigail rose and swung the kettle over the fire as Bill went to invite Ann inside. Ann frowned as she took in the whitewashed brick walls and bare boards. She hurried through the kitchen as though it would contaminate her if she lingered, even though it was, as usual, neat and tidy.

Seeing a well-dressed woman cross the threshold into the living room, startled everyone. Jim jumped up and asked Ann to come and sit by the fire to get warm. Ann greeted everyone and took his chair. Her face was stiff and unsmiling as she held her hands out towards the warmth and looked around the room. Her eyes drank in Sally's appearance, causing Sally's cheeks to redden as she smiled shyly at the visitor.

Ann thought how much she resembled herself at a similar age, but she felt no warmth towards her daughter, who was sitting on a step by a closed door, caressing her pet dog. Ann wasn't keen on animals, especially one that had growled when she'd first entered the room. She hoped it wouldn't come by her, and kept her handbag on her lap just in case.

'This is Mrs B ... Brown, she's my second cousin.' Bill stumbled over the introduction as he'd nearly said, Mrs Brooks. His face reddened, and then he continued with a smile for Sally. 'We thought Sally might like to come into town and have tea with us to celebrate her birthday if that's alright with you.' He looked questioningly at Abigail and saw her lips tremble as she nodded her permission.

'Would you like to go?' Jim asked Sally.

'Yes, oh yes please,' Sally said. Inside she was unsure about the attractive lady who seemed so out of place in their cramped living room. It didn't prevent her from being curious, and she wasn't about to miss an opportunity to go out for tea with her father and the mystery lady.

'Would you like a cup of tea before you go out in the cold again?' Abigail asked as the kettle came noisily to the boil.

Bill answered quickly. 'No thanks Abigail, he glanced at his watch, it's half-past two now so we won't stay. I'll bring Sally back at about six o'clock – would it be alright if I stayed here tonight?'

Abigail nodded. 'Of course, you know you're welcome to stay here whenever you like. I'll make the truckle bed up for Sally.'

Ann asked if she could use their bathroom, making Sally laugh. 'We don't have one of those.' She blushed then said that she had to go too and would take Ann with her down the yard. As they went through the kitchen, Abigail heard

Ann ask Sally if she'd prefer to live somewhere that had a bathroom. Sally said she'd love an inside toilet, but she liked living where she was.

'I'd hate it,' Ann said. How could a child of hers stand living among this squalor? She felt smugly superior when she considered the difference in the start that she'd given to Frank and the lack of comfort that Bill had provided for Sally. She saw no difference in the morality that dictated their actions.

Bill took the opportunity when he was alone with Jim and Abigail to explain who Ann was. He assured them that the visit wouldn't happen again and that Sally would be staying with them. He promised to tell them more later on as Sally and Ann might return any minute, and he didn't want Sally to know.

Abigail nodded and breathed a sigh of relief. She wouldn't have been able to let Sally go anywhere with the hard-faced woman who proved to be her mother. Perhaps Ann was kinder than she seemed, but Abigail didn't think so. However, Abigail trusted Bill and knew that Sally wouldn't want any other mother than herself. Nevertheless, she had butterflies in her stomach when she thought of losing her darling and held onto Tess's collar and stroked her head as they left.

38

Sally held Bill's hand as they pushed their way through the crowd in the markets and on to Lyons on the corner of New Street. It was an imposingly large, two-storey tearoom that was always busy on Saturdays. Sally had peeped longingly in the window as she'd shopped with Abigail, but they had never been inside. She gave a tiny skip as they crossed the tiled entrance into the foyer and stood looking about, fascinated. A polite waitress showed them to a table halfway down the crowded room that was buzzing with the sounds of crockery and chatter. Sally told Bill that she'd like to be a waitress when she was older. She thought they looked smart in their black dresses with the white collar and pinafore, and the frilled hatband that kept their hair tidy. Bill merely smiled, but Ann said Sally should set her sights higher; or be a skivvy all her life. Sally took no notice. She felt too excited to think solemn thoughts.

They were soon seated at a table that had a starched white cloth and a menu from which she could choose her meal. Sally asked for fish and chips, and Bill said he'd have the same. The air was redolent with tantalising aromas, and Sally flushed with the newness and excitement of it all. She sipped slowly at her ginger beer and ate her meal in as genteel a way as she knew how, wanting this to be a special memory, although she couldn't have explained her feelings to anyone except Tess – she felt very grown-up. Ann was quiet as she picked at her ham salad while Bill chatted with Sally about her birthday and school. Ann smiled at Sally's childlike pleasure when Bill gave her the bead necklace that he'd bought for her. Ann offered to help with the clasp as Sally struggled to put it on, but Bill stood up and fastened it, kissing her on the top of her head as she thanked him for the hundredth time. Ann felt a momentary flash of rejection but told herself not to be so foolish.

They continued to talk in a desultory fashion with Sally wishing Ann wasn't there to spoil her time with her dad, and Ann wishing Bill wasn't there so she could speak freely to her daughter. Ann had been listening and watching Sally and had concluded that she wouldn't mind them living together when she was a little older. Ann painted herself a rosy picture of how life could be with her daughter. She asked Sally some questions about her likes and dislikes and began to formulate a scheme whereby she'd wait until Sally finished school then she'd see if she could persuade her to come and live with her and be her helpmate.

'I think it's time to be getting back now Ann, and it's starting to snow again. Will you be alright if we walk with you to the station, and see you on to the train?' Bill asked.

'Of course, I will – I'm a big girl now.' She winked and smiled again at Sally as she gathered her gloves and handbag together, and then stood while Bill helped her on with her fur coat. When they were all ready to go, Bill, went to buy a packet of cigarettes. Ann looked thoughtful, and opening her purse took out a ten-shilling note. She tucked it down inside Sally's mitten and said in a conspiratorial whisper; 'Buy yourself something nice for your birthday, Sally.'

Sally didn't know what she should do; she'd never had so much money before and didn't know if she should accept it.

Ann saw her confusion and said reassuringly, 'It's alright – don't forget I'm related to your father, so we're related too.'

'I suppose we are,' Sally said, grateful to be given a reason why she should accept the money, 'thank you very much, Mrs Brown.'

Just before they waved goodbye to Ann, Bill asked Sally to sit on a bench and wait for him; then he'd taken Ann aside. Sally could see he was saying something serious and wondered what it was that made her give him a strange smile as she listened, and replied quietly while nodding her head. Bill returned to Sally and she waved as the train pulled away from the platform – leaving Sally wondering if she'd ever see the posh lady again.

Bill didn't seem to be very pleased when Sally told him about the money that Ann had given her, but she noticed when he said that she could keep it, his smile was almost identical to the one that Ann had before she'd boarded the train. He wouldn't tell Sally why he was smiling though and changed the subject by challenging her to race him as far as St. Martin's. By the time they arrived at the church with Sally winning by a nose, they were out of breath and laughing so much that Sally almost forgot Ann's existence.

It was on a visit to see his son two months later that Bill found out that it was Ann who'd stipulated Frank should think that they were both dead. He found it difficult to believe that anyone could be so vindictive and selfish. His anger at Ann's behaviour finally severed any residue of his understanding of her. He hated her and knew he'd never willingly see her again.

39

Sally called over her shoulder to the elderly lady who owned the local newsagent's shop.

'Alright Mrs Harris, as soon as I get home, I'll tell Mom you'll be round later this evening,' She opened the door, and the bell that alerted Mrs Harris when someone entered the shop began to clang. Sally had always enjoyed the raucous sound, though she knew some light-fingered people who lived in the district, would have gladly put it out of action. Fumbling to put her change into the felt purse that she had proudly made under Abigail's supervision, she bounced out into the road with Tess close at heel.

'Oi! Watch where—oh! Shit! Oh, bugger! The three plates of food that the youth had been carrying went flying up in the air and smashed onto the cobbles, scattering thick, white pieces of crockery splattered with lumps of potato, and surrounded by strings of dark green and yellow spring cabbage. Three skinny lamb chops covered in dark brown gravy were intermingled with bright, green peas, and had somehow managed to collect together forming themselves into a tent-shaped heap. Two metal dividers and a top cover rolled along the cobbles for a few inches, clattering and spinning noisily before slowing by degrees, and eventually coming to a halt. Tess started forward as the tantalising smell of the dinners overcame her training until Sally automatically put out a restraining hand and told her firmly to sit. Tess instantly obeyed but gazed askance at her mistress who stood shaking with dismay.

The young man had danced about as he'd tried to save the stack of plates from falling but had only succeeded in planting the heel of his boot firmly in the slippery mess as it landed, and endcd up sitting on his backside his flat cap askew.

A group of youngsters and a couple of older men passing on the opposite side of the road were laughing and calling out good-natured remarks.

'Hey mate what yer gonna do fer yer next trick?'

'Can we 'av a repeat, I didn't see 'ow yer did that.'

'Ooo, yer gonna be in some trouble when yer get back ter work.'

Sally stood still with her hands pressed over her mouth as she saw the damage she'd caused; her attention had been in the shop with Mrs Harris. From the minute she'd stepped out of the shop, time seemed to slow down. Sally watched individual strips of cabbage twirl about like ribbons in the wind as they slowly settled into the conglomerate mess that was spreading over a wide area of the cobbled street. She dragged her eyes to where the owner of the plated dinners sat, legs spread-eagled on the ground. She thought he looked comical with his cap covering his eyes. But it didn't make her smile.

He pushed his cap back into place so that it almost covered his short, fairish hair, and stared forlornly at the chaos in front of his feet. Then he noticed the stricken face of the young girl who'd backed away until she stood pressed into the shop doorway as though she was trying to enter it backwards. Sorry as he felt for himself, knowing he'd have to replace the dinners out of his own pocket, he suddenly saw the funny side of the accident. He proceeded to laugh uproariously, setting a startled Tess off to bark in unison.

Sally couldn't understand why he was so full of merriment when she felt close to tears. She turned and rushed back into the shop where Mrs Harris was still serving her customer.

'Whatever's the matter, love?' Mrs Harris fled round the counter and sat Sally down on a chair usually reserved for elderly customers.

Sally explained between sobs what had happened, and Mrs Harris went to the door and looked both ways along the street, but the young man had disappeared. She finished serving her customer, fetched a bucket of soapy water, a broom and a shovel and helped Sally clear up the mess. 'Best do it now before anyone else has an accident,' she said.

'Where's he gone do you think?' Sally asked.

'He's probably gone to fetch some more dinners for his workmates, now stop yer worryin' and get on home,' she said and patted Sally's arm.

Sally ran the short distance to her home, her plaits swinging wildly, and her green and white striped summer dress clinging to her tanned legs. She burst into the house, desperate to confess to Abigail her part in the debacle. Abigail laughed and told her to forget about it as accidents were always waiting to happen and catch people out.

By the next day, Sally had dismissed the accident and was getting ready to go shopping when there was a knock at the door.

'Quick, answer it before they wake Jim,' Abigail called softly to Sally.

40

Sally pushed a stray lock of hair back from her forehead with damp hands and opened the door. She thought her eyes were playing tricks on her as she recognised the young man who she'd caused so much trouble for the previous day.

A smile lit up his pleasant face bringing a gleam to his deep-set eyes. He doffed his cap and gave a small bow. 'Hello again, Sally,' he said and grinned at the look of surprise on her face. The recent sunny weather had sprinkled a few freckles on her nose and cheeks, which now glowed. The youth stood looking at her; he thought the freckles suited her. He hadn't been able to get her image out of his head since their unfortunate meeting.

'How d' you know my name?' Sally asked frowning. 'I don't have any money to pay for the dinners, and I'd have said how sorry I was, but you'd disappeared when Mrs Harris looked for you.' Sally felt close to tears and had turned to go and fetch Abigail when the young man put his hand on her arm.

'It's okay, please don't upset yourself, I've already replaced the dinners, it was partly my fault anyway, please don't bother about it. I had a bloody good laugh, and so did my boss when I explained to him what took me so long. Anyway,' he held out his hand and tried to look serious, 'I thought I should introduce myself before we bump into each other again. My name's Edward, Edward Griffiths, and I know you're Sally Tildesley.'

They solemnly shook hands, and Sally giggled as she said, 'I am sorry, but you did look so funny sitting on the ground with your cap over your eyes. How did you find out who I was?'

'Oh, it's easy when you're clever like me,' he chuckled, 'I went into the shop that you flew out of and asked old Mrs Harris if she knew who the beautiful girl with the long brown plaits was. She knew who I meant and said you were as beautiful inside as outside, and I wasn't to cause you any trouble. I had to convince her that I meant no harm before she'd tell me where you lived.'

'Well you're not so clever,' Sally said, and pushed her hair back from her face again to hide her blushes, 'my name's not Tildesley, it's Brooks, my Mom's name is Tildesley.'

Right on cue, Abigail asked, 'Who is it, Sally?'

'I'd better go in now – we're going up the town in a minute. It was nice of you to come and tell me everything was okay.' She turned to go back indoors.

'Can I come and see you again? I'd like it if we could be friends. Perhaps we could go for a walk to Bell Barn on Sunday if your Mom will let you?'

Sally hesitated. 'Stay there, and I'll go and ask her?' She went inside and explained who Edward was, but Abigail said she'd have to know more about him before they could go anywhere together. Sally arranged for Edward to come and talk to Abigail the next evening. He seemed happy with this and waved as he ran lightly down the yard, jumped to grab the top of the brick wall that separated their yard from the next street, flung his body over and rapidly disappeared.

Sally thought how kind he was and good looking too. She confessed to Abigail while they finished getting ready to shop, that she'd like to know more about him.

'You can tell you're growing up,' she said with a wry smile, 'don't be in too much of a rush, you've plenty of time.' She tugged humorously at her daughter's plaits, and Sally responded with a hug.

'I'll always be your little girl Mom,' she said playfully, and then seriously, 'you know I love you more than anyone else in the whole world, don't you?'

'I love you too my darling, now come on and let's go shopping before there's nothing left to buy.'

41

Abigail bustled round and handed Sally a worn, cane basket, folded a sturdy hessian bag into it and shrugged into her coat. Sally could feel Abigail's pleasure at the sentiments she'd expressed, but she had no idea that her words had touched Abigail as profoundly as they had. Abigail knew that Sally was as precious to her as Grace had been. If she had the power to prevent it, she'd never let Sally feel a minute of hurt.

Abigail's mind continued to wander as they started their short walk in the sunshine to the centre of town. She only half-listened to Sally's chatter, and responded to greetings from acquaintances with perfunctory smiles and waves, as she thought about Sally's meeting with Edward. She wondered if he was going to be the start of Sally's introduction to a world outside her control, where she could no longer prevent the realities of life from weighing Sally down and ending her childhood.

She continued to feel a sense of disquiet as they did some of their shopping, leaving the vegetables until they were on their way home. She knew many of the stallholders and barrow boys by name and was greeted continuously, and given the best fruit and vegetables to be found on the market. Even so, she was careful to ensure they got value for their pennies.

Although Sally was only twelve, she already had a slightly voluptuous appearance and a way of responding warmly to almost everyone she met. She was very popular and retained an appealing air of innocence that Abigail knew resulted from the fact that she'd been protected by herself, Jim, and her father from the deprivation that many of their neighbours endured.

Abigail sometimes felt appalled when she thought about the changes to her world. Since the war and the general strike, motor cars were replacing horse-drawn vehicles, houses now lit by electricity, planes could fly to Australia in less than a month, and electrified locomotives were replacing steam trains in some areas. Some things never seemed to change though, children still ran about in rags and went to bed hungry in filthy hovels.

She became aware that they'd reached St. Martin's church while she'd been mulling over her world's deterioration and expansion. She held Sally's hand as they went into the church and sat quietly for a while as they were wont to do each time they came into the town. Abigail found that she couldn't stop thinking about what the future would hold for Sally if they failed to give her a better start in life than the one that she and Jim had had. She didn't feel sorry for herself, but she thought about the way she'd worked hard all her life, and had little enjoyment except that which Sally gave her just by being with her and having such a kind and gentle personality. She failed to realise that Sally's loveliness was mainly a result of having herself as a role model.

Sitting in the familiar, tranquil atmosphere still gave Abigail a sense of peace. After a time, she felt she'd discovered answers to the questions she'd been asking herself. She'd never given much thought to when she would feel she had enough money to achieve her dreams; she'd just felt the need to save whatever she could. Being thrifty had paid off, and she'd managed to accumulate a tidy sum. Now she could use her savings to change Sally's future for the better.

Ever since Ann had visited with Bill and spoken disparagingly about their home; Abigail had looked with new eyes at the surroundings she'd taken for granted all her life. She'd always felt a sense of pride that their house was bigger had more rooms and was kept clean and tidy. Compared to their neighbour's homes, it was a palace. It had a tap plumbed in, walls that were in good repair and didn't run with water, as many in the yard did. That pride had disappeared. She'd begun to be more and more ashamed of their environment as she crossed the yard each day to their shared water closet. The thought of moving away from all that was familiar and owning property was terrifying, but she felt determined to talk to Jim and ascertain how he would feel about leaving his home. Abigail had been looking in the papers to find out the price of houses in districts that she'd never visited. She knew she'd saved enough money to buy a home towards the outskirts of Birmingham though she'd never mentioned her nest egg to another soul. Abigail wondered what her friend Ellen would think of the idea that was rapidly becoming her intention. She was determined to overcome any obstacles that might try to thwart her.

'Are you ready for the fun and games now?' Abigail nudged Sally, who was reading a religious tract left in the back of the pew where they'd rested.

'Lead on Macduff,' Sally misquoted and giggled as Abigail glanced back and pulled a funny face at her.

'You think you're clever now you've been reading some Shakespeare rubbish, don't you?' Abigail said, 'Well come and see how clever you are at getting Bert to knock a ha'penny a pound off our carrots.'

42

Abigail let her necklace repeatedly slide through her fingers. 'What do you think, Ellen?' she asked after sharing her feelings and plans with her best friend.

'Well, I agree there's some sense in what yow're sayin. It'll be a fresh start for yow, an' there's sum noice 'ouses bin built out that way. There's a noice park an' all. A course yow'll be livin' among the Irish y'know.'

'Nothing wrong with that is there?'

'No, I'm just sayin' wot's a fact.' Ellen sighed and looked tearful, 'it's nun of my business I know.'

'You've always been welcome to speak straight out Ellen, don't stop now, we'll remain, friends, no matter where I move to.' Abigail said. She knew how Ellen must be feeling as she was feeling choked too at the thought of leaving the best friend that anyone could wish for. She got up and crossed the room to hug Ellen. 'We're a couple of old dafties.' She smiled as she poured water into the teapot and set it aside to brew.

'O, I know, but I was just thinkin' if yow could afford the rent. It'll be a lot more than 'ere y'know.'

'I know, but I'm not thinking of renting a place Ellen, I intend to buy a house that we can leave for Sally to live in after we've gone. I'm going to talk to Jim about it tonight.'

Ellen chuckled. 'Well yow've worked 'ard and yow've bin careful, but I must say I'm surprised yow've got enough ter buy an 'ouse. More power ter yow're elbow.' She drew in a deep breath. 'I'll miss yow tho; we've bin 'avin our mornin' chats since before yow 'ad Sally t' brighten our loives.'

'Jim got that bit of compensation when he had his accident, so we've got enough between us to buy a nice place in the Sparkhill area. We'll miss you too, Ellen, but I'll still be coming into town twice a week, and I'll always come and see you, and I hope you'll visit us whenever you can. I know it won't be the same, but Sally deserves better than to live in our yard where she has to share with – well you know all that.' She sniffed and taking out a handkerchief, blew her nose and stared bleakly at her friend. 'I don't know about you, but I could do with another cuppa?'

'Ar, me an' all, I'm just bein' silly, tek no notice of me. Yow'll 'av' enough trouble when yow tell Jim what yow wanna do.'

43

'G'night Mom, night Uncle Jim.' Sally blew them a kiss and ran lightly upstairs, swiftly followed by Tess who had taken to whining if left alone in the kitchen. She went obediently to lie on her old grey blanket and watched as her friend cleaned her teeth with a mixture of salt and soot that she kept in a pot on the marble washstand. Sally undressed, pulled one of her pretty cotton nightdresses over her head, and climbed into bed. She enjoyed the luxurious feeling when she sank into the freshly shaken feather mattress that sat atop a flock one.

She didn't mind going to bed early even though it was still light; she was looking forward to seeing Edward again when he came to meet Abigail. She lay thinking about the good-looking young man who she guessed wasn't much older than herself, but found she couldn't recall his features. She could only see deep blue eyes that seemed to be continually laughing when he looked at her. He'd been dressed similarly to most other factory workers; except for the modern knitted pullover that he wore instead of a waistcoat. She wondered who'd knitted his pullover for him as she gave in to the Sandman and drifted into a deep sleep.

Downstairs, Abigail poured Jim and herself a glass of ale that she'd fetched in a jug from the outdoor earlier that evening. When they settled down, Abigail outlined her wishes to her husband, who listened with interest. She'd expected some opposition as she didn't think he would agree to leave the house where they'd been settled since their marriage twenty- two years ago. But again he surprised her by saying he thought it was a good idea in many ways. He didn't mind that she wouldn't be able to take him a hot meal each night. In fact, he didn't raise any objection at all.

They agreed that they shouldn't tell Sally or Bill their plans until they'd found out how to go about making their dream a reality. Jim seemed to be as pleased as Abigail about taking a step up in the world, and not just for Sally's sake either. When they went up to bed later that evening, they were closer than they'd been for quite some time. As they fell asleep, Abigail's last thought was to picture the indoor bathroom that they would have. Jim allowed his thoughts to enjoy what would become, his newfound freedom to entertain his lady friend without fear of Abigail or Sally interrupting him.

When Abigail met Edward the next morning, she decided she liked the openness of his face. While drinking a cup of tea, he told them that he'd be fifteen in a couple of months, was the baby of the family, and that he lived in Lombard Street next to the smithy.

Jim laughed when he knew who Edward's parents were. He said he knew his father, Harry, who usually cut his hair at the local barbers, and had drunk a pint with him on occasions when he'd seen him in their local. He'd never met Edwards' mother, Minnie, although he'd heard she

176

could be a right tartar when anything upset her. Edward entertained them for a while regaling them with stories of the things his sister's Gladys, Elsie and May got up to as they tried to avoid the wrath of Minnie. He told them that he had a brother called Percy who'd already left home to work in the stables of a family who owned a large estate near Wootton Wawen.

Abigail said it would be alright for him to be friends with Sally, and invited him to come and have a meal with them the following Sunday. 'But no silly behaviour young man.' She didn't explain what she meant, but Edward nodded as if he understood her meaning. Sally thought it was a very peculiar thing for her mother to say to someone who she'd only just met. 'Well we're off to church in a few minutes,' Abigail said, 'would you like to come with us?' Edward declined and indicated that he had chores to do at home. He left shortly after thanking Abigail for the tea.

Sally hadn't said very much while her mom and Uncle Jim were inspecting Edward, but she'd liked the way he made everyone laugh, and thought she would like to be friends with him. She followed his tall, lean figure out into the kitchen, and waved shyly as he repeated his disappearing trick over the wall.

'See ya.' He called as he dropped down into the next street, leaving Sally to wonder if he would return. She had a few other friends, but no one as interesting as he appeared to be to her young eyes.

44

Sally kept her new friend's existence to herself initially – she didn't want to look silly if he never showed up again. She needn't have worried; he came to the door the next evening and asked her to go and have a game of ball in the yard with him. Sally said she would, but she'd promised to call for Faith. Edward said that they could all play together. Some other local lads joined in, and they were all soon treating Edward as their leader. He knew just how to organise their games, and as he was older than the others, they followed his affable orders without fuss or resentment.

These days became a regular occurrence, and Edward didn't respond when one of the fathers referred to him as king of the babbies. Sally admired Edward's restraint as he just shrugged and continued to enjoy himself.

Bill told Sally that he thought Edward was a comical mixture and wondered why he wanted to come into their yard when he must have friends to play ball games with in his street. Sally smiled and said she was glad he was her friend, and that Tess liked him too.

'Well you just make sure he behaves himself, or he'll have me to deal with,' Bill said in a stern voice, but laughed when Sally looked puzzled, 'it's alright love don't worry about it, but if he ever does anything you don't like, promise me you'll tell me about it?'

'I'm not sure what you mean, Dad, but he's a good friend, and I don't think he would want to do anything I didn't like.' Sally had a good idea that her dad was talking about sex, but she'd no intention of admitting it. She trusted Edward, and he'd never made her feel even the slightest bit uncomfortable. But if he did, she knew she'd never want to see him again.

That summer Sally and Edward spent all their free time together. He went shopping with Abigail and Sally and carried their heavy bags of vegetables home. He went into St. Martin's with them on many occasions although he confessed to Sally that he'd no time for mealy, mouthed clergymen.

Sally was surprised that Edward didn't speak like her Uncle Jim until he explained that his parents didn't come from Birmingham. They came from Gloucestershire, and his mother became very annoyed if he didn't speak properly.

After they'd been friends for a couple of months, Edward took Sally to his house. They went to take some oranges that he'd bought at the market with the small allowance his mother gave him out of his wages. He'd become well known by the stallholders who were friends with Abigail, and they'd let him have the fruit cheap.

His job paid very little as he was the general run about at a small manufacturing company. He was inclined to be generous natured and often spent his few coppers on others, and Sally knew he'd spend every penny on her if she allowed him to. He got the message when he bought her some ribbons for her hair, and she firmly asked him not to buy her anything else. As usual, he complied with her request – he didn't want to lose her friendship.

Sally went to meet his family willingly enough but felt overwhelmed by the friendly banter from his sisters even though she said afterwards that she liked them. They were older than Edward by two, four and six years. Elsie was training to be a nurse. Gladys was a hand press operator in a Deritend factory that made buttons, and May the youngest, who was quieter than her sisters, remained at home to help their mother who took in washing and ironing.

Sally found that their home wasn't like her own. It only had one room downstairs, two upstairs and a cellar. They shared a tap with every other house in the yard. Sally didn't know how they all fitted in but was too polite to ask. When Edward opened the door and ushered her in without any warning to the occupants, Sally found herself in a small room that had a table with four grey, painted wooden chairs and a rocking chair set next to the range.

Two of the girls were reading, and another one was ironing a white shirt on half of the table being cushioned by a folded grey blanket with a piece of scorched sheeting on top. She went to the range and swapped the cool iron that she'd been using for a hot one, winding a cloth round the metal handle before picking it up and spitting on its base where the drop of saliva sizzled for a second then evaporated. Their mother was scraping carrots at the other half of the table. She stood up as Edward introduced Sally, and wiped her hands on a piece of rag which she threw back onto the table. She gave him a dirty look, said a terse, 'Hello,' turned her back and went noisily upstairs after telling one of the girls to finish the carrots and get them into the pot. Whatever was in the black pot that hung over the fire gave off an inviting aroma of onions and something that Sally didn't recognise.

Edward gave the oranges to his sisters and said quietly, 'Who's upset her this time, eh?' They all shrugged and pointed at the door which Minnie had closed sharply behind her. Edward understood. 'See you later.' He winked at Sally as they left.

45

He regretted taking Sally to his home and explained later that his Mom was probably listening behind the stairway door. She often did it to hear what they said so she could vent her spleen on any of the siblings that hadn't behaved as she would wish.

'Is she miserable?' Sally asked.

Edward shrugged. 'My dad's a lot nicer. He's often out cutting hair for some men who aren't able to go to the shop. He learned his trade when he was in the workhouse in Cheltenham with his mother and a brother and sister. His sister died while they were in there. He hardly ever mentions his family, so I don't know how they came to be there. That's where he met Mom. Oh, not in the workhouse,' he gave a silly grin, 'I mean after he came out.'

Sally didn't know what to say, she knew there were workhouses that destitute people had to go into, but they were terrible places according to her dad. She couldn't imagine being that poor with no one to help.

'Why is your Mom so cross today?' she asked and gave Edward a quick hug

'I don't think Mom likes Dad to be out so much, but it brings in extra money.' He explained with a shrug.

Biting her lip, thoughtfully Sally said, 'It's alright we can still be friends, but I don't want to go there again.'

Later that day, Sally told her mom how unpleasant Minnie had been. Edward, red in the face, said he wasn't thinking of repeating the experience, but added that his Mom wasn't always in such a bad mood.

They continued to meet at Sally's home where Edward was made welcome. He came to be treated like one of the family and spent more and more time there. Jim teased him about having to start paying rent. He couldn't know how much Edward would have liked to spend all his time living where Sally was. Abigail and Jim both thought the main reason he visited so often was to get away from his mother.

One evening Sally told Edward and Abigail that she'd made up her mind what she wanted to do when she left school. To Abigail's surprise and pleasure, her daughter asked if she'd teach her how to be a seamstress like herself. Sally had never shown much inclination to make anything. But she had often made herself useful by unpicking old clothes and removing tacking stitches to help her mom when she was busy with orders. Abigail thought it'd be a good idea, but told her she must ask her dad's permission.

Bill agreed that when Sally left school at Christmas, she should learn the skills needed to earn a living.

46

It was September and a glorious Indian summer weekend when Bill borrowed a motor car from one of his friends, and except for Jim who chose to stay at home with Tess, they all squashed into the car with Ellen. Sally delayed the trip by making many apologies to Tess and explaining why she couldn't go with them until everyone shouted at her to stop messing.

In high spirits, they went for a jaunt to the Lickey Hills just south of Birmingham. Abigail had packed a basket with hardboiled egg sandwiches and Ellen's wonderfully moist sultana scones. Bill had brought a small stove that ran on methylated spirits and a battered tin kettle and teapot that he'd picked up on his travels, so they were all set for a good picnic. After walking for a while among the dramatic pine-covered hills, the adults settled down to enjoy the sunshine. At the same time, Sally and Edward expended more energy by lying down and rolling swiftly down the gentler grassy slopes.

It was a novel experience for them all. The air was exhilarating and redolent with the scent of pine that exuded from the trees as they walked. Once they left their shade, the intense sunshine gave a magical glow to everything;

even the springy grass that their feet sank into appeared to be a brighter shade of green than Sally had seen before. She peered intently at the many species of wildflowers and wanted to know the names of them, but no one in their party knew more than a couple. Sally thought they were beautiful and was determined to find out what to call them. She was fascinated too by the many species of birds that she didn't know and kept calling out, 'Oh, look, what's that one,' until told firmly by Bill to give it a rest as no one knew. Sally looked back in later life and thought that this was when she first fell in love with England's countryside. Everyone chuckled when she wound her arms around a tall spruce tree, hugged it and told it how beautiful it was.

As they rolled down the hill, one of Sally's braids became tangled with some twigs, and that necessitated undoing the plait. Edward sucked in a quick breath as she did so. Her hair was long enough to sit on. It was luxurious, a shiny, chestnut colour that she usually wore in two plaits that swung about as if they had a life of their own. He said he'd re-plait it for her, but she laughingly refused to let him and ran swiftly back up the hill to where Bill and Ellen were lying with their eyes shut enjoying the sun. Abigail, whose hands were seldom idle, was crocheting a cotton table centre for a customer. Her fingers flew as she chatted happily to Ellen.

'Mom, will you do my hair for me?' Sally grinned at Edward as he pulled a daft face at her. His thoughts were in turmoil whenever he looked at her lately, but he knew she only saw him as her best friend, and he was careful not to let her see how he felt.

'Come and sit down both of you – you're getting all hot and sticky.' Sally flopped down by her legs, and Abigail braided the three tresses back together.

'Put your hat back on now, and you too Edward,' Abigail said, then took her straw hat off for a few minutes to waft her face.

'I'm hungry, Mom, can we have our picnic now?'

Bill had put the kettle on to boil sometime before, and the water was hot enough to pour into the teapot.

'There'll only be enough for one cup each, I'm afraid.'

'Better than nothing,' Abigail said. She wet her lips with the tip of her tongue.

Ellen sat up and reaching for the basket began to unwrap the clean white cloth that held the sandwiches.

'Phew smell,' Edward said and wafted his hand in front of his nose.

'Yow dunno wot's good fer yow.' Ellen laughed at his wrinkled nose and offered the thickly cut and buttered egg sandwiches around.

When they were all replete Abigail said, 'Alright be quiet now because I've something important to talk to you about.'

Everyone gazed intently at her serious expression as she told them what she and Jim were planning.

'Well?' She looked with raised eyebrows from Bill to Sally and back again hoping they would approve.

Bills face beamed. 'Sounds good to me Abigail,' he chucked Sally under her chin, 'but you won't be getting too posh to want me for your dad, will you?' He continued to laugh as he teased her, but Sally didn't crack her face.

'What's the matter, love?' Abigail reached across the makeshift picnic blanket to her daughter and held her hand.

'Come on, what's bothering you – don't you want to have a bigger house with a bathroom?'

Sally's voice wobbled. 'Where will we be moving to?'

'Well, with Ellen's help I've found a house that your uncle and I would like to buy in Sparkhill, opposite a lovely park and by some shops.' She watched Sally's face as she blinked away a tear. 'That's alright love we haven't bought it yet. I wanted to ask you and your Dad how you'd feel if we moved house. It would be alright Sally, Edward will be able to visit as often as he likes, and you'll be leaving school yourself soon so things will change anyway won't they? It's lovely out that way, and the trams run to and from town quite frequently.'

Bill also tried to reassure her that her life would be better when they moved. But she kept shaking her head. Sally found it impossible to believe that anything would be better than staying where everyone knew her. She was so familiar with the surrounding squalor and pervading smells that she never gave them any thought. They were just part of her life, a life that she loved.

Edward tugged at her plaits and looked for permission at Bill who nodded. He held out his hand and said, 'Come and walk with me, Sally.' He pulled her up onto her feet. 'We'll be back soon,' he said to Abigail and winked.

When they returned, Sally knelt by Abigail. 'I think it'd be a good idea to move Mom, I know you're doing it for me, and please don't think I'm ungrateful. Edward said he'll come and visit, and bring Faith with him sometimes. I know I'll soon make new friends too.' She leaned her head against Abigail's ample bosom.

Abigail hugged her tightly. 'It'll be alright y'know love, and nobody likes change at first.'

'Yow're a good lass, yow deserve better than t'stay behind my post office – yow'll see, it'll be luverly.' Ellen wiped a hand across her own eyes and smiled. 'I'll miss you too; I suppose I'd better get used to speakin' like this now you're going to be posh.'

Everyone laughed as her voice rose higher and higher in an attempt to speak in a highfalutin way. It broke the tension in the closely-knit group, and after another short stroll, they packed everything up and prepared to return home. In the distance, they could see a few houses and a large building that Bill said might be at Rubery, but he wasn't sure. In the car, as they were going home, they caught glimpses of vast stretches of water that they found out later were called the Bittell reservoirs. Sally asked if it was the seaside much to everyone's amusement.

They all thanked Bill for a lovely day out, but as they went in, it was to find both Jim and the fire had gone out. Tess whined and jumped up to Sally.

'C'mon then,' she ruffled her pet's fur enthusiastically, 'let's take you for a walk.'

Bill didn't stay for the promised cup of tea; he hurried off to return the borrowed car. As he drove along, he idly wondered where Jim had gone.

47

Abigail was on her knees, scrunching newspaper to kindle the fire when Sally sang out 'G' morning Mom, happy Christmas, here let me do that.'

'Hello love, happy Christmas, no it's done, you should've stayed in bed until I'd heated some water for you to wash.' Abigail beamed at her daughter who at nearly fifteen years of age, was becoming an attractive young woman.

'I couldn't; I'm dying to open my presents, and give you yours.' She pranced over and planted a kiss on top of Abigail's head. Then she unwound the piece of cream net that held her mom's hair in place.

'Well, nothing's changed. You know its breakfast first, and then we'll all open our gifts together. Your uncle's gone to take Tess for a quick walk in the park. He'll be back soon. You'd better get yourself dressed, young lady. Boil some water and take it up to the bathroom.'

'Okay.'

Sally looked longingly at the gaily wrapped presents under the Christmas tree, but obedient as ever disappeared into the kitchen, her long plait swinging against her fluffy green dressing gown. In years to come, she thought how much she'd enjoyed that day even though she couldn't remember her presents. She felt that it had been her last Christmas as a carefree child.

It was just after Sally's birthday when she was reading a book by Louisa M. Alcott that Abigail called to her from the kitchen. 'I've something important to tell you. I'll be with you in a minute.'

Sally frowned and chewed at her bottom lip. Her mom sounded solemn. She knew that Abigail hadn't been feeling well since Christmas. She seemed to have been living on fresh air. When Sally questioned Abigail about her health, she said not to worry because it was only women's troubles. Then she would quickly change the subject. Sally slumped onto the sofa and winged a silent prayer to the God that her mom had taught her to love, begging him to make her mother feel well. The prayer only made her feel stifled; she got up and went to look out of the window.

Abigail smiled softly and gave Sally a quick hug when she walked stiffly back into the living room.

'Back hurting again, Mom?'

'No love just my bones are getting old, come and sit here by me.' Sally grinned and snuggled close as she sat down, squashing Abigail against the arm of the sofa. 'Gerrofme you daft bug and be serious a minute,' Abigail said, while gently pushing Sally off with her elbow.

'Okay, what's the excitement for?' Sally asked.

Abigail smiled. 'I've found employment for you, and you can start first thing Monday morning.' She gazed expectantly at her foster daughter. Sally's face had become suffused with an unbecoming red. Her dejected expression surprised Abigail.

'Well, cat got your tongue?'

'Where, erm what? I don't know how to do anything except sewing,' Sally felt bile sting the back of her throat, 'hell, Mom, I thought I'd be staying at home with you, and helping with your orders. You said my sewing's been good enough, and I've been working hard for you, you've never complained. Why do I have to go out to work?' She got to her feet and walked over to the fireplace, as tears began to flow. Maybe Abigail had become tired of her being around her all day?

'Now you look here my girl, never mind hell Mom, you are acting silly,' Abigail said. She crossed the living room in two strides and placed her arm around Sally's shoulders. 'I know you don't like mixing very much, but I can't bear to see you have the type of life I've led. I want you to get out into the world, and meet new people, and perhaps visit different places. I won't be here forever, you know.'

Sally's crying ceased as she peered into her mom's tired eyes. 'Are you ill Mom?' She sniffed and pulling a handkerchief from up her sleeve, mopped her eyes. She clenched her fists across her chest at the thought of living her life without her foster mother. Her dad was hardly ever about these days, and Uncle Jim seemed to be out frequently too.

'No, you silly bug, I've told you I'm fine, but I've got to go some time, and I want to see you settled and happy before I do. Now stop carrying on, and I'll tell you all about it.' Abigail pushed Sally towards the sofa and sat beside her. She took a deep breath and said, 'You'll still be sewing my love – you're a very accomplished needlewoman – why would I find you anything else to earn some money of your own?' She clasped Sally's slim hand in her warm, capable one. 'You'll be sewing at Mr Dyson's establishment just down the hill.'

Sally's troubled eyes glazed over as she tried to recall who Mr Dyson was. 'I don't know where you mean Mom,' she frowned and focused on Abigail's wrinkled, pink cheeks, 'Mr Dyson?'

'You know – the undertaker.'

Sally jumped to her feet. 'I'll be working with dead people?' She glared at Abigail. 'I can't, not dead people!'

Abigail laughed and explained that she would be sewing shrouds, and wouldn't have anything to do with bodies. Not given to sulking, Sally agreed to try the job after being reassured that she wouldn't have to stay if she didn't like it. How could I bloody well like it, Sally thought, but refusing to go to work, didn't cross her mind. The word bloody was often on the tip of her tongue these days. When she'd been at school, all the girls her age had sworn profusely when adults weren't about, but she knew to keep the word in her head. Abigail would have been shocked if she'd said it aloud.

'Mind you give it a fair trial though,' Abigail wagged her finger, 'you've stayed at home for longer than most girls can.'

Sally went to the stairs with a parting shot at her mom. 'Okay, okay, I suppose I should say thanks, but I don't want to go. You should have talked to me about it first.'

'Let's have less cheek my girl, just be grateful I care enough to try and ensure your future happiness.'

Sally was grateful that her mom had arranged the job for her, but she felt full of doubt that she could branch out on her own. She blew a kiss to her mom as she climbed thoughtfully up to her room.

48

Once she became accustomed to the smell of embalming fluid that permeated the building, Sally found that she did enjoy her work. She shared a sewing room with another girl called Christine, who was a year older than herself. Christine was a plain-looking girl with a pronounced overbite that caused her to speak with a lisp. She had thick blond hair and such a comical way of expressing herself that Sally liked her. She told Sally many amusing stories of her family and their escapades. When they shared their lunchtime, Sally would usually ask to hear the latest pranks and disasters that made up her friend's everyday life.

Christine had three brothers and four sisters, and they all lived in a small house behind the park. Sally was fascinated to hear that a set of elderly grandparents also shared their dwelling. She didn't think she would have liked to be so cramped and have to share a bedroom. Christine laughingly told her that she was spoilt, and after considering their differences, Sally had to agree that she was privileged; although she'd never known her birth mother.

When they knew each other well enough, they started to chat about boyfriends and speculated about sex, but Sally's cheeks flamed when Christine asked bluntly, 'Have you done it yet?'

Sally replied sharply. 'No, I bloody well haven't, I'm staying a virgin till I meet Mr Right. Have you then?'

'No, but I don't want to wait until I'm married neither. I want some fun before I settle down and have kids.'

'You might get pregnant anyway.'

'Not me, I know things,' Christine said. They jumped up as Mr Dyson called out that their lunch break was over.'

Sally's machine handle flew as she fed the gauzy material under the needle, but her mind frequently strayed back to their conversation. She sometimes had daydreams lately where she was standing at the top of a ladder, and a handsome man caught her as she fell. She knew he was attractive – but could never quite remember his face – just his strong arms holding her and caressing her loosened hair. Maybe she should have a bit of fun too Sally thought, but she had never met anyone that she wanted to hold her like that. She shook her head and tried to concentrate on her sewing before she caught her fingers under the needle.

After that day, Christine and Sally shared many intimate details about their hopes and dreams and shared much laughter too. Sally grew to love her company and readily agreed to accompany her new friend to the picture house the following weekend.

'You never know who we'll meet,' Christine said, with a lascivious leer making Sally chortle. It caused her to jerk the material that she was sewing which snapped the machine needle.

'Damnation! I wanted to finish this lining before I went home.' Sally fussed about looking for the sharp end of the offending needle. 'You go on ahead, Christine, and I'll catch you up.'

'No, I'll wait, don't want some bogey man getting you on the way home.'

Sally thought how much fun Christine had brought into her life and began to worry that Edward might not like her going to the picture house without him. She didn't want him to come with them, though. It was all new to her; she'd never wanted to spend much time in anyone's company before except her family and Edward. The realization hit her that Edward had never allowed her to be with others of her age. She scowled.

'C'mon stop daydreaming,' Christine said, 'I don't know where you'd gone to, but you should have seen the look on your face. Proper fierce, what were you thinking about?'

'Curiosity killed the cat, you know,' Sally said.

'Ah, but satisfaction brought it back.'

'Well, this time it'll stay dead.' Sally stuck her tongue out at Christine, who raised her eyebrows but didn't continue her curious banter.

Not much later the girls shrugged their coats on and strolled out of the back entrance calling a bright, 'G'night' to some of their fellow workers. They wended their way home arm in arm, both tired but happy.

'What about Saturday?' Christine asked, 'shall we go and see Mr Hitchcock's new film, *Blackmail,* I've heard it's terrifying, but in some of it the actors talk.'

'Talk?'

'Yes – you know – we can hear them speaking, not just read the words.'

'Sounds funny to me, but yes, let's give it a try.'

'Alright, I'll meet you at the bus stop at two o'clock. Don't you be late.'

'Don't you be late neither.'

They gave each other a quick peck on the cheek and waved as they parted. Making plans to do something different had left Sally feeling happier than she'd done in ages. She couldn't wait to tell her mom what she'd arranged. She was doing what Abigail had wanted her to do, enjoy living.

49

Edward did not take the news that Sally was going to the picture house with her friend, very well. He became miserable and tried to persuade her to let him accompany them, but Sally said that Christine had asked her first, and may not like him to join them. She couldn't bring herself to say that she didn't want him to go with them. It would hurt his feelings. He scuffed his shoes on the doorstep, as she calmly refused his demands to let Christine down. She usually teased and cajoled him back into a good mood, but this time she told him firmly that he could clear off home, and sulk by himself. They parted without a backward glance as Sally went inside. She knew that Edward's sulks never lasted very long and her heart felt light as she patted herself on the back for not giving in to him, as she so often did. When she settled down in her comfortable bed that night, she thought about the difference in their feelings towards each other.

Edward had often told her that he loved her and wanted their relationship to become more than just friends, but Sally knew that she didn't return his feelings. He was her friend, and she loved him dearly, but she couldn't imagine being intimate with him and asked him not to talk to her about their future together. She'd told him that she intended to be a virgin when she married, and so far, Edward had kept his passions in check. Sally drifted off to sleep with an uneasy feeling that there was soon going to be a time when he would not be so easily discouraged. Would they be able to remain friends?

The sparkling snow had been falling steadily for a couple of days; the fat flakes were becoming thicker by the minute. Appreciating how difficult their journey would be Mr Dyson sent his workers home early. It was Friday, and he wanted to get off home too. Christine and Sally linked arms and trudged companionably to where their paths diverged at the entrance to the park. They gave each other a peck on the cheek as usual, and said, 'T'raa, see you on Monday,' as they parted company.

Sally walked a few feet further, tentatively placing one booted foot in front of the other now that her support had gone. Suddenly Edward appeared in front of her. Sally looked up at his dear familiar face and smiled. 'Hello you, where did you ...' Her greeting died; Edward had a strange look on his face. He didn't reply but gripped her arm tightly, and then pulled her roughly into the park. 'What d'you think you're playing at, leave go of me,' Sally struggled to free herself from his iron grip, 'bloody well let me go.' She aimed a kick at his shins.

'Shut the fuck up and walk will you.' He continued to force her along the path – half supporting and half dragging her through the snowdrifts. His breath was coming in ragged gasps as he repeatedly shook her to make her walk properly.

Suddenly Sally became quiet, stopped resisting and walked as well as she could. 'Where are you taking me, I'm cold Edward, I want to go home,' she said. Her teeth chattered.

His face was grim as he pulled her off the path into a small copse of bushes hidden from the road. Ignoring her cries and her floundering protests – he shoved her ignominiously against a silver birch tree – causing snow to fall in a powdery white canopy over them.

'Stop it, Edward, stop it,' Sally shouted. The snow was in her hair and eyes, blinding her. She used her woollen mittens to clear it as it rapidly melted on her hot cheeks. He wasn't her Edward at this moment, and she didn't know what he was going to do. 'Get off me, leave me alone, you bastard!' She yelled at him. The snow spluttered from around her mouth. Edwards's face was frighteningly close to hers as he pinned her arms to her sides. He kissed her, forcing his tongue deep into her mouth until she gagged, and struggled harder to push him away with her knees.

Suddenly she was free. She staggered and fell, sobs pouring in gasps from her bruised lips.

'Oh, my God, forgive me, I'm sorry, I'm sorry.' His large, scarred hands were covering his face as though he couldn't bear to look at her.

Sally peered up at him. She pulled herself up unsteadily to her feet, raised her right hand that still held her lunch bag, and smacked him across his head with all the force she could muster. He staggered backwards but remained upright.

'I'm sorry, I'm sorry,' he cried, 'I don't know what's happening,' Sally could see the tears glistening in his eyes. 'It'll never happen again, Sal, I promise.'

'You won't get the chance.' Sally pushed hard into him, and he staggered back against another tree as she forced her way past Laurel bushes that flicked snow lazily at her. 'Bastard,' Sally yelled. She felt numb and was shivering violently as the word bastard played over and over in her mind. How could Edward, her best friend, mistreat her, hurt her physically and mentally. How could he, how could he, she stormed while she fled as fast as the heavy snow would allow her frozen feet to move. She glanced back a few times to see if Edward was following her. He stayed in the bushes – she hoped he'd stay there forever.

When Sally finally reached home, she leaned against the sidewall of the house for a few minutes to compose herself. She could smell the evening meal that her mom was cooking. She went inside to be greeted by comforting normality.

50

'Hello love, come by the fire; you look frozen.' Abigail took in the picture of winter that was her lovely daughter. Her rosy cheeks were radiating with health: and her bow-shaped lips spread in a loving smile. Then as she pulled off her knitted hat, her lovely face was surrounded with a halo of glinting hair. My goodness, Abigail thought, she's become a stunning young woman. Where's my little girl gone?

Sally kissed Abigail and then settled herself close by the fire with Tess's head in her lap. 'Is that bread pudding I can smell Mom?'

Abigail chuckled, she knew Sally didn't expect an answer. Cinnamon bread pudding was often on the menu as was the sausage and mash with fried onions which was nearly ready to serve.

Sally caught hold of Abigail's hand and sniffed the palm for as long as she was allowed before Abigail used the same hand to give her a gentle slap. Her mom's palms often smelled of onions, no matter how much she washed them. Abigail fried onions every night to flavour her gravy. It was one of Sally's favourite smells.

It felt good to laugh together, Sally thought. It took away some of the hurt that Edward's behaviour had caused. Sally's anger had more or less dissipated by the time she went to bed, but she was restless wondering what tomorrow would bring.

By Saturday morning, she had dismissed the thought that she would tell her mom how Edward had manhandled her. She knew that Abigail and her uncle Jim would be furious and may even decide that they shouldn't be allowed to see each other. At sixteen years of age, Sally was inexperienced and had scant understanding of the relationships between men and women. Although she no longer felt angry, she was still hurt and puzzled by Edward's use of force towards her and determined that he would never again be allowed to treat her as though he owned her.

Wearing a suitably hangdog expression, Edward arrived out of the blue Sunday morning just as Sally and Abigail were getting ready to leave for church. Sally glared at him but didn't want to make a fuss in front of her mom. She contented herself by rehearsing what she would say to him when they returned from church. When they eventually were able to have a private conversation, Sally accepted his humble apology but made him believe that if he ever hurt her again, it would be for the last time. Sally had the sort of nature that wanted unpleasantness to disappear as soon as possible. She took his hand. 'Okay, let's forget it, come and play cards.' Edward looked sheepish, but soon their laughter rang out as usual.

Edward knew Sally meant what she said, but he also knew that he had a destructive streak of jealousy in his nature. The flash of hot anger that spread wildly through his

202

body as he'd seen Sally show some affection towards another person had frightened him. Edward knew he'd lost control, and now always tried to reassure himself that it wouldn't happen again. He loved Sally much more than she realised. Being two years older, he'd had some experiences in his life that he was aware she knew nothing of as yet. His passionate nature smouldered just beneath the surface, but he knew if he didn't show restraint, he would lose her forever. He couldn't bear to think of it. It felt like a sharp knife pierced his chest each time he contemplated being without her.

As the days passed, Sally found herself thinking increasingly often about sex and wondered what it would be like to love someone so much that giving herself to him would feel right. She slept restlessly and felt her face flame when her imagination sometimes ran wild, causing a jolt of warmth to spread through her belly and set her legs tingling. Sally wondered if she wanted Edward to carry on kissing her, but knew that wasn't the case – she only wanted Edward as a friend. She didn't even like the manly smell he exuded when he was too close to her. Sometimes the image of her uncle Jim having sex with the woman in his hut entered her head, but it was rapidly pushed back into the depths. Everything seemed to be happening so quickly; she felt that her emotions were being dragged all over the place, and there was no one she could tell how she felt. Her dad was becoming a stranger since he'd moved to live in Leicester to be near his brother. She knew, however, that she would be too embarrassed to let him suspect how troubled she was. Her thoughts turned to her aunt Claris, who she hadn't set eyes on for a couple of years. She decided to visit her; she might be able to confide in her and get some answers. Making plans for her visit, and looking forward to an adventure drew Sally into a deep untroubled sleep for the first time in days.

51

Sally sat on the window seat as she stared out of her neat bedroom at the houses opposite. The sun was still shining, sending brilliant, dancing reflections across the ultra-clean windows, but Sally saw nothing. She was rehearsing what she would say to her mom when she could pluck up the courage to go downstairs. She chewed fretfully at a thumbnail until it ripped from side to side. 'Bloody, bloody hell,' burst from her downturned mouth as she automatically reached for an emery board. Her recent visit to Aunt Claris had given her more answers than she'd bargained for.

She'd had such high hopes of her aunt being able to help her to understand her emotional turmoil but the visit hadn't gone as she wished. After listening patiently to Sally's outpourings, and offering some sound advice, Claris had put an arm around her niece's shoulder and said, 'You need to grow up Sal and see what's under your nose.'

Dumbstruck, Sally's gaze had lingered on her aunt's serious face. The silence between them had become a perceptible wall – blocking the air – until Sally felt she couldn't breathe. She'd jerked away from the embrace.

She frowned. 'What on earth do you mean – grow up – and see what's under my nose?'

Claris had unearthed a crumpled letter from the depths of a battered black handbag that she'd used ever since Sally could remember. Her aunt hadn't been one to waste money, and spending it on herself; she considered to be a waste. She'd dropped the bag noisily onto the floor, smoothed the blue sheet out, and passed it to her frowning niece. Tears had welled as Sally slowly read the contents and then clasped the paper to her chest. She hadn't wanted to believe the words that her mom had written, but she'd known that they must be true.

Claris had listened to Sally's sobs until they eased, but she was crying too as she'd explained that Abigail had insisted that she keep her secret. She didn't want Sally to know until she had to. Claris had felt Sally should understand because she hadn't been able to persuade Abigail to see a Doctor, and perhaps she would listen to her daughter.

On her return journey, Sally's eyes were swollen and bleary with tears that seemed to be finding their way onto her cheeks ever since she'd left her aunt's. She'd stood unsteadily as the train approached Snow Hill station, and then wound her way carefully past her fellow passenger's legs, anxious to see if Abigail had come to meet her as she'd said she might. She half hoped that her mom wouldn't be there; she would want to know why she'd been crying. Sunk as she was in her misery, and feeling a draught, Sally attempted to look out of the train window. She realised too late that the breeze was from the opposite window. Her head had crashed through the glass which had flown outwards in a disappearing shower. It had cut into the borrowed straw hat that she was wearing as she jerked her head back. Blood had soaked into her glove from a small cut on her forehead as she'd dropped to the floor, and heard herself, and others in the carriage scream before rushing to her assistance. She'd struggled to get up just as the train had come to a standstill opposite where her mom was standing, moving her head to and fro as she searched the passing carriages.

'Oh my goodness,' Abigail had jerked the carriage door open, 'what's happened to you?' She glared at the young man in a tweed suit who had helped Sally to her feet and was holding a large white handkerchief to her forehead. 'What have you done to her?' she said.

The man had held out his hand to assist a bemused Sally onto the platform, saying, 'You may keep the handkerchief young lady, and I'd advise you to check if a window is open before you thrust your head out in future.' He'd then turned to Abigail and said in a formal tone, 'I have done nothing Madam, only assist her as required.' He'd winked at Sally, and tipped his felt hat in Abigail's direction as he strode to catch up with the crowd climbing the long flight of steps to the barrier where the ticket collector stood. Abigail had hugged her daughter as they inhaled the sulphur smell of the billowing white steam that the train was belching forth.

'Who was that man – do you know him?' Abigail had asked. Sally shook her head; she had been too upset to notice him.

'C'mon Mom let's get home,' she'd said, 'you look tired. It's only a small cut, and I can't wait to see Tess and have a cuppa.' She'd smiled, and taking Abigail's arm tucked it into the crook of her arm and started forward.

Slowly they'd followed the kind stranger out of the station and wended their way home after Sally dropped the tattered hat into a bin.

They'd sat in companionable silence for most of the bus journey. Sally answered all her mom's questions about her visit to Clarissa, but she didn't mention the devastating information that her aunt had given her. She did notice for the first time how much her mom had aged. Her skin had taken on a yellowish tinge, and new spidery lines showed around her eyes, and across her soft cheeks. Her stomach, always hidden behind a voluminous wrap-around apron, had been covered by a navy dress and was noticeably distended. Sally couldn't believe how blind and selfish she'd been. She'd squeezed Abigail's arm and apologized for ruining her hat.

Abigail had shrugged her shoulders and said, 'Oh, don't you worry about the hat, it's a good thing you were wearing it, or it could have been your head that got cut worse. You're a dozy begger though not seeing the window was shut that's all I can say. You should be more careful love; I shall have to keep you at home in future.' She'd laughed as Sally pretended to protest, but her daughter had never felt less inclined to laugh.

Jim had arrived home shortly after they did and Abigail rushed around getting his tea on the table as he'd said he was going out again later with his mates. Sally surreptitiously studied his face as he sat by the fire reading the newspaper. She thought how much she'd grown away from him since the night she'd discovered his secret liaison. They'd never spoken about it, but Sally figured he must have known she had seen what was going on that night. Her stomach ached with unspoken dislike as she wondered if he knew how ill Abigail was, or if he even cared. He didn't seem to want to be at home with them anymore. Sally suspected that – going out with his mates – was an excuse to see his fancy woman. She mentally shrugged her shoulders and promised herself that she would look after Abigail and do whatever it took to make life easier for her. She wondered too if her dad knew. It was several months since he'd managed to come and visit. He wrote occasionally, but his letters didn't say much. Sally felt a pang as she realised how much she missed him. He needs to know she thought as she ate her sausage and mash tea.

After Jim had gone to work, Sally called, 'Mom, come and sit down, and I'll do the dishes in a minute.' The clatter ceased as Abigail came into the living room, and sat down wearily in Jim's chair. She finished drying her hands on an old towel and looked quizzically at Sally's serious face.

'Okay,' she said, and sucked her teeth to dislodge a tiny piece of sausage skin caught in the gap between two of her remaining incisors, 'what's Claris been telling you?' She leaned her head back against the grease-stained antimacassar and sighed.

Sally gulped back a sob, her hands clasped tightly in her lap, 'You're ill Mom, why haven't you told me?'

'Now, now love, it's just women's troubles,' Abigail said.

'No Mom, tell me the truth,' Sally said, 'how can I help if you won't talk to me? I'm grown up now, I go to work and earn my keep, and I need to know Mom – please.'

Abigail settled lower in the chair and chewed at the inside of her cheek. 'Alright love, but no one can help I just have to get on with it. I saw Dr Sadler while you were away, and he said there's nothing to be done, it's gone too far.'

Sally held her breath. 'What has, what's gone too far?'

Abigail hesitated as though saying the words aloud would make it more real, 'I've got cancer love and...'

Her shoulders slumped as Sally started up and flung her arms about her mom's neck. They clung together and rocked in their shared heat, hearts breaking as they each thought of a future without the other.

'I'm so sorry Mom; I should have known –'

'No, I shouldn't have left it so long,' Abigail sucked in a shaky breath, 'I was a foolish woman to be so scared, and now it's too late, and I haven't long Sally.' She started to speak again, but Sally put a hand gently across her mouth.

'I could have helped more instead of being so wrapped up in myself.' She stroked Abigail's grey hair that was wound into plaits around her ears and snuggled into her neck where she inhaled the scent of the woman that was her world.

Abigail broke the silence as she pulled away from Sally and said with a firm shake of her head. 'No, my love, you've no idea how much you've helped me just by being here. I've been so lucky to have had a second chance at being a real mother,' she winced as she straightened her back, 'we both have to be strong now and let nature take its course.'

Sally moved away and sat down slowly on the sofa, silently screaming rejection of the loss which she was already feeling. Her mothering instinct taking over, Abigail went again to sit beside her daughter and pulled her close. Sally could feel how much thinner Abigail had become and how hard her abdomen was.

'There, there my love, I'm glad you know, I won't have to hide how I'm feeling anymore,' she grimaced as she said in a whisper, 'sometimes the pain is terrible.'

Silence reigned again until Abigail stood hands on hips, and gave a short laugh. 'Alright enough of this silliness, there's plenty of life in me yet, let's get on with it.' She walked quickly into the kitchen, and Sally followed. As they washed the dishes, Abigail said, 'At least when I've gone you'll have a home of your own, so I know you'll be alright.'

'You're not to talk like that, I won't care what happens to me if you leave me, Mom – let's get on with the pots – and we'll sing shall we?' They laughed and started to sing *"*Roll out the Barrel" in unison, but entirely out of tune, as though it could put their world right. Sally knew her safe, secure world had ended, but she had to try to help her mom to live.

52

Less than six months passed before Abigail lost her struggle to survive. She died at home with Sally's warm, pink hand clasped in her wasted, blue-veined one. Sally refused at first to believe that she could go on living without the love and guidance that had always been hers. She and Ellen had spent three months nursing Abigail at home. Jim had moved into Sally's bedroom, and she had slept next to Abigail on a truckle bed. Jim did what he could, but he felt both unable and unwilling to assist in her nursing. He was hardly ever at home and seemed restless and was abrupt whenever he was spoken to. Sally felt her dislike for him expand into an insoluble ball pressing on her ribcage. She wished in the end that he'd just stay away. He made her feel sick.

She only left her mom's side to go to work, and at the end, when Abigail was racked with pain and continually slipping in and out of consciousness, Sally felt a sad relief when her mum finally died and went to the heaven that she was confident was waiting for her.

Sally thought no one could ever fill the void that her mom's passing had left. She sent a telegram to her father, desperate for his support. She needed to see him and hold on to his love. The answer was a bombshell. It was a letter from her uncle Arthur telling her that Bill couldn't come as he was in prison. Arthur reluctantly explained that Bill had committed bigamy. He'd married a woman called Frances Lester that he'd met in the local library. Frances's brother had somehow found out that Bill's wife was still alive, and after a massive row had reported him to the police

Sally was stunned. She didn't know what to do with herself and didn't know where to turn. How could her mother be alive? How could her dad let her think that she was dead if she wasn't? Sally had never felt so utterly alone before. She wanted to cry, but all her tears seemed to have turned inwards, and gushed like an icy waterfall into her chest. She pictured herself freezing to death, as the cold spread throughout her body, and she began to shiver uncontrollably. She sank onto the floor the crumpled letter clutched tightly in her hand. Time passed – until everything melted – then she cried.

At Abigail's funeral mourners were standing inside and outside the church. The vicar from St. Martins took the service, and the only person that didn't cry was Sally. She had no tears left to shed.

Abigail's friends from the market had rallied round and put on a simple spread in the church hall to mark her passing. There were many people there that Sally didn't know, but she never forgot the outpourings of love for her mom.

To Sally's amazement, her uncle Jim left immediately after the church service was over, and did not appear at the graveside. She lied when asked where he was, and said he'd been taken ill. She knew in her heavy heart that she would never forgive him for his insult to the woman who'd been his faithful wife for so many years. She had to live in the same house, she had nowhere else to go, but she fervently wished he'd been the one to go instead of her mom. Guilt flooded her for thinking such a thing – but she didn't care.

Sally was in bed when she heard her uncle come home. She pulled the covers over her head and cuddled her pillow. Her disturbing thoughts mixed between the loss of her mom and the lies that her dad had told her. Sleep was a long time coming.

53

Although Mr Dyson had arranged Abigail's funeral cheaply for Sally and told her that she could return to his employ when she was ready, Sally declined his kind offer. She wanted to make a fresh start and applied for a position in a factory close to home. She started work as a hand press operator. The factory was dirty, noisy and smelled of oil and hot metal, but the atmosphere was great, and Sally soon found that she enjoyed it. It was impossible to think about losing her mom, or anything else for that matter, with the banging of the presses and the squeal of lathes turning out small engineering parts. She soon learned to sing along with the other girls as they swung the long-curved handles. It helped them to keep a good rhythm.

Sally would never agree to go out with the young men that frequently pestered her. Their attention met with smart banter that she quickly developed as a barrier to intimacy. Sally made friends swiftly with several colleagues in the machine shop. She was hardworking and easy-going, and always had a willing ear or a pair of hands ready to help out. But she was known as the girl with the sad face by those who worked in other departments.

Edward still spent as much of his free time with Sally as she allowed him to, but she kept him at arm's length. She blamed her disinterest in his company, on tiredness and having to take care of her uncle Jim and household chores, but Edward knew she was making excuses. He hoped that time would bring her closer to him again. He didn't want anyone else, it had always been Sally for him, he could wait, but he knew better than to say this to Sally.

Sally's life settled into a pattern of hard work, eating, sleeping and walking Tess. It left her little time to think or feel. The predictability of her days comforted her. Sometimes she felt guilty that she no longer cried herself to sleep every night, but she was sensible enough to know that it wouldn't have been what her mom wished her to do.

Feelings of animosity towards her uncle continued, but he was rarely home in the evening. He invariably washed, changed his clothes, ate his tea and went out, returning after she'd retired for the night. They spoke when necessary, but lived as separately as possible. It suited both of them.

Two months after the death of her mother; Bill came to live with them. At first, Sally was delighted, but she soon found that he had changed, he was no longer a happy person. He was still softly spoken and caring towards her, but he was apathetic towards any conversation regarding his plans for the future. He refused to talk about his time away, or the reason why he'd been in prison. When Sally tried to speak to him about her mother and elicit any information about her, or her whereabouts, or the lies that he'd told, Bill would shrug his shoulders and leave the room in silence. Sally felt hurt and angry, she had a right to the truth she told him, but he was unapproachable on the subject. After many fruitless attempts, Sally decided to bide her time, sure that he would come around eventually. It wasn't that she wanted to see her mother, just not knowing the truth tormented her.

To her knowledge, Jim hadn't even asked Bill for answers; just accepted the fact that he was there and paid his share of the bills. Sally had hoped that her uncle and her dad would slip back into their old companionable ways. But Jim continued to follow his nightly routine, and Bill spent his evenings in his bedroom or pottering about in the garden. Neither gave a hand with chores around the house, and Sally became increasingly tired and annoyed at having to take care of them and work full time. The atmosphere in the home became tense, and Sally missed her mom more than ever. Alone in her room, at times, she found herself talking aloud to her and begging her to show her how to make things better. Sometimes she thought her mom answered inside her head, and it helped.

Sally was a reasonable person with a kind nature. Still, her frustration and tiredness culminated one day in her shouting – 'Well do it your bloody self then – ' in reply to Bill's complaint that the shirt he needed to wear needed washing properly. Bill was shocked and dismayed at his normally easy-going daughter's response. She was instantly apologetic, but it was a wake-up call, he noticed for the first time how tired Sally looked. She had dark circles under her eyes, and her face had taken on a translucent appearance. Remorse filled him, and he drew her gently into his embrace.

'I'm sorry love; I've been a thoughtless bastard, so wrapped up in my misery I couldn't see.' He sighed deeply and pulled her closer, rocking her as if she was once again his beloved baby.

Sally felt herself relax against him as weary tears oozed from under closed lids. They sank together onto the sofa and stayed hugging for a while until Bill pushed her gently away. Sally dried her eyes on her sleeve and looked into the face that she loved more than any other since her mom's death.

'Dad, please tell me what happened, is my mother alive?' Sally said.

Bill hesitated and ran his hand through his hair. 'Yes, I think she still is, but I don't know where she is.' He stood up and started to walk away, changed his mind, and turned to face his daughter, then blurted out, 'I married a lovely lady, and I knew I shouldn't have, but I hoped your mother was dead. She should have been – she was an evil bitch. I went to prison for bigamy so she must be alive, but that's over now, in the past, I can't tell you anymore,' his hand swept across his forehead, 'I don't want to talk about this ever again Sal – it hurts too much.' He walked to the hallway, but hesitated at the door and said over his shoulder, 'No more questions, Sally, I mean it. I love you, but I can't bear anymore – Abigail was the best mother you could have had.'

Sally went to her father, reached up and placed her arms around his neck. 'I love you too, Dad, it's not important as long as you're okay. I'm sorry things didn't work out for you.'

'Thanks, love,' Bill said and went upstairs.

Sally went into the kitchen followed by Tess who wagged her tail briskly as she gave her a large bone to gnaw on. She took the lid from the pan of lamb stew and wafted her hand as the steam threatened to burn her face. She didn't know if she felt happy or sad to learn of her mother's existence. But knowing she was alive raised so many new questions in Sally's mind: she couldn't help wondering what she looked like. What had she done to make her dad feel so strongly? When did they part? Was she to blame? Where had she been all these years? And where was she now? But the question that she kept returning to was why didn't she love her daughter? Sally finished her chores automatically; her brain never stopped whirling. Had her aunt Claris known what happened – did she know who her mother was? Sally tried to stop thinking about it but found it impossible. She resolved during that evening to respect her dad's wishes but planned to visit her aunt as soon as she possibly could.

After Bill and Sally's talk, the atmosphere in the house lightened. Nothing changed as far as Jim was concerned, but Bill gave Sally a hand where he could, and his mood seemed to have improved. The laughter returned, and Sally enjoyed her father's company as they played cards or read most evenings.

A few months later Bill surprised Sally one evening after they'd had tea. He had been taking casual labouring jobs since his return, but he now told Sally that he'd jumped at the chance of a long-term bricklaying job back up in Leicester. Sally was sad to see him go but happy that he would be staying with his brother.

As the front door shut after their hugs of farewell, Sally sank into the chair by the fire and closed her eyes. She was relieved to think that her life would be a little easier now and drifted into a dreamless sleep, the first in many months. She wouldn't have slept well if she'd known what the next day would bring.

54

Loaded up as she was with groceries bought during her lunch break, Sally struggled to insert her key in the lock. She was late arriving home, her uncle Jim's tea wouldn't be ready, and he would be annoyed. She knew he was off out again that evening, not that she minded; she preferred the house to herself with just Tess for company.

Stopping to greet her dog with a quick pat and a cheery, 'Hello my beauty.' Sally placed the full hessian bag onto the hall floor, shrugged off her coat and aimed it at the coat stand. More haste less speed, she admonished herself as it promptly deposited itself on the floor. Not troubling to pick it up she grabbed the bag, hurried past the stairs, pushed the kitchen door open with her backside, and dropped the bag with a thud onto the terracotta tiles. Potatoes rolled lazily across the floor unheeded as Sally gazed open-mouthed at the woman standing by the back door, drying her hands on a tea towel.

She could see the woman with her eyes, but her brain refused to take in reality for a second. The woman coolly surveyed Sally then after a few seconds, she raised her well defined, dark eyebrows and said, 'Hello, you're late.' A slight smile hovered around her mouth, lifting her prominent cheeks, but her green eyes belied the warmth of her lips. She finished drying her hands, bent and began to pick up the fallen vegetables.

Sally came to life. 'Leave them,' she said. 'Who are you, and what are you doing in my kitchen?'

The woman straightened, tucked strands of her mid-brown hair behind her small ears, and said boldly with a French accent, 'I live here, it is my kitchen now.'

Sally took a step back, did she hear these words? She opened her mouth to tell the woman to get out when recognition dawned on her. Sally started forward; temper surged, hot lava boiling up in her chest. She grabbed the woman by her arm and thrust her towards the back door. 'Get out, get out you filthy trollop!' Sally's voice became shrill as she shouted words that she'd never had reason to use before.

The woman jerked herself free and staggered back towards the sink. 'I knew you'd seen us all those years ago, leave me alone you silly girl, I'm here to stay, and you can do nothing about it.' Recovering her balance and with her lips twisted into a sneer, she said, 'Now why don't you be sensible, and let me get on with cooking your uncle's dinner?' She turned her back dismissively.

Sally's heart was beating so fast that she felt sick and light-headed. Memories of the night when she'd seen her uncle and this woman in his hut assaulted her. Feelings that she'd never thought herself capable of were building inside her. She wanted to throw her out of the house, but she knew uncle Jim must have brought her into the premises. She whirled, ran into the hall, picked up her coat and handbag, and fled out of the house. She vaguely heard the front door

221

slam behind her, and Tess's sad whine, as she ran down the path and turned towards the park.

Angry tears soaked her face; her breathing became laboured, forcing her to slow her pace to a walk. She crossed over the Stratford Road and leaned against the park wall by the gates. She didn't know what she was going to do; she was having difficulty unscrambling her thoughts. Passers-by stared, but Sally didn't see them lost as she was in her screwed-up emotions.

'You alright love?' The elderly gentleman leaned heavily on his ram's head cane and peered into her blank face. He stretched out his hand, and tentatively touched her arm as he repeated his question.

Sally's eyes brought him into focus. She looked bewildered.

'Erm, do you need help love?'

Sally pulled her herself together and said, 'No – thank you, I've just had a bit of a shock that's all.'

'Anything I can do?' the man asked.

'No, thank you, please don't worry about me. I thought a walk in the park might help. I'm a little out of breath – I'll be alright in a minute.'

'Why don't we walk a little way together, and perhaps you'd like to tell me what has upset you so?'

Sally took a step away from him and inhaled deeply. 'Please don't think me rude, you're very kind, but I need to be alone right now.'

He smiled and said soothingly, 'Alright my dear.' He raised his well-worn hat and continued strolling toward the city.

Sally watched his receding back, she wasn't ready to tell a stranger her business, but she felt calmer and grateful for his kind intervention. She walked into the park and sat on the first bench. She thought that her life had become one long question. How could he bring his fancy woman to live in their home? Mom scrimped and saved to buy that house to ensure my future Sally fumed.

After a while, her anger disappeared like the breeze that stirred the bushes. But worry about the future soon had her weeping quietly into her handkerchief. She dreaded going home, but where else could she go? She wished her dad hadn't returned to Leicestershire, but he had, and she hadn't anyone else close by other than Edward. She didn't want to involve him knowing he loved her; it wouldn't be fair to give him false hope. She didn't feel that way about him; she never had and didn't think she ever could. More and more questions and thoughts tumbled like transient butterflies in her head – questions to which there didn't seem to be any answers.

Sally was unaware of the passage of time until she noticed that the numbers of people walking their dogs and generally strolling about had lessened to the odd one or two. She tried to stop feeling sorry for herself, she knew she'd led a sheltered life, but circumstances had changed. Making a promise to become more self-sufficient and ready to brave whatever awaited her at home, she began to walk from the park.

55

Filled with mixed emotions, with her heart beating a tattoo in her chest Sally again opened the front door to her home. As she stepped into the hall, her uncle came out of the sitting room. He smiled tentatively and said in a steady voice, 'Sal, come in 'ere please I wanna talk to yer.'

Sally hesitated, she wanted to refuse, but old habits of obedience came to her rescue. She looked into his ruddy face, unsure if he was angry or embarrassed, and followed him into the sitting room where she thought the woman would be waiting for her. Relief flooded over her when she saw it was empty except for her uncle who was now sitting in his chair with Tess lying curled up on the hearth-rug fast asleep.

Sally stood in the doorway, watching Tess's eyelids flutter as she followed her dream creatures.

'C'mon an' sit down,' Jim said,

She sat on a comfortable chair opposite her uncle. He looked sad and kept his gaze on Tess as he spoke.

'I'm sorry, Luv, I wanted to tell yer before Yvette moved in, but I put it off too long an' I'm afraid 'er jumped the gun. I knew yer wouldn't loik it.' He shifted in his seat and looked directly at Sally's deadpan face. She didn't respond so he went on quickly, 'we've bin seein' each other fer a long while, and I can't blame 'er fer bein' fed up of waitin' 'til the toim wuz roit.' He took a deep breath which drew his shoulders back, then slumped forward and waited.

Sally snorted and looking him in the eyes, said, 'How could you, how could you bring your fancy woman here? Mom's not gone six months yet.'

'Old on, 'old on and listen,' he fetched his pipe from the mantle shelf, 'she ain't me fancy woman she's me wife. We got wed a month ago, and she's bin patient enough.' He proceeded to fill his pipe with intense concentration giving her a chance to let the unwelcome news sink in.

Sally could not believe she heard correctly. She jumped to her feet and began pacing between the window and her chair. There was a loud pounding in her ears, and she felt light-headed – she thought she might faint. She plonked down onto the chair again, and after a couple of minutes silence, she said in a controlled voice, 'You married that trollop —why?'

Jim contemplated the draw on his pipe. 'Calm down Bab, she's no trollop; we've bin seein' each other fer years, I'm sure yer know that.' He looked knowingly at Sally, his eyebrows raised.

'Yes, of course, I knew,' Sally said, 'but why did you have to marry her?' She could feel herself trembling and headed towards the door.

'C'mon, Luv it'll be alright you'll see. Yer wunt 'av ter work an' come 'ome ter keep 'ouse anymore. Yvette will see ter all that.'

'Why ...? Sally held her hand up – 'no, I don't want to know.' She turned as she left the room and looked at her uncle's once-loved face. 'I'll leave as soon as I've somewhere to go.' She gave in to sobs as she ran upstairs with Tess close on her heels. She was aware that her uncle had been saying something as she left the room, but she didn't want to hear anything else. She was in a nightmare; her whole world seemed to have collapsed about her.

'Damn him, damn them to hell,' she said as she flung herself down on the pink bedspread that her mom had made. She cuddled up to Tess. Her pet made small sympathetic noises as Sally stroked her silky fur. Gradually her tears subsided, and she calmed down, allowing her heartbeat to slow. Her feelings see-sawed what could she do? She was alone.

Her stomach grumbled, and she remembered that she hadn't eaten since lunchtime, but she couldn't bring herself to go down to the kitchen or face her uncle or that woman yet. She drank water from the carafe on her bedside table then spent a long, wakeful night trying to plan. She considered asking her aunt if she could live with them for a while, but decided that she didn't want to be a burden. She didn't consider going to her father; sure that her uncle Arthur wouldn't have room to take her and Tess in. She wished they were near and could give her some advice.

As soon as it was light, Sally crept downstairs, fed Tess and let her out into the garden for a run. She made toast and a pot of tea which she took up to her room. Once she'd eaten, she lay back on the bed and fell into an uneasy doze. Yvette and her uncle woke them as they left the house. She watched with her usual kind thoughts twisting into an unpleasant tirade, as she peered from behind the nets to see them link arms as they walked away. Sally wondered where they were off to, but realised that it didn't matter, and briefly wished they'd never return. She didn't want to think

226

such wicked thoughts, and tried to blank them out of her mind.

Although Sally didn't know what she should be doing, she knew she couldn't stay. It would be more than she could bear to see the trollop take her mom's place.

She started to sort her wardrobe and chest of drawers out; carefully placing neat piles of clothing on the floor until she could buy a suitcase to pack them in. She'd arranged to meet Edward in town at midday, and couldn't wait to tell him what had happened and ask for his advice. She had no one else so she would have to talk to him about everything.

Feeling despondent she left the house after telling Tess she'd take her for a walk when she returned.

56

Saturday was always a busy market day, and this one was no exception. Sally loved the hustle and bustle and usually spent some time chatting to the stallholders who had known her since she was tiny. Her thoughts dwelt on what she felt were insurmountable problems, so today she noticed no one as she hurried through the busy crowd of shoppers on her way up to New Street. She couldn't stay with her uncle even if he wanted her to, but she felt ill-equipped to be on her own. She'd never missed her mom as much as she did now.

Abigail hadn't left a will, so Sally knew she had no legal right to stay in the house that now belonged solely to her uncle. More than anything else, she felt sad and hurt by this as her mom had told her repeatedly that she'd only bought the house to ensure that Sally had a secure future.

Sally tried not to let bitterness overcome her, but when she thought that Yvette, who'd been fornicating with her uncle for years while her mom was alive, might inherit everything that her mom had worked hard for, it felt like a knot in her stomach. She desperately wanted to talk with her dad or her aunt about it, but she had to go to work the following Monday, so she knew that was impossible.

Relief at reaching Edward's side brought fresh tears raining down her face, and Sally brushed them away impatiently as Edward drew her into the familiar warmth and pleasant aroma of Lyons tea shop. They sat at a corner table and as soon as they'd ordered a pot of tea and buttered toast Sally's plight spilt from her narrowed lips into Edward's willing ears. Initial outburst over, Sally mopped her eyes with an embroidered handkerchief, looked at his worried face, and said, 'What shall I do, I can't stay there with them can I?'

He shook his head. 'No, you bloody well can't.' He reached for her hand across the table and gave it a comforting squeeze. 'It'll be alright– it will – I'll make it okay.'

Sally allowed him to hold her hand briefly, then gently withdrew it and began to pour the tea. 'It'll be going cold,' she said. They sat absorbed in their thoughts; comfortable with silence while they ate. Suddenly Edward reached across and again took her hand firmly in his neatly manicured one. Sally's cup clattered into the saucer as he drew a deep breath and spoke in earnest.

'We could get married Sal, you'd come to love me, I'd look after you, you know I would. I've always loved you.' Scarlet in the face he peered intently into her startled eyes. 'Say yes, Sal, please say yes.'

Sally shook her head, withdrew her hand and said, 'I can't Edward, I'm sorry, but you know I don't love you like that. I wish I did, but I wouldn't make you happy. Please be my friend,' she said quietly, 'I'll always need you to be that.' She drew her gloves from her shabby, black handbag, and started to rise from the table.

'Alright Sal, I'll be your friend forever, but I'll keep asking,' he smiled. 'You might change your mind one of these days. Please sit down love – I've got an idea that might help.'

'I know how I feel Edward, and I'm sorry. I don't want you to keep hoping. You should find someone else who will love you.' Sally sat down.

'I don't want anyone else – you let me worry about my happiness. Anyway, do you want to hear my idea?' Sally nodded without enthusiasm.

'What about my aunt Frances? She's looking for a companion.'

Sally's eyebrows drew into a frown. 'Who?'

'My mom's sister, she lives alone in a big house just off Stratford Road. She's got money. She married Uncle Phillip. He had something to do with banking in London until he died from a heart attack while running to catch a train home. Not that I know why he would be in a hurry to get back to Aunt Frances, according to Mom, she always treated him like dirt. Whenever I've visited, she's always been okay, but apparently, she likes a drink and can become quite belligerent, and swears a lot when she gets drunk.'

'Sounds nice,' Sally frowned again, 'a companion, what does that mean?'

'Erm, well I think it's someone who will live with her, keep her company, and fetch and carry for her. I know she has a very nice lady who does the cleaning and washing, so you shouldn't have to do any heavy lifting or dirty work.'

'But that would mean I'd have to give my job up,' Sally said.

'Mm, yes Sal, but you'd have somewhere to live as well as earning money, and you wouldn't have to stay there if you found something better.'

Sally shook her head. She didn't want to leave the job that she enjoyed, and Edward's aunt Frances didn't sound any more pleasant than his mother. But she reasoned, it would get her away from Hillfield Road.

'She might have found someone else now or changed her mind,' Sally said.

Edward shrugged. 'She might have done, should I find out?'

Sally nodded and smiled. 'You are kind to me, and I don't know what I'd do without your friendship.'

Edward's return smile was falsely bright as he said, 'You're worth it. I'll go tomorrow and talk with her. I have a feeling you'll be just who she needs. What about the swearing though Sally, apparently she can be quite foul-mouthed.'

Sally laughed. 'I haven't lived nearly all my life around Cheapside, and listened to the costermongers, without being able to ignore bad language now have I? I'm sure she can't say anything worse.'

'Okay – now c'mon let's go and have a walk around the rag alley, and take your mind off it all.'

'Yes, but what If she doesn't like me?' Sally wasn't sure she could face a belligerent person, even a sober one.

'We'll face that if it happens, one step at a time, eh?'

57

'You stupid girl, how many times do I have to tell you?' Frances drew herself up to her full height and seemed to take pleasure in admonishing Sally for pouring her tea before adding milk to the cup.

'I'm sorry Aunt I'll try to remember in future.' She ran from the room and brought back a fresh cup. Her hands shook as she poured the tea just as Frances liked it. Her employer took the proffered drink without a word and turned her back on Sally's retreating form.

Sally reluctantly called her employer, Aunt, as required by Frances. Initially, she was grateful for the job even though she had to leave Tess with her uncle Jim. He'd promised to look after her until Sally found a place where she could have her. Their parting had been civil, but Sally had not seen Yvette who'd stayed away.

Sally's bedroom at Frances's house was pleasant. There was a single bed, with a white frilled bedcover, and pink and white floral curtains which complimented the light wood wardrobe and dressing table. Frances must have taken an interest in her home at one time. Now she seemed to take little interest in anything, and Sally was glad to escape from her whenever she could.

She felt no warmth toward Frances whose demeanour was arrogant and reserved with both her and Mrs Smith, the tall, softly spoken cleaning lady. Sally was not reluctant to work hard and willingly carried out her daytime chores of ironing, and fetching and carrying as required by her employer. However, she began to earn her money as the afternoon wore on. Frances expected a glass of whisky to be in her hand at five o'clock precisely. Sally soon recognized that around four o'clock, her employer would become agitated, picking fault with everything. Things that wouldn't usually raise her eyebrows became sticks to beat Sally. Frances usually calmed down after the first glass full had passed her lips. After the third glass, Frances insisted that Sally stayed at her side. It became Sally's nightly torment. Frances always talked about the same things. The drunker she became, the more her outpourings deteriorated into an invective regarding the way life had treated her, and her husband's failings. Specifically, those concerning his death that had left her alone. At first, Sally had tried to talk with Frances, but Frances's reaction had been to scream at her to shut up as she'd no idea how much she'd suffered. Sally never tried again to cheer or reason with her. But this nightly diatribe became increasingly hard to bear as Sally chose not to share her burden with anyone.

Mrs Smith and Sally had become friendly, and Sally felt she could have trusted her, but as she observed little of the interaction between herself and Frances, Sally kept quiet. She wished Mrs Smith stayed later as their employer's irrational behaviour distressed her deeply, and made her cry at some point daily. Sally knew she'd been sheltered from much of the harsh realities of life by her mom, and was grateful, but often had to tell herself to grow up and grow a thicker skin. She found her own advice hard to follow, and she'd come close to telling Edward what was troubling her a few times but didn't want him to feel responsible for her, so she stayed silent.

After a couple of weeks, her employer began to abuse her physically as well as verbally. It started with a sly pinch as she passed her a book, and then rapidly escalated into an occasional slap or punch. Frances always apologised after her malicious behaviour, which usually took place when she was well on the way to being drunk. Sally didn't know how to deal with it – she'd never experienced such spite before.

One evening about six o'clock Mrs Smith returned unexpectedly to collect a parcel of linens that she intended to soak overnight at her own house. She found Sally sobbing in the kitchen with a blood-covered tea towel held to her face.

Mrs Smith's nostrils flared as Sally showed her the gash in her cheek where Frances had thrown a glass at her for not replenishing it quickly enough. She broke down completely at Mrs Smith's kind concern and went on to divulge all the hurts her employer had inflicted.

'Right, get yer things together yer coming home with me. Don't worry; we'll sort it. Spiteful, frustrated old bag. Well, we'll both 'av' ter find new jobs, eh?' She put her arm around Sally and then gave her a gentle push. 'Go on then, get yer things. I'm goin' ter tell 'er.'

Sally felt relieved to be told what to do and did it. In no time she'd collected up her few belongings and felt desperate to leave the place where she'd been so unhappy. She couldn't hear what Mrs Smith was saying to Frances, but the raised voices soon tailed off, and Mrs Smith, red in the face, returned to the kitchen.

'C'mon then, let's go and leave her to pickle herself,' she said.

58

Sally's mind was again in turmoil as she followed her new friend out into the watery, evening sunshine. She tried to express gratitude for her intervention as they walked along Warwick Road towards the River Cole. She said she didn't know how to repay her as she'd caused her to give up her job at a time when jobs were very hard to come by.

'What will Mr Smith say when you turn up with me in tow?' Sally asked. What was to become of her; who else was going to employ her?

'There's been no Mr Smith since just after Alfie was born – he died. I don't even know why. He just keeled over one Sunday while we were eating tea.' Mrs Smith spoke in a matter of fact manner interrupting Sally's worrying train of thought. 'It's been hard bringing up my two boys on my own, but I've managed. They're good lads, and they've been lucky enough to stay in work when most poor buggers can't find a job for love nor money.'

'Mrs. Smith –'

Mrs Smith patted her arm. 'Call me Gran. Now stop worrying, and we'll let tomorrow take care of tomorrow.

Sally stood awkwardly by the door, overcome with shyness as Gran proudly introduced her two sons. 'This young hooligan's Ted.' She flipped his ear gently, and they both laughed. Sally raised her eyes to the flushed face of a nice-looking young man. She guessed that he was around twenty-five years of age. An unfashionably long forelock of mid-brown hair partially covered his attractive face. Sally thought he looked kind as he reached up and pushed it back onto his head. He smiled at Sally. 'And this one's Alfie, my youngest, and he's a bloody nuisance too.' They all laughed. All except Sally, who seemed unable to breathe, let alone laugh. Gran touched Sally's arm. 'This is Sally she's been through a bad time the last few months, so she's going to stay with us for a while. Mind you treat her gently.'

'We will.' The men chorused and almost fell over each other to take her case from her.

'Hey, hey, don't kill her with kindness – let her get into the room. Come and sit by me.' Gran sank gratefully onto a large sagging sofa covered with bright cushions.

Sally felt unable to move as she looked into the laughing eyes of the youngest man. She'd last seen him when she was feeling extremely foolish, having put her head through a train window. Their eyes met and seemed unwilling to separate. She expected him to say he already knew her, but he didn't. Neither did Sally – she became unconscious of time passing – until Gran spoke again.

'C'mon Sally, don't be a goose, they won't bite. Will you take her case up to my room Ted? She'll be sleeping with me,' Gran said.

Alfie took Sally's coat and whispered in a teasing voice as she passed him. 'I might.'

She kept her head down, trying to hide her blushes. She could feel the heat radiating from her cheeks as she sat beside Gran, who in the process of unlacing her black shoes, had noticed nothing of the exchange.

'I'll put the kettle on; you'd like a cuppa wouldn't you Sally.' Alfie winked at her and went into the kitchen; calling back to ascertain if Gran wanted to soak her feet. Sally's eyes followed his neat figure as he left the room. No one had ever affected her in this way she thought and blushed again as an unbidden picture of herself entwined in his arms entered her head.

Later that evening when they'd eaten a fish and chip tea Gran regaled her sons with the circumstances of Sally's appearance and their loss of employment.

'Nasty old bugger, we'll look after you, won't we Alf?' Ted said.

Alfie nodded. 'It'll be like having a sister. We've always wanted one haven't we Ted?'

Ted agreed enthusiastically, and he missed the slight edge of sarcasm in his brother's tone. It wasn't wasted on Sally, though. She wondered as the evening wore on why neither of them had acknowledged their previous meeting. She hoped it was Alfie's intention not to embarrass her. It was her reason for keeping quiet.

Subsequently, Alfie behaved like a brother to her and made no mention of his teasing when she'd arrived. Without a word said, both Sally and Alfie continued to conceal their previous meeting.

Sally settled quickly into the comforting warmth of the happy family. Her happiness was complete when Ted and Alfie fetched Tess to live with them. They all liked her dog and felt it was worth the argument that had ensued when Yvette initially refused to part with her. Jim had solved the problem by firmly telling Yvette that Tess belonged to Sally.

Ted told Sally that Jim seemed pleased she had settled with the Smith family. He'd sent his love and a message for her. Sally merely shrugged; she wouldn't allow herself to unbend and consider responding to his request to see her.

Tess soon began to sleep in Ted and Alfie's room – Gran had strict rules regarding dogs on beds. She turned a blind eye as far as their bedroom went, and Sally didn't mind sharing her dog, she was just glad to have her back.

59

Before too long, Sally began to feel at home and content with her life once again. She soon understood that everyone shared household chores with equanimity plus a little wrangling on occasions. Ted arranged an interview for Gran at his works in Tyseley, and she became employed as a canteen assistant. The wage was paltry, but she was grateful to have a job.

It took several weary weeks, and miles of walking and begging for work before Sally was in the right place at the right time. Meanwhile, the Smith family readily supported her. She felt uncomfortable about them keeping her, and promised herself she'd pay them back somehow when she could.

Eventually, when she applied for work, for the third time, at Brook Tool Company nearby, she was lucky and replaced a woman who'd had to leave because she was pregnant.

Ted was an experienced tool setter and Alfie, a junior buyer for Serk's radiator manufacturer. They both knew how lucky they were to be doing jobs that they enjoyed and expected to stay with their companies for the remainder of their lives.

They all chipped in for household expenses, their share worked out by Gran according to their income. Sally offered to pay more, but Gran refused, kindly dismissing her indebtedness.

Sally shared a bedroom with Gran and found she enjoyed the intimacy. Seeing her dressed in her voluminous winceyette nightgown, and her salt and pepper hair neatly plaited to below her waist made Sally smile, and follow suit. Gran always went upstairs first, undressed, and then shut her eyes while Sally undressed – she said it wasn't decent to get ready for bed together – her late husband had never seen her undressed in all the time they were married

Gran had many more sides to her character than Sally had seen. One night there was a knock on the door after they'd all gone to bed, and Ted called up the stairs that Gran was needed as Mrs Florence was in labour. Gran was well-liked in the neighbourhood, and Sally had known her to be almost asleep on her feet at times, but she never refused to go and help when needed.

Ted taught Sally to ride an old bike that was in the outhouse. After many laughs and false starts with him holding onto the saddle and running up Seeleys Road with her, she got the hang of it, and they spent many evenings riding a few miles just for the joy of feeling the wind in their hair.

There were three bicycles, but Alfie always refused to accompany them, saying in his cheerful way that he was waiting until he'd bought a car when he'd take them all out. Ted reckoned he wasn't fit enough to keep up with them. But even Ted's friendly tormenting didn't get Alfie to change his mind. Sally wasn't sure if Ted might be right; Alfie appeared to be short of breath at times. He took pains to hide this from them all, so Sally didn't feel that she could mention it, even to his mother.

Many evenings they played card games that one or other of the brothers taught her. When Edward joined them making a foursome, Partner Whist was their game of choice. Edward objected when Sally partnered anyone but him, and Sally privately told him not to be so stupid. Edward apologised and kept his negative thoughts to himself, but he continued to be on the lookout for any sign of intimacy between Sally and the men, he too, now liked to spend time with.

At times Edward seemed to be so twisted up inside with his thoughts about Sally that he scared himself and wondered what he might do in order not to lose her. He'd asked her to go to the cinema with him recently, but she'd made an excuse. He'd become eaten up with jealousy and had to fight hard to control it.

Gran refused to play cards – waste of time – she always said, but she enjoyed the badinage while she was knitting for some new baby. There was always some new baby.

Sally became used to being with Alfie daily but still felt a panicky sensation in her stomach when they accidentally touched hands or stood too close. She liked to look at him; drinking in his teal eyes that always seemed to be smiling teasingly at her. His blond curly hair which he kept slicked down with Brylcream during the day, tempted Sally to pull each piece and watch it spring back into place. A temptation she always resisted even when he'd just washed it. She knew it would cross some line and feared to expose the way his nearness affected her. She often wondered if Alfie had any idea how she felt when around him. She didn't think he had an inkling; he only ever treated her in a friendly, circumspect manner.

Her feelings toward Ted were different, and she came to look on him as the brother she would have liked to have had. He would often stroke her hair as he passed and had even offered to brush it for her on one occasion. She'd refused, but his kindness and attention to her welfare left her feeling warm and comforted. She hoped that Ted felt nothing more than friendship for her; she knew she couldn't love him in that way. Not in the passionate mind consuming way that she had come to love Alfie.

Sally would have been embarrassed, had she known how difficult Ted found it to keep his love for her a secret. He thought he should give Sally time to grow up a little and felt that she was probably promised to Edward anyway, they seemed to be such close friends. He also thought he was too old for Sally to want a relationship with him. Edward was a much more suitable candidate, but this very thought brought a painful flash of envy.

As the days passed from an exceptionally wet summer into equally miserable autumn, Sally enjoyed taking each day as it came, not worrying what the future held for her. In December she visited her aunt Claris to coincide with her father's visit. Neither Clarissa nor Bill had much to say about Sally's current living arrangements. They were just glad that she was happy. Her aunt teased her at first about having three young men dancing attendance on her, but this stopped as Sally blushed furiously and turned away.

'You can tell me anything love, but I won't press you,' Clarissa said and hugged her. Sally felt unable to confide how she felt about Alfie to anyone, so she laughed and hugged her back. They were interrupted by Abi, who was still as fascinated by Sally as she had been when she was tiny.

'There's nothing to tell.' Sally said and turned away to talk to her cousin. She sounded convincing, but she knew she'd lied. Even these few days away from Alfie felt unbearable though she was glad to be with people that she loved.

Throughout the return journey from Carissa's, Sally's stomach churned with the anticipation of seeing Alfie again. She hoped he would be waiting for her on the platform but, as the train screeched to a halt and the steam began to clear, she could see it was Ted's welcoming face that met her quickly smiling eyes.

Ted beamed at her as he took her case, gave her a peck on the cheek, and then grasped her elbow firmly as they pushed their way out of the hectic station. Sally was pleased to see her friend, but only half-listened to his enquiries about her trip away. She was reliving her initial meeting with Alfie on the train and wondering why she'd felt none of the confusion that she now felt when they were close. She'd barely noticed him then; now she never had his image out of her mind.

60

Sally shrieked, no, stop it, stop it as a second then a third snowball went whizzing over her head and smashed into the wall of their house. Alfie scooped more snow into his gloved hand and compressed it into a soft ball. He laughed uproariously as Sally turned and also scooped up a handful of sparkly snow. She threw it at him with all her might, but it was wildly inaccurate, causing Alfie to walk steadily towards her with his snowball held out menacingly. It was Sally's turn to laugh, half amused and half scared that he would rub the snow into her glowing face. Alfie had achieved the reaction that he desired, and threw the snow to the ground as he reached her outstretched arms that were making feeble attempts to ward him off.

It was the first fall of snow that year; coming at the beginning of April it seemed to have young and old alike taking full advantage of the crisp unseasonable weather. Shrieks of laughter came from youngsters tobogganing on purloined trays along Seeleys Road. Neighbours' voices carried clearly on the cold air, sounding more raucous and happier than usual, as they called greetings to each other. Gran had sprinkled salt to help passengers alighting from the frequent trams that stopped outside her house.

In her haste to get away from Alfie's playful behaviour, Sally burst too quickly through the back gate into their small garden. She skidded on the soft snow and fell unceremoniously to the ground with her skirt riding above her knees. Alfie held out his hand and helped her up. He wasn't smiling as he asked if she was alright.

Embarrassed, Sally shook her head and started to walk gingerly towards the kitchen door. As she reached the step, Alfie gently dragged her back into his arms and held her close.

Sally heaved a sigh and relaxed against his chest as he said, 'That's the second time I've helped you up from the floor,' Sally could feel his hot breath tickle her ear as he whispered, 'and I've loved you ever since the first time. I never thought I'd be lucky enough to see you again.' He eased her willing form around to face him.

'I love you too, Alfie,' Sally said simply. They stood holding hands, gazing in wonder into each other's deep, deep eyes. They kissed.

For Sally, it was the most wonderful feeling she had ever known. She had pictured it happening, but never really thought it would. Her heart did somersaults in her chest, and her eyes closed. When they broke apart Alfie said breathily, 'I've wanted to kiss you for such a long time love.'

They kissed again, and as they separated for the second time Alfie went down on one knee into the snow, looked up into her bemused face and said, 'Will you marry me, my love?'

Sally felt as though every bone in her body had melted away, leaving her feeling weak. She held tightly onto his hand and knelt beside him. 'Yes, oh, yes, of course, I will. I love you so much.'

Alfie's smile lit up his face. 'I'll always try to make you happy Sal I promise.'

Sally kissed his cheek. 'I know you will, and we will be happy.'

Seeing her shiver, Alfie said, 'C'mon let's get you inside and warmed up.' He stood, pulled Sally to her feet and led her through to the kitchen.

'Mom and Ted aren't home yet; I'll just make up the fire, and we'll have a cuppa.' They soon had the fire throwing out some heat and Sally began to take her coat off. Alfie held onto her arm. 'Here, let me.' He took her coat and hung it up with his own, behind the door. He pulled off her boots and put them in the hearth to dry, and then did the same with his own. His socks were wet through so they came off as well. He sniffed them exaggeratedly and said, 'Phew, I hate the smell of wet wool.' He placed them on the fender to dry, swung the kettle over the cheerful flames, and spooned tea from the caddy into the teapot. He held onto her hand again as he went into the kitchen to fetch milk. 'You'll have to come with me; I can't let you out of my sight just yet in case it's a dream, and I wake up.'

Sally went without demur; she was bursting with happiness, but couldn't seem to sort out the jumble of thoughts in her head, or the new feelings which rampaged through her body. She wondered what Gran and Ted would think about it, but felt sure that they'd be pleased. She began to worry about Edward's reaction – he'd always hoped she would eventually fall in love with him no matter how many times she contradicted him.

247

Her worries fled as Alfie sat on the sofa and pulled her onto his lap. After a few more kisses and cuddles, reality began to impinge on Sally's mind again. She pulled back from him and tried to stand, but he held onto her.

'Told you I'd never let you go again.' He thought how beautiful she looked with her face flushed from their embrace, and her hair that was threatening to fall loose from the braids that wound into circles around her ears. They looked a little like hairy doughnuts Alfie thought and told her so. Sally tittered then sobered as she explained to Alfie how worried she was regarding Edwards's feelings about their engagement.

'Leave Edward to me,' Alfie said and persuaded Sally to sit beside him again. He placed a comforting arm around her shoulders and drew her close. 'If you like we'll tell him together, he's coming here on Saturday, isn't he? I've time to buy a ring to put on this lovely finger. He held up her left hand and kissed each fingertip. Any preferences, would madam like diamonds, rubies or emeralds?'

Sally blushed. 'I don't mind what it is as long as it isn't too flashy – I don't care if I don't have a ring.

Alfie's face became serious. 'Well I mind, if my ring is already on your finger, he'll see it's pointless to argue, and that you've made your choice. He'll have to accept it or fall out with us. I don't think he'll do that; you've been friends a long time, and you've tried to convince him that you would never marry him, haven't you?'

61

Sally nodded solemnly. 'What d'you think your Mom and Ted will say? Will they mind?'

Alfie leaned his head back against a cushion. 'Don't be daft Sal they'll be tickled pink to know you're going to be a permanent part of this family. You'll see, our mom already loves you, and before you arrived, I've never known Ted to be as happy as he is. You and Tess have given us all a present to treasure.' He let go of Sally's hand and got to his feet, walked over to the range, lifted the kettle from its hook, poured boiling water onto the tea leaves and gave them a good stir before replacing the lid, and standing the pot on the hearth.

'You'll see, it'll be alright my love, now come and give me another kiss while that brews. Mom and Ted will be here any minute and frozen I bet. The temperature's dropping. I shouldn't be surprised if it freezes tonight.'

They had just enough time for a kiss or two before Gran called as she came in the front door. 'Hope you've made the tea you two, I'm half frozen.'

She entered the cosy living room and nodded like a wise owl as she saw that Sally's hand was held firmly in Alfie's. Her eyebrows rose, and she chuckled as she divested herself of her long coat and held out her hard-working hands to the fire. 'Like that is it?' she gave a benevolent smile, 'I wondered if you'd ever get around to it.' She chuckled again and dropped wearily into her chair, then leaned towards the glowing fire and continued to warm her hands. 'Come on love, pour us a cup, I'm parched, feels as though me tongues stuck to me teeth.'

'Is that all you've to say about it then, Mom?' Alfie asked.

'Well, a cat with one eye could see which way the wind was blowin' between you two.' She took a steady look at their puzzled faces and gave them a reassuring smile. 'I couldn't be happier; you make a lovely couple. Now, will you please pour me a cup of tea and tell me all about it.' She sank back into her seat and closed her tired eyes for a few minutes.

Alfie and Sally explained to Gran in fits and starts about the snowballs and Sally's fall in the garden, she nodded throughout the garbled account, but when Alfie told her that they'd become engaged her eyes flew open, and she clapped her hands like a child. 'Oh, Sal, I'm delighted that you will be my daughter-in-law. When are you thinking about then?' Gran asked.

Alfie looked askance at Sally, who shook her head. 'We haven't even discussed it yet, and I'll have to see if Dad will sign for me – I'm sure he'll be pleased. You'll be the first to know Gran. I love you, and I'm so grateful to you for allowing me to be a part of your family.'

'Now shush,' Gran said, and smiled, 'you can come and help me prepare the vegetables, we're having corn beef hash, and that'll bring us all down to earth won't it eh?'

'You stay right where you are Mom, and we'll do the tea won't we, Sal?' Alfie said.

They went into the kitchen, leaving Gran to rest in the warm. The chores took longer than usual, but Sally and Alfie were too absorbed in each other to notice how the time flew.

Ted arrived with a wet Tess in tow a little later and on hearing their news offered his congratulations, gave Sally a peck on her rosy cheek, and slapped his grinning brother on his back. He rubbed Tess vigorously with her old towel before she sniffed at Sally's hand then lay down in front of the hearth.

'I'm pleased for you both, when's the wedding to be?' he asked, looking from one to the other.

'Not decided yet,' Gran said, bringing about hoots of laughter as they all thought she was fast asleep and had been speaking in hushed voices.

Sally was relieved that both Gran and Ted were pleased for them, but she retained a pending sense of doom when she thought about Edward's reaction to their news.

Hopefully, Alfie was going to be able to make it alright as he'd said, she thought as she snuggled down beside Gran. They both put their cold feet on their hot water bottles to warm them. Gran slept as soon as her greying hair touched the pillow, but it took Sally a while as she couldn't stop her brain from whirling, happy thoughts vied with worries about Edward. She fell asleep thinking about how perfect their life was going to be as one big happy family. The image blotted out Edward's possible response to her happiness.

In the next room, Alfie wondered how he'd managed to be lucky enough to have a girl like Sally fall in love with him. It took him a while to fall asleep too – the chilly air had triggered one of his coughing fits. He hoped he wasn't keeping Sally or his mom awake and was glad that Ted was already asleep; he usually grumbled if Alfie kept him awake with his coughing.

Ted lay still, feigning sleep. He was heartbroken – he loved Sally too – now he would never have a chance with her. It had been love at first sight on his part, but he never dared to tell her. He'd known she preferred his brother. He'd seen the way her soft blue eyes always followed him when he left the room. He wanted them to be happy, but he wished it had been him that she'd loved. Eventually, he fell into an uneasy sleep vowing he would never let them know his true feelings.

62

The whole family became very upset the following month when Tess became ill with Canine Distemper and was too sick to be saved. The vet charged a hefty price to put her to sleep. 'It's the best you can do for her.' He told them, shaking his shiny, bald head in a sorrowful manner as he held out his pink hand for his fee.

It wasn't long after that wretched event that Gran decided she needed to give her son a warning as he and Sally had been spending every minute together outside work time.

'Good God Mother,' Alfie said, 'do you think I'm an idiot? I wouldn't treat Sally so cheaply.' He glared at her worried frown.

'Well I'm only reminding you; a tuppenny bun can cost fourpence if you're not wise. It's no use you being angry with me; I wouldn't be doing me duty if I said nothing. So go on, get to work, I've said me piece.' She turned away, pulled a shawl around her broad shoulders and bid her son a fond farewell as she left for work.

Sally came downstairs with a frown on her face. 'Why were you shouting at your Mom?' She rubbed the top of his arm as she went into the kitchen, her eyes automatically strayed to the corner where Tess usually lay.

Alfie felt tired; he'd had yet another restless night, his cough pulling him frequently from a sound sleep into startled choking. He wondered if perhaps his mother was right, she'd asked him to see Dr Hughes, but he'd not wanted to waste hard-earned cash just for a cough. His mother's wise words regarding both his health and Sally had upset him. Her concern was appreciated, but Alfie felt he was old enough not to need telling. He smiled at Sally as she returned to eat her bread and milk by the fire.

'It was nothing love – nothing to worry about anyway. Mom was telling me that I should take more care of myself now that we're to be married. She worries about my cough and wants me to see Dr Hughes, but I don't trust doctors, they give me the willies.'

'Well I agree with Gran you should see him. Promise me you will,' she said and cuddled up to his warm body.

Sally could hear another paroxysm as she left the house and felt determined that when she returned from work, she would try to persuade him to be sensible.

Alfie continued to ignore all the sensible advice, and towards the end of June, he collapsed on his way home from work. As he neared the house, he fell to his knees, incapacitated by the violence of a coughing fit that he was unable to stop. Alfie began to tremble when he saw his white, linen handkerchief stained with bright red blood. After a while, with the help of a passing neighbour, he managed to get to his feet.

'You're looking bad Alfie,' Mr Benton said, as he held onto his arm, 'let's get you home, eh?'

Although the coughing had ceased, it had left Alfie too weak to walk unaided. He clutched desperately onto the river bridge railings.

'Alright son, hold on there, I'll fetch Ted,' Mr Benton said, and ran towards Gran's house.

Together they half carried Alfie the short distance home where his mother ministered to him while Ted ran to fetch Dr Hughes.

'Now there's no use you carrying on like that,' Gran said, 'he's going to be alright. You heard what the doctor said; he just needs to rest and get plenty of fresh air. He's going to see if he can get him a bed in Yardley Green. They've just started them new-fangled sun ray treatments there. He'll be his old self soon enough you'll see.'

Sally mopped at her red-rimmed eyes. She'd been stoic and helped do whatever was necessary when she first saw how ill Alfie was. But now he was asleep in bed she'd given way to panic, and sat rocking backwards and forwards, tears squeezing through her shaking fingers as she hid her face.

'I can't bear to lose him, Gran, he's my whole world,' she said.

'We're not going to lose him; consumption isn't what it used to be. Lots of people recover these days.' Gran tried to sound cheerful. She patted Sally awkwardly on her bent head, but inwardly she was just as frightened. Her Alfie was so full of confidence and good humour that she thought nothing could take that away, but she hoped that he hadn't left it too long before seeking treatment. His cough had become so much worse recently. Gran didn't see any point in upsetting Sally further, so she kept her fears to herself.

Gran gave her notice in at work and stayed home to nurse her son. Although it was hard to manage, there was rarely a time when Alfie wasn't receiving care or company from Gran, Sally or Ted. Edward popped in sometimes and sat with Alfie giving them a chance to do other things. They got on very well considering Edward's hopeful intentions regarding Sally.

He'd taken the news of their engagement calmly, congratulating them and wishing them well, but he'd said nothing about it to Sally when they were alone. He still treated her as his friend, but never arranged to meet her as they used to. He seemed to be more Alfie and Ted's friend than hers. Sally was glad their relationship had changed, but occasionally she missed their close companionship.

63

Alfie's bed was now downstairs. He had the most nourishing food that they could afford, and windows were frequently open to allow in as much warm air as possible. They were all careful to speak in a positive way to him, but Gran told Ted that she didn't think there was anything else they could do that would help to speed his recovery.

The local chemist dispensed soothing draughts prescribed by Dr Hughes, but he hadn't managed to find Alfie a place at the fever hospital. There were so many people needing treatment that he would have to wait his turn. Gran knew that there were sanatoriums that could help, but they couldn't afford to send him there. It saddened her but made her all the more determined that he would get the best treatment possible at home.

After about a month of this regime, Alfie began to feel healthier. He was becoming bored with everything and protested that he was now well enough to leave his bed. Sally and he had become closer than ever while he was bed-bound, their relationship had developed past the kissing and cuddling stage, but they still managed to keep their passion under control. Lying in bed with little to occupy himself had allowed Alfie's imagination to run wild, and he found it increasingly difficult when they were alone to curb their intimacy.

Sally too found saying no, to his half-joking request to share his bed, almost impossible. She longed to feel his hands on her bare flesh and blushed at the unbidden visions that intruded on her thoughts. There had been several nights that she'd encouraged Gran or Ted to stay with them when they had made other arrangements; afraid that she would give in to the temptation that plagued her.

By September, the nights had grown cold, and Sally sat shivering, as she kept Alfie company despite the coal fire that was always alight. Gran was at a neighbour's helping with a birth, and Ted was spending the weekend with relatives, so she and Alfie cuddled up together on his bed.

'C'mon get in, you'll freeze out there,' he said, holding the bedclothes open.

Sally laughed, gave an exaggerated shudder and tumbled willingly into his arms. 'Now just you keep your hands to yourself, Mr Octopus. I only want you to keep me warm.' They snuggled up together, pulling the blankets right up to their chins. 'Luxury,' Sally sighed as she shut her eyes. She'd been at work all day and as she became warm, began to drift off to sleep.

'Hey, stay awake, I want to talk to you.' Alfie moved her round to face him on his thin arm.

'About our wedding?' She opened her eyes and grinned widely at him. 'I think we should make it as soon as you can walk. What do you think?'

Alfie shrugged with difficulty. 'No not about that love. He chewed his lip thoughtfully. 'I'm not sure I'm going to make it.'

Sally leaned up on her elbow and looked him in the face. 'Oh, Alfie, don't say that you're much, much better, you know you are – it's not like you to be a pessimist.'

'You think so, but I know how I feel. I want to get better, but I have this awful feeling in my gut that I'm not going to.'

Sally drew his head towards her and kissed him on the lips. 'Shh, I won't let anything happen to you. I love you so very much – you're just feeling down tonight. You'll feel better in the morning when the sun shines.'

'You could make me feel better now.'

'Oh, Alfie you know we mustn't, what if I got pregnant?'

Alfie ran his hands down her arms and across her breasts. 'Well we're getting married anyway aren't we?' he whispered. His hands became more daring, making her breath come in short gasps.

This was the point where one or the other would generally call a halt to their lovemaking, but this night was different. Their frustrations and worries over the last few months finally spilt over. They made love with all the intensity and passion their bodies could stand, carried away by a compelling force that shook their beings.

Afterwards, Sally arranged her clothing and herself under the bedspread and lay back against Alfie. They slept, not even waking when Gran returned home in the early hours. Seeing them clothed, but fast asleep, she smiled indulgently and went to her bed.

Although Alfie and Sally had kept their emotions under control after that night together, it had drawn them incredibly close. They spent every waking minute possible togcthcr – usually holding hands and talking. Thcy planncd to get married the Saturday before Christmas. Alfie had laughed and looked roguishly at Sally when she said she couldn't get married in white. He'd said that she better had – everyone would think the worse if she didn't. She'd agreed, and bought a beautiful length of satin from her mom's friend who had a stall in the rag ally. She wished her mom was there to help her make her dress but believed that she could see her from her place in heaven, and would be happy for her.

Sally had asked her friend, Faith, to be bridesmaid, and Alfie had known that Ted would be his best man. It wasn't to be a big event, just the ceremony, and then a buffet back at Gran's afterwards for a few close family and friends.

For the remainder of her life, Sally relived the night of passion that she'd shared with the man she loved. She was forever grateful that they'd had that closeness as Alfie had been right. He didn't get better. Two weeks later, he died.

One evening as they sat together on Alfie's bed, he suddenly had a coughing fit that was violent and prolonged. He covered the bedding and Sally with copious amounts of blood. Gran came rushing in, but his heart could stand no more, he rapidly became unconscious and died within minutes, with Sally and his mother holding tightly onto his hands.

Sally felt she had plunged into a nightmare. She'd always attended church, but now she cursed her maker. It was impossible to believe God would be so cruel if he loved them. Why would he take Alfie away she raged when he was kind and good? She promised herself that she'd never say a prayer or set foot inside a church again.

64

No one felt like celebrating Christmas, and at Gran's suggestion, Ted decided he'd go and spend a couple of days with friends he'd known since childhood. He'd felt utterly lost since Alfie's death. They'd always been as close as brothers could be; it was as though Alfie had been his motivator. He spent most of his time when not at work, in his room. He said very little, usually leaving his mother and Sally to keep each other company in their mourning.

Sally went to work, and returned home, with Alfie's name and face continually chasing around in her head. She didn't want to leave the house where she could picture him clearly, run her hands over surfaces that he'd touched and sit where he'd sat.

Gran tried in vain to get Sally to accompany her when she went to assist at a birth, but Sally always refused. She didn't need to explain that it would take her away from time to sit and relive her happy days with Alfie. Gran knew. Her heart was heavy as only a mother's heart can be, but she had a more prosaic way of coping with the loss of her precious son. She found that helping others with life's trials enabled her to come to terms with her grief.

Returning early from one of her charitable outings, Gran walked in on Sally who was having a strip wash in front of the fire. Sally was as usual lost in her thoughts as she dipped the flannel in and out of the enamel bowl, and didn't hear Gran enter the room.

Gran smiled indulgently, but her smile turned to a puzzled frown as Sally stood with no clothing to hide her figure. Sally startled and grabbed the nearby towel as Gran said quietly, 'Putting on a bit of weight aren't yer Sal?'

Sally's face glowed scarlet as she tried to cover her protruding belly.

'You're in the family way aren't yer?' Gran's Birmingham accent became quite pronounced when she allowed it to, 'now how did that 'appen, eh?'

Sally sighed deeply. 'I was going to tell you Gran, but I wanted to be sure. Please don't be angry with me.'

'I'm not angry love, just puzzled. Get yourself dressed, and then we'll talk. I'll put the kettle on.' She went into the kitchen and shut the door to give Sally some privacy

Sally stemmed her ready tears, dressed quickly in a pink, flowery nightdress, and cleared away her washbowl. She wasn't anxious about what Gran would have to say, but she now knew for sure that she was having Alfie's baby. Gran's face had confirmed her suspicions. As soon as she'd missed two consecutive months, she'd thought she might be, and the notion had buoyed her up. She wanted this special reminder, this tangible proof that his death could not destroy their love.

'Well I'm just glad that Ted's away,' Gran said, as they sat drinking their tea together. She raised her brows at Sally.

Sally's cup clattered in its saucer as she looked her friend in the eye and haltingly told her what had happened between herself and Alfie.

'I'm not too surprised,' Gran said, nodding her head, 'and not sorry either. We'll love this grandchild of mine, won't we?' She smiled at Sally, who had visibly relaxed at her kind, accepting words. 'What're we going to do about it though – there'll be lots of tongues wagging you'll see, there's nothing some people like better than to feel superior when someone else is in trouble.' She refilled their cups and sat back down.

'Perhaps I need to leave and go somewhere I'm not known,' Sally said. Her head drooped as she pictured leaving this sanctuary where she'd been so happy and loved.

'You'll do no such thing me girl. You'll stay here, and we'll face what stones get thrown – together. People can think what they like. I'll be proud to hold me, grandchild. Anyway, I don't think folk around here are going to say too much to my face. I'm not known for being backwards at coming forward,' she ended with a chuckle.

Sally looked sheepish. 'I'll be known as a fallen woman, but I can't be sorry, I loved Alfie so much, and I'm glad I still have a part of him to keep with me.' She stood up, and grinned at Gran, grateful for her wisdom and support.

'I know you did and I'm glad too. Enough, let's get some sleep we've work in the morning.'

As they settled down for the night, Gran said, 'G'night Sal,' then as an afterthought 'you know Ted's very fond of you, don't you?'

Sally pictured Ted's caring face for a moment. She was very fond of him too, but it was soon replaced by Alfie's smiling one as she fell asleep, with her hand placed protectively over her belly.

It was Christmas Eve when Sally told Edward that she was expecting. Myriad expressions crossed his face as he absorbed her unwelcome news. Then he said 'Marry me, Sal, I'll look after you and the baby. I'll bring it up as my own. No one needs to know that it's not mine. Please Sal – you know I've always loved you.' Edward gripped her shoulders none too gently in his urgency to get her to agree.

Edward had felt hurt and churned up inside when Sally and Alfie announced their engagement. He'd always thought that she'd learn to love him as he loved her. For him, there was no one else. He'd been out with a few girls, but after a couple of times, he'd stopped seeing each one. They weren't Sally. And now circumstances had changed he felt sure that Sally would turn to him if only he could convince her of the depth of his love for her. He was willing to take on the baby and try to love it. She must see sense and marry him, he thought.

65

To his dismay, Sally backed away, shrugging his hands firmly from her shoulders. 'I don't know what to say, you know I don't love you like that. I can't marry you. It wouldn't be fair, why should you be responsible for Alfie's baby?'

Edward looked stricken; he was upset and angry that she'd rejected him yet again; he'd convinced himself that she would see it was the best thing to do. He sputtered in a tightly controlled voice. 'Well, what are you planning to do? Have you told your dad yet? How will you manage?'

He thought she must surely hear the thudding in his chest. He wanted to shake some sense into her. He needed her and was determined to pursue her until she gave in. He knew he had to tread carefully though, or he'd frighten her off for good.

'No, Sally replied, no one else knows except Gran,' she turned away and walked towards a cupboard beside the grate, 'she'll stand by me. I don't need to rush into anything.'

'If you change your mind, Sal, just let me know – I'm not going anywhere.' He shook his head and managed a smile.

'Shh!' she said and placed her finger to her lips as Ted called a greeting from the kitchen entrance. 'Ted doesn't know, and he doesn't need to know yet either. We'll talk about this later.' She knelt and unearthed a neatly wrapped present from behind the sofa and thrust it into his hands. 'Don't open it until the morning, go now.' She gave him a small push on his shoulder as Ted strolled close to the fire while blowing on his cold hands and rubbing them together to warm them.

He smiled at Sally as he said, 'I decided that I wanted to be with my two favourite girls for Christmas. Mom knows, she's on her way round from next door, she'll be here in a minute.' He lowered himself down onto the half-moon shaped, rag rug. 'Are you staying a while, Edward? D'you fancy a game of cards?' Sally's and Edward's jaws dropped. Ted hadn't wanted to do anything since Alfie died.

'Sorry mate, I promised I'd get home early to give a hand with fixing things for tomorrow. Mom wants bloody paper streamers hung up; lord knows why. There's little to celebrate in our miserable house,' he grimaced, 'well it's miserable when she's there anyway. I'll see you on Boxing Day – perhaps have a game then eh?'

Ted nodded and said dolefully, 'I suppose ... Merry Christmas anyway.' He picked up one of the fragrant fir cones that Sally had perfumed with pine, sniffed it and stared into the pleasantly crackling fire as Sally showed Edward out.

'Sure you won't change your mind, Sal?' Edward asked, as he began to cross the road to the tram stop.

Sally shook her head and waved, as relieved to see him go, as she was glad to see Gran appear, from her friend's house next door.

'You've told him then?' Gran asked, as they went into the house and shut out the chill wind that wanted to follow them.

'Mm, yes, and he asked me to marry him again. He said he'd bring up Alfie's baby as his own, but I don't believe him capable of doing that. He becomes so jealous over little things, and I'm scared that he would grow to resent the baby and throw his kindness back in my face. I know he's been my friend for years, but I've seen how his jealousy can make him behave irrationally,' she sighed, 'I wish it were that simple, but it's not and,' she found tears begin trickling down her cheeks, 'I don't love him, I could never forget Alfie.'

'Hey, you two I'm in here, you know. What's going on? Who don't you want to marry?' Ted called from the living room.

Gran left Sally in the front room and went to talk to Ted, who was looking expectantly at the door as she came in.

'Sally's expecting Alfie's baby,' she paused, allowing this news to sink in.

Ted shrugged. 'Well, I'm not surprised she's been looking peaky for a while.'

He jumped up and went quickly in to Sally, put his arm around her, and said as he led her to the hearth, 'It'll be alright Sal, we'll look after you, won't we Mom?'

'Of course, we will,' Gran said.

Ted paused for a moment. 'I'll be an Uncle; and a good one too,' he gave a wide grin, the first one they'd seen in a long while, 'trust Alfie to give us a parting shot eh?'

267

Later that evening Ted rustled the newspaper he'd been reading, causing both Sally and his mother to cease the knitting in which they were absorbed. 'What's this you were saying earlier about Edward Sal? Has he asked you to marry him?'

Sally explained briefly, and Ted snorted. 'Well, I think you're right. You'll be fine here with us.' He disappeared behind his paper. He wasn't entirely sure why he hadn't offered to marry Sally himself, but the thought of her turning him down too was more than he could bear; far better to have her as a close friend. He would look after Sally and the baby.

Christmas morning Sally woke to find beautiful, thick ice patterns decorating her window. Some resembled lacy leaves and ferns that grew in the park, some like snowflakes as they settled singly before pressing down on their companions. She brushed her fingers lightly over the crisp picture then scraped herself a peephole with her nails so she could look out into the quiet street below – it was pristine. She stroked her belly and spoke tenderly to her unborn baby, trying not to let her grief communicate itself to Alfie's child.

She washed quickly in the icy water from the ewer and hurriedly dressed, the tantalizing smell of bacon cooking spurring her on to join Gran and Ted where she knew there would be a blazing fire. For some reason that she couldn't quite fathom, all seemed well with her world. 'C'mon my darling,' she whispered, as she walked carefully downstairs, 'let's go and eat, I'm starving, and I bet you are too.'

66

A month later, Sally's dad and her uncle Arthur visited for a couple of days and stayed in a small local hotel. They didn't say so, but Sally was grateful that they'd come to make sure she was alright. Bill hadn't been angry with her, and he'd said very little about the pregnancy except it was a pity that Alfie had to die. Sally knew though, from a conversation with Gran after they'd returned to Leicestershire, that Bill was happy at the thought of becoming a grandfather. Both he and her uncle had given her some money to help buy things for the baby. They left after promising to visit again after the child was born. They didn't mention the fact that they were also going to visit Frank.

Once again, life settled into a familiar routine: work, home, and occasional visits with old friends. Ted didn't go out much, he usually sat reading, and listening with indulgent laughter to the excitement a finished baby garment would bring to Gran and Sally; the two people that he loved more than anything or anyone else. There was so much poverty in the surrounding properties, with many families having no wage earner or prospects of finding

269

employment that these garments often found a different home.

'We're the lucky ones,' Gran said, 'it won't hurt our little one to have one less matinee coat will it Sal?' Only too happy to pay back some of the kindness she'd received, Sally agreed, though she stroked each item lovingly before she parted with it.

As her bump grew, Sally was unable to hide her pregnancy, allowing people to speculate about her condition. She'd expected some adverse reaction, but not the venom directed at her on a couple of occasions.

She coped by ignoring the people involved until a woman she barely knew had referred to her baby as a little bastard and spat on the cobbles.

Sally lost her temper and smacked her full in the face, sending her staggering into the road. The visibly shaken woman pulled herself upright and began to scream at Sally that she should be ashamed to be seen out in her condition, and she'd have the police on her.

Sally was appalled by her reaction. She'd never so much as lifted a finger in anger to anyone – not even Frances no matter how spiteful her past employer had become. She ran the rest of the way home in floods of tears while holding on protectively to her belly.

She was relieved that no one was home as she sank into the fireside chair, gasping for breath. The baby was restless, pushing up little rippling hills that showed through her clothing. She stroked her abdomen gently, trying to soothe and reassure the child as she said aloud, 'No one's going to call you a bastard again my darling if I can help it.'

She scolded herself for not stopping until now to think what the stigma of being without a father would mean. The baby didn't deserve to suffer for the love its parents had given one another.

Before Gran arrived home, Sally had made her life-changing decision. If Edward still wanted her and the baby she'd marry him, the sooner, the better.

Despite Gran's sermon, that to marry in haste meant to repent at leisure, Sally and Edward wed at Birmingham Registry Office as soon as the obligatory twenty-nine days' notice had expired. They had a few hours off work and met up with Faith and Ted in Edmund Street. These two much-loved people were their witnesses at the brief ceremony. Edward gave Sally a bunch of African violets which she clutched in front of her bump so tightly that her hands ached. If it hadn't been for Faith's girlish giggles and good humour the marriage would have been a very sombre affair. Sally did her best to appear happy as did Ted, but they both found their painted-on smiles hard to maintain.

Ted was kicking himself thinking that maybe if he'd dared to ask her, Sally just might have agreed to marry him instead. He knew she wasn't in love with Edward, but by the time she'd told him her intention, he thought it was too late for him to tell her how he felt.

Edward was elated – he'd won her at last. He knew Sally had only agreed to marry him because of the baby, but he didn't care, confident she'd come to love him as he loved her. He didn't need to have anything to do with the baby, just give the child his name.

When they left the registry office, Faith went home to her two children who were being looked after by a friend. Sally, Ted and Edward returned to work by tram. They couldn't afford to take any more time off. Gran had said she would put on a bit of a tea for them to celebrate on the following Sunday. Sally felt that was more than enough.

Although Sally was upset because it was Alfie's image that was clear in her mind while she made her vows to Edward; she didn't regret her decision to put her baby first. She was very fond of Edward and hoped that he might be right, and she would come to love him as he desired. She promised herself that she'd show her gratitude, and be the best wife she could be to him.

Initially, they stayed with Gran. Ted willingly gave up his room to the married couple and slept for a few weeks on the sofa. But Sally found it very difficult to be such a burden to her friends.

Edward had told his mother the truth about the baby, and she'd said to him that he was a bloody fool, but he didn't care, he had what he'd always wanted.

On their wedding night, Sally had begged Edward to wait to consummate their marriage until after the baby was born. But he'd insisted, ignoring her embarrassment at the possibility they would be heard.

He turned out to be a considerate and tender lover, and to Sally's amazement, her body responded to his lovemaking, blotting out Alfie's image for a short time.

67

It suited everyone when Edward managed to rent two rooms on the first floor of a Victorian house on Stratford Road near to Stoney Lane. It had quite a few stone steps leading up to the front door causing Sally to pull a face and baulk at climbing them.

'C'mon you can do it, I'll help you,' Edward said. He took her arm, and they slowly made their way to their rooms.

Sally put her arms around his neck and kissed him on the lips for the first time of her own volition. Then said as she sat down on the bed, 'Thanks love, I'm not sure I could have hoisted this big bump up the stairs on my own.'

Edward laughed as she patted her abdomen and grimaced. 'You should know by now that I'll always be here to help you,' He leaned in to smell her hair; something he loved to do as the outdoors smell seemed to stay trapped in the coiled tresses that he thought were beautiful. Sally had said while they were staying at Gran's that she'd like to have her hair fashionably bobbed, but Edward was horrified at the thought and forbade her to do any such thing. Shc'd willingly obeyed; she'd wanted to please him and thought it wasn't important enough to fight over. Edward was

273

delighted that Sally had taken the initiative with a gesture of affection. Was she coming to love him, he wondered, while they organized their possessions into some semblance of home?

Sally had some items put by for her Bottom Drawer; the bundle contained things that would be useful when she got married. She'd been squirrelling odd pieces of linen and a few items of crockery, bought cheaply on the market, ready for her marriage to Alfie. Even though it wasn't as she'd planned, she was now glad of them. With the help and donations from relatives and friends: basic furniture, a bed, a table, two chairs, and a chest of drawers meant that they could start their married life in relative comfort.

Much to Sally's relief, Edward played his part as an expectant father convincingly, creating a shared intimacy between them. As he watched the ripples across her belly and felt the baby move, he realised he was genuinely looking forward to the birth.

The second week in June arrived and with it came Gran. She stayed to help Sally as she gave birth to her daughter. It wasn't a difficult birth, and Sally was soon fretting about lying in bed.

Edward fell in love with the pretty dark-haired child on sight and sat rocking her whenever he could. Sally was delighted, but Gran admonished him on more than one occasion saying, 'You'll spoil her, you see if you don't.'

Edward just laughed and took no notice at all. He never seemed to tire of separating her fingers and toes and gazing in awe at her tiny, shell-like nails.

After the second day of lying in, Sally took matters into her own hands, and while Gran was out shopping, dressed, and was sitting on the edge of the bed feeding her daughter, when she returned.

Gran tut-tutted a few times, called Sally a headstrong bugger, and said she'd make tea for them both, shaking her head as she turned away. 'You wouldn't have been allowed to get up if you'd been in hospital my girl, but you're young and healthy so ...'

Edward suggested that they call their baby Barbara. Sally loved the name, and they christened her Barbara Ann Griffiths in the heat of a gloriously sunny day in July. Sally put aside her vow, never again to enter a church, she didn't want her daughter to be different from her peers. She had, however, refused quite vehemently when Gran tried to insist that she make arrangements to be churched before the christening. The thought that she should be cleansed following her daughter's birth gave her another reason to become an agnostic.

Sally and Edward found that they liked living on the busy Stratford Road. There were plenty of shops where Sally was able to buy whatever they needed. She was within walking distance of Gran's house, so she was able to see her quite frequently. She valued her advice with Barbara, and Ted was turning out to be a wonderful uncle, just as he'd promised – ready and willing to help when necessary.

Since leaving school, Edward had worked for the same small, manufacturing company situated just off Bradford St. He'd started as a general runabout, and then after a few years had learnt how to operate a lathe. He was a hard worker who'd become skilled in many of the processes needed in the manufacturing of small metal items, and was now earning a good wage as a foreman. He was content to have Sally and Barbara waiting for him at home. Since Barbara's birth, Sally seemed to be happy too. Sometimes as Edward worked, he would count his blessings, bringing an involuntary laugh gurgling up in his throat. His mates' ribald teasing only made him feel happier, as he returned their remarks with, 'G'on you're only jealous.'

The rooms that they rented weren't ideal. Sally had to bump the pram up and down the steep steps unless there was someone else handy who would help her to carry it into the hall. Some of her neighbours moaned that it blocked their right of way. Edward told her not to worry; he'd deal with their complaints. He must have done so as Mrs Jenkins, an elderly lady, who lived in the room that was opposite to where the pram had to stay, smiled whenever she saw her, and no more complaints ever reached Sally's ears.

'What did you say to make her so amenable?' Sally asked her smug-faced husband a few days later.

Edward grinned. 'Oh, you know, just used my good looks and charm.'

Sally pressed him for more of an explanation, but he grabbed her around her waist and covered her face with kisses until she stopped asking. After Edward had stopped tickling her until she could laugh no more and begged him to stop, Sally realised that they were content together. Barbara was their talcum powdered glue – she held them both in her thrall.

Bill came to stay at Gran's during Christmas, and they all spent the whole of Christmas Day and Boxing Day vying to see who could keep Barbara's attention for the longest time.

276

'Go on you silly load of bugger's,' Gran said, as they passed the good-tempered baby around, 'you're treating her like a toy.' But she was careful to have her share of cuddles. Barbara was a blessing – she was a part of Alfie for everyone – except Edward who thought of her as his child.

68

Their happiness was short-lived; when she was nine and a half months old, Barbara contracted Gastro Enteritis from which she never recovered.

Edward did not know what to do. He thought that Sally would never get over the shock of losing her baby. He couldn't seem to get through to her. She became withdrawn, barely ate. She only slept fitfully and would wake abruptly, weeping noisily.

Sally couldn't believe that she'd lost Alfie's baby. While Barbara was alive she'd felt that she still had a part of him to love – now she had nothing except her memories. It wasn't that she couldn't sleep, she didn't want to sleep, afraid that even her memories would quickly fade. It was already testing to remember the details of his face. She didn't want that to happen to Barbara's face too. Her arms ached for the weight of her child, and her breasts leaked continuously. Even the Epsom salts she'd taken didn't seem to help dry up the milk.

When Edward came into her room, she wanted to scream at him to get out and leave her alone. She did so on one occasion, shouting, 'Why don't you fuck off and leave me alone.' Edward's face crumpled into tears. Sally immediately regretted her outburst. She hadn't sworn at him since the awful day in the park. Sally didn't usually swear and had never seen Edward cry. 'I'm sorry, I'm sorry, please don't cry Edward,' she said and burst into tears herself.

'You aren't the only one who's lost our daughter,' he whispered, rubbing his rough fists across his face.'

'I know, and I'm sorry, it's just so hard to bear. Come and lie by me – I do love you,' Sally said.

'I don't need to tell you how much I love you, Sal, you already know,' Edward said, as he lay in her arms.

Shortly after this, Gran persuaded Sally to drink milk laced with brandy to help her sleep, but it had little effect. She eventually asked Doctor Hughes to call, hoping he could tell them how to help her. He gave them a prescription for a sleeping draught to have made up at the chemist, but he said that there was little else he could do.

He took Edward aside and said, 'Time will help Sally and you, but there's nothing like filling the cradle again to ease a mother's grieving. I'd advise you to ensure that Sally quickly becomes pregnant again.'

Edward didn't tell Sally until over a year later what the Doctor's advice had been, but it proved to be good. When Sally held her second daughter in her arms, she tucked her firstborn away in her heart. They named their new baby, Margaret Alma. She didn't take the place of Barbara, but she brought her love with her. Edward felt the same rush of love that he'd felt for Barbara and again became a doting father.

As Sally's state of mind and figure improved, she wished she'd not been too self-conscious about her pregnant state to join in the street party that had taken place in Seeleys Road in May, to celebrate the Silver Jubilee of King George and Queen Mary. There had been organized fun and games for children and adults. Tables had been shoved together and covered in red, white and blue crepe paper: local children ate sandwiches, cakes, jelly and ice cream, treats that were supplied by their parents. As she'd watched from Gran's window, Sally had been amazed by the way everyone had dug deep into very shallow pockets to provide such a spread. Now she wondered if she was feeling a little isolated having given up the camaraderie of factory work and deliberated if it would be possible to go back. She didn't think that Edward would agree, so she tried to be content with her lot.

One day when Margaret was three months old, Sally was tucking her gurgling infant into her pram when her neighbour stopped her.

Mrs Jenkins laid a hand on the pram handle and said in a whisper, 'Now I don't want you to think I'm nasty,' she glanced nervously at the flight of stairs that led up to Sally's rooms, 'but I don't think you should let Mrs Field look after Margaret.' She glanced again up the stairs, a worried expression deepening the furrows across her mouse-like face with its large front teeth.

Sally stood with her mouth gaping. Mrs Field was a very nice, middle-aged woman who lived in a bed-sitting room above Sally and Edward's bedroom. On a couple of occasions, she'd been kind enough to mind Margaret for an hour or so while Sally shopped. Sally hadn't been looking forward to hauling the pram out into the rain and had been very grateful when Mrs Field volunteered her services.

She shook her head doubtfully at Mrs Jenkins. 'Why would you say such a thing? She's been nothing but kind to us.'

Mrs Jenkins pushed open the door to her room, grasped Sally's arm firmly, and dragged her forcefully inside, shutting the door quietly behind them.

'Whatever's the matter?' Sally asked. Her voice was unusually sharp – she didn't like to leave Margaret in the hallway on her own.

'Oh my dear, I don't usually speak ill of people, you know that, but I have to warn you.' She swallowed audibly, her hands shaking as she peered intently into Sally's surprised face. 'I'm sure you don't know,' she licked her dry lips, 'Mrs Field has advanced syphilis. That's what is wrong with her nose; some of it has been eaten away.' She paused and nodded several times as Sally's hand clutched her chest. 'That's why she keeps it covered up – she wants people to think her nose is burnt. It's what she tells those who ask, but I was a nurse for many years, and I've seen it.'

Sally stepped back from her, she knew instinctively that Mrs Jenkins was telling her the truth, but she didn't know what to say or do. She took a deep breath 'Thank you for telling me, but I really must get on now. My friend will be wondering where I've got to.' She fumbled with the doorknob and almost fell in her hurry to get back to her sleeping baby.

Mrs Jenkins shut the door, then opened it immediately. 'You won't tell her that I've told you will you?' she said, and again glanced at the stairs.

'No, no, of course, I won't.' Sally opened the stained glass and wood front door as Mrs Jenkins shut herself inside her room.

69

When Edward arrived home to their empty rooms, he thought that Sally had left him; she'd always been there with a meal waiting for him. He looked into the bedroom and saw with gut-wrenching relief that both hers and Margaret's clothing were still where they should be.

He knocked on Mrs Jenkins door, but there was no answer even though he could hear her wireless quietly playing cheerful music. No one else appeared to be at home in the building either. He hurried to Gran's where he thought he might find her. Sally met him at the door and threw her arms around his neck as she drew him into the front room.

'Don't be angry,' she said, 'I couldn't stay there a moment longer.' She told him what she'd learned from Mrs Jenkins.

'I've told her she's silly,' Gran called from the living room, 'but she won't listen.'

Edward shook his head. 'I'm not angry,' he smiled as he stroked her hair and then cuddled Margaret, 'but what are we going to do Sal, we can't stay here, there isn't room.'

Sally's lips narrowed stubbornly. 'You'll have to find us somewhere else Edward; I can't risk exposing Margaret to some awful disease; we've lost one child I'm not going to lose another,'

'Come and have some tea lad,' Gran called, 'it'll be getting cold.'

They went into the living room. Edward's head hurt as he gratefully ate the liver and onions that Gran had kept warm in a colander set over a pan of steaming water. He was so relieved that Sally still wanted to be his wife that he felt he'd do anything she asked. He racked his brain for a solution. Decent rooms that they could afford were hard to come by. He didn't know what he could do. He looked up as Sally sat nursing Margaret by the fire. He loved them so much; at times, his heart felt as though it would burst with it.

Gran proved herself to be the best friend that anyone could wish to have. When Edward had finished eating, and they were all drinking tea, she said in her gruff matter of fact voice. 'Sally and the baby can stay here Edward while you find somewhere else for all of you – Ted won't mind. It isn't the best solution maybe, but it's the best one I can think of if Sally is determined not to take Margaret back to live there.'

'Come home with me Sally,' Edward said. He sat forward in his chair and ran his long-fingered hands through his hair. 'I'll tell Mrs Field to keep away from you and Margaret. I'm not bothered if she's offended.'

'No, I just can't,' Sally shuddered and held Margaret close to her breast, 'I know I'm stupid, but I can't bear the thought of living under the same roof as that horrible woman.' Edward looked dejected as Sally shook her head vehemently.

'Hold on Sal; you don't know how she caught it, it may not have been her fault,' Edward said.

'I don't care how she caught it, and I don't care if I'm unreasonable, I'm staying here until you find us somewhere else to live.' Sally looked defiantly at her husband, her face suffused with angry red patches.

'Okay, calm down, you're upsetting Margaret.' He took the baby, who'd started to wail at the raised voices, and began to make soothing noises as he sat back down with her. She quieted, and Edward said, 'Alright Sal, have it your way, I'm too tired to argue.'

After a couple of weeks trying to find somewhere suitable for his family to live, Edward became more and more dispirited. The places that they could afford were little better than damp, dismal hovels with outside water closets. They would be living in squalor. In despair, he went to see his mother, who now lived in a modern Municipal house in Sunningdale Road, Tyseley. He didn't think that she would help them, but both Gladys and Elsie had married and had their own homes, only his youngest sister May lived there so he knew there would be room.

He was nonplussed when he told his mother the pickle they were in, and she immediately said, 'I don't blame Sally I wouldn't stay there either, brazen 'uzzy, she didn't get that filthy disease by herself now did she?' She lifted the lid on the scrag end of mutton that was simmering on the stove. The delicious smell filled the air making Edwards's stomach clench. 'Do you want some,' Minnie asked, abrupt as ever.

'Yes, please, Mom, I'm starving.' At that moment he could have flung his arms around her and hugged her, but he knew it wouldn't be welcome. She loved her children, but she wasn't an affectionate woman and had always warded off physical contact even when they were very young. Sure that she hadn't changed; Edward sat at the table and ate his fill.

Minnie waited until they'd finished eating before she said, 'I don't know Sally very well, but I'll not see you living in separate places. You can all come here until you find somewhere, or perhaps the Council can find you somewhere if we're overcrowded or something.'

'Thanks, Mom, I appreciate it,' Edward said.

'Well you'll all have to sleep in the small room, I can't see May wanting to give her room up,' she tilted her grizzled head to one side, 'perhaps she might have the baby in her room for you, you'll have to ask her.'

Edward had an idea that he'd have his work cut out to persuade Sally to move in with his family, but she just had to see sense, he couldn't stand being without them.

He needn't have worried as Sally readily agreed. Even though she wasn't keen on his mother, she liked May and his father, Harry. She'd missed the warmth that she'd shared with Edward and wanted them to be together again. Fortunately, there was a large garden shed where they were able to store their furniture.

Minnie seemed pleased to have them to stay, and Edward was optimistic about the temporary arrangement. Sally made an effort to get on better with her mother-in-law, and all seemed well again for a while.

70

Sally sat on the side of their bed being careful not to ruck the silky, flowered eiderdown that belonged to her mother–in–law. She drew her gaze away from the window that showed the miserable April drizzle and anxiously studied her husband, who was washing away the grime from his workday. He hated having dirty hands and cleaned his nails meticulously every evening.

Without turning his head, Edward started to talk. 'Looks as though the new King will be alright he certainly seems to care about us working class, they were saying at work today … '

'Edward, I need to talk to you,' Sally said. She was fidgeting with her handkerchief and chewing the soft tissue inside her lips.

Edward carried on cleaning his nails. 'Okay, I hope it's not about you and Mom again – is it?'

It seemed that all he heard lately was moans from one or other of them or anxious talk from his dad about the likelihood of there being another war. He breathed a sigh, and his shoulders slumped.

Sally echoed his sigh. 'No, but it'll cause trouble with her that I do know.' Edward turned to face her and saw her gloomy, set expression. He finished drying his hands and then sat beside her, digging her playfully in her ribs. She shrugged him off, got up, and took a couple of steps to the window and looked out.

Edward caught her by the hand and drew her down beside him again. 'What's up with you, eh? Cheer up it can't be that bad, can it?' He spoke in a jocular fashion, but he knew the cramped, overcrowded way that they were living was getting everyone down. There'd been quite a few heated exchanges between Sally and his mother recently, especially as Margaret was very whiny while cutting her teeth. Sally often resorted to putting her in her pram and taking her for long walks away from her mother-in-law, who was easily annoyed and not afraid to show it.

'Come on, love, what's the matter?' Edward stroked her silky hair.

'Stop!' Sally held onto his hand tightly, 'I think I'm pregnant again'.

Edward let out a noisy breath. 'Well that's nothing to be upset about, is it. We said we wanted another one, didn't we?'

'Yes, but your mom ...'

'Never mind, it's none of her business; I know it'll be difficult, but we'll manage. We need to get a place of our own.' He hugged her and patted her stomach over the top of her corset.

Sally hugged him back and leaned her head on his shoulder; a crushing weight had disappeared from her heart.

'When d'you think, eh?' He nodded, and raised his eyebrows, a wide grin parting his full lips.

Sally's face became troubled again. 'I'm not sure, but I think it'll be at the beginning of November. I dread to think what your mom will say.'

'Well you stay here, and we'll soon find out, won't we? Better to get it out of the way.' He went downstairs and broke the news to Minnie, then waited for the fireworks that never came.

She shrugged, put down the vegetable knife that she'd been peeling potatoes with and said, 'It happens.' She got up and threw a shovel full of slack onto the fire to damp it down, and then turned from the subdued flames to face her son. 'You'll have to leave here though – get a place of your own – you know that don't you?'

Edward nodded. 'I'll go down to the housing again on Monday if the boss will let me have a couple of hours off.'

'Well you tell them you've got nowhere to go, and I'm not 'avin you here any longer, that'll move you up the waiting list. Now call Sally to come and have her tea, May will be back in a minute, she's only walked up to the station to look at the timetable. Don't know what the fascination is; she isn't going anywhere.' She shook her head and laughed as she went into the kitchen from where the aroma of lentil and bacon bone stew wafted out in an invisible cloud.

Towards the end of her first trimester, Sally miscarried. At first, she was distraught, but Gran told her that it was nature's way of not allowing babies, who perhaps hadn't formed properly, to be born. It happened to quite a lot of mothers. Sally was comforted by this and held on to the fact that she had Margaret, who was becoming very entertaining and affectionate and much less whiny now that she'd cut a few teeth. Edward was very disappointed; he

289

had hoped that this pregnancy would give him the son that he wanted.

As time passed, he frequently had to intervene between Sally and his mother. He didn't always think the argument was of his mothers making either, but he invariably stood up for his wife.

71

The majority of that Christmas holiday, Sally, Edward and Margaret stayed at Gran's where the loving-kindness of their two friends further highlighted their untenable situation. Ted often arrived home with news of the latest preparations being made by the government in case there was war again with Germany. Hitler was increasing the German army and persecuting Jewish people and other minorities in any way he could, he reported. Gran wouldn't allow him to say too much as Sally became very anxious at the thought of another war which would cost the lives of yet another generation. She knew that Edward would be involved too, and felt that she couldn't bear to lose someone else.

Edward had been barking up the wrong tree with his prediction that King Edward VIII would be good for the country when just before Christmas 1936 he astounded everybody by abdicating. Even Sally was shocked at the news, and she had never taken any real interest in the goings-on of the Royal Family, she didn't feel that they were real people, but in some deeper part of herself knew she was jealous of their privileged life.

On his mother's advice, Edward had omitted to inform the Council that Sally had lost her baby, and in January 1937 to their delight, and everyone's relief, Sally and Edward were handed the keys to a new Council house not far from his mother's.

Sally's heartbeat quickened as she set eyes on their first real home. It was just off Fox Hollies Road at the end of a small cul-de-sac and situated opposite a grassed island. It had a large front garden and an even larger one at the back that led to the railway embankment between Spring Road and Tyseley station.

Two good sized living rooms led off the hall. The kitchen, which boasted a sizeable white crock sink, and a corner gas boiler was accessible through a door from the living room. Everywhere smelt new. Two steps dropped down from the kitchen door to the rubble-strewn, muddy garden. As Edward surveyed the empty expanse, his mind envisaged row upon row of vegetables that he would grow. Sally spent their first few hours, skipping from room to room admiring the front bay window, the three bedrooms, and a very modern bathroom.

The couple sat against the wall in the room that was to be their bedroom making plans for where the furniture would go, and how they could make their house a home. Then as it began to grow dark outside, they made love on the bare floorboards.

'I'll always love you Sal, and I'll try for a job at Lucas's. We'll need more money to make the place comfortable, and look nice,' Edward said, as they lay in spent closeness.

'I love you too, Sally said, snuggling down onto his strongly muscled arm, and I know you'll always look after us. Sally shivered, it was dark outside, but a half-moon shining through the square paned windows cast shadow patterns on the chimney breast wall. 'I think we'd better get dressed and arrange for our bits and pieces to join us, don't you? Your mother won't want to mind Margaret for too long will she?'

Minutes later the happy pair were running hand in hand over the railway bridge that separated Acocks Green from Tyseley. With their blood still zinging, they hurried to let Minnie and May in on the details.

Friends and relatives again rallied round to help them get settled. Elsie's husband, Bernie, a six-foot-seven strapping fellow borrowed a flatbed trolley from a friend, and almost single-handed carted their few items of furniture from Harry's shed to their new home. Harry insisted on giving him a few bob as a thank you. Bernie refused to take it initially, but he'd been out of work for a few months, and money was tight.

Edward was taken on as an experienced machinist at Lucas's and brought home considerably more money than he'd been able to earn at his old factory. It suited him well as Lucas's was within walking distance. He was sorry to say goodbye to his workmates but knew it was for the best, so amidst promises to keep in touch, he swapped one set of noise for another.

Sally made curtains from bright chintzy material for each of the windows and cut up old coats bought for coppers from friend's stalls in the rag market. She and Edward sat for hours each evening making rag rugs from old hessian sacks and cut up cast-offs, using half a wooden dolly peg as a tool, they soon helped to warm and brighten their home.

Sally wasn't the world's best cook, but did her best to produce cheap, tasty meals that she'd learnt how to make from her mom: stews, chips and egg, sausage and mash with fried onion gravy, and shortcrust pastry plate pies were her mainstays; with bread pudding, spotted dick, sago or rice puddings a few times each week as treats. She didn't mind cooking, but cleaning was something she only undertook when necessary.

Washing was the chore she hated the most. It was hard work while seeing to the needs of her daughter, and it left her feeling somewhat exhausted. She was always thankful when the weather was dry and bright, and she was able to dry a line of washing without having to fetch it in and put it out again between showers.

Except for wash day, Sally walked with Margaret in the pram down to the village to buy whatever shopping they needed for the day. She was never a chatty person; her very generous breasts were a source of embarrassment to her, making her shy with strangers. But a friendly smile and a twinkle in her eyes made her popular. People often stopped to pass the time of day with her. She made and remained lifelong friends with a family of three spinsters and their good-humoured father, who lived at the top of her road opposite another married sister called Betty.

Alice, Ede and Olive were all alike, just over five feet tall and blessed with ample figures. Although Sally came to be very fond of them all, Ede became her best friend and confidante. They often arranged to shop together and at times laughed uproariously while watching Margaret's antics.

'You're like a couple of cackling hens.' Mr Horton, Ede's father, often told them.

But they knew he enjoyed their happiness and loved Margaret as though she was his grandchild. He never said so, but Sally had the distinct impression that he wasn't keen on Edward. He always made an excuse to go out or sit in their front room with his racing paper whenever Edward called round to fetch Sally and Margaret home. Sally wanted to ask him about it, but couldn't pluck up the courage to put him on the spot, so she kept quiet.

72

One day Edward came in from the garden to find Sally sitting on the sofa darning a pair of his socks. He laughed, took the sewing from her hands and picked her up swinging her round in a circle almost banging her head on the corner of the cooking range wall.

'Put me down, put me down,' laughed Sally, 'you'll make me wet myself.'

Edward deposited her gently onto the settee and pretended to be out of breath. 'You know love you've made me the happiest man in the world.' He stroked her hair then knelt before her knees, leaning his head into her lap. He rubbed his cheek against the rough texture of her grey skirt and inhaled deeply, enjoying the fresh scent that was a mixture of her warmth, and her favourite Lily of the Valley eau de cologne.

As she stroked his head, she felt overwhelmed by the devotion that he'd shown towards his family. She sighed; it saddened her that he felt so much more for her than she still did for him. Her resolve never to let him know her true feelings strengthened. Sally knew she'd managed to convince him of her love, and she'd never willingly disillusion him she promised herself for the umpteenth time.

Margaret was in danger of becoming spoilt, Gran warned, as she was loved and indulged by everyone. Her hair had become a mop of light brown curls, and her face always had a chubby grin that brought chuckles of delight from her parents. Their house was rarely quiet until they were all asleep. Sally appreciated the friendship and the help Gran and the Horton family gave her. They frequently took Margaret off her hands for a while so she could get on with whatever needed doing.

Except for Elsie, Edward's eldest sister, and Gert and Albert, his great-aunt and her husband, Edward's family was conspicuous by their absence. There hadn't been a falling out exactly, but there was little help or friendship offered or requested. Sally thought that Edward and his mother were too alike for them to be close. Both were leaders with strong opinions and ways of getting things done. He had little in common with Gladys or May, and Sally was glad that they didn't see much of them, although she couldn't say why as they had never exchanged a cross word.

Elsie and Bernie lived relatively near and often came round for a game of cards or dominoes. Lexicon was the latest craze, but Sally preferred the old games that she'd grown up playing. On these evenings, which they all looked forward to, Elsie and Sally would indulge in a Babycham each while their husbands nursed a couple of pints of Ansell's brown ale. They took turns providing the cheese sandwiches that they enjoyed for supper. Elsie would bring hers already made up, wrapped in greaseproof paper with some chopped onion to top them. They considered themselves well blessed to be able to forget about the threat of war for a few hours.

Edward continued to adore his daughter, but he sometimes wished she'd been a boy. He spent whatever time he could with her, but it didn't amount to much. He was working long hours, and each evening as soon as he'd had his tea, he'd be busy in the garden. It no longer resembled a muddy building site. He'd sectioned it off into two plots, one where he'd planted vegetables, and the other where he'd dug in an air raid shelter made from arched corrugated iron sheets. Everyone was erecting them wherever possible, and there was a strong feeling that they would need them too.

Although the structure was fundamental, Edward had built in two narrow beds and had supplies of blankets, water and candles ready, just in case they were needed. He spent money they could ill afford on purchasing a wireless to keep up with the news.

It was money well spent as far as Sally was concerned, she listened to anything that was being broadcast on their wooden box, often shushing Margaret so that she could hear her favourite programmes.

'I don't understand too much of what they're talking about though,' she confessed to Edward, who smiled indulgently.

He didn't admit that quite a bit of information went over his head too. Neither had heard of many of the places mentioned.

In September, Sally and Gran met up at Ede's to celebrate the news that there wouldn't be a war as Mr Chamberlain had signed a peace agreement with Hitler.

'Don't you believe it, there's too much evil going on over there, you mark my words,' Mr Horton said, scooping Margaret up onto his bony knees where she snuggled up with her thumb immediately entering her mouth. After a minute, she offered her other thumb to Mr Horton who declined with a kiss on her cheek, and a broad grin on his face.

'Oh, don't be such a pessimist,' Alice said, 'just be happy you'll be able to sleep safely in your bed.'

Mr Horton said no more, just nodded knowingly, and began to play round and round the garden on Margaret's palm, making her giggle when tickled by the man she called Granddad.

That night Sally closed her book sharply enough to make Edward glance up and said, 'What do you think Edward, is there going to be a war or not?' Her voice was calm, but inward panic threatened. She'd just finished reading *The War of the Worlds* by H.G. Wells, and though she knew it wasn't real, it had seemed so realistic that she'd been trying to imagine a real war.

Edward placed his detective novel on the arm of his chair, and thoughtfully scratched the short beard that he'd recently allowed to grow. He didn't want to worry Sally, but he thought that there probably would be hostilities between Germany and Britain no matter the agreements reached.

He said in an offhand way. 'I think there may be Sal, but I don't think it'll be anything much to worry about.' He lit a cigarette that he'd rolled up earlier and blew the smoke out through his nose. 'Anyway, I need to read this,' he picked up his book, 'it's got to be back at the library by tomorrow, so stop worrying and go and check on Margaret, I thought I heard a noise.'

He spoke abruptly, and Sally felt a bit put out by his apparent lack of concern. She flounced from the room – shut the door and put out her tongue – pulling a silly face as though he could see her. Giving a silent laugh at her childish behaviour, Sally climbed the stairs, her worries put aside for the time being. Edward chose to ignore her behaviour; at least she would be able to stop being concerned about the future for the time being he thought, unknowingly echoing his wife's thoughts.

It was a relief to Edward when Mr Chamberlain declared that Britain was at war with Germany. He was glad that the shilly-shallying was over. Sally was terrified that she would have to evacuate Margaret to stay with strangers in the countryside, but Edward agreed that she should stay at home.

Early in 1940 Edward could be restrained no longer and joined The Royal Engineer Corps. Being quick to learn, after basic training, he was promoted rapidly through the ranks. He soon stood out for his leadership qualities, and when asked if he would like to train as an electrician at The School of Military Engineering in Ripon, he jumped at the opportunity. The training was intense, but an apt pupil, he passed his exams with high marks, and after a short home leave was posted to Leatherhead where he was able to put his new knowledge into practice. Further promotions followed until he became a Regimental Sergeant Major.

Although Sally had been distraught when Edward joined up, she secretly came to enjoy the break from married life.

She longed for his strength, however, when the Luftwaffe began their air raids that same year.

73

Daily living became harder and harder for Sally as with most people. Sleepless nights spent ensuring Margaret was safely in the air-raid shelter and the need to queue each day for food took their toll. She felt deeply indebted to her friends for all the support they gave her. Ede would often sleep at Sally's house to keep her company, and at times they'd watch the night sky with fascination as tracer bullets and searchlights formed strangely beautiful patterns overhead. Sally quickly became able to tell if the overhead plane was – one of ours or one of theirs – by the drone of the engines. She was grateful that Mr Horton, who was an air raid warden, always checked in on them to make sure they were safe.

On August 25, a cloudy Sunday night, bombs were dropped on Birmingham without respite and some of the houses in their small cul-de-sac were hit; including the Horton's next-door neighbours. The next morning Sally left the air raid shelter where she'd spent a terrible night. She'd cuddled Margaret while the high pitched whistle and explosions of falling bombs had ensured that they had no sleep – sure that they would be killed. She cried when she saw the devastation and realised how close they'd come to losing their friends, and their lives.

She put a protesting Margaret in the pram, and after picking her way through the knee-high smoking rubble, half ran, half walked to Greet to satisfy herself that Gran was unharmed. She felt a lump in her throat when she spotted Gran's house was undamaged.

Gran opened the door slowly, and she looked tired. Sally hugged her fiercely. 'You're okay, thank God.'

'Oh, my dear, I'm fine. I was worried about you and Margaret. The bombs seemed to be dropping Tyseley way.'

'It's okay they didn't get the goods yard. I think the bastard Luftwaffe missed their target; they'd have been after the railway lines,' Sally said.

'Come on I'll make a cuppa love,' Gran said, as she helped Margaret from the pram and Sally sank into an armchair.

Later, when Sally walked home, she saw more of the damage that had been wrought by the bombs. People were salvaging what they could from the destruction. An eerie air of calm hung over the bombed buildings. She could hear shouts of encouragement and the occasional laugh from a group of people in Stockfield Road where two houses were sagging and leaned dangerously towards each other. As she started to hurry past the blacksmith's, Sally was amazed to see that he was busy making something that she didn't recognise. She paused for a moment so that Margaret could enjoy the sight, the smell, and the hiss of the water as a hot metal object plunged into it. Margaret watched with fascination and asked for a repeat. The blacksmith laughed and rolled his eyes at her causing Sally to laugh too. She thought how peculiar it was that amid all the devastation, something so every day should continue as though nothing was amiss.

A few yards further on she came to a factory site on the corner of Fox Hollies Road where nothing remained standing – it must have been a direct hit – the crater where the bomb had struck was still smoking. She'd been past it many times, but couldn't recall what its purpose was, but she guessed it might have been manufacturing mattresses from the unburned bits of ticking strewn on the ground. The smell was awful, and it reminded her of the time when she'd singed one of Edwards shirts because she'd been distracted while ironing – this stink was much, much worse though. Thankfully Margaret had lain back and fallen asleep even though she had protested several times that she was too old to be in a pram. Sally hurried past and ran the rest of the way to her road. One look brought her to tears as two bodies were pulled from the wreckage of a house. These were people that she'd chatted to daily, and she felt helpless. Many people were milling about searching amongst the rubble. Sally averted her eyes and walked unsteadily home, where she rocked Margaret in her arms for some time as she cried out her fear and her sorrow for her neighbours. Margaret started to cry too, and stroked the tears from her mother's face. Sally found it hard to understand what the war was all about, no matter how much people explained it to her. She went to bed that night and knelt and prayed; something she hadn't done for many years.

When Sally went into the city centre for the first time in a while, she was dumbstruck as the bus passed through so much destruction. The centre had been badly hit in April; some of the Victorian buildings that were so familiar to her were reduced to twisted steel and rubble. She was distraught when she saw the damage done to the market hall. The stone walls, steps and pillars were still standing, but the beautiful glass roof had gone, as had most of its interior. Around her was devastation, but in its midst, the street traders were still plying their wares, determined that life should go on no matter what Hitler threw at them. To her relief, she saw that St. Martin's church was still standing. But couldn't bear to look at the damage that it had sustained. After buying a few necessary items, she took the bus back home where her daughter waited with her friend, Ede.

'I told you not to go, didn't I? It's a bloody mess,' Mr Horton said, as Sally mopped her eyes while describing what she'd seen.

'I wish I'd listened, I'm not going back again – ever,' Sally said.

Mr Horton laughed. Go on with you; it'll get re-built better than before, you'll see.'

It'll never be the same though,' Sally said.

'Well, there'll be more to come before this lots finished, just you try and stay safe, eh? Here give these to Margaret, she's out in the garden with Alice, and stop moping we're going to give as good as we get, and win.' He handed a bag of sweets to Sally as she dried her eyes and gave him a grateful smile.

74

The money that Edward sent home was more than Sally had ever had before, so she put aside as much as she could. She'd had a good role model in her mom. Her sensible upbringing had stood her in good stead when the rationing of butter, sugar, bacon, eggs, and other groceries had bitten deeply. She was able to feed herself and Margaret well.

Sally was always pleased to see her dad when he visited about once a month, sometimes accompanied by his brother, and always accompanied by their ration books. After a short stay, they would then go on to visit friends in Wolverhampton. She never knew which friends these were, and chose not to enquire. She'd learned, when young, that Bill wasn't keen on questions.

Towards the beginning of 1942, Bill's visits became more frequent. At first, Sally thought it was to see Margaret, but he stayed with them for less and less time before going to Wolverhampton. She eventually became curious and risking his disapproval questioned him more closely about his friends. He searched her face as he told her that he had a lady friend who lived there. He added with a grin that he was thinking of moving in with her.

'Yippee, that means we'll be seeing more of you,' Sally exclaimed.

Bill laughed. 'And I'm going to join the Home Guard there. I'd still like to do my bit as long as it isn't killing people. I can help to ensure that she's safe.'

Sally kissed his cheek. 'I'm proud of you; when am I going to meet her?

'Perhaps one day when I'm settled,' he said, looking a little sheepish.

'Oh, go on with you – I just hope she's nice – what's her name?'

'Olive Green – I think her parents had a warped sense of humour,' he said, looking very boyish. Although his skin was weather-beaten from working in the open, he carried his fifty years very lightly, and Sally told him so.

Even though there was a war going on and neighbours were losing not only their homes and possessions but their lives too; Sally no longer felt afraid. She'd survived so far, she reasoned, so perhaps her life was meant to go on. She counted her blessings every night and prayed to God that the war would soon be over, and life could return to normal.

In many ways, her life wasn't unhappy, she knew that she was one of the lucky ones, but she wanted the madness to cease. She adored her child, who was turning into a bookworm, had good friends, and enough money. Edward was doing well in the army, and he was able to come home on leave quite frequently.

A few weeks later, Ted was home on leave and listening in to one of his mother's and Sally's, hopes and fears talks.

'Don't become too complacent, everything changes, and not always for the better,' Ted said, peering over the top of his newspaper.

'Hush up,' Gran said, 'and come and have some cake.'

Sally and Gran had saved some of their ration coupons and put on a bit of a spread. Sally and Margaret were happily tucking into their second slice of homemade cake that tasted delicious; even though it was short on both eggs and butter.

Sally passed him a slice and kissed the top of his head as she started to help clear the table. She had no idea how that brief show of affection had made him feel as she said, 'How d'you fancy coming to visit Edward's aunt and uncle on Saturday with me? Give me a hand with Margaret; I know they'd like to see you again.'

'Do you mean the couple that are caretakers of those offices in Cherry Street?' Ted looked doubtful; he'd met them a couple of times, and wasn't enamoured.

'Oh please come, I've promised them I'd visit and take Margaret, they haven't seen us for ages, I feel guilty, but I hate going to town on my own now.'

Ted couldn't resist a plea from Sally and reluctantly agreed to go with them. He regretted his compliance when a well-dressed older woman walked up to him on their way through town and thrust a white feather into his hand. Sally was upset and swore at the retreating woman.

'Cheeky bleeder, just 'cos you aren't in uniform, how does...'

'Oh, don't let it worry you, Sal, I certainly won't. She's just a stupid, ignorant person living in the past, take no notice.' Ted shrugged and clasped Margaret's hand again. She'd let go, startled at the onslaught of the strange woman.

Seeing the bewilderment painted on her face, Ted tried to explain but found that he became bogged down.

'Just take no notice love, she's just an idiotic woman, he said.

'Yes she is, but she shouldn't be so nasty,' Margaret said and squeezed her uncle's hand.

Sally couldn't stop thinking about the injustice of the woman's actions. Ted was in the army, and he didn't care about being accused of being a coward. But what about the men who weren't in the forces through no fault of their own, she thought, how would they feel?

For the first time in her life, Sally wanted to do something about what had happened. She couldn't believe that the woman had any right to behave as she had; she knew it had happened frequently during the Great War, but the feminist movement no longer believed in the unfair practice.

After a few days mulling it over, Sally wrote a lengthy letter to the editor of the *Birmingham Mail* explaining what had happened and how it made her feel. She never received a reply but was gratified to see an article shortly afterwards condemning the handing out of white feathers, and reminding people that not all men in civvies should be in uniform.

'Hello there,' Ede smiled at Edward as she beckoned him into the hallway. 'Sally there's a handsome man in a very posh uniform asking for you,' Ede called out to her friend who was playing with the family cat on the floor in the living room. Sally jumped up in surprise, she knew it must be her husband, but he wasn't due for home leave until the following week. She hurried into the hall. Edward looked handsome, and very much the distinguished NCO. There was something different about his uniform, Sally noticed, but she couldn't quite put her finger on it.

'Hello, darling.' She moved into his embrace and returned his ardent kiss. 'What are you doing home?'

'Fetch Margaret, and I'll tell you when we get home. Where is she?' he asked. Margaret would typically run to greet him when she heard his voice.

'She's in the garden, Mr Horton made her a swing for the apple tree,' Sally said.

'Daddy,' Margaret cried. She'd heard his voice, raced in and threw herself at Edward's legs

'Eh, steady on, you'll have me over,' Edward said, laughing at her enthusiasm, 'get your coat we're going down home.'

'Alright tell me what's going on?' Sally prodded, as they walked the short distance to their house; waving to a couple of neighbours on their way.

Edward touched the end of his nose playfully. 'You'll know soon enough, let me get in and get these boots off.'

Sally asked no more questions until Margaret had been fed and tucked up in bed. Her protest that she was old enough to stay up another half an hour fell on deaf ears as usual.

'Are you going to tell me what's up or not?' Sally said and frowned at her husband. He looked tired as he sat in his armchair by the fire.

He spoke in a choked voice. 'I'm only here for two days, love. I've been transferred to the Royal Electrical and Mechanical Engineers Corp, and I'm being posted to where I'm most needed. I don't know where yet, but it's abroad – somewhere hot – we now have light uniforms to wear.' He took a deep breath. 'I don't want to leave you and Margaret Sal, but I don't have any choice. Fucking, bloody, sodding war,' he burst out and put his head in his hands.

Two days later Sally and Margaret watched tearfully as Edward, receiving a salute from the uniformed driver, got into a khaki coloured jeep with open sides, and started his unwilling adventure.

Neither had any idea that it would be almost three years before they would meet up again, and their feelings would be very different.

75

Before Edward left for his posting, he showed Sally a simple way for them to communicate secretly with each other. They worked out a code by picking individual pages and lines from *The Wind in the Willows*. In this way, he was able to inform her that he had been redeployed to Ceylon. He never attempted to tell her anything about the war with Japan, so other than infrequent private love messages; she was ignorant of his day to day tribulations. She never knew how he'd managed it, but she was overjoyed when she received a small wooden crate containing rich aromatic tea. There was no letter with it, and no sign where it had come from, but hidden at the bottom were two small ebony elephants, and a photograph of Edward dressed in a smart, white uniform and standing by the side of a jeep. His hand was indicating the letters SALMARED painted in white on its side. Initially, Sally thought it must be a Tamil word, but laughed at herself when it dawned on her that it was a word made up of their names. It touched her that even from the other side of the world, his thoughts and love were with them. She couldn't wait to show Margaret and tucked the photo away in her handbag.

After admiring the photograph of Edward, Ede accompanied Sally to fetch Margaret from school. They hurried down Warwick Road past St. Mary's church and were on time to meet her as she came out of the Westley Road entrance of Acocks Green School. When she showed the photo to her daughter, Margaret quickly planted a kiss on it, leaving wet marks on her father's face before Sally could stop her. Margaret clapped her hands as Sally pointed out the significance of the initials. They all chattered away as they stood in the queue at Wrenson's grocery shop with Margaret asking questions that Sally or Ede did their best to answer. Aware that they were overly noisy, Sally told Margaret to be quiet and promised that if she didn't speak again until she spotted a dog with no tail, she could have sixpence.

She remained dumb, eyes on stalks as they walked up the hill towards home. When they turned the corner into Broad Road, Margaret stopped walking and folded her arms. 'There's no such thing is there, Mom?'

Sally laughed and apologised. 'Well it kept you quiet anyway, and if you're good, I have got a lollipop for you after you've eaten your tea.'

Mollified Margaret skipped a few yards ahead towards the end of Westfield Road.

'Mind the 'orse road,' Ede called sharply.

'Only one doll and put your coat on now,' Sally admonished her daughter. They were going to spend the day in town at Gert and Bert's, and Margaret wanted to take all her precious toys with her.

Gert had written Sally a lovely letter asking her to come, and visit. Sally wasn't too keen on taking Margaret on the forty-four bus into town to visit relatives that she wasn't keen on, but she hadn't been since the time that Ted had accompanied them, so she felt unable to refuse. There was something about both Bert and Gert that seemed to be a trifle shifty. They always dined well and never seemed to have a problem with rationing. Sally wondered if they were involved in the black market, but she didn't want to know.

Once again, there was plenty of lovely food, and as they all tucked in, Gert told them that they were expecting her nephew to visit later that day.

'You haven't met Harold, have you, Sally? He's my youngest sister's lad; he lives in Mold in North Wales, but the company that he works for have seconded him to Olton while the war's on. I'm not sure what he does, but he's needed there. It's not far from where you and Edward live, is it?'

'No, we've never met.' Sally looked away and rolled her eyes. She was reluctant to meet anyone new. She was feeling tired after a disturbed night. Margaret had woken from a dream about a big pink pig that was trying to eat her leg, and it was some time before Sally was able to calm her.

Sally needn't have been concerned; Harold came across as a charming young man who spoke with a lilting Welsh accent. He had acne, but it didn't make him shy. He shook her hand vigorously, hugged his aunt, and then endeared himself to Margaret by making a coin disappear from his hand and appear in one of her ears.

As the afternoon wore on and it looked as though it might rain, Sally thanked Gert for a lovely time and said she should be thinking about taking the bus home. Margaret was becoming tired too, and not a little grumpy.

'Oh, don't go yet, I'm sure Harold will give you a lift home, won't you Harold?' Gert said.

'Yes, of course, I'd be delighted. The car's only just up at the end of the Street. I'm working in Olton at the moment, so it's on my way home anyway. We should go soon – it looks very unsettled outside.' He playfully tangled his fingers in Margaret's hair, but she shrugged him off and went over to her mother and leaned against her legs.

'Can we go home now please – on the bus?' Margaret said in a tired voice.

Sally looked relieved, 'Yes darling I –'

'I'll fetch the car; will you be ready by the time I'm back?' Harold said.

'Are you sure you don't mind, we could easily go on the bus, it's not started raining yet – perhaps it won't.' She didn't fancy being in a small car with a stranger even if they were distantly related.

'Of course, I'm happy to be of service,' Harold said, and ran off down the stairs, past the darkened row of offices, beneath the flat. Sally passed Margaret her coat, and after saying goodbye, they walked slowly down the stairs to where Harold's car was waiting for them, its choke pulled out, sending fumes belching from its exhaust.

Sally was relieved when Margaret asked if she could sit in the front seat. She quickly agreed and squeezed herself into the back of the small, Ford Anglia car.

76

When they pulled up outside Sally's house, she intended to thank Harold, and settle Margaret down as quickly as she could, but before she could say anything, Harold walked round to her side of the car and helped the sleepy child from her seat. He held onto her arm as he locked the car. Sally stood, mouth slightly agape wondering what he intended.

She attempted to take Margaret from him; stammering her thanks in a rush of words that she could never remember afterwards.

'It's okay,' Harold said, 'I'll help you in with her, you look all in.' He smiled disarmingly as he started to walk down the path to the front door.

'No, it's really alright, Harold, I can manage,' Sally said firmly. But Harold ignored her and continued down the path. She pushed past him, put her key in the lock and opened the door – nearly going headlong over the doormat in her haste to avoid letting him in. She reached for Margaret again, but he shepherded her before him, causing Sally to step back out of their way. He then entered with a protesting Margaret and shut the front door. Sally felt very uneasy having him in the house – she knew that Edward wouldn't like it – and she didn't want him there.

'Come on, Sally, let's get young Margaret to bed, and then you can make me a cuppa before I go home if you don't mind that is.' He smiled and let go of Margaret's arm. Margaret staggered as he released her from his firm grip. He laughed and then walked over to the window where he stood looking down the garden. 'Nice bit of land you've got here. Has Edward been growing beans and peas?'

Sally knew he could see the tall sticks standing up like tent poles where late beans that she'd planted were still flourishing. She didn't know what to do to get rid of him, he was family, and she didn't want to be ungrateful, but she was becoming very concerned. Margaret was nearly asleep on her feet and said, 'I'm going up now, Mom, okay?'

'Mm, yes,' Sally said, 'I'll be up in a minute to say goodnight, don't forget to brush your teeth, love.' She turned to Harold and said, 'I think you should go now. I'm exhausted; would you let yourself out, and I'll see you next time at your aunt's.'

She turned away and went to the stairs. She stood with her hand on the newel post for a moment trying to decide if she should go next door and ask for help. But she couldn't just leave Margaret on her own, and anyway she was worrying unnecessarily He would go soon if she were firm with him. She climbed the stairs slowly and went into the bathroom – she needed to pee. She lingered as long as she felt she could. She hadn't heard the front door close and knew that she had to go and face Harold and insist that he left immediately. When she looked in on Margaret, she was asleep. Sally leaned down and kissed her daughter's silky hair. She felt worried, but she wasn't sure what was worrying her. He seemed a nice enough chap, he hadn't done anything untoward really, but she felt quite strongly that something about him wasn't above board.

She ambled down the stairs holding onto the wide bannister; her heart was drumming in her chest as she pushed open the living room door and went in. Harold was sitting in Edwards chair flicking through an old *Life Magazine* that had been lying on the floor where she'd left it.

'There you are,' Harold said, 'I thought I was going to have to make the tea.' His friendly smile allayed Sally's fear somewhat.

'I'll make the tea, then you'll have to go, I don't want the neighbours talking about me,' she said, trying to keep a light tone to her voice. 'My friend from up the road usually pops in for a cuppa about this time. Listen out for the door, will you?' Harold nodded and continued to read the magazine.

Sally went into the kitchen and closed the door behind her. She was acting silly; he just wants a cup of tea then he'll leave. She hated the way he made her feel so uncomfortable and wondered if he'd believed the lie about Ede popping in.

'Thanks,' Harold said, as she handed him a flowery cup and saucer, 'aren't you having a cup?'

'I'm not thirsty, and I've got to fold all this washing ready to iron in the morning.' She didn't look at him as she pulled clothing from the wooden horse, and placed it carefully on the table. She sensed rather than saw that Harold had come to stand right behind her. She stepped away from him, but he followed her and placing his hands on her shoulder, tried to draw her towards him. Sally stood her ground.

She threw his hands off her and moved to the other side of the settee. 'I don't know what you think you're doing, but you'd better leave right now.'

'Come on, I want you Sally, and I know you want me too,' He said. Sally couldn't believe what she was hearing.

'You must be mad. I want nothing to do with you, now fuck off and leave me alone. You wait 'til I tell Edward about this, he'll fucking kill you. Get out, go on, go,' Sally said. She pushed him towards the door into the hall with all her strength.

Harold sidestepped, and punched Sally in the face knocking her back against the kitchen door. He stood looking at her then seemed to reach a decision. He grabbed her arms and pulled her off balance onto the floor. Sally struggled to get up, but Harold punched her again and again until she passed out. When she came to it was to feel Harold as he penetrated her. His breath was hot on her face —he gruntingly thrust in and out—while mauling her now naked breasts.

Sally had never felt fear like it; she went limp, afraid that if she cried out, he might kill both her and her daughter. It was over quite quickly, and Harold rolled off her. He stood while wiping himself on his handkerchief and adjusting his clothes.

'You shouldn't have led me on, and you wanted it. I know you did, and you're nothing but a prick tease.' He was red in the face his spots standing out alarmingly as he tried to excuse himself.

Sally didn't move. 'Just get out you bastard,' she said, through clenched teeth.

He threw his soiled handkerchief onto her face, 'Let me know when you need seeing to again – you know where I'm working,' he said. He stepped over her and went out, slamming the door behind him. Thankfully Margaret slept through it all.

Sally was never again, so glad to hear a door shut.

77

Sally gagged and knocked the handkerchief off her face. Her thoughts were like tangled skeins of wool clogging up her brain. She remained where she was, lying on the icy linoleum – she didn't feel the cold – just a dull emptiness inside her. Time ticked by undisturbed until her numbness began to fade, and she felt a draught of air hitting her exposed body. She sat up gingerly, pushed her breasts back inside their support, and buttoned her pink blouse. Her knickers were around her ankles, her skirt and underskirt pushed up above her thighs. She gave a thought to the sad fact that she had no stocking that might be laddered. The idea almost made her smile – almost.

She held onto the back of the settee and pulled herself upright. Her face throbbed, her lip was split, and she tasted blood as she swallowed.

As soon as she felt able, she adjusted her lower garments and hobbled to a chair by the table. She sat with her head resting on her hands; she could feel hot tears start to sting her bruised eyes as they gushed down her pale cheeks.

Question after question ran through her mind. How had she let this happen? Was it her fault? Had she shown him any encouragement? On and on, she tormented herself until she felt a wave of anger wash over her. She wanted to kill him, how could he do what he had? She hadn't shown any interest in him. He'd seemed so friendly and helpful with Margaret – but her memory jolted, she hadn't trusted him. Deep down, she thought she should have known.

She stood and looked in the oval mirror that hung on the wall by the hall door. Her left eye was swollen, almost shut, and her other eye didn't look much better. She began to walk toward the kitchen door, intent on having a wash and making a cup of tea when a familiar knock sounded on the front door. She knew it was Mr Horton coming to check on them.

Her footsteps dragged—she couldn't let him see her like this—but she answered the knock, opening the door a few inches. She knew he wouldn't go until he'd made sure that she was alright.

'Hello ... please don't look at me,' Sally held her hands over her face, 'will you fetch the girls for me?' She started to sob, the promise not to let this rape get to her that she'd made while lying exposed on the floor, fled as she saw his concern.

'Whatever's the matter, love?' He couldn't see her face; there was no light. Everyone knew better than to draw attention to their road.

'Please, Mr Horton, I'm desperate, please fetch them now.' Sally leaned against the doorpost – she felt too weak to stand.

'You go and make a pot of tea love, and I'll be back in a couple of minutes.' He hurried off, and Sally sat down gingerly on the stairs, her hands in her lap.

She didn't have to wait long before all three of her friends arrived breathless and anxious.

Sally leaned her head back against a cushion while Ede placed cold tea compresses on her eyes.

'Can you tell us what's happened, Sal?' Ede asked and gently patted Sally's arm as they listened intently to her. Between their gasps and her fresh outbreaks of sobbing, she managed to tell them how Harold had beaten and raped her.

There was a nearly a minute's silence after she finished speaking, then all three sisters expressed their horror.

Ede stood up. 'You need to go to the police Sal – c'mon let's get your coat – I'll go with you, Alice and Olive can stay with Margaret.'

'No, I'm not going anywhere,' Sally said. She shook her head slowly and then gulped the tea that Olive had made. She winced as it touched her mouth.

'But he can't be allowed to get away with it Sal,' Ede said, taking Sally's trembling hand in her chubby one.

'It's no use I just couldn't – I don't want anyone but you three to know. I was foolish to let the bastard bring me home. Please don't try to make me, I couldn't go out looking like this, and I need a bath.' She shuddered and looked at each of the three women in turn.

'Okay,' Alice said, 'I know it's a bit late, but I'll light a fire, and it'll soon have the water hot enough.' She raked the ashes, and shovelled them into an old bucket, then reached into the coal scuttle and began screwing newspaper into short lengths and placing them in the grate.

When the fire was roaring up the chimney and starting to heat enough water for Sally to bathe, Ede said, 'I'll stay here tonight,' she stood up slowly letting go of Sally's hand, 'we'll see how you feel about it in the morning. I'll just go and fetch my things. Will you be alright for ten minutes?' Sally nodded and winced at the sudden movement.

'Can I borrow your camera Olive?' Ede asked her sister.

Olive nodded. 'I think there's still some film in it, are you taking a photograph of Sally's face?'

'Just in case we need to show what state he's left her in – vicious bastard,' Ede said.

Sally started to protest but thought better of it; she wanted to let her friends organize her, and their kindness soothed some of her hurt.

'Will you take Margaret to school in the morning?' Ede asked Alice.

'Of course,' Alice said, 'we'll come up home with you, and give Sally a chance to catch her breath,' she touched their friend's face gently, 'your poor face Sal, I could cry for you; the bastard, how can men be such animals?'

'Not all are,' murmured Olive, as they went into the hall.

It was nearly three weeks before Sally ventured outside again. Her friends had been wonderfully supportive, one or another would do the shopping, take Margaret to school and fetch her home every day.

Sally's bruises had almost disappeared; now showing faintly as dirty yellow marks. She continued to refuse to report Harold; she didn't want the neighbours or Edward to find out how foolish she'd been. She swore to her friends that she'd never go to Gert's place again. She didn't want them to know what had happened either just in case they told Edward.

It was some time before Sally ceased to jump whenever there was an unexpected knock at the door. She got into the habit of looking through the front room window before she answered. As the external bruises faded and her lip healed, she forced herself to stop dwelling on the past, and their lives eventually returned to normal, at least on the surface.

78

At the beginning of that very cold December Gran, Sally, Margaret and Ted, who was on leave, bundled themselves up in their warmest clothing and went by bus to Cannon Hill Park. Sally made boiled egg sandwiches which she told her daughter was lunch for them and the ducks. Sally and Gran chatted away while Ted ran about playing a ball game with Margaret as if there was no age difference between them. Whoever dropped the ball had to go down on one knee, then throw and catch the ball with one hand behind their back. It was causing shouts of laughter. Margaret had not been out after school for a while, and Sally felt guilty. She'd only thought of herself and not spent very much time considering her daughter's needs – hence the visit to the park.

After about an hour, Sally shouted them to come and eat. They pelted towards her, both more than ready for some lunch. Sally opened the greaseproof wrapping on the sandwiches and passed them around. They were all munching away merrily when the smell of the boiled eggs made Sally feel nauseous. It was a smell that always amused everyone. It's just like farts Margaret often said before being shushed by the adults. Sally usually quite liked the eggy smell, and she'd felt fine while making them up, but she could feel bile rising into her throat as the stink of sulphur wafted over her.

'Eh, love, what's the matter, you look pale. Are you going to be sick?' Gran asked, brushing crumbs off her long black skirt onto the ground.

'No I'm alright just a bit of a tummy upset; perhaps that bit of fish I had last night was off.' Sally rubbed her stomach. 'I think perhaps we'd better call it a day. The cold's beginning to get into my bones anyway and I don't want to be poorly on the bus.' She stood up and stamped her feet.

'Come on then I'm gettin' a bit chilly as well,' Gran said.

Sally managed to control her nausea on the way home, but she was glad they had gone to the park when Margaret smiled broadly at her.

'Thanks for taking me Mom I've had a great day.' Margaret said, as they left the number one bus in the village, and crossed the road to wait with Gran and Ted for the bus that would take them home. Sally smiled and kissed the top of her daughter's head.

'What about me?' Ted asked, pulling a cheeky face and leaning his head forward. They all laughed at him and his playfulness. Gran and Ted had kisses all round as they said goodbye, and then Sally and Margaret watched, waving madly as the forty-four bus pulled away. Margaret tucked her arm in Sally's, and they walked home in companionable silence. Sally still felt a little unwell and thought that perhaps the crisp air might help.

By the following week, Sally knew she didn't just have an upset stomach; she had morning sickness. She was pregnant. She sobbed as she listened to a new song on the wireless called "We'll Gather Lilacs." She knew there wouldn't be any gathering of lilacs for her, whatever happened.

Christmas 1942 came and went. Sally no longer felt unwell, and she was bursting with energy. The house had never been so clean and tidy. Inside though, she was filled with dread at the thought of telling Edward that she was having a baby. She knew she wouldn't be able to hide it for much longer; she was starting to show. She understood from when she'd been carrying Margaret that she shouldn't lace herself into her corset as it might make labour more difficult and possibly damage the baby, so that wasn't an option.

Early in January Sally arranged to go to the cinema with Ede to see *Brief Encounter* with Trevor Howard, an actor that Ede liked. Alice readily agreed to babysit. She loved looking after Margaret, not that she needed much looking after these days.

Sally deliberately hadn't told her friend about her predicament in the hope that she would miscarry, but she knew that it was time to enlighten her. When they left the cinema, they linked arms and started to walk home. Sally reluctantly launched into telling Ede about the pregnancy. Talking about it made it seem real for the first time, and Sally found herself crying useless tears once again. She dashed them fiercely away with her hand, determined to cope in a better way with her problems.

'Oh my Lord, oh, I'm so sorry, Sally,' Ede said.

They stopped walking and leaned against the wall of Stone Hall, a mellow looking building attached to the

Senior School. Sally lit a cigarette for them both and passed one to Ede, who took it and inhaled as though her life depended on it. She didn't know what to say, or do to help her friend and said so.

'There's nothing anyone can do I'm going to have to tell Edward, aren't I? I can't bear the thought, and he's over there doing God knows what, could be killed anytime and I've let him down so badly.'

'Don't say that, don't even think it. You know it wasn't your fault, Harold's a relative, how could you have known he'd be a bastard?' Ede swore vehemently.

Ede's defence of her touched Sally deeply; her gratitude was reflected in her eyes as she surveyed her friend's kindly face. 'Thanks for that Ede, but I still don't know how I'm going to tell him.' She sighed deeply, ground out the cigarette end on the pavement, and then picked the nub up and threw it over the garden wall. Ede followed suit.

'Come on home; it's too cold to stand here any longer, let's get Olive and join Alice, four heads are better than two,' Ede said.

Sally related the news to Olive and Alice. When the initial shock had worn off, they sat drinking hot tea and eating a luxury piece of buttered toast while they all tried to think how best to write to Edward.

'Well, I had the picture, which I took of your black eyes, developed, so you can send him that,' Ede said. 'Why don't I write and tell him what happened, instead of you?'

Sally shook her head. 'That's kind of you, but it has to be me, the photo would be helpful though.'

After another half an hour passed without any feasible ideas, her friends left, promising to give her whatever support she needed. Sally went to bed with all the fruitless

329

suggestions, though kindly meant, spinning around her tired mind.

79

Writing to Edward proved to be less painful than Sally had imagined. It proved to be a cathartic experience. She sent him the photo and informed him in a matter of fact way what his nephew had done to her. She told Ede after she'd posted the letter that it felt helpful because she'd re-lived all the horror of that evening without crying, or feeling too sorry for herself. Waiting for Edward's reply though was nerve-wracking. Sally rushed into the hall, looking for some post at the slightest noise.

As the weeks went by with no word from Edward, the constant worry affected Sally and Margaret's daily lives. Following nights when Sally had little sleep, she found it difficult to drag herself out of bed in the morning and see to her daughter. Fortunately, Margaret was turning into a bit of a treasure, not only would she get herself ready for school, but she often made breakfast of toast, or fluffy egg made with egg powder, for them both.

When the letter did arrive one Saturday morning in March, Sally was lying on her bed with her eyes shut. Margaret came running into the bedroom, jumped energetically onto the bed and cried, 'It's a letter from Dad, wake up. Wake up, Mom; it's a letter, can I open it, please, please, can I Mom?'

Sally sat up immediately and took the letter from her outstretched hand. 'No, you can't you noisy bugger, clear off and shut the door on your way out.' She spoke more sharply than she intended.

Margaret went out and slammed the door behind her. Upset because she didn't know what she'd done wrong; her mother didn't usually speak to her like that unless she'd done something awful. Feeling confused Margaret went into her bedroom and flung a book across the room onto her bed, and rapidly followed it. She was feeling tired of her mother's strange behaviour; she didn't know why Sally was often crying or why she was so short-tempered these days.

Sally went to the bathroom, leaving the letter unopened on the bedside table until she returned. She sat on the edge of the bed and tore the envelope open with shaking hands. She quickly skimmed its contents, and then read slowly through it again.

███████

March 4th, 1943

Dear Sally,

I know it's taken me an age to reply to your letter. I've been in ██████████ *didn't get it until a few days ago. I'm horrified at what Harold did to you. You must have been in a lot of pain. Thank god for Ede etc.*

What I don't understand is why it's taken you this long to tell me about it. It's hardly something you could keep quiet about, is it? It makes me wonder if this is really what happened. Did you flirt with him? Is that why he got the idea that he could screw you?

I've been away a while, did you feel the need of a man? Is that what this is all about? Why would you let him into the house? I don't know how you expect me to feel, but I took on one man's bastard, I'm not taking on a second you can be certain of that. You'd better make sure it's not there when I get home.

Give my love to <u>my child.</u>

I do love you Sal, but at the moment I'm struggling to think why.

Edward

After reading it through twice, Sally tore the letter into shreds and tossed them onto the dressing table. She was furious, furious with him for not believing her – but even more so –for calling Barbara a bastard. He'd not been talking about her like that when persuading her to marry him, or when he'd said he loved her as his own. She felt as though he'd killed Barbara with his own hands. She sobbed, a painful lump blocking her throat. Her tears were not for herself, but her memories of Alfie and his child.

The child, Sally, was carrying shifted uneasily inside her. Reminding her it was there, and pulling her out of her misery. She blotted her tears and forcefully said aloud, 'No more, fuck him, I don't need him.' The content of his letter wasn't entirely unexpected, she knew he had a jealous nature, but she was devastated by the words he'd written. She decided that from then on, she'd stand on her own two feet; she didn't need a man to look after her.

Later that day Sally showed the letter that she'd taped back together to Ede. She shook her head as she handed it

333

back to Sally. 'I hoped he'd be more understanding Sal, and I'm so sorry, what are you going to do?' she asked.

Sally leaned forward and placed her empty teacup on the table. 'Well I know what I'm not going to do – I'm not apologising or crying any more. It wasn't my fault – I did nothing to provoke his attack. Edward can go to hell as far as I'm concerned. I don't suppose he's been an angel while he's been away he's too fond of his cock.' As she said the word cock, Ede gave a sharp intake of breath and caught Sally's eye. They both burst out laughing.

'Well good for you, we'll get through this – you won't be on your own Sal. What are you going to do about the baby?'

'Have it adopted,' Sally said slowly, 'I think it's the best thing to do. It'll be hard because I know I'll love it. It's not the baby's fault how it was conceived, and it deserves to be loved by two parents. I've thought a lot about it; if Edward comes home still feeling the same, God knows what he might do. I've Margaret to think about, haven't I? It's not fair for her to have to put up with his temper, and I know he'll never let me leave him even if I'd anywhere to go. It's not as though I have a mom to go home to, is it?' Sally breathed deeply. 'Mom scrimped and saved so that I'd have a home of my own, but when Uncle Jim died, he didn't leave a will, and everything went to that gold-digging French bitch he married. I know one thing though I'm not feeling sorry for myself anymore. I've more backbone than that.'

True to her word, Sally organised a private adoption with a couple who lived in a large detached house in Sutton Coldfield. She'd been introduced to them before her confinement and believed they would make good parents.

Sally made a promise to them that she would never make herself known to the child, and Mrs Malvern said she would send her some photos occasionally.

When her son was born, Sally held him for a couple of minutes before handing him to the adoptive parents via the midwife who had made the introduction. As she held him in her arms, Sally was overwhelmed with love for him. He was so beautiful she wanted to change her mind and keep him, but all the reasons that had made her decide on the adoption were valid.

Gran held her close while she cried afterwards, patting her back and reassuring her that it was for the best. But Sally knew she'd never get over the heartrending parting with her flesh and blood to other people, however caring they were. Sally wrote briefly to Edward to inform him of the birth and adoption. Her letter was terse and factual. She couldn't imagine ever living happily with him again.

Two days after Sally signed the adoption papers finally letting her son go, a letter arrived from Edward apologising and telling her not to have the baby adopted. But Sally was glad she'd already signed. She wouldn't have wanted her son to be unloved, by the man who brought him up, and she believed that Edward would treat him differently to the way he treated Margaret.

Margaret was the only one to ask where the baby had gone as Sally became noticeably thinner. Sally told her that she'd only been doing a favour for friends who couldn't have children of their own. This story seemed to satisfy her. She was many years older before she heard the truth from another child at school.

80

As Sally had feared, the husband who had gone to war wasn't the same man that came home on leave in 1945 following his deployment to England. After greeting Margaret and Sally pleasantly enough, he sent his excited daughter out to play in the garden. It was cold, but he insisted, so Sally ensured she was wrapped up warmly and told her to come in when she called. Margaret opened her mouth to complain but quickly closed it – she didn't dare challenge her father. Sally returned to the living room and surveyed her husband as he sat in his braces by the fire – his jacket was placed neatly over the back of a dining chair.

'She can't stay out there too long, you know, it's freezing,' Sally said. She sat on the sofa and waited for him to speak.

'I want you to get in touch with Harold and tell him that you want to see him, but don't tell him I'm home.' He sat forward in his chair; his eyes narrowed in his deeply tanned face.

'Why, what are you going to do, ask him if I'm telling the truth?' Sally said. Her eyes wide as her nostrils flared.

'No, but I do want to talk to him, and I'm bloody sure he won't come if he thinks I'm here,' Edward said.

'How do you expect me to contact him then, I've not seen him from that bloody day to this – and I never want to set eyes on his face ever again – I could kill him for what he did to me.'

'Calm down; you know where he works, don't you? You can phone him.'

'Edward,' Sally said, her foot tapping up and down, 'I've never even used a phone box before. I wouldn't know how to phone anywhere.'

'Well I'll have to teach you then won't I? Because you're going to do it, and you're going to do it today.' Edwards sounded quite crazy as he spat the command out.

Sally had never been frightened of her husband before, but she felt a small stab of fear now. She nodded and stood up. I'll do what you want, but I'm going to call Margaret to come in she must be cold. And I don't see why he'd come here after the way he left.'

Edward snorted and gazed unwaveringly at her. 'Well, you'd better persuade him then hadn't you, because if I have to go and fetch him – you'll be sorry.'

Sally swallowed hard, she didn't know what Edward meant by that, but it sounded like a threat. She couldn't believe how much he'd changed. She called Margaret to come in and get warm by the fire and shivered as her daughter tumbled inside, bringing the cold air with her.

'Get your coat,' Edward said. His menacing tone had disappeared. He turned to his daughter. 'I'm taking your mom for a walk, stay in the house, we won't be long.'

They walked in silence to the phone box where Edward looked up the phone number of the firm where Harold had said he worked. Sally crossed her fingers hoping that he'd have returned to Wales, but his boss called him to come to the phone. Edward tilted the receiver so that he could hear both sides of the conversation.

Harold was stunned to get the call and sounded suspicious as he asked Sally why she wanted to speak to him. Sally told him in a small voice that she was lonely, and would like him to visit that night after Margaret was in bed – just as Edward had instructed.

Harold agreed with a brittle laugh. 'I told you you'd need my services again,' he said. Sally felt sick. She ended the call, and they went back home with her stomach churning as she wondered what Edward intended. He told her coldly to wait and see. Edward had heard every word but still didn't apologise to her and only spoke to her when necessary. Sally responded in a like manner; she felt at a loss to know how to behave as she felt so intimidated by Edwards coldness.

'I think I'll go up the road to see Ede,' Sally said after Margaret was asleep.

'No, I want you here. You need to show my fucking nephew into the front room then make an excuse to leave him on his own. Do –you – understand?' Edward asked.

Sally nodded and went upstairs out of his way where she spent her time mindlessly collecting washing together. She wanted Harold to hurry up and get whatever was going to happen over. She thought that Edward might be intending to give him a slapping, and on some level, she was pleased that he might feel some of the pain that he'd inflicted on her.

As planned, when Harold did arrive and looked enquiringly at her with a smug grin on his still spotty face, Sally said, 'Hello,' with a bright smile, and then held the door open for him to go into the front room. Instead of following him in, she said she needed to go to the bathroom. She closed the door and went into the living room. Edward pushed past her and strode into the other room, shutting the door quietly behind him.

Sally put her ear to the living room door she could hear voices, but couldn't make out what they said. Then there came a sound like flesh hitting solid flesh. It went on for a few minutes with muffled groans and cries emanating from the room. Then all was silent.

A minute later, Edward fetched Sally into the front room where Harold was lying in a heap on the linoleum. Edward turned him onto his back with his booted foot. His face was a bloody pulp – he was groaning quietly. Edward dragged him to his feet and stood back. 'Now apologise to my wife,' he said.

Harold cringed as Edward took a step towards him. 'I'm sorry, I'm sorry,' he mumbled out of profusely bleeding lips.

'Not good enough, on your knees,' Edward ordered. His face was a mask.

'Harold fell to his knees with a resounding thud. 'I'm sorry, I'm really, really sorry.'

'Look at her, you bastard – that's my wife.' Edward said, through clenched teeth.

Harold raised his head, his face was a mass of small cuts where Edward's ring had landed – his eyes were almost swollen shut, but he tried to look at her.

Sally felt appalled. She'd wanted to see him hurt, but the reality was sickening. She turned, left the room and went to sit on the top stair.

Edward ordered Harold to take off his clothes, except for his underpants, and then threw him bodily out of the house.

He'd already warned him not to go to the police, and Harold had no wish to test what the results of such a course of action would be. Neither Edward nor Sally ever saw him again, and he never knew that he'd fathered a child.

Later that night when they went to bed, Edward slapped Sally hard across her face as they had sex. 'That's just in case,' he said, 'now you've had one for that little runt you'll have another one for me.'

Sally found out the meaning of hate that night. As dawn broke, she leaned up on her elbow and wondered with a gut-wrenching ache where her friend had gone. He must have died when he was in Ceylon. Undoubtedly, something had happened to harden him while he was there. She wished she'd never met him and was glad to see the back of him when his leave finished.

81

Churchill announced that the war in Europe was over on May 8, 1945, and the whole country rejoiced. Their road was no exception, children and adults sat down together in the street at tables arranged around the grass circle. The grass had been cut very short, and the pig bins, where they all put scraps, had been removed and hidden to cover the smell of rotting food.

Sally and Margaret joined in by adding their contribution: hard-boiled eggs, paste sandwiches, and jelly with evaporated milk to pour over the top. Some people carried a piano out of one of the houses, and much fun was had singing at the top of their voices while downing as much ale, soft drinks, tea and Camp coffee as was possible.

As the evening wore on, people carried an effigy of Hitler and threw it onto a massive bonfire where it burned amidst cheers and fireworks. Potatoes were baked in biscuit tins thrust into the glowing ashes. Sally told Gran that it was the best she'd ever tasted, and Gran agreed wholeheartedly.

Lisa was born earlier than expected in November. Sally didn't have time to put newspaper on the bed or have much of anything else to hand. Gran helped her to give birth to the heaviest of her children; she was ten pounds four ounces according to Gran's scales and covered in a layer of vernix.

'All the fish and chips you've been eating,' Gran said, with a chuckle.

From the first contraction, until Gran lovingly tucked them up in bed together, only half-an-hour had elapsed. Sally was delighted with her chubby daughter even if she was the revenge baby. They decided to name her Lisa May. Margaret was excited to see her little sister, who she instantly adored. She was a great help and spent many hours rocking the pram and talking baby talk to her.

Edward was demobbed and arrived home on a rainy day in September 1946. Sally rapidly found out what it was like to live with an ex R.S.M. who'd had a batman. Everything had to be just as he wished, or there was trouble. He barked his orders out and expected everyone to jump up as soon as he wanted anything. Although Margaret loved him, she became very wary of him and stayed out of his way as much as possible.

Sally found she could barely move for him until he started back to work at the Lucas factory in Formans Road. His breakfast had to be just as he liked it: a clean cloth on the table, milk in a jug, and knife and fork laid out just so. It was the same formal table setting with his dinner too. Margaret sat at the table and ate her meals with her parents, but she had to remain silent unless questioned.

As Christmas approached, Sally could stand the strain of this behaviour no more. She told Edward that she was leaving him as soon as she could find somewhere to take the children. He could see by her face that she meant what she said and begged her not to go.

'I know what I've been like Sal, I'm sorry, believe me, I'm sorry. I'm finding it hard to adjust to the real world. I don't want to lose you and the children. I've already been without you all for so long stuck out in the fucking jungle.'

He'd told Sally some of the conditions that the soldiers had faced while in Ceylon. Many of them, including himself, had seen minimal action: but the constant battle with ants, the heat, and snakes and scorpions, and the news of the Japanese moving ever nearer had been mind destroying. He'd been in Colombo during an air raid, but it was quickly over and never repeated. He said that boredom and missing home comforts were the worst parts of his war.

Sally hesitated then went into his outstretched arms and sat on his lap. 'I don't want to leave you, but I can't stand seeing Margaret becoming frightened to put a foot wrong, or me either for that matter,' she got back up, 'I'll give it until after Christmas then I'll see, but something has to change,' she said and left him to mull her words over.

Although Edward didn't seem able to stop his unreasonable behaviour entirely, Sally could see that he was trying, and did her best to get closer to him again.

82

The following November in 1947, their third child was born. They named her Cassandra, but she rapidly became known as Cas. She was a tiny scrap with hair so blond that it was almost invisible. Edward hadn't taken very much notice of Lisa when he came home, but he played with Cassandra whenever he could find time between work and outdoor chores.

Something always needed to be done. Edward emptied the shelter and used the corrugated iron to build a shed where he kept rabbits to supplement their food. Along one side of the shed, he made a hen house where they kept chickens that fed on potato peelings and Layers mash, so they provided fresh eggs daily. The girls often helped where they could. The weeding amongst the vegetables that Edward was growing was never-ending. Sally came up with rewards for them; usually a stick of rhubarb to dip in sugar cupped in a piece of greaseproof bread wrapper.

'Go on then, but don't come back for more,' she always said, but they knew she didn't mean it.

The garden supplied them with many treats including succulent Loganberries that grew on the wires that fenced off the railway embankment. Rhubarb leaves were used as play hats, or cut up and mixed with mud then served for pretend meals. They were in trouble though if they pulled up a small radish or tiny carrot, or allowed their ball to stray onto the vegetable patch.

Punishment for minor misdemeanours was very often cleaning out the rabbit hutches. Lisa was in trouble frequently, but she was secretly happy to have this task. She liked the silky feel of their coats, their big eyes, and the way they raised their tails when they were startled. As much as she loved them, she didn't see them as pets, and tried not to become attached to any of them; she knew they were a source of food.

One day when the school boilers had broken down, Lisa was sent home from school early. She found her father in the kitchen during his lunch hour with a rabbit hanging from a nail by the living room door in the kitchen. He was gutting it for the pot.

'I'm going to wash this skin and then tonight I'll teach you how to cure it. It can be your job in future,' he said.

Edward had meant it to be a punishment, but he knew it wasn't going to be when Lisa said, 'Oh good. I'll enjoy learning how to make a good job of it.'

Far from being upset Lisa was fascinated and learned at an early age how to skin the rabbit and cure the pelt with saltpetre and alum. She then made fur muffs and slippers for them to wear.

Her mother kept a book noting the pedigree of each rabbit to avoid inbreeding, but she never had anything to do with their slaughter.

Sally thought that she and Edward had been getting on better over the last couple of years, and went out of her way to be pleasant. Now watching the girls through the window as they weeded carefully between the rows of carrots and onions, she said, 'Sometimes I can't believe how our family has grown while my back's been turned.'

'I know what was going on while my back was turned,' Edward said and picked up the book he'd been reading when she entered the room.

Sally felt as though he had smacked her in the face. That's it she thought, I've had enough. She said nothing but started to squirrel away what money she could from the housekeeping each week – going without wherever possible. Their belts were still tightened after the war, but she tightened them further.

She shared her plans with Gran, who advised her not to make any rash moves. 'We'd have you here Sal, you know we would, but now that Susan and Ted are married there's no room. Susan's expecting you know. She's not showing yet, so she isn't saying much, but I know,' she winked. 'You know that I'll help in whatever way I can though. He's changed hasn't he, too big for his boots now.'

'He's certainly the big I am now, and I'm sick to death of it, but I know you can't help Gran. I'm pleased that Ted's settled and going to become a father. It'll suit him,' Sally said.

The Horton family had said more or less the same things when they saw Sally. She hadn't been out with her friends so much over the previous twelve months. She'd been trying to please Edward and doing her best to help him to cope with the aftermath of the war. But she decided she wasn't going to cut herself off anymore from the people who'd been her salvation during those terrible years.

Edward treated her more like a possession than someone he loved. Well, she wasn't his to use as he saw fit.

83

Just before Queen Elizabeth's Coronation, in 1953, the family's circumstances changed. Gran died after a short illness and Ted and Susan moved into a newly built flat by the bus terminus. Sally was distraught but couldn't allow the loss of the person, who had meant more to her than anyone except her children since Abigail's death, to stop her functioning. She had to continue her daily routine and Edward had become more and more demanding after his diagnosis of bronchial asthma. He'd had a persistent cough that had troubled him while he was in Ceylon and it had been getting worse over the last few years. His breathing was so bad at times that a panel of doctors recommended early retirement. He was able to retire from Lucas's and claim sickness benefit.

There were days when he was very poorly and stayed at home, but often he would be out doing work for people that he knew. He didn't declare any income he received for these temporary jobs, and Sally lived in fear that he would be caught working while receiving sickness benefit. But Edward had no qualms about it.

One day when Sally heard that a neighbour had gone to prison for committing fraud, she tried hard to get Edward to see sense.

'Don't you think you'd better stop doing odd jobs? Think of your health – and you could end up in prison,' she asked him

'Sod that, I suffered for my country, I deserve recompense. I'll decide what I should or shouldn't do, stop bloody nagging,' he'd said.

Sally never mentioned it again. She'd gone into the kitchen where she kept all her treats. She had whipped bonbons and chocolate éclairs in the peg bag, and her current Mills and Boon book stashed in the cupboard where she kept the ironing.

When the old man, as Edward, came to be called by his family, went out on one of his jaunts or to the Royal Legion Club, Sally played cards or board games, especially, Spades, Partner Whist, and Gin Rummy with her children and sometimes their friends.

She was very competitive, and if caught with the ace of spades in her hand, she'd shout, 'Oh, not a bloody gen,' much to everyone's amusement. Other nights they watched television together, and it wasn't long before Sally wouldn't miss an episode of *What's My Line* or *Alfred Hitchcock Presents*. Sometimes she'd go to bed after enjoying being so scared that she'd watched the drama unfold from behind a cushion. The girls stayed up with her and concentrated more on her reaction than the programme. They teased her unmercifully. Sally returned the favour sometimes by chasing them down the garden and threatening to swipe them with a wet fish that she'd bought at the market. She loved the closeness that existed between herself and her children. They compensated for the revulsion that she now felt for Edward as he sat hawking and spitting into the fire while he watched television.

To both Sally's and Lisa's surprise, Edward's face lit up when the letter arrived to say that she had passed the eleven plus examination. He agreed to her attending the local Grammar School and even forked out some extra money towards her uniform. Lisa was the first in the family and their road to go to a grammar school.

She went into her bedroom to try on her uniform as soon as they returned from the town. She was admiring herself in the mirror when Cas arrived.

'Quick, he wants you downstairs,' she said.

'Oh no – oh God – what for?' Lisa asked.

But her sister shrugged her shoulders. 'I don't know, but you'd better come downstairs quick.'

Lisa arrived in the living room and stood in front of Edward's chair wondering what on earth she'd done wrong this time. Her mouth dropped open when her father handed her a ten-shilling note and said, 'That's for passing your eleven plus, I'm very proud of you, buy yourself something nice.'

Lisa took the money and muttered her thanks. She wasn't used to being praised by him and left the room as quickly as she could. Sally wasn't sure that further education for girls was a good thing, but she too told Lisa that she was proud of her. Cas also passed the same exam in due course and followed in Lisa's footsteps, but she did not get given a reward.

When Margaret was twenty years of age, she fell in love with a young Irish man who she met at work, and although the three sisters were very close, it was quite a surprise for them all. As she was underage, she needed her father's consent to marry, but Edward, as usual, was being unreasonable and refused.

'For God sake Edward,' Sally said, 'it only needs consent from one parent, and I'm not standing in their way, I'll sign the bloody thing.'

'You hadn't better – I'm warning you – she's too young,' Edward said.

Sally said no more, but she went against his wishes and gave her consent. She also attended the wedding with Ede. Edward knew nothing about it until the ceremony was over. Sally was happy that her eldest daughter had married a personable young man even though she knew she'd miss her company. But when Edward found out what Sally had done, he became enraged and smacked her across her face. She considered that her defiance had been worth it. She had no regrets.

As the months passed, Edward was frequently at home due to his illness, and in time, he taught Lisa and Cas to play Cribbage, a game they came to enjoy, but both girls soon learned not to win too many times, as he would become childishly annoyed and invent chores for them to do. They kept out of his way as much as possible.

Sally was stunned one evening when Edward was about to go out, he smiled and said, 'Make yourself presentable Saturday night, and I'll take you to the Legion.'

He'd never offered before, but shrugging off her suspicion regarding his motives the following Saturday she took pains with her appearance and went with him. After that night, they went together most weekends, and she thoroughly enjoyed herself. He introduced her to some of his friend's wives, and Sally became friendly with two of them, Beryl and Ivy.

At the club, her husband was known as a polite gentleman and behaved like one too. His manner and behaviour made her smile inwardly. Both Ivy and Beryl thought he was perfect, and Sally never betrayed him; she knew she'd never go there again if she did.

From the way Ivy's eyes would light up whenever she saw Edward, Sally had a suspicion that they had been having an affair at one time. She thought it may still be going on, but it didn't interest her. Ivy was someone she liked to talk to, and she wasn't about to curtail her enjoyment.

Ivy's husband, Ernie, died from a heart attack a few years after Sally got to know him, and in his will, to their surprise, he had left his Lanchester car and his brassware business to Edward. He had no children; Ivy didn't drive and had no wish to take over the company. She said she was happy for Edward to have it. He inherited a considerable amount of stock, fancy mirrors, fenders and small brass ornaments. As he had sometimes accompanied Ernie on his rounds, Edward knew the suppliers and retail outlets too. He was excited to have his own business, and worked hard, when he was well enough, to build it up into quite a lucrative one. He couldn't bring himself to relinquish his Panel money though.

Sally and the children were glad that Edward spent less and less time at home; he was either touring round his customers or spending nights out with his other women. This suited Sally as when he was at home; his mood and temper became worse the more he drank. He kept a bottle of whisky by the side of his chair and often drank from the bottle until he was too unsteady to climb the stairs. Sally usually covered him with a blanket and went up to their bed, relieved that the whisky had stilled his abusive tongue.

84

Lisa picked up the phone from the corner of her desk. 'Lisa, Mrs Hammond wants to see you in her office,' the office manager said.'

'Okay, do you know why?' Lisa asked, but her boss had already ended the call. Lisa replaced the receiver and reached for her handbag. Mrs Hammond was head of the administration department in the lawnmower factory where Lisa had worked for the last six months. When she knocked tentatively on Mrs Hammond's office door and entered, she knew that it was something serious by the expression on the middle-age woman's face.

'Sit down, Lisa; I'm afraid I have some bad news for you.' Mrs Hammond paused and peered at Lisa's white face from behind her pebble spectacles. 'I'm afraid your father has been taken ill, possibly a stroke, and you need to go home. I've asked the van driver to take you there.' She took a deep breath. 'Go and get your things, David will be waiting for you.' She stood, walked around the desk, and placed her hand on Lisa's shoulder. 'Take as long as you need dear just ring me when you are ready to come back. I'm so sorry to give you this awful news,' she said and patted Lisa on her arm.

Lisa stood up a little unsteadily and said, 'Thank you.' Then she walked back to her office in a daze. She carefully folded her red, headscarf into a neat triangle, tied it firmly under her chin, and shrugged her coat on. She left the office amid good wishes from her colleagues and gratefully accepted the lift home.

'Where is he, how bad is it?' she asked and gave her mom a fierce hug.

'Oh Lisa,' Sally raised her head, 'it's bad, Doctor Sen hasn't been gone long. He doesn't expect him to get over this. He didn't think that sending him to the hospital would be wise. It's not been unexpected, you know, his heart has weakened with all the coughing. He's sleeping at the moment. It happened while he was still in bed.'

'I'll just go up and check on him – why don't you make us some tea?' Lisa said.

As soon as she opened the bedroom door, Lisa knew he'd already gone. There was an eerie silence instead of the harsh sound of his breathing. She felt for his non- existent pulse as she thought she should, and then looked down at the face that had dominated their lives and sighed. She bent forward and kissed his forehead – it already felt cold to her warm lips. The room had a sweet sickly smell to it, but she had no wish to know what the source was. She turned, left the room, and descended the carpeted stairs. She noticed the dust that had accumulated on the wide skirting board – I must give that a brush she thought. Their recently installed, black telephone sat on the table in the hall waiting expectantly. As if in slow motion she rang the Doctors number.

Family and friends attended Edward's funeral just a couple of months after his fifty-fourth birthday, but no one shed a tear until the blue velvet curtains closed and the coffin started on its final journey. Then Sally began to cry. She wasn't crying for her husband; she was crying for her childhood friend. As they heard their mother's choking sobs, his daughters began to cry too.

Faith, Sally's friend from childhood, who she only saw once in a while, had volunteered to stay behind to make sandwiches and cut up pork pie for the mourners. After an hour or so of handing round cups of tea, glasses of beer and the odd glass of sherry, Sally thanked everyone for coming. Gradually, in ones and twos, the house cleared. Margaret went home to her husband, who had refused point-blank to attend the funeral of a man he so disliked, leaving her siblings and Sally talking in a subdued way about times past.

About nine o'clock, Sally said, 'Well I'm glad that's over – I'm off to bed.' She climbed the stairs, wondering how she'd feel without the person who'd been a friend, a husband, and a pain in the backside for so many years. She found herself wishing that she knew what had caused Edward to change so much while he was in Ceylon. Surely it wasn't that she'd been raped she thought, he'd known it hadn't been her fault. Sally wondered if he might have left a lover or even children; he would have missed them as much as she missed her son. She deliberately put the question aside as she knew she'd never find the answer.

As she nodded off, Sally wondered sleepily what the future held, but she didn't dwell on it; just promised herself that she'd never again need an emotional relationship with another man. She slept soundly hearing nothing of the gale-force winds that were trying to rip the leaves that were already fading, from nearby trees.

85

Sally didn't miss her husband. She appreciated her freedom. There was no one to bark orders at her or throw shoes as she went into the kitchen.

She took up old-time dancing with Ede and another neighbour who also lived alone. She loved it, and as she gained some confidence, she went on dancing holidays, staying in hotels at places she'd never hoped to see. Her daughters gave her money for her birthday, and to mark other special days. They knew she would prefer this to any other present as it allowed her to indulge her newfound hobby.

Unexpectedly, and to the delight of everyone, after Margaret had been childless for ten years, she presented Sally with a granddaughter. Mary brought back welcome reminders of all the love that Sally had had for her babies. She never said no to babysitting, and Mary loved her nan nearly as much as her parents. Almost twelve months to the day that she had Mary, Margaret had another daughter. They called her Angela. She was as beautiful as Mary but strongly resembled her father with dark hair and green eyes, whereas Mary was turning out to resemble Sally.

Sally rushed round to Margaret's as soon as she was home, and said with tears in her eyes, 'Thank you for my new grandchild she is beautiful, and I never expected to have one let alone two. I know you'd given up hope until you popped Mary out, and I'm so proud of you, my love.'

'You're right, and it's a miracle. But I want it to stop now,' Margaret said, and laughed, 'enough is enough.'

'Well, don't blame me if I start to haunt your house, will you?' Sally drew Margaret to her and kissed her cheek. Can I hold her?'

'Of course, you can, and you can visit every day if you like. I could do with the help.' As Sally cuddled Angela close, she wished that both her mom and Gran could have been there to see her happiness. It brought a lump to her throat, swiftly followed by tears.

Sally took Margaret at her word and visited often. Lisa and Cas jokingly complained one day that between her dancing, their nieces and their granddad they hardly ever saw her at home.

Sally had recently taken to visiting her father quite frequently as Olive had passed away just before Margaret gave birth to Angela, and he was finding it difficult to manage on his own.

When she next visited him, she said, 'Why don't you come and live with us, Dad?'

'No my love you don't want to be burdened with me, where would I sleep, it'd mean Lisa or Cas having to give their rooms up. No, I'll be alright here,' he said.

'Now don't be a stubborn old bugger you can have the front room as a bed-sitting room, that way you'll still have your independence,' Sally said, 'and it'll help pay the bills, and I'll enjoy having you close. You don't have to decide right now, but think about it, okay.'

It didn't take too much more persuading by Lisa and Cas before Bill gave in and moved to where Sally could keep an eye on him. It suited them both, and they often sat companionably watching television during the day. Sally had become addicted to *Crossroads*, a soap opera about the day to day running of a motel in the Midlands. Lisa and her mom never missed an episode of *Doctor Who*, if they could help it. They both thought Jon Pertwee, with his head of thick, white hair, very attractive.

When Lisa married Alan Harman in 1967, she agreed to give up work and help in the home. Alan was five years older than Lisa, tall, slim, and sported a beard. Lisa thought that despite the difference in hair colour and eyes, he was her Jon Pertwee. Sally took to Alan right away, and as he drove a Morris Minor car, their lives became more comfortable.

Shopping was no longer a real chore, and Sally relished the trips out to places she'd heard of but never visited. Her favourite spot where they picnicked was Warwick Castle. To her, it conjured romantic times, but Lisa, her practical daughter, laughed and pointed out the horrible conditions she would have had to endure if she had lived then.

Lisa gave birth to Sally's third grandchild on the anniversary of VE Day in 1970. She was named Katy, bright as a button, and a real charmer. It was almost two years later when Sally was nursing Katy on her lap that Lisa noticed that her mother's left leg seemed to be shaking.

'Don't make a fuss, Lisa, it's nothing I've probably trapped a nerve that's all.' Sally put Katy down into her playpen and went into the kitchen. Lisa followed her.

'Alright Mom cut the crap, how long has it been like this? I thought you were shaking when you were sitting at the table yesterday. You might as well tell me the truth I need to know what's wrong.'

Sally shrugged her shoulders and gave Lisa a hard look. 'It's nothing I tell you it's been doing it for a couple of weeks on and off. It'll go as soon as it's come you'll see. I don't want to see a doctor either, so stop going on about it.'

It was Lisa's turn to shrug her shoulders. 'Alright but if it's not gone by next week I'm making an appointment for you, alright?'

The shaking didn't stop, and after having tests, Sally had a diagnosis of Parkinson's disease. She'd never heard of it. 'Do you mean I have St. Vitus dance?' she asked the specialist.

'No that's a different neurological disease, but the symptoms are similar. The nurse will give you some pamphlets when you leave.' He nodded to the nurse who'd been standing behind Sally, and Lisa then turned back to Sally. 'I don't think the disease has progressed far enough yet for you to need any medication. Not to worry, we'll keep an eye on you.' He ceased talking and looked down at papers on his desk.

Sally and Lisa knew it was time to leave his office. Neither fully understood what the doctor had said to them, but they felt too intimidated to ask.

Sally seemed to shrink into herself. She didn't understand what was happening to her. She cried at first, but as her symptoms didn't appear to become any worse after a few weeks, her fear faded, and she came to accept her illness, somehow feeling it was a punishment that she'd brought on herself. No amount of talking to Ede or her other friends convinced her otherwise for a long while.

Ede persuaded Sally to continue with their dancing evenings, and she went to a couple of sessions. But she imagined that people were talking about her, so she refused to accompany her friend again. Sally missed the dancing and felt she'd let Ede down, but she preferred to stay home reading one of her romantic novels, or watching television. Sometimes she played her records of Mario Lanza and Albert Ketèlbey, and they gave her some comfort. She scarcely went out for the next twelve months, glad of her friend's visits, but she had no wish to meet strangers.

86

At the end of 1973, a letter arrived from Susan, Ted's wife, to ask Sally if she would visit as Ted had cancer, and had been asking about her. It had been a couple of years since they'd last met and Sally thought that Susan wouldn't have invited her unless Ted didn't have long to live.

'Come on, Mom, I'll take you, gives me an excuse to show off my new car,' Lisa said.

It took a bit of persuading, but Lisa took Sally to her friend's home. Half an hour into the visit, Susan and Sally went into the kitchen to make sandwiches and tea. Lisa sat and talked to Ted, who was in a wheelchair by a large picture window which overlooked a somewhat overgrown garden. Suddenly Ted reached down the side of his chair and took a photo from his wallet. He thrust it into Lisa's hand. 'Put it in your bag quickly; I don't want Susan to see it.'

Lisa glanced at a picture of a lovely young woman with brown hair which had been plaited and wound around her ears. She had a luxurious fur collar on her coat which snuggled up to meet her hair. She quickly did as Ted had asked. 'Is that Mom?'

'I loved her, you know, I always have, and I've carried that photo with me all my life. I never told her.' He looked incredibly sad as Susan came back into the room, but his sunken eyes lit up as Sally followed her.

When they were seated back in the car, Lisa showed her mother the photograph and told her what Ted had said.

Sally looked thoughtful then said slowly, 'I think I knew how he felt really, but he was like a brother to me. I'm glad he never told me, it would have made things awkward. I'm pleased to have been able to see him and say goodbye.' Lisa held the photo out to her mother, 'No you keep it, love, I don't need it—you can show it to my grandchildren —tell them how beautiful I once was.'

'You still are Mom,' Lisa laughed and started the car.

Time passed peacefully. Cas now had two little darlings, lovely children with very dark hair and brown eyes. Her husband was a bit of a darling too, but Cas loved him despite all his faults and ensured they all visited frequently. Sally was never happier than when her growing brood of grandchildren visited her.

Early in 1974 Bill became ill. It was late evening when Sally went into his room after he knocked on the wall to call her. Sally put the light on and walked up to his bed.'

'What's the matter, Dad?

Bill was dripping with sweat, his eyes unfocused, glassy. He held on to Sally's shaking hand and whispered, 'Get that dog off that bloody piano it keeps playing with the keys. And shut the curtains the circus folk are looking in the window, nosy bastards.'

'Oh my God Dad, we need to get you into the hospital.' Sally called to Lisa to phone for an ambulance.

It was a relief to Lisa and Alan when they knew that Bill had pneumonia. They'd thought he was losing his mind. But Sally had a good idea of what was wrong and dreaded the possible outcome.

Alan took time off work and drove Sally and Lisa to visit Bill at Selly Oak Hospital the next day.

'C'mon Mom,' Cas scooched along the double bench by Bill's bed, 'sit here, he's been awake and knew I was here, but he's just nodded off again.'

Sally kissed her daughter and sat down. Her shaking was now very noticeable as Lisa drew up a chair.

'How long have you been here?' Lisa asked her sister and dropped a kiss onto her hair.

'Not long, how did you get here, taxi?'

'No, Alan's just parking the car he'll be up in a minute,' she smiled at Cas.

She is like Mom, Lisa thought, and jumped a few minutes later when a nurse said, 'Only two visitors at a time please.'

Lisa pulled a face at Cas, and they chuckled.

'I'll be in the waiting room, swap when you want to.' Cas kissed her mother again and left the ward as Alan entered. 'Come with me,' she said, and taking him by the arm led him out.

Cas had only been gone a few minutes before Bill opened his eyes and smiled when he saw Sally. She was holding his hand and causing him to tremble too.

He looks very old and so tired, Sally thought. She noticed that the tattoos on his brown arms had faded into pale shadows of their once brilliant colours. She stroked the snakes that he'd pretended would bite her if she was naughty when she was a little girl.

'How are you feeling, Dad?' Sally asked.

Lisa bent over and kissed him on his forehead.

'Better, but I want to come home,' he whispered.

'I know, but you need to wait until the doctor says you're better,' Sally said.

Bill grabbed her arm in a surprisingly firm grip – his canula was almost wrenched from his arm. 'Sally, I'm sorry,' tears rolled down his cheeks – he wiped them away, impatiently, 'I should have told you ... your brother.' Her dad let go of her arm and sank back into his pillows.

Sally thought he was hallucinating again and patted his arm. 'It's alright, Dad, go back to sleep, it'll all be okay.'

He sighed and began to cough feebly. 'No it's not, I should have told you,' he said again. 'Take my wallet home and look in it. I hope you can forgive me.' Sally could hardly catch what he was saying as he drifted into a deeper sleep.

'Will you get his clothes for washing and his watch and wallet?' Sally asked Lisa, 'I don't know what he means, but I'll have a look anyway when we're home.' Lisa nodded and walked around the bed to his locker.

They took it in turns to sit with him for the remainder of visiting time, but he didn't wake again. Cas and Lisa agreed to meet and visit their granddad the next day while Sally rested at home. Margaret was working and couldn't go in the afternoon.

Sally was too tired when they arrived home to do anything more than watch television for a while. She ate some soup with floury dumplings that Lisa had cooked that morning then had an early night. Lying in bed, she tried to read a paperback copy of *Jane Eyre*, an old favourite, which she held in her right hand to minimise the shaking. I was difficult to concentrate. She felt as though her world was collapsing about her ears. If it weren't for her children, she wouldn't know what to do. She went to sleep suddenly, her book falling out of her limp hand onto the floor with a bump that she didn't notice.

87

After breakfast the next morning, Sally thought about her father's strange behaviour and sorted through her black handbag after struggling to open the gold clasp that had always been so easy to undo. She pulled out his brown, leather wallet; it was cracked and worn and smelled of stale tobacco. Sally smiled, remembering him using the same one when she had been young. Inside she found a five-pound note and a couple of ones. There was a photo of her as a young child. She studied every detail of the image of the toothy grinning child and then placed it on the table by her plate. Delving further into one of the back sections, she found an off white envelope. Intrigued, she opened it – a photograph of a boy who looked about twelve years old – fell onto the side of her chair. She picked it up and stared at it. She didn't recognise the lad, but he looked a little familiar. She felt inside the envelope and found a piece of paper. On it was written, the names Frank Brooks, and Ronald and Mabel Birch with an address in Coventry. She searched the rest of the wallet carefully, but there was nothing except a couple of old bus tickets.

She called Lisa in from the kitchen where she was feeding Kaye and showed her what she'd found. 'Is this what he meant, is this my brother?' Sally felt light-headed. How could it be – did her dad mean that he'd fathered a child with another woman she wondered?

'Well,' Lisa paused peering closely at the photo, 'he does look like Granddad, and he has the same eyes as you – I suppose he could be your brother. Granddad was very upset, wasn't he?' She bit her lip and let go of her daughter who'd been struggling to get down. 'I wonder who Ronald and Mabel Birch are.'

Sally scratched her head. 'I'll be buggered if I know, I've never heard of them. Ask your granddad when you go this afternoon, and don't forget his clean pyjamas,' she said as an afterthought. She didn't think this Frank was her brother; why didn't her father tell her before now if she had a brother? She'd always wanted a brother or sister – he knew that. She remembered now with a start how he'd lied to her about her birth mother; what other secrets had he kept? A tiny kernel of hope inserted itself into her mind. Perhaps she did have a brother.

They were distracted from further discussion by the antics of Katy as she toddled over to the dining table and tried to climb onto a chair.

Cas popped in to visit on her way home from her job as a medical secretary at the General Hospital. She too thought that the lad in the photo looked a little like their grandfather.

'I love a mystery,' she said and nodded sagely, 'I bet it's true, the crafty old bugger, we'll have to find out the truth won't we Mom?'

Sally shrugged. 'I hate the thought that Dad's been so secretive, but I would still love to have a brother. It's not too late, is it?' She smiled as both her girls hurried to hug her.

The next day as Lisa and Cas arrived at the hospital, they were accosted by the ward sister as they passed her reception desk.

'You're Mr Brook's grandchildren, aren't you?'

'Yes,' Lisa replied, 'how is he?'

'He's sleeping at the moment, but I'm afraid he is very poorly. Dr Michaels would like to talk with you or your mother, could you wait here while I tell him you've arrived?' She indicated seats against the pale green wall, and went into a side room returning with a pleasant-faced, tall young man in a white coat; a stethoscope moved briskly across his chest as he walked.

He shook hands as he introduced himself and then escorted them into his office. When they were seated, he explained, as clearly as possible, that Bill had cancer.

'I'm sorry to tell you this, but he is dying, the cancer is widespread. I imagine that he must have been in pain for some time. Has he never complained?'

Both Cas and Lisa shook their heads, gazing in stunned silence at the doctor's puzzled expression.

'Are you sure you have the right person?' asked Lisa when she eventually found her voice, 'Granddad's always seemed so fit for his age.'

'I'm afraid there is no mistake, I doubt that he will recover from pneumonia which could be considered to be a blessing in disguise. I think you should prepare yourselves for the worst. I'm so sorry.' He stood and gestured for them to follow him into the corridor, where he asked a volunteer to get them a cup of tea. He then shook hands again and left them to walk down the ward to their grandfather's bedside.

When he woke, Bill was very groggy and disorientated; Lisa decided they shouldn't ask him about Frank. He was too ill to be bothered with anything that might upset him again.

Sally visited Bill each afternoon for the next three days. Other family visited too, but Sally never conceded her seat to anyone. She held on tightly to her father's hand whether he was awake or not. On the second day, Bill went into a coma, and on the third day, he died.

Sally was distraught; the immense stress she had been under during her father's illness had caused her disease to worsen. She collapsed and was admitted for a few days into another ward at the same hospital. She was prescribed Sinemet, to help to alleviate the increased tremor. When she was allowed to go home, she was reticent and noticeably depressed. Everyone did their best to raise her spirits, but nothing anyone did seemed to last for long.

Bill's funeral was the last straw for Sally. Even after two months had passed, she was still finding it difficult to motivate herself to do anything but read library books. She spent more time, than her family thought was good for her, sat quietly looking out of the window into the garden. Lisa spent as much time with her as she could and one day when she handed her mother a library book that she'd dropped on the floor. Sally said, 'You know, Lisa, I loved my Dad very much, and I know he was rambling, but I can't help wondering if I do have a brother. If it's true, though why wouldn't he tell me?' She shook her head, and continued with a frown, 'I know it's not true, but I wish I'd had one if only to stand up to Edward for me – I don't even know if my mother is still alive.'

371

'Would you like me to try and find out for you?' Lisa asked.

Sally nodded her head. 'Yes, love I think I would like that. I've been thinking about it a lot.'

Lisa put her arms around her mother's shaking shoulders and drew her head onto her chest. 'I'm sorry Mom, I know what you mean, I would have hated to be an only child, but I'm sure Granddad would have told you when you were young if it had been true. Try not to think about it; it's only making you feel miserable. Think how much we all love you, and want you to be happy.' Sally sniffled but seemed to be comforted.

88

Early in June without mentioning their plan to Sally, Alan drove Lisa and Cas to Coventry. Lisa had been mulling it over and felt determined to try to get to the bottom of the mystery that their granddad had left them. When they arrived, they were a little reluctant to walk up the path and sat in the car, looking at the house.

'What if they won't talk to us?' Cas said.

'Oh come on, I haven't driven all the way here for you to chicken out – they won't bite – go on,' Alan said.

'Well you come in with us then,' Lisa asked her husband. He refused.

She put her tongue out at him and laughed cheekily as she and Cas let themselves out of the car.

'Mm, I could live here,' Cas said, listening to the sparrows twittering in the hedges.

'Me too, just look how lovely the house is. Well-kept too.' Lisa gazed admiringly at the way the January sunshine reflected off the bricks sending little flickers of light into her eyes. They strolled up the gravel path admiring the neat borders where the green shoots of bulbs were just peeping through the soil.

They looked doubtfully at each other as Lisa rang the doorbell set into the side of an attractive glazed door. There was no answer, and they both gave a heartfelt sigh. Lisa rang again keeping her finger a little longer on the bell push. The door opened, and a neatly dressed, somewhat elderly lady looked enquiringly at them, 'Are you Jehovah's Witnesses?' she asked politely.

Lisa smiled. 'No,' she shook her head, 'are you, Mabel Birch?'

'Yes, what is it you want dear? Are you selling something?' she cocked her head to one side, her crooked nose reminded Cas of a Flamingo. She tried not to laugh, but her eyes danced with suppressed mirth.

'Do I know you?' Mabel asked warily.

Lisa smiled reassuringly. 'No, we've never met, I'm Lisa Harman,' she said, and put her hand on Cas's arm, 'this is my sister Cassandra. We're Sally Brooks' children, and we wanted to ask you about Frank Brooks. Does he live here?' Lisa paused, 'does the name mean anything to you?'

Mabel looked at her fingertips and then at the two young girls. 'Yes it does, you'd better come in,' she said and wended her way along the hall leaving them to close the front door.

Lisa and Cas followed her into the front room, their feet sinking into a brightly patterned carpet, and glanced around curiously. Highly polished furniture and a comfortable three-piece suite filled the room. Money hasn't been an issue here Cas thought. Lisa only had eyes for the worried-looking lady who'd perched herself on the edge of a well-upholstered armchair.

'Have a seat – now what do you want to know?' she asked, her lips a thin line. Like the edge of a knife, Lisa thought and hoped that Mabel's temperament wasn't so sharp.

Cas looked to Lisa, who summoned up her courage and told her why they were there.

'And you think I know where this Frank is, do you?' she gave a brittle laugh. 'Well, I don't suppose it matters much now if I tell you. Frank is my son. I rarely see him these days as he lives in Pontefract,' she gave a wry smile, 'I'm not his birth mother you see, and I didn't much like his choice when he married. I'm afraid we had words. She looked directly into their eager faces and gave a cackling laugh before continuing her story in an ordinary voice. Both Lisa and Cas wondered if she was disturbed, 'I promised his mother that I'd never tell him who she was. Ronald and I – he's dead now – told Frank she'd died giving birth to him. His father was supposed to have died in the First World War in France. She insisted on it; otherwise, she wouldn't have let us have him.' Tears sneaked from under her wrinkled lids; she pulled a tissue from a box on a table by her side, dabbed at her face and went on speaking. 'We so wanted a child. We'd have promised her anything.' She sat back in her chair, completely out of breath.

'Are you okay?' asked Cas while trying to untangle the jumble of information they had just heard.

'Yes my dear, I don't suppose you'd make me a cup of tea, would you?' She looked quite pale as she pointed towards the kitchen.

'Of course, I will,' Cas smiled, and went from the room.

A couple of minutes slipped past marked by the tick of a handsome Wag at the Wall clock that graced an alcove.

'Who was Frank's birth mother?' Lisa asked, 'was it, Ann Brooks?'

'I couldn't tell him could I, not after saying that his father had been killed fighting in France,' she started to wail and spluttered, 'I couldn't, he'd have hated me for telling him such lies – both still alive – both alive, I couldn't, could I?' she held her hands out to Lisa.

Lisa thought she was somewhat disturbed and tried to calm her down, 'No, you couldn't – of course, you couldn't.'

'Is Bill still alive?' Mabel asked, 'I haven't seen him since Frank married and went to live up north. Frank didn't know that my cousin Ann and Bill were his real parents. They never told him, and I couldn't, could I, could I?' she sounded very distressed.

Lisa shook her head and said no more. She was thankful when Cas brought a tray of tea in, and poured a cup for each of them. Mabel held on to her saucer as though it was a lifeline.

'What about Ann, is she still alive?' Lisa asked gently, after filling Cas in on what had transpired while she'd been in the kitchen.

Mabel seemed to be deciding whether to tell them anything more, she hesitated, and sucked at her false teeth. 'Erm, she died two years ago so she can't mind what I say now can she? But I can't tell Frank, can I?' she shuddered. Tea slopped into her saucer.

'No,' said Lisa firmly. She felt sorry for this old woman who seemed riddled with guilt, 'but I think he might understand if he knew how you'd been coerced into lying, don't you?'

'Oh, do you think he might, do you really?' Mabel grasped at the possibility that her son might forgive her.

Lisa nodded. 'It's a pity that our grandmother isn't alive; I would have liked to meet her,' Lisa said falsely. She thought about how she'd have hated the selfish person who hadn't cared about either of her children.

'Her other children are still around though.' Mabel dropped this bombshell into their incredulous ears.

'Wha'…what d'you mean?' asked Cas her voice squeaky, astounded at the very thought.

Now that Mabel had started to tell her secrets, information that had been eating at her tumbled out. 'Oh yes, she lived for many years with a man that she couldn't seem to get enough of, she had two children by him. A boy and a girl, his name's George, the girl was called Louise, but she married when she was sixteen and went to live down south somewhere, Ann told me. Glad to see the back of her she was.'

'Where does George live then?' asked Lisa trying to take in all this incredible news.

'I know he still lived at home when his mother died because he came and fetched me to her funeral. I suppose he's still there. It's a big house in Wolverhampton. I've got the address in my bag if you'll pass it to me. It's over there by the sideboard.' Lisa passed her bag, and Mabel wrote the addresses of both George and Frank on a page from her book, tore it out and passed it to Lisa.

'You will tell Frank that I couldn't help it, won't you. I adolised him.'

'Mabel, of course, we'll tell him, now you stop blaming yourself, and we'll let you know what happens, okay,' Lisa said.

Mabel had a smile on her face as she waved goodbye to the sisters after Lisa promised to keep in touch.

89

'I was about to send a search party in,' Alan joked, as they headed back home. He'd been expecting the girls to be full of information when they came out, but they weren't very forthcoming, they seemed bemused by their distant cousin's revelations. After a few miles, they sketched a picture for him, and he promised to take them to the house in Wolverhampton the next day. As it was a Sunday, they hoped to catch George in.

'It's okay if you don't want to come, I can drive us there, but you know your way around better than me, Lisa said, hoping he would go with them.

'No I'll take you, never know what you'll run into,' Alan said.

'Thanks, darling – now remember,' Lisa said, 'not a word to anyone, especially Mom, until we know more. I don't want to get her upset or excited unless we know for definite that what Mabel said is true. She seemed a bit loopy, didn't she?'

'Just a bit,' Cas emphasized the words.

Alan again opted to wait in the car when he could see that the house was in a pleasant area where he felt that the girls would be safe knocking on a stranger's door. George turned out to be a grumpy but accommodating person. He didn't resemble Sally, but some of his mannerisms did.

When it had sunk in who they were, George said he had no idea his mother was married to anyone else. Lisa broke the news in as diplomatic a way as possible that Bill and Ann were never divorced.

George laughed until his eyes twinkled. The girls couldn't understand what was causing his outburst until he spluttered, 'The lying old cow.' When he'd calmed down he went on, 'Well I don't want to shock you, but she was an old cow. She always maintained there had never been any man in her life before Raymond, our father. These days we'd be taken into care. Your mother had the best of it being brought up by someone who loved her.' His demeanour became very serious as he inquired, 'What's she like, your Mom?'

'You'll have to come and meet her and see for yourself. She's lovely, kind and funny and we love her very much,' Lisa said.

George nodded energetically. 'I'd love to.'

'What about your sister, where does she live? Do you think she'd like to meet Mom too?' Cas asked.

'Yes, I'm sure she would, but she lives in Worthing on the South Coast so it might take a bit of arranging. I'd be happy to take you down there so you could tell her what you've told me.'

George wanted to meet Sally that day, but Lisa persuaded him to wait until they'd contacted the rest of the family. She explained about Sally's illness and said she'd prefer not to get her excited with half a story.

They made arrangements for the following weekend George phoned his sister Louise, but he didn't tell her that he was bringing two nieces with him. They booked into a small B & B where George had stayed before. The girls were delighted to have the chance to talk with their uncle on the long journey, and he turned out to be as amusing as their mother and not at all grumpy once they got to know him. They both liked him, and when they met their aunt, they loved her too. She resembled their mother, almost a smaller version with chubbier cheeks. Her white hair curled in just the same defiant way and her blue eyes twinkled too. The transference of love was easy and instant.

After telling George off for not warning her, she welcomed Lisa and Cas warmly and introduced them to her son and daughter who were intrigued by the surprise family members. Lou, as she was known, wasn't shocked by the news that she was illegitimate, and agreed that their mother had been a very selfish, uncaring person. She laughed when her brother repeated his assertion that she was an old cow.

'I left home as soon as I could,' Louise said, and then nodded across at her brother, 'I don't know how he stayed with her. Thick-skinned aren't you?' she teased him.

90

The following weekend George drove them up to Pontefract. He was anxious to meet his half-brother and said he preferred to tell him details of their tangled lives, face to face. When the three of them entered the outdoor pursuit's shop that Frank owned, Lisa and Cas recognized him immediately. He was the image of Bill.

George told him that they'd come from Wolverhampton to meet him, but refused to disclose any details other than to say it was to do with his mother. Frank looked dubious but agreed to meet them at the local pub after the shop closed. They left, as he had a customer waiting. The three of them spent a fascinating afternoon having lunch and wandering around the shops and the castle ruins.

Later, they sat drinking around a shiny copper topped table, and Frank heard the story of his birth and their relationship. As soon as George told him he was his half-brother, they threw their arms around each other and became choked with emotion. Frank didn't doubt for a second that it was the truth. Then when the greeting was over, Lisa showed him photographs of Bill and Sally. They were astounded at his resemblance to his father; it could have been the same person, just a younger version. They were even more surprised when Frank told them that he had known Bill since he was a lad, and had met him many times as a family friend. He listened with interest until they mentioned that Sally had Parkinson's disease, but they were shocked when Frank burst into tears, put his head down on his arms and sobbed. When he was back in control, he explained that he'd always been sad that he didn't have any siblings, and was desperately upset to think that now he'd found he had two sisters, one of them was so ill. He was also distraught to hear how his foster mother had been manipulated by the woman who he knew as Mrs Brooks and seemed determined to try to make things right between them.

When they returned home, Lisa and Cas couldn't wait to tell Margaret what they'd discovered. She was intrigued and delighted for Sally's sake. It took a bit of planning, but on a brilliant summer's day at the beginning of July, Frank, George and Lou met up at the Westley Arms Pub near to Sally's house. Lisa and Cas met with them and provided the transport to Sally's house where a secret buffet-style meal waited. It was challenging to keep all the planning from Sally, but they had managed it, she knew nothing.

Sally was relaxing in the garden when the girls placed chairs around as though they were about to join her.

'Hey, you noisy bugs come and sit down, we're talking.' She tutted to her friend, Ede, who was in on the surprise.

Lisa signalled to Ede to distract Sally. Ede started talking about the railway lines and pointed down the garden.

Lisa showed her aunt and uncles through the kitchen, and down the steps onto the crazy paved patio.

'Mom, I've brought some relatives to meet you,' she said.

Sally looked up, and her jaw dropped in surprise to see three strangers standing in her garden. Ede got up and went into the house. Lisa followed her. They joined Margaret and Cas who were gazing out of the window. They all had tears in their eyes as Sally looked in wonder at her siblings, beaming faces.

THE END

Sally-*Secrets and Lies*

Acknowledgements

This is the book that I began many years ago only to put aside after a friend read the first few chapters and commented that there was 'No oomph.' I think he meant sex. I was too young to ignore his opinion. It was much later after I became confident enough to write what I wanted to and not what other people thought I should, that I continued with this family saga. I enjoyed the journey.

May Stephens, my lovely mom and an avid reader, I hope you can read this book wherever you are. I know that you would enjoy spotting snippets from stories that you told me over the years. Thanks, Mom.

Thanks also to my friend of many years, Kay Aston aka Duck, and Hannah Williams, a very special granddaughter, for reading my first draft and giving me feedback and encouragement. It was much appreciated, and your comments were valued.

Thanks, as always, goes to my Susie for her help with editing and formatting. I couldn't do it without your patience.

A big thank you to William Sutcliffe, Jenny Colgan and Fiona Mozley, who were speakers at a Writers' & Artists' conference that I attended. You all gave me sound advice and the courage to keep on writing as I wished.

Last but not least, sincere thanks to each one of you who have bought my book. I hope that you enjoyed it.

Lesley Elliot

By the same Author:

The Copper Connection

In May 1995, life changes forever for twenty-one-year-old Heather Barnes when an abhorrent crime fractures her life. Not willing to rely on the justice system, she vows to exact revenge. Is she strong enough to carry out her plans? Is she smart enough to avoid detection? We follow the highs and lows of her family life and relationships as she grows from a helpless victim into an independent, resilient woman. Will she ever be capable of putting the trauma behind her and finding the happiness she deserves, or will her need for vengeance destroy her?

Printed in Great Britain
by Amazon